A Piece of My Heart

HARPER & ROW, PUBLISHERS

New York   Hagerstown   San Francisco   London

RICHARD FORD

A Piece of My Heart

I am grateful to the University of Michigan Society of Fellows, who supported me generously while I wrote this book.

R.F.

Portions of this work originally appeared in *Esquire, Michigan Quarterly Review,* and in somewhat different form in *The Paris Review.*

FIRST EDITION

Designed by Dorothy Schmiderer

Library of Congress Cataloging in Publication Data

Ford, Richard, 1944–
    A piece of my heart.

    I. Title.
PZ4.F69877Pi   [PS3556.0713]   813'.5'4   75-5536
ISBN 0-06-011362-6

---

76 77 78 79 80 10 9 8 7 6 5 4 3 2 1

Kristina

Prologue

W.W. came down over the levee in the rain, his old Plymouth skidding out of the ruts and his gun barrel pointed wildly out the window, still warm from being shot. He looked down on the boat camp through the willows and for a moment saw nothing but the house and the dock shielded in the rain, though he had watched from a distance as Robard's truck had topped the levee three minutes ago and disappeared over the side, and had come on after him. He drove more slowly through the willows as the rain began to let go harder. Fat droplets plowed down the rifle barrel and dripped on his pants, though he didn't notice. He saw Robard's truck finally, sitting down in the cover of the low limbs, steaming and ticking in the rain. He left the car, left it rolling until it rolled into the back of the truck, and stepped cautiously toward the dock, still in his baseball uniform, where a blond boy was standing over the water with a rifle held barrel-to-toe, watching an empty boat drift down the lake corridor toward the shallows.

When the boy sensed the presence of someone else, he whirled and threw up his rifle and pointed it squarely into his belly.

"Now who the hell are you?" he said, the corners of his mouth quivering so that he seemed to want to smile.

W.W. looked out on the water, fingered the warm trigger guard, and wondered if he could shoot the boy and somehow in the scrap avoid being shot himself. He decided he could not, and smiled.

"I'm W. W. Justice from Helena."

"What are you doing in your baseball uniform and totin a rifle, W.W.?" the boy said, displaying the absence of three front teeth, behind which could be seen his tongue at work trying to fill up the space.

"I come after Robard Hewes. I guess you hadn't seen him."

"Come who?"

"Robard Hewes."

"Well, W.W.," the boy said, flicking the corners of his mouth with his tongue and letting the tip of his rifle sink back to his foot, "I never did hear of him. But I'll tell you one thing."

"And what's that?" W.W. said.

"I just did kill a man here, wasn't a minute past you drivin up."

"Who'd you kill?" he said, watching the empty boat dawdling in the rain breeze.

"Damned if I know. Whoever it was, though, didn't have no business being here. I'll tell you that. I'll tell you that right now."

PART I

Robard Hewes

1

In the dark he could see the long tubular lights nose down the mountain toward Bishop. They crossed the desert after dark, leaving Reno at dusk and slipping across the desert at midnight toward Indio. He sat in the front room in the dark and stared through the doorway, smoking and listening to the beetles swarm the screen and the air sift through the window. Someplace away a cab-over ground down and started across the meadow to the mountains. In town he could hear a car horn blowing a long time and tires squealing, and then it faded and sank back into the night. He breathed a plume of smoke in the dark and ran his fingers through his hair.

"So," she had said, "how long will you be gone?" setting the dishes on the window sill and staring out into the purple light. "What's it going to be like?"

"It'll be all right," he said. "I'll be back."

And she had turned, her thick hair over her shoulders, blacker than his, and disappeared into the house without another word. As if she had just caught herself being lured into an arrangement and had drawn back to save herself on an instinct she had forgotten existed, since for eight years there hadn't been a reason to save herself. He had listened to the door shut.

In a while he had gotten up from the table and switched off the bulb and gone to wait until it was good dark and he could leave in the cool.

He wondered, sitting alone there, just what you do. When your husband up and just steps out of the life you have with him, after living eight years cultivating a dependence that he won't suddenly up and drive away into the night without saying why, what do you do? What alterations can you make? He felt he would have to settle with whatever adjusting she had done, when he came back. He tried to think of some other way, and decided there wasn't one.

He blew smoke in the darkness. A car came along the dirt road, its headlights tracking the shoulder, the radio playing so that it sounded very close to the house. The car reached the end of the road, turned back into the desert, and the music floated away.

At nine o'clock he walked to the back of the house, switched on the bulb, filled the kettle, and set it back on the flame. The kitchen smelled cold, though it was warmer than in the other rooms. The stove smelled of gas. He rinsed the Thermos and set it upside down on the sink. He took down the powdered coffee and sat at the table and waited.

He remembered sitting in the little two-room warming house in Hazen, waiting at the table for the doctors to come from Memphis. He had rinsed the mugs, set them in a line on the wood counter, each with a spoon, set down the tin of powdered coffee, and begun waiting for shooting time, warmed by the gas ring and the bulb light shining at the corners, bending shadows into the back room where the cot was. He waited in the cold until the doctors came down the car path, their heavy cars swaying and rocking, throwing their high beams across the field to the corner of the woods, where he could see through the half-glass door, red cinder eyes flashing and disappearing into the trees.

He had waited at the window until they came inside, old men in long wading boots and canvas coats, and took the pan off the stove and made the coffee while the men's voices filled the room, laughing and coughing until it was warm, and he had slipped away to wait on the cot until he could see the window whiten and the first silver haze behind the treetops, and herded the men across the field in the stillness toward the timber so that the cabin sank and became just a single light and finally disappeared in the burnt flakes of sunlight. In the cold the men grew silent and morose like lumps of soft coal, plodding into the trees, their boots squeezing together, until the ground gave way to water. He had set them in the boats and waded down into the flood, towing them through the trees until he could hear the ducks squabbling and conniving a hundred yards farther in the deep water. High up he could see their imprint trading cleanly on the pale sky. He set the men out there, held the boats while they stumbled out into the thigh-high water, spoke the directions they ought not go, toward the channel of the creek, then left them wading noisily through the water, laughing in the shadows, until he could not hear them and had towed the boat back to the ground.

He had gone back then across the field to the house and waited, dozing under the light, until the morning had grown up bright and glassy. Then he walked back across the bean rows to the boats, where he would find one of them, always one, returned, lolling in the shallows, asleep and blue-lipped, a strand of yellow hair across his temple, asleep before light had ever come. He towed him sleeping back into the timber, through the black water to where the others were shouting and roiling the water and shooting, to where the ducks were down and bleeding on the lilting surface, swimming in circles among the trees.

He had waited there in that shack for the doctors to come from Memphis, or the fish salesmen to drive from Gulfport and Pass Christian, or the Jews from Port Arthur, driving all night through Louisiana and arriving before light, puking in the muddy yard, and bellowing in the night. He had waited there mornings, thinking of nothing, waiting for whomever old Rudolph took money from (a thousand dollars a head) and sent out, rinsing their spoons and sliding away noiselessly out of the light into the cold back room, waiting to take them in for the ducks.

Until that ended, after three years, without even a notice to old man Rudolph, or a message. He had slipped off with Jackie, under the nappy lights, blue and gauzy as if a chill fog had settled in between them, driving through Little Rock after midnight, all the way to Bishop, where he felt enough distance was opened between him and the shack and the fields and the whole life there that it would be too hard to go back. And when that distance was finally made, he felt safe.

He spooned coffee into the Thermos and poured water until it steamed in his face. He corked it, jostled the bottle, and snapped off the light. He walked back to the front room, sat by the door and listened for Jackie, for her breathing, for any sign, a groaning in the bed staves to indicate she was there, since she had gone without a word and closed herself in the room and never made a sound once the light was off inside. He sat, the chair squeezing in the dark, and waited, listening for the frailest sound. He could feel the breeze channel underneath her door, the gentian running east through the house back to the desert. He stood and walked to the window ledge, picked up his paper sack of rolled-up clothes, and went to the screen and looked across the plateau toward Bishop, dissolved in the night, the road to the mountains invisible except where a pair of elongated lights twisted down off the valley.

He thought that if your life was filled with beginnings, as he had just decided today that his was; and if you were going to stay alive, then there would be vacant moments when there was no breathing and no life, a time separating whatever had gone before from whatever was just beginning. It was these vacancies, he thought, that had to be gotten used to.

He lifted the latch and walked across the porch toward the truck. Jackie lay asleep, hearing him walk across the boards and the wet grass, heard his shoes in the gravel, and the nail settle of its own weight back into the eye of the latch, heard the truck heaving and hissing. And she lay still, unwakened by the sounds, unaware he was leaving, aware only of the sounds and of the cool air rippling the sheet and flowing out under the doorway into the room where, if she had awakened suddenly and sat startled in the bed, she might have called him, thinking he was there, sitting in the darkness smoking, and believed that all this had never happened.

2

Early in the morning he had lain awake in the gray light and let it all revolve through his mind again carefully.

Twelve years ago he had lain under the eaves at Helena in the little rose-wallpapered room, alert to the ticking through the cypress timbers, hearing the weight on the stairs, the coarse shuffling through the door, and turned his head toward it but couldn't see.

"All right," he said, startled, a heavy sweet smell riding the darkness. "I can't see you now. Who is that?"

"It's me," she said, letting her quilt subside and releasing the gardenia smell into the room. "I can't wait no longer."

Her knees bent into the bedding as he was trying to climb to see her in the dark, and only saw her breasts rolling toward him and disappearing, and her arms taking him up and holding him until, when he tried to talk, he could only say, "Honey, honey." And that was all.

In the morning she stood and kneaded her eyes and swung her arms through the dusty light, her underarms pale and dark at once. The bed smelled sour.

"Robard," she said, stretching her fingers through her damp hair. "You wake up now." (Though he was certainly awake.) She stared at him, her lips everted, and he strived to move his eyes, inch by inch, toward the painful sloping sunlight.

"I got a riddle," she said.

"A what?" he said, smelling the sheets all around him.

"How come the birds wake up singing every morning?" She smiled and set her teeth edge to edge.

"What?" he said, not hearing it right.

"Cause," she said, sticking her full belly out and smiling.

9

"They're happy to be alive one more day." She laughed out loud.

And all at once her expression changed and she looked at him as if she had never seen him before and was surprised to find him lying there. And he had seen paleness in her eyes, some disappointment he couldn't calculate but could feel commencing, like some dead zone inside her had uncovered all at once. He thought that it was the print of something lost, something irretrievable, though it was all he knew, and he felt that was only part of it.

A year ago a letter came unaddressed and sat a month in general delivery before the card came warning him to pick it up. It said:

> *Robard:*
> *We are in Tulare now. W. W. pitches. Come and see*
> *me please. I still love you. Your cousin. Beuna.*

After a month in the mail slot, it smelled like the same gardenias, thick and rank, flagging to the onionskin so his neck prickled when he smelled it, and he decided then that he had to go, if it was just to see what was there, and could work on explanations later.

He had sat beside her in the Tulare fairgrounds in the smothering night heat and watched W.W. on the brick dust under the lights expel one spiteful pitch after another that no one could ever hit or even halfway see, the last six batters going back without bothering to swing, so that the game was over in an hour and a half.

Beuna had on a red sunsuit printed with elephants running, the halter pinching her breasts up so that he doubted if she could swallow all the way down. Her stomach had forged over her shorts and he thought then that she was much fuller now, after twelve years, but ripe like a peach orchard pear, and womanish in a way that he had never ever seen before and never even really imagined to be possible. She sat beside him and slowly pressed her bare thigh against his until he began to feel like some great whirling gyro were being turned against him. And she never once uttered a word nor made a sound, and for the hour and a half he had sat as though some hot current were passing into his leg, turning a circuit through his body and passing out through his fingers, taking all his strength and resistance as it went.

When she released him, she set her head sideways and stared at him, holding him, like the high point on a compass.

"Robard," she said, her voice sounding like a bubble rising up out of the cramped insides of her throat. "I love you."

The first banquet of grandstand lights fell dim, sinking them in queer afternoon shadowlight.

"All right," he said, looking across the dingy field for some sign of W.W., knowing he was baiting calamity by even being there.

"I'm *so* wet," she said. "My God!" She fished her hand in his trousers and squeezed him there until he felt a noise down in his throat that wouldn't come loose. "Robard?" she breathed, bringing her mouth to an inch from his ear and squeezing as hard as she could. "Do you love me?"

"All right," he said, unable to get his breath.

"Is that all?" she said, her eyes pinching up meanly and her grip relaxing so that he had time to feel his saliva get thick as gravy.

"You do what you can," he said, sucking air through his nose, trying to keep his throat constricted.

"Well," she said reproachfully, staring at her toes on the next riser down. He could hear W.W.'s voice calling out of the dark across the field. Behind him other voices were laughing. Suddenly she had him again, foisting her hand in his trousers as if she were driving a nail and until he felt like some awful vision was about to appear in front of him. The last standard of lights died off, huddling them in a wretched darkness. "Since you put it thataway," she said slowly, "I guess it'll be fine."

On the road back across the desert he began to try to settle things. In general, he knew, things didn't end in your life because by all sensible estimations they *ought* to. Or because people involved did things or changed places that would ordinarily make carrying on any longer a natural hardship. Because once a force got a start in you, it grew and took on dimensions and shadings and a life separate and sometimes as complete and good as your own. And if a man would ever sit down and study his life in a practical, good-sense way, he would see that, and understand that nothing in his life *ever* ended. Things only changed and grew up into something else.

In three weeks a letter arrived at general delivery written on drugstore stationery. It said:

> *Robard:*
>
> *We are not in Tulare now, but are in Tacoma, Washington. It ain't nice here and rains. He played good at Tulare and pitched at Oakland one time, but everybody got a hit, and he rode the bus up here the next day and I come by car. It is just a big ditch behind our little house and I am afraid it will flood and drownd me. I don't know what will happen to me now but something will. Smell this. I love you still more. Beuna.*

He held the paper up to the light, standing in the long, airy vestibule of the post office, and smelled the paper where the writing was, and took the letter quick out to the gutter and tore it to pieces and let it flutter through the grate into the dry sewer mouth.

In two weeks a letter came postmarked Helena, Arkansas, with a message written on Holiday Inn stationery. It said:

> *Robard:*
>
> *I am home. W.W. says he will pitch at Oakland again and is still at Tacoma playing kid games. His mind will change. I love you more. B.*

He had sat on the steps of the post office thinking about W.W. set up in a strange little bungalow in Tacoma, W.W. wondering what could happen to a man's whole life in the space of one week and how he could get it all back on track and pry Beuna loose from her stepfather's house and get her back where he was so he could have a chance at Oakland again, where somebody could see him.

A week later a letter arrived that simply said:

> *Robard:*
>
> *W.W. has seen the light. I knew. . . . Beuna.*

He figured she must have made a bet with herself that she could treat it all like she was the victim and he was the culprit for wanting to stay and pitch baseball, and she had won it.

And after that a letter every week from Helena pleading with him to come, always on the same rose onionback, with loud promises and whatever smells she felt were useful to what she was asking. And he had stayed and stayed and put each letter in the grate and tried to forget about it.

Though he wondered just what it was he had seen years ago and seen up in Tulare the instant he said, "All right," when she was hoping for something richer, and what it was that made her strand W.W. out in some strange foreign country, just so he'd quit doing the *one* thing he knew to do. Twelve years ago he might have believed it was just some act of girlishness she played at, brought along by the fact that she liked mingling with her own cousin ten feet out of reach of her mother's headboard—and that *that* right there had caused enough private turmoil to make some show of remorse creditable. And the only thing like remorse that she knew then was to make herself look cast down by something mysterious she couldn't explain and that in all the commotion going on at 3 A.M. there wouldn't be time to talk about. Except that didn't work out. It had gone on too long to be just girlishness. And when he had seen her in Tulare, she had fixed on him with her pale flat eyes like a specimen she was studying, and there had been again the same forlorn miscalculation he had always seen, just as though it marked a vacancy she was beside herself wondering how to fill.

3

At five-thirty he had gotten up, dressed, and driven up the Sierra to Mammoth and sat in the truck while the light got darker and turned green just as the rain commenced through the fog. At six-thirty the foreman drove up in a company truck, climbed up into the bed wearing a yellow rain suit, and read off a paper that said the job was closing because the state had to make a study.

The foreman said a job was open at Keeler laying pipe for a feeder to the aqueduct, and anybody wanting to sign ought to make the noon list. Men started moving off even before he had finished, heading for their trucks, anxious to get out of the drizzle and down to Keeler before the list filled and they had to scrounge. When the foreman had finished reading the paper, he stuffed it in his pocket, climbed back in the truck and drove off.

He walked back to the truck thinking he could drive back and eat breakfast with Jackie and think about going to Keeler when he'd slept.

He drove out from Mammoth back to the highway south. Up the Sierras the rain was pulling apart, opening gaps to daylight. He was beginning to think that there were some things he hadn't understood. From the first, eight years ago, when he had left Hazen and transported himself and her across the country, and had started to pick work where he could up the Sierras, he had been as desperate as anybody, and every bit as panicked when a job shut down, and had gone off to wherever there was another one opened. And he had felt the same panic starting, listening to the foreman, the same creepiness the others had disappeared with to Keeler to patch into whatever was there. Except he couldn't go off and start opening ditches and pitching pipe without having made a choice. When the first job closed in Lone Pine eight years ago, in 130-degree heat, he had panicked. And the first thing he remembered seeing was men rushing like they were bolt out of a cannon. And he'd gone with them because he'd gotten caught up and couldn't resist. And all that rigmarole, he thought, had just given the panic something to work on, and switching jobs up and down the Inyo had come to seem like the best solution because it was *a* solution, and that was better than nothing.

Though after eight years now, he thought, he ought to wonder if it was the best solution anymore, and in fact if it had ever been. If he wanted the job he could just drive down in the morning and stand at the site until somebody goggled over in the heat, and step in without any questions.

So that what he was thinking about, of course, was Beuna. All those years of running desperation and internal commotion getting jobs and being anxious might have been just a lot of useless barging around, like a man with his sleeve in a thresher. And that whatever she had infused in him back in Helena, twelve years ago, hadn't been dormant, given all the activity it seemed to have sponsored, but just misunderstood.

The rain had spread out into a silver sheet below the fog. The truck struck out from under the clouds to the light and started off the long grade toward the desert, where he could feel the air already hotter, two thousand feet up off the flats. The road he could see down below bent across an oval meadow demarking the edge of the Sierra and the desert. A file of poplars divided the meadow along the shoulder connecting the toenail of mountain to the outskirts of Bishop, which sat off a ways in the purplish mist halfway down the horizon.

But what happens to you, he wondered, worrying already— what happens when she manages to infect you with something dangerous, keeping it alive for years on the strength of gardenia odor and a few flourishing letters? What happens when you recognize it's important—what you did and what she did and would do, and when and how and to whom, and that it's left you with a kind of ruinous anxiety that just one thing will satisfy?

He took the long curve down into the stretch of shaded road toward town. It worried him, because he knew that things in your life didn't disappear once they were begun, and that your life just got thick with beginnings, accrued from one day to the next, until you reached an age or a temperament when you couldn't support it anymore and you had to retire from beginnings and let your life finish up on momentum. And he wasn't to that point yet! So that whatever she had fostered inside him couldn't be counted on simply to retire, but to protrude into the middle of everything indefinitely and give everybody a bad time, unless serious adjustments were made to transform her and it into something he *could* live with, in the way everybody lived with things.

He drove into town to the front of the post office and stopped, thinking, in the heat, that seeing Beuna as an impediment or as something to be survived was only one way of looking at her, and not by any necessity the way she was. He stepped in where the air was cool and dry. The lobby was a long empty arcade with wired-up skylights that clouded the room with submerged shadows. He picked up the letter at the registry and walked back out into the sunlight, looking up the street to see if he saw anyone he knew. He thought about breakfast and decided to let it slide.

He stuck the letter under the visor and started back toward the mountains. He drove out across the meadow until he crossed the Works Progress bridge at Inyo Creek and stopped and got out and walked back to the railing. The breeze stiffened and flicked the page, and he read the words over and over, poring over them, his lips forming the words each time. And after a while he walked down in the yellow and green checkered light and stepped into the sedge and laid the envelope on the surface and watched it turn and dance away until it snuffed like a flicker of light. He puzzled for a moment at the letter, the page fluttering in his hand, and suddenly folded it into quarters and backed out of the wet grass. He climbed the bank and crammed the page down inside his instep and started back toward the truck.

He thought again that to see Beuna as an obstacle was only one narrow-minded way of looking at her. And not the only way. Since another was to think that he was not finished with this part of his life yet, wife or no wife, this part left with Beuna, and with women in general, and that there was still this much left, this much of an opportunity to do with the way he wanted, and that thirty-four was still young, inasmuch as you only got to live one time and this was his time right now.

4

He drove down into Arizona and slept in the afternoon behind a motel in Flagstaff. He got up at four o'clock and drove straight until dark, and slept on the truck seat outside Bluewater, New

Mexico, and woke up in the high sunshine and drove into Grants to eat breakfast. At Grants he stepped out in the breeze, between the highway and the Santa Fe yards, and watched cattle cars being switched onto the main line from south Texas, the cattle asleep on their feet in the cool tinted air. He watched the train get made up and disappear out to the east, then drove to Albuquerque and up again across the purple lip of the Manzanos back into the desert.

Out of Santa Rosa a Buick convertible was pulled down off the road and a blond woman in white pants was standing beside it in the sun, shielding her eyes with one hand and waving the other hand lazily as though she were signaling someone up the road. The Buick had had its left taillight bent in, and the warning signal was flashing dimly in the sunlight. He looked up the highway to see if someone was standing back up on the shoulder, but there was no one, only the black imprint of Santa Rosa quavering on the low table of the desert.

When he stopped, the woman quit waving and rested her hand on her hip, but kept her eyes shielded with her fingers. He got out and walked along the car, looked down in the back seat and saw it strewn with beer cans, some with beer spilling out.

"Sun's real bad for your features, know that?" the woman said indifferently, removing her hand so he could see her small face.

"What'd you do to it?" He motioned at the car.

"He says the pump's busted, but I don't know nothin about it. I know it stopped." She pinched up a piece of her blouse and pulled it away from the skin.

"So where's he gone?" he said.

"Variadero, building a hamburger palace." She shaded her eyes again and studied him as if she had heard something she hadn't liked. He slid in and waggled the key.

"It wouldn't do *me* no good to go turning nothin." She stepped up into the shade of the car and plumped at her hair.

He tried the key. The motor turned over nicely, but quit short of starting. He held the accelerator down and twiddled the key back and forth trying to spark it, but it wouldn't fire, and he finally stopped and squinted at her standing outside in the heat. She looked a lot like a lot of women he'd passed up, little blue-star ear studs, hot skin that made her look older than she was. It made him just want to slide away.

She stiffened her mouth. "Half them's Larry's," she said, flicking her eyes away. "He drinks his breakfast on the way to work, I drink mine on the way home." She laughed. "I don't pick up no hitchikers, though."

"Nobody said you did," he said, staring at the big chrome dashboard trying to figure if one of the gauges was measuring what was wrong with the engine.

"I don't, either," she said.

"That's good," he said, and climbed out. "Look here, I can't get your boat fired up." He flicked the sweat off his chin.

"What the hell am I supposed to do?" she said, glaring out at him.

"I'll take you down the road," he said.

"Curvo," she said, raveling her mouth into a smirk.

"How far is it?"

"What difference does it make if you're going that direction?" she said.

"None," he said, and started back toward the truck.

She reached inside, yanked up a split package of beer, and came behind him. "I got my valuables out," she said, and laughed.

"You going to leave it blinking?" he said, looking unhappily at the beer.

"Hell with it," she said, and climbed in the truck.

She sat high up on the seat, her hand flounced out the window letting the breeze flit between her fingers. She was different the first moment she got in the truck, a little more fragile a framework, he thought, than she had been standing outside beside the car. She had a small round bruise underneath her ear which she worried with her fingers, and every time the wind stripped her hair back against her temples, he got another look at it.

"Air temp makes a difference," she said, watching the hot air through her fingers. "They put 'em in trucks."

"Is that right?"

She looked at him, then turned her face into the breeze.

"What is it your husband does?" he said.

She cranked the window up and gave him a stern look. "Hod carrier. He's eight years younger than I am." She reached forward, ripped the package of beer a little more and set a can on the glove box door. "California's the other way, ain't it?" she said, pulling the top.

"Is that right?"

"You done stole something, ain't you?" she said, letting her head roll against the window frame.

"Off."

"You ain't stole *nothin*, then. I steal *off* every day, but it don't get me anyplace." She laughed. "You think I look old?"

He looked at her short neck, and he tried to make out he was estimating. "How old are you?" he said.

"That ain't the point," she said, having another drink of the beer and setting the can on the armrest. "That ain't the god-damned point. Point is, how old do I *look*? Old? You think I look old?" She watched him carefully to see if he was thinking over telling a lie.

"No," he said.

She raised her head slightly and widened her eyes. "I'm thirty-one. Do I look like it?"

"No," he said, thinking that if he had one guess out of a hundred possible ages, thirty-one would've been second after forty-one. "That means the old man's twenty-three."

She gave him a surprised look. "I ain't worried about that," she said.

"Nobody said so."

She took another drink of her beer. "I take him to work in the morning and come get him in the evening. Them little town bitches come wherever he's at and switch their asses in his face, but they know I'll be pulling up there in my white Buick at six o'clock holding a sack of beer in one hand and something better in the other, so he don't have to go nowhere to have fun but with me. I'm the goddamn fun," she said.

"Where is it you live?" he said, snuffing his cigarette.

"Rag-land." She pointed off into the desert, where he could see the gauzy pancake hills in the south.

"How far you drive every day?"

"Seventy there, sixty back," she said. "I mix it up."

He started figuring miles and looked at her and added it up again, and looked forlornly down the highway. She took a last long gulp of beer and let the can drop between her legs, pinching her mouth in a hard little pucker, as if she had just decided something.

"That's a hell of a ways," he said. "I'd let them switch their ass if it was me."

"You worry about you," she said. "I own the Buick. If I want to drive it to the moon, I will."

She turned away and stared at the desert. He figured he'd just get out of it while he had the chance and make a supreme effort to keep his mouth shut.

"I just don't want to lose him," she said slowly, speaking so softly he had to look at her to see if she was talking to him. "I've had about as much trouble as I can stand," she said. "I'd just like to have things easier, you know?"

"Yeah," he said.

She pulled another beer out of the package and peeled off the top. "We ain't been married but four months," she said, taking a tiny sip and rotating the rim against her lip. "I had a husband to *die* on me seven months ago. TB of the brain." She looked at him appraisingly. "We knew he had it, but didn't figure it would kill him quick as it did." She smacked her lips, looked at him again, and wrinkled her nose. "Flesh started falling, and I had him in the ground in a month."

She gradually seemed to be taking on appeals she hadn't had, and he decided just to let it go.

"In Salt Lake, see?" She was getting engrossed and tapping her beer against the window post. "We was in the LDS, you know?"

He nodded.

"I was the picture, you know, the whole time we was married." Her face got stony. "And after he died they all came around and brought me food and cakes and fruit and first one thing, you know. But when I tried to get a little loan to buy me a car so I could go to work, they all started acting like somebody was callin them to supper. And I had been the picture of what you're supposed to be. I let 'em have their meetings right in my house." She drew her mouth up tight. "Raymond was born one—see? But I was raised on a horse farm outside of Logan."

She took another sip of beer and held it in front of her teeth and stared at the desert. It was past midday. The sun had turned the desert pasty all the way to where the mountains stuck up. He watched her while she looked away, watched her breasts rise and fall, and maneuvered so as to see the white luff of fabric between her blouse and her shoulder showing the curve of her breast, and it made him feel a little shabby and a little bad and he disliked himself.

The woman let her breath out slowly. "I had a friend that had that Buick, just sitting in his garage." She kept looking at the desert. "I told him if he'd let me pay it off a little bit every month, I'd buy it. I always wanted a Buick, and it never seemed like I'd get one. It's queer to have to get down before all your dreams start coming true." She looked at him and her nostrils got wide. "Anyway, I quit the LDS right there," she said, "and got the hell out of that Salt Lake City. Let me just tell you, don't be fooled by them. They're cheap-ass, I swear to God."

He looked at her blouse again to see in the little space, but she had swiveled sideways of him and the space was gone, and he let his eyes wander on back to the road.

She tapped the can against her teeth. "I think I'm better now," she said. "Less quick to judge. It ain't easy to have a window on yourself." She slid back in the seat with her arms folded across her stomach as if she felt better. "Where you going?"

"Arkansas," he said.

"Where's your wife at? Did you leave her home to take care of your babies?"

"I didn't say I was married," he said, feeling itchy.

"I know it." She sighed. "You ain't hid *nothin*, have you?

You're right up on top with everything." She smiled.

"I guess not," he said.

"I ain't getting after you," she said.

"Ain't nothing to get after," he said. "How come you to get married again so quick?"

"Bad luck," she said, and laughed and made her shoulders jerk. "Why don't you drink a beer? I'd feel better if you drank one."

He took a look in the mirror and saw nothing but the markers flashing back. "I'm fine," he said.

She pushed a ring top out the ventilator. "Let me slide over— don't nobody know me at Curvo anyway."

She shoved across the seat and socked her head against his shoulder and put her heels on the dashboard. She let the can of beer, a soft tuft of foam pushing up through the tap, rest on her stomach, and arced her fingers around his thigh. And all he could think was that he wasn't going to do anything to stop it.

She held the half-warm beer can up to his face and rolled it back and forth. "Larry likes that," she said, smiling. "It makes him relax."

He looked at her hiding up under his shoulder, her green eyes with the tiny black centers peeping at him, and reached around her so that her face was drawn up against his chest.

"Do I look thirty-two?" she said, her eyes mounting with tears.

"God, no," he said. "You think I look thirty-four?"

"You're married," she said.

"So are you."

"That's right," she said. "Let's don't talk about that now." One of the tears broke and wobbled onto her lip.

"I want to know how you got married again," he said, holding the truck to the road.

She hugged him so the tear got wiped off, and got her arms around his stomach. "Oh, I went to Albuquerque with my car and moved out to Alameda. You know where that is?"

"I ain't been there but twice," he said, feeling warm inside.

"It ain't far," she said. "I took a little house by myself and drove to work every night at Howard's. I call it Howard's." She drew one fingernail up his leg and made the back of his neck cold. "So

I was driving my car one night along this road where there wasn't any light, drinking Ezra Brooks. And got off the pavement somehow and hit this guy straight on and killed him, just mowed him like a weed. He never even knew what hit him. He just went down *boom.*" She flopped her hand upside down on his thigh. "Just like that. I didn't even have time to honk. I stopped and went back and seen he wasn't moving, and felt of his heart, and it wasn't even fluttering, and I figured it didn't take a nurse to know he was dead. But there wasn't a drop of blood on him nowhere. He was clean as when he'd put that suit on. So I walked off down the road to the Amoco to get one of them boys to call the police. And. thank God I had thrown my Ezra in the ditch, cause when I was walking up the road some drunk slowed down and tried to pull up behind me, and instead of getting beside me, the bastard hit me, and knocked me in the ditch and broke my leg. Son-of-a-bitch just kept going, with me all broke to pieces. It wasn't until the police came along and found *my* car and the guy I hit that they saw me in the ditch up the road bawling my head off."

She looked up at him hopefully.

"So how'd you end up married?" he said.

She drummed her fingers on his leg. "Cause they cramped us up in St. Dominic's Hospital on account of a flash flood in the mountains." She puckered her lips and didn't say anything for a time. "Put all them people in the hospital, and I had to share a room with a man. And that turned out to be Larry. He had his hernia operated on from carrying bricks. And quick as he got out, he started bringing flowers, and we started going one place and another when I got out, and we just sorta caught on. Ain't that romantic?" She smiled.

"How long did all that take?" he said.

"Two months, give a week," she said, "portal to portal."

"That ain't too long," he said.

"Life rushes," she said, and eased her hand up and unzipped his pants. "I'm tired of talking," she said, watching her hand tour around in his trousers as if it were after something that wouldn't keep still.

23

5

Curvo was off the highway ten miles on a gravel track that made a giant curve east and then north again and marooned the town, which was only a red clapboard building, two glass-bulb pumps, and a file of butchered outbuildings, with the desert open all around to every direction. He could see that all the outbuildings were cages of various sorts, patched in with coiled chicken wire to permit inspection from the outside. The largest coop, a square weathered shed built of sawed two-by-fours with the door removed and fresh chicken wire basted over the opening, had a newly stenciled sign that said ZOO.

He stopped between the pumps and the building and looked out the woman's window waiting for someone to come out. The building appeared to be a store, and the plate window was flocked with red fishing bobbers and plaquettes of leader line, and a pair of split cane fishing poles crossed corner to corner. A rooster crowed from down among the cages, and he heard it flap its wings as though it was trying to get away from something.

"Where is everybody?" the woman said, lifting her hair off the back of her neck. "Some kid works here—I seen his old flat-bed last week. Beep the horn." She grabbed at the wheel, but he caught her.

"I'll get out," he said, taking a look back at the cages. "What's your name?" he said.

"Jimmye," she said.

"Jimmye what?"

"What's yours?" she said, aiming her chin at him.

"Robard."

"What is it?" she said.

"Robard."

"That's a damn poor name."

"You're real sweet," he said, shoving the door to.

He walked down the row of cages, looking in each one to see if someone was squatting inside tending to whatever was locked up. In the zoo pen there was nothing but a few scraps of wrinkled cellophane and a gamy smell like something had just died inside. The second cage was a high four-poster frame built of creosote posts, covered with chicken wire and full of raccoons, two fat ones and eight or nine little ones piled into one corner. All the raccoons stopped and stood looking at him, then all at once went back to climbing the cage. In the third cage a maroon, black, and gold rooster had removed himself to the top branch of a fresno bole that had been dragged in from outside and gouged in the ground on the side farthest from the raccoons. It looked to him as if the coons were avid to get at the rooster, and were only waiting to find some tiny fault in the mesh that would turn the tide in their favor once and for all. The rooster was eying everything guardedly, his beaky head snapping from one little coon face to the next, in case one came squeezing through the wires, when he'd have a whole new set of worries.

The woman all of a sudden honked the horn and held it a long time so that the quiet in the yard was exploded. He grabbed a piece of dirt and flung it at the truck.

"What-in-the-shit!" the woman yelled inside the cab, her head erupting out the side, her mouth broke open. "Who's bombing me?"

"Cut out that blowing. You ain't helping nothin."

"I'm hot as shit!" she yelled.

"We're all hot," he said, frowning and feeling desolated.

She ducked her head back in the truck and disappeared below the back window.

A latch snapped at the end of the row and a little girl in jeans let herself out of the last cage and walked up squinting in the sunlight, as if he were someone she was accustomed to. She drew her hair away from her ears, catching it high up with a rubber band, making her face look perfectly round.

"You got a mechanic?" he said, looking behind her to see if anyone else was coming up out of the cage. The girl was wearing a shirt with arrow pockets and mother-of-pearl buttons that belonged to someone bigger than she was.

"What's the matter?" she said, her face arranging itself into a little frown.

"I don't know," he said, looking back at the truck, hoping the woman wouldn't lay down on the horn again. "These here your animals?"

The girl surveyed down the row of cages as if she were trying to make up her mind. "Yes," she said.

"They're nice," he said, taking another uneasy look at the truck and trying to think how to bring up getting her Buick worked on.

"You want to see Leo?" The girl cocked her head into the sunlight so that she could see him with one eye only.

"I seen him if that's him," he said, pointing at the rooster.

"That ain't him," she said, smiling slyly. "He's back yonder." She motioned behind her.

She walked back to the cage she had just come out of, past two box pens that were empty, and stopped outside the last one and pointed in at a big rufous-colored bobcat lounging in the dust, staring at nothing. The girl looked at the bobcat and then at him as if she was expecting a compliment. He studied the bobcat a minute, feeling a little cold commotion inside that had to do with wild animals and the suspicion of what one could do to you before you got turned around. At the bottom of the cage, almost at his feet, there was a big long-boned jack rabbit resting on its haunches, eying the cat quietly, its skinny ribs shoved against the wire so that tufts of fur gouged through in tiny hexagons.

He looked at the girl, waiting for her to say something that explained.

Leo began panting, and strings of thick clear spittle slid off his tongue into the dust. He seemed unconcerned with the rabbit, though the jack seemed intensely concerned with him, and stared at him, its skinny ears flicking around nervously and its nose testing the air as if it were gauging the seriousness of its predicament.

He stood back and stared at the rabbit, and didn't say anything, though after a minute he noticed something about Leo he hadn't seen before. The right back paw was missing at the low joint, the stub matted with thick reddish hair and sprawled behind the other one as if it contained the same big padded paw.

"What come of his leg?" he said, catching his knees and staring at the cat's empty leg.

"Borned bad," the girl said, looking at Leo the way he'd seen a salesman look at used cars. "Hillbilly give him to my dad in Missouri. Found him in a hollow log, starving." She wrinkled her nose as if there were something nasty about it. She squatted on her heels and wiggled her fingers through the wires and called the cat, who rolled over onto his back and squirmed in the dust and stretched his forelegs straight up in the air. "C'mere, Leo," she said, and the cat relaxed and looked at her with his head upside down, eyes half open and gleaming. The rabbit looked at her intently and squeezed back into the corner where she was.

"He thinks I'm calling him." She giggled. "Don't he wish."

"I wouldn't doubt it," he said.

The rabbit went back to measuring the distance.

"You see my coons?" she said, standing and walking up the row to where the coons were decorating the wires.

"I saw 'em," he said.

He looked back at the rabbit and had an impulse to kick the gate open, but the cat bothered him, lounging in the dust, half awake, waiting for somebody to make just such a move. He followed the girl back up the row.

"Got the two old ones," she said, "and the rest just come by themselves." She looked at him as if she were waiting to see what he would say. "I'll sell you one for sixty cents."

He could smell foulness drifting out of the first cage. "Don't think so," he said.

"Yes I will," she said, looking at him professionally.

"I'll buy that rabbit," he said.

"Ain't for sale," she said, and looked out across the empty road and slowly bent her line of vision toward the truck sitting in the dead sunlight. "That your truck?"

He studied the truck. It looked like it had been dropped out of a passing airplane. "Yeah," he said.

"Can't you fix your own truck?"

"Lady's car needs fixin. Ain't the truck."

"Lonnie won't be back here before tonight," she said. "But he won't work on nothing. Be too dark. He won't have the right light."

"Who else is there?" he said, feeling put off.

"Nobody," she said. "He's in Tucumcari. Be roaring drunk when he comes back. Won't work on nothin."

He looked at the sun, cerise and perfectly round, pushing a porous shadow from the raccoon cages over the tips of his toes, and thought it might be two-thirty.

"Is that the woman in the truck?" the girl said.

The back of the woman's head was visible in the oval window. She was working on her face in the rear-view.

"That's her," he said.

"You'll have to spend the night then, or go to Tucumcari," the girl said, turning back to the cages. "There ain't no mechanic from here to there. There ain't nothing up that way." She pointed up the road into the desert. "Lonnie'll be good in the morning. He'll fix it. He ain't but twenty-two, but he ain't a fool."

"Where's your daddy?" he said, looking up at the desolated back side of the house. A white tub washer was set outside in the dirt with one leg bent up.

"Gone," she said, and pursed her lips.

"Are they dead?" he said.

"They gone to Las Vegas. They ain't come back."

"Do you expect them?"

"I guess," she said, and looked at him indifferently.

He was getting nervous. "What time is it?" he said.

The girl consulted her wrist watch, a thin silver strippet with a face as small as her shirt buttons. "Three o'clock," she said. "We got a room. Got a fan in it if Lonnie ain't sold it."

A breeze lifted off the desert and passed through the cages and carried the raccoon foulness back in his nostrils.

"I got to clean that empty cage," the girl said, wrinkling her nose to let him know she could smell it.

"What was in there?" he said.

"That there rabbit," she said, moving a strand of her yellow hair from across her temple where the breeze had left it.

He looked back at the rabbit hied up against the wire, studying the bobcat strangely. A tiny vein of panic opened inside him. "Lemme buy that rabbit," he said quickly.

She frowned. "Leo gets hungry when it gets cool," she said. "That rabbit don't know that, though."

"I bet he's figured it," he said.

She giggled and let him know it didn't make any difference what a rabbit knew. The breeze worried the stray short hairs above her forehead and made her look grown.

"What's your name?" he said.

"Mona Nell," she said, wagging her shoulders and forcing her hands down inside her pants pockets. "What's that woman's name?"

"I believe she said Jimmye."

"That's my daddy's name," the girl said, and laughed.

He looked at the truck and the woman sitting high up in the seat, her back facing him, teasing her hair in the mirror. He felt like he ought to get away, and at the same time felt helpless to maneuver a way to go about it.

The girl giggled again and squatted and began teasing the raccoons, who were piled up against the chicken wire.

He walked back to the truck feeling as if the girl had applied pressures on him that he couldn't quite put his finger on, but that had him whipped.

"Where the hell is everybody?" the woman said, scowling out the window, her hair plumped up and her eyes purple as a bruise.

"Gone," he said softly. "Won't be back till night." He leaned on the window sill and looked back at the girl, squatting in the dust.

"That's the shits," the woman said. "What the hell am I

supposed to do if I got to get Larry at six?" She fattened the corners of her mouth.

"Looks like two things," he said, staring at the ground. "Ride to Tucumcari. That kid said there's mechanics there. Or stay put and call somebody. You can get Larry to come get you."

She frowned at him as if she didn't like hearing him say the name. Her eyes got small. "They got a telephone?"

He looked at the eave of the house and saw a trunk line strung to the road. "I guess," he said.

She looked at the wire. Perspiration had formed in the roots of her hair. "Son-of-a-bitch, Larry Crystal," she said.

It occurred to him that she had just said her last name.

"He'll be off with his piss-ant brother drinking beer quick as he sees I ain't coming. That's the trash he is." She lowered her brow as if she could see all that was coming.

The first truck to pass the station hissed through the curves and ground out into the road—a tandem hauling diesel smoke into the desert. There was large writing on the sides through dust and coagulated grease, WHACK MY OLD DOODLE, and below that, TAKE ANOTHER LITTLE PIECE OF MY HEART, as though one line followed on the other and made good sense. He looked at the writing and scratched the back of his neck and wondered what that meant. He thought about asking her to have a look at it, but she looked mean and he decided against it.

"What time is it?" she said.

"Something till," he said.

The girl was down at the far end of the row of cages and was cooing to the bobcat, saying his name over and over in a sweet voice.

"Let's get out of here," she said.

"Where we going?" he said.

"A tourist court up at Conchas. You and me is staying in it. Let's git."

He looked at her to let her know he was considering it. "What about the car?"

"Shit on *it*. The car ain't going nowhere."

He rested his forehead against his wrists and stared at the dirt, trying to think about what to do. "I thought you *was* worried about it," he said.

"Let's get out of here, all right?" she said. "Worry about that tomorrow."

"What about . . . ?"

"What about shit!" she said. "Leave my business to me. If I need any advice, I'll ask your little cunt you're so hot about."

"I ain't hot," he said, keeping his head sealed against his wrist and spitting in the dust.

She got quiet, and he decided to let things be quiet awhile.

"I'm waitin," she said.

"What're you waitin on?" he said.

She glared, and her eyes darkened in the middle, and he understood it was the way she looked when she wanted to seem angry.

She sat staring straight out at the long curve in the road, breathing deeply. The breeze switched and came up from behind the building. The girl sat on her haunches, making a high-pitched hooting noise like a dove. He figured the woman needed time to figure out he wasn't going to have himself ruled by somebody that didn't mean anything to him, no matter what the reward was, or even if it meant giving up the reward.

"Ain't no need being mad," he said into the hollow of his arm.

She looked away.

"Ain't no need to go somewhere else."

"I'm past the point of carin," she said, letting her shoulders relax.

"They got a room right here," he said.

She looked at the long red building, then at him and back down the road.

"The boy can look after the car in the morning," he said, feeling things sliding away from him.

She caught a corner of her lip between her teeth and drummed her fingers. "They got a air temp?" she said.

"Fan," he said.

Her pale face seemed to pale more while he looked at her, like coarse cloth held to the sun.

"Might as well," she said, looking out in the desert toward the hazy cactus figures pinpointing the horizon, and sighing. "We can't dance in this heat."

6

The girl led them inside the house, where it was murky and cool, and stood behind a store counter before an old ledger book. The room was lit by whatever light could angle through the flocked window, and by a mint-colored bulb in the cold case at the back of the store. He had to get near the page to see to sign, and when she pointed the place, he looked at the book for a moment and signed "Mr. & Mrs. S. Tim Winder," using the ballpoint chained to the ledger. The only other registry on the page was at the top, written in square penciled letters that said "RAMONA ANELIDA WHEAT, THE QUEEN."

The girl led them between two steepled rows of Vienna sausages and Wheat Chex, through a green portiere and up two flights of stairs to where it was quiet and hotter, and where it smelled to him like an icebox that had been locked up and left in the heat. Sunlight illumined a square of green linoleum, and the room drew together inside like a kiln. There was a brown metal bed, a serpentine bureau with a doily, a chair, and a string-pull ceiling fan with one blade removed.

"You better open a window," the girl said, blinking in the heat and holding her ponytail up to let off the hot air. "It'll cool off when the sun moves. You'll be hollerin for a blanket."

"Ain't there no toilet?" Jimmye said, looking desperate in the heat.

"That fan works." The girl reached on her toes and yanked the string. The motor hummed as if it were straining against resistance, and the blades stayed still. "Pot's downstairs," she said. "We got two."

He went to the window, pried it up, and stood back to allow in the breeze, but there was no moving air. The truck looked abandoned in the lot, sunshine gleaming off the hood. He tried to think about what had gotten him up this far, up into this room when he should have been on the highway halfway to somewhere, and he couldn't figure it at all.

"Ain't there no sinks?" the woman said.

"In the pot," the girl said. "I'll put a glass in there. Lonnie'll be back tonight. You'll hear him cause it'll be a noise when he does. He gets drunk as cooter brown."

"I can't wait," the woman said, flouncing on the bed. "What else does he do?"

"Nothin," the girl said, and let her jaw fall open and shift back and forth while she stared at the woman. "Check-out's eight-thirty. You get charged another day." She threw the key at the dresser and slammed the door before the woman could speak.

"A.M. or P.M.?" she yelled, but the words got slammed in the door. "Little split-ass. A kid pimp—ain't that the shits," she said.

He stood staring down at the truck.

"I know you," she said, laughing and bouncing lightly on the bed. "You got the eye for that little twat."

He walked across and stood in front of the bureau and looked at her and sighed, his hands in his pockets, wondering whether it would do just to leave her sitting, go off for a Grapette, and never show back.

"What're you lookin at?" she said, and slumped on the side of the bed, watching him meanly.

He shook his head.

"What're you shaking your ugly head at?"

"Not anything," he said, trying to quit thinking.

"You think you're some hot young stuff, don't you?" she said.

"I hadn't thought about it," he said.

"Oh, yes, you *did,*" she said. "You thought you were too good to screw me, but I got some bad news for you—you weren't." Her eyes had gotten round again and she looked frightened. "You're right to my level. It may of took you a while to get here, but you're here, by God." She retired to her elbows.

"Where'd you get that colored mark on your neck?" he said.

"He give it to me," she said proudly. "It ain't a *mark*. Don't you know what a hickey is, Robert? Did you think somebody'd been beatin up on me?"

"I didn't think about it," he said.

"I guess not." She poked around after the mark, as if she thought she could feel it.

The fan had begun circling. He picked up the chair and brought it to the side of the bed. He sat with his elbows on his knees and his face collapsed in his hands. She smiled at him and he knew she knew everything.

"You gonna stay mad at me?" he asked quietly.

"I ain't mad," she said. "You ain't nobody."

"That's right." He listened to his breath escaping between his fingers.

"You ain't hidin *nothing*—are you, Robert?"

"No," he said.

Her smile sweetened and flesh collected in a little pouch under her chin.

"How come you're up here with me? I'm a married woman," she said. "Ain't you married?"

"I guess," he said.

"Ain't you got no sense of right?"

"I guess not," he said.

"This here's adultery, boy," she said, smiling keenly. "Who's it paying the bill?"

"Whoever wakes up second, I reckon," he said.

She pressed in his direction, letting her legs scissor a fraction. "You going to strand me, are you, Robert?" She let her calves rub his knees, her pants pushing above her ankles.

"What's-his-name'll be to get you," he said.

"Sure will," she said. "You better hope he don't find you here, or there'll be shit to fly."

She kept smiling, and he had the impulse to get out the door and not stop until he had reached the line to Texas.

"He won't find nobody but you," he said.

She pushed off her elbows and straddled him, her pants

squeezed up on her knees, her eyes wide. He set his hands along
her calves and wedged them inside the material, and felt the cords
in her thighs. She lay on the spread, breathing evenly and letting
her head wag side to side.

"He won't find me," he said. His throat was dried up.

She hummed in her throat and turned her face so that she
stared at the metal uprights above the foot of the bed.

He unbuttoned her pants and slid them around her thighs. Her
skin was bluish. She hissed through her teeth as though it were
a pain commencing. He laid her pants over the chair back and
pushed his hands up her legs. She bridged her neck and sank her
elbows in the ticking.

"Robert?" she said, her arms laid out, her hands made into fists.

"What?"

"Do you think I look thirty—I mean, with you looking at me?"

The linoleum buckled. He tried to get himself onto the bed and
pay attention to what she was saying all at the same time.

"No, sweet," he said softly.

She drew her legs up and eased his hand, faced down the
bedspread and smiled.

"You don't look twenty where I'm at," he said.

"I ain't mad at you no more," she said, her voice lost inside her
throat.

"That's sweet," he said. "Now that's real sweet."

7

At seven o'clock it had turned gray down in the east. The coons
were against the wires, staring at the sun sagging by degrees. Leo
lay quietly, eying the rabbit, who had dozed as the day cooled and
was not awake, the breeze pushing back lightly against the hatch
of his fur, laying bare a smooth white undercoat.

He lay beside the woman in the brown light feeling the breeze
draw through the room, pulling the curtains and plucking the

flesh on his arms. The screen slammed and he could hear the girl move out in the yard, cooing at the raccoons. The woman shuddered and he looked at her expecting her eyes to open, but she lay still, breathing as if she were barely alive. He could smell the sage on the breeze, a faint burning aroma in his nostrils, and he could hear the raccoon claws clamber down the wires to the child.

"You make me feel kinder towards the world," she had said, and he couldn't figure out why, and lay with his chin in the pillow, listening.

"Don't you feel that way all the time?"

"No." Her lips were to his ear. "I get contrary, get people in trouble."

"Don't he make you feel good?"

"Larry does. Sometimes."

"How come you want to foul up with me?"

She turned on her side and crossed her arms beneath her chin. "I don't trust him," she said, as if it were something she always knew, but had just realized.

"You're up there every day," he said. "What ain't there to trust?"

"If I *wasn't* up there, he'd be humpin some bar bitch like he is right now."

"But you *are* up there," he said.

"And there's a lot of tonk bars between Rag-land and Variadero, too—see?" she said.

He graveled his chin in the pillow and tried to figure that out. "Looks like you got him jumpin the creek."

"You're sweet," she said, and gave him a kiss on the shoulder. "I love him. But I can't trust him not to wipe me out."

"So what does that mean?" he said.

"I got to cheat on him so he don't have a chance to leave me like I was in Salt Lake."

"That don't make sense," he said.

She smiled. "If I cheat on him a *little,* and he knows I'm liable to anytime, then it balances me—see? He can't feel like he's put nothin on me, cause he knows I'm probably putting something on him already. It gets dangerous when you feel like you can fool the other one anytime you get ready and not pay for it. Everything starts splitting. You got to stay balanced."

She ran her fingers through the hair on his belly. "I want you," she said in a queer high voice.

"Wait now," he said, picturing Larry laying bricks in Variadero and wondering where his wife was while the sun was going and whether or not she was liable to show up, or whether she was stopping over in some tonk bar and not making it in until tomorrow. "Does he know that's how you're playing it?"

"Let's don't us talk," she said, grabbing him up in her tight little fist and rolling her eyes back. "I need it right now, understand?"

"But wait a minute," he said.

"No waits," she said. "No waits."

When she had gone to sleep he lay and stared at the ceiling, spattered with the gold tinsel of water seepage. He understood that when it rained, it rained until the boards soaked and the water shot the walls and set the house floating like an ark. He dozed and felt himself drawn to a powerful commotion as though the sky were driving through the cages, drowning animals, filling the truck bed, and buoying him inside until it was necessary to hold the bed staves to be saved from drowning. There were lights in the yard, flashing through the panes across the wall in his room, revolving rectangles of light across the wall, and he had sat up startled and faced them and heard the groan of someone's pickup and two doors slamming and the soft lilt of voices in the yard. He walked out on the low plank porch and stood where his mother was watching the two men angrily while they talked one at a time in quick low tones, trying to avoid her eyes and get the story told and get gone. They stood silhouetted in the truck lights that fanned the grassy spiderwebs, and for a while his mother stared at them while they talked, watching them intently, snapping her eyes over one and to the other, holding them unmovable until they finally talked so fast the words ran together into gibberish.

And after a while she just stared past them into the headlights, and they finished and left. The way the woman told it, his father had gone up into the hills early in the evening to attend a service, and took the woman with him in his car. And three-quarters of the way up the long grade, full of roots and chuck holes, winding up the Bostons toward the top of Mount Skylight, where the tent was supposedly staked on a high knob, the old car had failed where they forded a creek, a ribbon of spring water squirreling down the mountain toward the Illinois River. The woman said she got out and went into the bushes while his father stayed and monkeyed with the dashboard wires, trying to get the car going before it got night. And when the woman came back from the bushes, it had begun to rain, "an unimaginable rain," she said, that smacked the sides of the car like a lanyard, and the water rose over the bottoms of the doors and swirled and shot past the car so that a strong man couldn't have walked through it without falling. And she said she could see him inside humped over the dashboard studying the wires and fuses, unaware, she guessed, that the creek was up or that it might not do to be out in it. She herself, a plump, slope-eyed woman from Tonitown, said she never imagined what the outcome would be, and went up and squatted underneath a plum bush to wait for the rain to stop and the creek to subside so they could go on to the church, which turned out to be accessible by some other road. And as she sat, the water got dark and creamy, and rose, and pieces of split-off pine timber came down the chute, and she got wringing wet watching the limbs batter the car and the water rise to the door locks. She said she believed Mr. Hewes did sense something was not right, because he opened the window and said something to her that she couldn't hear and tried to open the door, but the water was against it and the other side was busted from before she knew him. And she said that he closed the window and looked out, laughing and grinning and making funny little signals with his hands, signals she said she couldn't make out any better than what he'd said. She said for a long time, maybe ten minutes, the two of them sat and looked at each other, she on the bank under the plum bush, wet, and he shut inside the car with the ugly water raging around, smiling and making signals, perfectly dry. Until, she said, the water seemed to wash over the car all at once, without a wave or a tree limb to hit it, or any inkling that it was losing purchase, and just suddenly, rolling, it rolled over and the water over it and it out of sight into the darkness.

Robard felt himself to suffer the long breathless suspension, suspended between the moment of purchase and the moment when whatever it was had knocked him unconscious and made it feasible for him to drown in the floor of his own car, so that he felt that at any moment at all he could expect the impact and the long slow daze that ended by dying.

8

Behind the house the clouds had piled against the sky. The sun had gone and left the sky indistinct and pinkish. In the east it had been dark a long time. He lay still in the smoky light. There was a chill in the room, and he could hear the girl outside teasing the raccoons onto the rungs of the cage. He rose quietly, dressed in the corner, and carried his shoes out the door. On the floor outside the girl had laid a blanket, and he brought it inside and spread it over the woman, covering her until her fingers clutched the basting and she drew it around herself and slept on. He slipped down the stairs into the store, where the cold box glowed and the compressor hummed in the gloom. He took a candy bar out of a plastic jar and a soda from the cooler and stepped into the lot, where the air was slow with the fragrance of sage.

The little girl looked up when she heard the screen slap, and went back to tempting the raccoons when she saw it was him.

"You got a Butterfinger?" she said, keeping her eyes averted.

"And a Grapette," he said, squeezing candy out of his teeth and taking a look down the cages.

"Seventeen cents," she said.

Her hair was full of fine gold threads mingled with what was almost white. "I set you a blanket out," she said without looking up. "It'll get cold. I knocked but didn't nobody answer."

"We must've dozed," he said, taking an interest in what he could see of the cat's cage, but feeling reluctant to go down to it.

The raccoons nibbled and licked the girl's fingers when the celery was gone. The rooster perched on a low branch and studied the raccoons curiously, as if he couldn't understand anything about them.

"What about your rabbit?" he said, stuffing the candy paper in his pocket.

"What about him?" she said.

He glanced down the list of cages. "His time must be about up?"

She giggled and pulled a cellophane bag of peanut hulls out of her shirt pocket and began feeding hulls to the coons one at a time. "His time came and went," she said.

He looked at the girl quickly, feeling bested. "I thought you said he didn't get hungry till the sun went down." He walked up toward Leo's cage.

"I can't tell Leo when to get hungry," she said.

"I didn't hear nothin," he said, looking up at the window with the chintz curtains flagging gently outside.

"Leo don't make no noise," she said. "Sometimes the rabbit makes a little peep, like a bird, but usually it just gives in and don't say anything."

Leo was lying against the back wire tearing off a piece of the rabbit's haunch and beginning to chew it deliberately. He searched the ground, but there was no sign of a struggle in the dust, as if the rabbit might have made a dash when Leo decided his time had come. There were two skid tracks where Leo had dragged the rabbit back to his own precinct, and it occurred to him that the rabbit might just have died of fright. After sitting in the sun all day staring at Leo's eyes, the final seconds might have been too much for him, and when he saw Leo get up, it may have been over right then. The long wait must have got him. Leo gurgled at a sinew and pawed it with his front feet, stretching it backward until it snapped.

He felt an awful anguish and looked at the girl, who was watching him, squatting in the dirt. He felt maybe somebody ought to sit down and talk to her, and tell her she wasn't doing things right, give her an idea on how things ought to be. Except it wasn't his business and there couldn't be any use making it be. If she wanted to feed rabbits to wildcats, then there wouldn't be any way on earth to make her quit, since somebody had taught her that that was a thing to do. And there wasn't any changing that.

"What time is it?" he said.

She looked at her wrist watch. "Seven-forty. Dark by eight," she said.

He saw the sky was steely down to the horizon. A flicker of bat slipped through the air and disappeared.

"Lonnie won't be back till late," she said.

"Do me a favor." He rubbed his fingers through his hair.

"Depends," she said.

"Tell that lady"—he eyed the window, inside of which the air was dark—"I had to leave."

The girl got up off the ground and dusted her jeans and stuffed the cellophane in her shirt pocket. "Who's paying?" she said.

He opened his wallet and took out a bill.

"Three dollars and seventeen cents," she said, watching the empty Grapette bottle dangle off his finger.

"Keep the rest for the favor," he said.

"She ain't sick, is she?"

"Tell her I said I had to take off. She won't care."

"She ain't going to like it," the girl said confidently, rocking on her heels.

"She won't care," he said.

"What *you* say," the girl said, and glared at him. "You ain't foolin nobody."

"I know it," he said, moving toward the truck.

The girl stared at him coldly.

He could see the last stippets of gold in her hair. He took a look at the window and saw the curtains swell into the breeze, and started for the truck. He dropped the bottle in the oil can by the pumps, and the girl watched him a time, then broke for the house, her ponytail licking her shoulders as she disappeared in the store, the screen door whacking shut. He could hear her hit the inside stairs. He let the truck idle, watching the door as if he were waiting for the woman and the girl to come boiling out like bloodhounds. But no one came, and he let the truck idle out onto the road. He watched the house in the mirror while it sank, and it satisfied him to think that when the woman woke she could as soon feel kindly toward the world, and toward herself, and toward Larry and maybe toward him.

At eight-fifteen it was dark. He passed Tucumcari, a strip of dairy bars and gray stucco buildings with lights frozen in the darkness. He watched the drive-in lots and along inside the lighted cafés for someone that might be the girl's brother, some kid standing up against a building waiting to get sober. He watched for a flat-bed truck parked back in the gravel lots, but there was nothing to fit what he had made up in his mind, a boy holding a bottle by the skinny neck, staring cross-eyed at the sky as if he hadn't figured out some mystery that plagued him. He stopped at the east edge of town and ate Mexican food and a bowl of custard and drove the thirty miles into Glenrio and from there past the signs into Texas before midnight.

9

In the night he had driven over the flat husk of Texas to Oklahoma. After two o'clock his legs cramped and his eyes got tricky, framing figures on the fringe of the road caught in the headlights, then vanishing when the truck got into them. At two-thirty he hid the truck in a pecan orchard, slept an hour on a sawbuck table and woke in the cold odor of green pecans, pressed dew in his eyes and started into Arkansas.

The letter in his shoe said:

> *Robard. I have me a plastic bag and a way to use it once I see you in your flesh. It can't wait forever. You have got to come and get it. This here is me. Beuna.*

Underneath her signature was a mark on the paper where she had pressed something wet, then allowed it to dry before folding it in the envelope so the paper was wrinkled and blotched a fishy yellow shade, but wasn't stuck together. Around it she had drawn a circle in ink with an arrow pointing down from the words "This here is me." It made him feel hot inside. Though it was true enough that after that hotness expired nothing else was certain. The best he could remember, Helena was a weedy cotton plant on the skin of the delta. He had stayed around in 1959, working the Missouri Pacific in Memphis and deadheading down to save rent, boarding with his mother's cousin two days a week, and whomping Beuna both nights in the attic, then spending the day slipping around waiting for dark. All of which added up to maybe fifteen days sum that he had ever spent in Helena, Arkansas, which made him nervous when he let his mind play on it. Since fifteen days was almost too little an acquaintance to hope to come back after twelve years and carry on what he was hoping to carry on in the midst of everybody and have it work out the way he wanted without there being a slip-up somewhere and somebody noticing some irregularity. And he figured the only thing to do would be to be fast enough and cute enough when the time came to get out before the shooting started.

He had gone about settling some things before he left Bishop, standing at the screen, explaining to himself that in behalf of being smart, he couldn't afford any reliances, since there wasn't anybody to rely on and since there wasn't any reason to believe the place or anybody in it would turn out any better or kinder or any more understanding than they had been when he tried to make it honest, working for old man Rudolph, and had gotten squeezed out by the innate stinginess that infested the place and everybody in it like an air that you couldn't breathe, but couldn't live without. He had just told himself that very thing over and over standing at the door waiting for good dark to settle, and by the time he left Bishop, he had it fixed in his mind.

Except that back behind whatever little plans he had was at least the reliance that the place *would* hold him up long enough to do what he came to do, pay him, in a sense, for having been born there and having put a good-hearted attempt into staying when it was clear nobody like him ever *should* stay. And the moment he figured he had kept that reliance, in spite of all he had schooled himself to believe, he had had the strongest unfaltering feeling he had made a mistake somewhere, and that the thing he ought to do was turn around and go back without another say-so. Except it was way too late by then, and he couldn't ever turn around now, not after getting this close. And it would all have to be worth it.

10

In Little Rock he ate breakfast and got back outside in the chill to the phone booth. He took off his shoe, got the letter, and flattened it on the shelf where he could see. He got Helena and wrote the number at the bottom of the letter just below where it said "This here is me," and dialed the operator. The phone started ringing a long way off. Morning traffic came slowly. He watched two policemen saunter out of the café and stand looking at the truck, talking like they thought they wanted to buy it, then laugh at something and drive out of the café lot.

The phone was answered by a voice several feet from the receiver. "All right," the voice said.

"Beuna?" He could barely get the word audible.

"What do you think?" she said. He heard the receiver strike something hard as if she were trying to hammer more words out.

"Who is this?" she said, her voice drifting away then reviving. "W.W., it better not be your asshole trick."

"It's me," he said, feeling the words stop up in his throat.

"I'm hanging up," she said. He could hear her pounding the plunger. "Get the sheriff," she said.

"It's Robard," he whispered. And everything seemed to slide back, like a whole panoramic world had moved into the background, leaving him in the calamitous center, alone and unprotected. A fishy sweat crept up in his palms, and his short hairs got stout.

"Who?"

"Robard."

"Oh, shit!" she said, as if some foulness had happened where she was.

"Beuna?"

"Where are you? God!"

"Little Rock," he said, switching hands and wiping his face.

"I'll come meet you," she said, all out of breath.

"No," he said. "I'll *be* there. Don't do nothin."

"Robard, I've been so awful," she said, sobbing. "It's giving me the shakes to hear you."

"Don't do nothin," he said. His hands started trembling.

"Robard?"

"What?"

"I'm gonna come on the phone."

"Don't now," he said.

"I'm going to, it's just doing it."

"Don't, just don't do that, goddamn it now!"

"I can't help it, things comes on you."

"No!" he yelled at the receiver.

"Robard?"

"What?"

"Can we go someplace? It ain't got to be far."

"We'll see," he said. His mind sunk into gloom, as if he were caught in some commotion he needed to control but couldn't quite make slow down.

"Robard?"

"What?"

"I got my little bag?"

"I remember." He could see the little bag, without knowing exactly what could happen with it.

"We're going to have to go to Memphis to do it. There's these rooms in the Peabody Hotel that's got shower baths with eight nozzles that shoots you everywhere at once."

"All right," he said, gasping.

"Robard?"

"What?"

"I want to do it in that thing with you."

"We will," he said, wondering what you did. "I'll call you."

"W.W. ain't here days. He's workin at the BB plant and playing ball at Forrest City. He don't come back until late."

"All right," he said, his mind whipping. "I can't come today."

"You got you some girl?"

"No," he said, pressing his head against the window glass and leaning until the booth started to groan and he had his entire weight concentrated on just one cold spot of glass.

"Why can't you?"

"Look, I'll call you," he said.

"You ain't got to bite my head off," she said.

"I got to go."

"Do you love me?"

"I can't talk about that."

"You said 'All right' the last time. I remember."

"What else you want me to say?"

"I don't know," she said in a small voice. "Say 'All right' again and that'll be enough."

"All right."

A silence opened through the line.

"Just think about that," he said, "and them shower baths."

"God," she said, moaning. "You're going to make me come."

"I'll be there," he said, wanting to get out.

"Robard?"

"Huh."

"Is something the matter with you?"

"Nothing is," he said. He folded the letter with one hand and stuffed it in his shirt pocket on top of the Butterfinger wrapper.

"I thought something was the matter," she said.

"Everything's wonderful," he said.

"It is," she said. "Don't you think everything's wonderful?"

"Yes, hon, I do."

"I do," she said sweetly. "Now that you're here, I do. Everything's been so awful."

"I'm hurrying," he said, unable to get his breath again.

"Oh, good God," she said, and hung up.

11

He stopped in Hazen to buy cigarettes and walked toward where the old man kept his rooms. Hazen was fifty miles from Little Rock, a rice prairie town along the Rock Island, a white stone grain elevator by the tracks, a few cages and poultry houses catering to duck hunters, and a smatter of houses and mobile homes in the oaks and crape myrtles, and all the rest save a pecan orchard given up to the rice, planted in tawny, dented fields to the next town, twenty miles in all directions.

By the time he had come up from Helena eleven years ago and gone to work for Rudolph, watching his sluice gates in the summer and sitting out winters in the little shotgun house the old man had built as a warming house for the duck hunters, Rudolph's troubles were all over with and there wasn't anything left for the old man to do but sit up nights and wonder about it.

He crossed the Rock Island tracks and walked down the right of way through the suck weeds and across the gravel path to where he could see the white plank house with the old man's rooms recessed in the dark corner under the south eave. He could remember the old man slumped on the broken shingle of his mattress, his undershirt catching the pale light in the room, coughing and snorting and staring across the empty floor, trying to think of something to say by way of important instructions, before he sent him back to the pump house to tend the gates. He could hear the landlady downstairs, rattling the tiny trays she used to coddle the old man's eggs, while Rudolph rested his belly on his thighs, drifting in and out of sleep, waiting for the word to come into his head that he could give and that might make sense to somebody. Finally he would murmur something low out of the cavity of his chest, some gate to close or spillway to wind open for an hour or a ditch to inspect for seepage, anything to keep the help moving water from place to place. The old man would stop and snort and gaze out in the dark, and he would slip down the stairs, through the hot kitchen, and take out across the cold fields. Like that.

When he had first come up from Helena there had been, he remembered, a man named Buck Bennett who had worked for old man Rudolph, hired to run local fishermen off the reservoirs, patrol the roads, and see over the property when he wasn't too drunk to find the deputy's badge the old man paid for, or too drunk to keep his old jeep out of the bar ditches, where the old man promised it would remain, since he wouldn't let a wrecker come on the property to pull him out, though he said Buck could come and look at his jeep whenever he wanted to if he had any doubts about its still being there.

Buck would come down late in the evening, drink a pint of whiskey, and sit on the one claw-toed chair the pump cabin had and talk about the old man.

Buck said that the old man had come down sometime in 1941, from Republican City, Nebraska, had sold his half of his father's pig farm to his brother Wolfgang and moved himself and two steamer trunks on the train to Little Rock and put himself up in a commercial hotel at the foot of the Main Street bridge and bought himself a Buick coupe and drove all over the country between Little Rock and Memphis looking for cheap land. And after not very long, Buck said, he bought eight hundred acres of swamp fifteen miles back out of Hazen, land that no farmer had even thought to abandon, much less cultivate, since La Fourche Creek ran straight through the middle of it and flooded every spring, leaving a solid counterpane of silt and randy water on top of the entire parcel so that even the rice farmers had given up on it and just kept it for duck hunting. He said that Rudolph, who was in his thirties and strong as a bulldog, had gotten hold of the land and practically gnawed every tree on it with his own teeth and built up a maze of bar ditches and ramparts and iron sluice gates to channel the water out of the lows and into an old dead-tree reservoir he dug out with three World War I scoopers. In a year's time he had gotten the land set up to be a farm, built a two-story shingle house and a metal windmill, and transported an Austrian man and his family down from Republican City to live on it and run the farm, and promptly moved himself out of the commercial hotel and into the R. E. Lee on Markham Street and fell in love with the lady who owned it and six more like it in Memphis and Shreveport, and whose husband had been drowned falling out of an inner tube on Lake Nimrod, leaving it all to her.

Buck said that before very long Rudolph had communicated his feelings to the lady, a small wiry red-haired woman named Edwina, and that they were married in the hotel lobby with a bang, and that right away Rudolph moved up to her suite on the eleventh floor and started ordering baskets of fruit and cases of whiskey and running the bellboys up and down the elevators bringing him one thing after another, until Edwina had to tell him the hotel was for other things than just to make him happy.

When the farm started making more money than he could count (though not more than he could save), Rudolph began carrying Edwina's friends to shoot ducks on the big reservoir or back in the woods where he had left the water standing in the winter. Though, Buck said, every time he did it he arranged to get mad and raise hell with everybody for driving too fast on the gravel roads that he had graded personally, or for killing suzies instead of greenheads, or for some infraction of the rules that he was making up as he went along, and finally ran all her friends off entirely when they wouldn't do things the way he wanted them done, though Buck said it was hard to figure out just how that was. He began carrying an old steel-barrel 12-gauge across the seat of his car as a convincer when he came on somebody he didn't like or wanted to run off. And all the time living in Little Rock like a caliph and staying up in the suite drinking Evan Williams and eating fruit and ordering people around including Edwina, and making everybody wish they had never seen him.

Buck said it didn't seem like any time until Edwina had him divorced and married herself off to an Italian named Tarquini who was fifteen years younger than she was and wore his suits halfway up his asshole, and whom Rudolph had taken out to the farm two separate times before he found out what was happening on the days he stayed at the farm by himself and left Edwina to her own devices. Buck said Tarquini was just some interior decorator from Chicago that Edwina had hired to re-deluxe her hotels, but couldn't resist getting in the sack with since she and Rudolph weren't seeing things eye to eye.

In the settlement Rudolph made Edwina donate him a room in the R. E. Lee for life and one free meal a day, and when it was over he went back down to Hazen, where he could go to the farm when he wanted to and drive his old grader down the roads and along the bar ditches and run everybody off he didn't like and spend time figuring out just what had happened to him.

Buck said he guessed the old man probably used the farm to get back at Edwina by just never inviting anybody she ever knew or that he ever knew when he knew her to hunt with him, and by paying him, Buck, to take people in and out all winter for a thousand dollars a season and letting that information get back to Edwina by mentioning it to the waiters in the dining room when he came into town to eat his free meal and stay in his free room.

He said the old man would come down to the cabin late at night and have a bottle of Williams and an old R. E. Lee Hotel glass and pour Buck a level and watch him drink it, then sit back and cry like a baby. Buck said he had to just keep on drinking until it was gone, because he couldn't stand listening to the old man cry and tell the story over and over again. Finally, he said, he'd tell Rudolph his was just a clear case of bad timing, and then go to sleep. The old man sat there, he said, staring out the screen door into his rice fields not able to sleep because he had a problem he couldn't understand. And Buck said that he never would have drunk so much if it hadn't been for all those nights.

He walked around to the side of the house and knocked on the door, thinking he could ask what had happened to the old man and go on. The old woman came to the screen and smiled as if she recognized him, and said Rudolph still had his rooms.

He thought he ought to forget it and go back. He smiled at the woman and she pushed open the screen and he got inside before he knew it and she pointed up the narrow hallway to the upstairs, and he went up. He felt like he was making a mistake acting like he wanted to see the old man when he didn't want to at all, and was disappointed to know he was alive still, when he shouldn't have been alive at all. The door at the top was closed, and a thin pane of light radiated over the sill. He could hear the woman reading her newspaper out loud in the kitchen and the sound of her chair groaning.

He knocked and the old man said to come in, standing in the middle of the room under a hanging bulb, wearing poplin pants and no shirt, staring wild-eyed as if he were getting ready to make a charge. He looked heavy-chested and bent to one side, his white hair stuck up in tussocks over his ears. He regretted ever coming inside.

The room was sour. The old man looked at him intently, as if he thought he recognized him, the way the old woman did, but couldn't be sure.

"See Minor," he said suddenly, "about the work. Don't see me."

"No sir," he said, and pressed back against the molding of the door, thinking about getting out.

"Who is that?" Rudolph said, and stepped up under the bulb.

"Hewes," he said. "I used to work on number two."

The old man got a step closer. "Took off without saying whoop-dee-doo, too," the old man shouted, like it had happened last night. "I come out a week later wonderin where in the shit you was, and there was my house wide open, lights burning, propane still in the pipes." He took a step back and humped down beside his desk table. "What do you say about that?"

"I had to leave of a sudden," he said, fixing his eyes on the single closed window behind the old man's head.

"Well, there ain't no more house!"

"What come of it?" he said.

The old man squinted as if he had just decided he was really somebody else. "Remember Buck Bennett?"

"Yes sir."

"Buck Bennett was a crazy son-of-a-bitch. You remember that?" The old man smiled companionably as if he could see Buck at that very moment drunk and falling down.

"I guess," he said.

"He was a drunk, now." The old man reached down and jerked his white sock up and plowed at his nose. "He took five bone sawyers from New Orleans back in there on two, forgot to light the jet after he'd turned it on. The bone sawyers got there drunk, and they all sat down to wait for shooting time, and every one of them went to sleep and didn't wake up. They found Mr. Buck's cadaver on the bed with a doughnut in his hand. He musta eat that doughnut and went to sleep, and all the rest of them just sat out there at the table and put their heads down. They didn't even get a doughnut." The old man pawed his face and gawked as if it had been a great inconvenience.

"When did that happen?" he said, trying to envision Buck's old face, and unable to work it back out.

"December, six years ago," he said quickly. "I didn't see the bastard for two or three days. He didn't come to get my instructions. So I figured he was drunk, and went out to his house and there they all six of 'em was, and the place smelled like hell. There wasn't no way to get it out of the boards. So I went out, after they had carried them all off, with a gallon of gasoline and put a match to the son-of-a-bitch, and burnt it down and plowed it under." He smiled. "So there ain't no more house. I put soybeans in there right where you lived."

"What do you do with the hunters?" he said, still trying to fathom up Buck's face.

"Put 'em in Minor's house. He's got sense to keep a fire lit. I don't employ no more drunks." The old man's tiny blue eyes seemed to hold tears in them.

"Buck said he wouldn'ta drunk so much if you hadn't brought him the whiskey," he said.

"He's a goddamn liar," the old man shouted, rising out of his chair, his eyes snapping. He grabbed the backing on the chair and squeezed it until the cane cracked. "Buck was on the goddamned hooch the first day I seen the bastard, and it was hooch that killed him by muddying his goddamned mind so he couldn't even remember to light a goddamned pilot."

"He figured you give it to him so he couldn't do anything else and so you wouldn't have to pay him nothing. He couldn't do nothin about it, Mr. Rudolph, but he knew it."

"Buck went to California—you know that, don't you?"

He watched the old man's face twist out of one angry expression into another one.

"He went out there and learned how to be a soak and come back here and tried to turn it into a skilled trade," the old man said.

"Some people ain't lucky," he said, watching the old man grow madder and madder, and feeling better.

"Some people don't know when they're good off." His eyes flashed. "They have to fuck it up. What're you doing here, Hewes —trying to fuck up something?"

"I wanted to look at you."

"What the hell for?" The old man was hunched up underneath the bulb, glaring.

"If I had a good idea, I might just think about twistin your head off."

The old man smiled instantly. "Old Buck might not of known

very much, but he knew how to kill hisself good enough. You don't even know how to do that, Hewes." Rudolph's smile broadened until he could see dark splotches on his gums.

He looked at the old man in the cone of scaly light, leering out at him, until he felt the urge to go away and come back in the night and burn the house down and everything with it.

He went back out through the kitchen all the way to the truck without stopping. But when he got in, he tried to think about Buck killing himself, waking up in the cold little house and looking out and seeing nothing at all, knowing that in an hour or a half hour the doctors would be there, and there was nothing to look forward to beyond sitting there with the old man while he stared at the fields and cried, until he himself went to sleep and the old man sat there mumbling half-awake about Edwina and Tarquini and how he let it get away from him. And he thought that might finally just *have* been enough to make him turn on the propane and go to sleep, that it was all just a kind of weariness, and the best thing to do was to go to sleep. He sat in the truck and tried to think what all that meant to him. And he sat for a long time, listening to the trucks hiss on the highway to Memphis, and decided that while it made him feel bad, it didn't mean anything to him, and didn't affect his life at all.

12

When he had worked in the switchyards at Helena, the old heads used to say that once the river had been where the town was now, and that the town was set up on the Kudzu bluff that overlooked the present town, and where the town of West Helena is now. They said one night the river simply changed its course, removing itself five miles to the east, leaving a thick muddy plain for the residents of the bluff to stare at and get nervous about. They said little by little the people on the bluff ventured down and started establishing themselves where the river had been, and building stores and houses. And after a while everyone moved down and they changed the name of the town to West Helena and called the new one in the bottom Helena. The men in the yard called this movement The Great Comedown, and swore that the town, by coming off the bluff, had exercised bad judgment and would have to suffer misfortune because, and it seemed to make good sense, the town now existed at the pleasure of the river, and they believed anything that owed to the river would have to pay, and when it paid, the price would be steep.

When he had told Beuna she gave him a pained look and said, "Ah, shit, Robard. We're all dying sooner or later. Them assholes think they figured the reason. But I'm satisfied there ain't no reason."

He got to Helena at noon and drove straight down the bluff into town, the sky pale and hot, and kept straight on through, uneasiness brewing inside him. The streets were wove up with country people in town for lunch. He thought everybody who noticed the truck was noticing him, and anybody who noticed him was a threat. He watched the doors and the alley mouths, in case W.W. should suddenly come striding out of some beer bar and stand mooning at something in the traffic he thought he recognized but couldn't figure why, but *would* if he had another minute to ponder it.

When he had shown up in Tulare, W. had gotten gloomy, as though some bad idea was trying to hatch out in his mind that he wasn't going to let live because of the slowing effect worrying had on his fast ball. Instead W. had gone around moping and frowning and acting as if he had a quince in his underlip and couldn't talk, but was still highly agitated. He had tried to stay where W. could see him anytime he wanted to, thinking that might dewire whatever W. was trying to figure, but couldn't quite get clear.

In the hot grandstand he asked her if she thought W. might be thinking, and she laughed so hard her flesh had gone into violent quivers. "What with?" she said, in the meanest voice she knew. "His mind ain't nothin but a baseball. Baseballs don't get suspicious, far as I know."

Except, he figured, watching people traipse back and forth

across Main Street in the sunshine, W. might not turn out to be so altogether slow if he found out what was happening to his wife while he was screwing parts in BB guns. All those years when he could've been cashing big pay checks, but instead ended up building air rifles for three-eighty an hour and pitching Industrial League at Forrest City, might just have built a big reserve of unrelieved nastiness that he could start relieving if he could just catch somebody diddling his wife and figure out a way of getting a shot off.

The only alternative then was just to be smart and *stay off*. He had figured that out long ago. But waiting for the light, thinking everybody who walked in front of the truck was having a look at his license plate and a longer look at him, he could see just how much business he didn't have idling around town. He would have to come after dark, collect Beuna, and run her to someplace where they wouldn't have to jump up every time a bug hit the screen or start grabbing clothes for fear it was W.W. coming to pick up his cleats or leaving his pail before going off to hit fungoes. He figured he had to park the truck, back in to a wall, and not get near it until he had to, since every time he got in it he ran a risk, and every time he got in it with Beuna, he was pleading to get shot.

He pulled through the intersection, stopped, and made an inspection back up the street, thinking if he waited he just might see a face. When he didn't, he got out, stepped inside the drugstore, bought a newspaper, and drove full tilt out of town, keeping bandaged to the road.

A mile and a half past the last motel, he stopped at a drive-in and parked on the side away from town. The restaurant was a little pink cinder-block with a red and white keyboard awning strung out the back. A girl came down under the awning, took his order, and went off. A breeze picked up off the fields, stirred the dust, and made the awning groan and sway over the struts.

He opened the paper and stared at the Help Wanteds. There was a job in Helena to install linoleum tile, another one in Helena for a drag-line crew with the Corps of Engineers, a job to relocate in San Bernardino, a job in Elaine to guard somebody's land, offering two meals and a room, and a job running a stamping machine in the BB-gun plant.

He hinged the paper over the steering wheel and stared out under the awning toward the fields, back of which he could make out the low perimeter of light green softwoods, beyond which was the river. The awning buckled softly in the breeze and the sun rolled behind the clouds, and he could smell his sandwich frying in the cinder-block kitchen. He tried to think just what it was he was doing. Without even intending, he had gone straight for a job, just like finding one was bone-hard necessity. It was aggravating. Because what was supposed to happen to Jackie, lying back in her room thinking God knows what? Making plans not to see him again, gone by now to where he wouldn't ever find her? It had seemed to him that when breaks came in your life, the decisions got made ahead of time. Judgment was supplied and the sides were weighted and one got chosen on balance. And that was the way he understood life got run, not counting the unforeseen. When he left Hazen, it had been at the end of a long time spent thinking and puzzling. Sides were added and the answer found, though it came in the middle of the night and seemed like foolishness even though it wasn't. But he wondered if decisions didn't really get made in reverse, acting one way, then supplying the reason based on the number of people who got maimed or made happy. And if it wasn't just ignorance to think decisions got made any other way. In this very case, there seemed to be no decision to make at all, only things to do for which he could supply reasons later, when he saw how it worked. So that the only thing he could do about Jackie, lying back there making plans, was just to see what happened and write a postcard.

The girl came back, supporting a tray with a beer and a sandwich. She smiled and fitted the tray to the window and wiped her hands on her pants.

"You going to want something else?" she said, tearing a check off and laying it on the rubber mat. She had a little wisp of mustache on her lip that she bleached.

"Which way is that BB-gun plant?" he said, trying to make her out through the condiments.

The girl stared back toward town and pointed. "Thataway," she said, frowning toward Memphis.

"Then which way's E-laine?" He licked the mayonnaise off the rim of the bun.

"Thataway," she said, pointing down the highway that ran in front of the drive-in and disappeared into the softwoods. Her cheeks were rouged up and she had peppered brown all around her nose to be freckles. "Twenty miles," she said. "Ain't nothin but a store and a quit gin, and some old man's fishin camp over the levee. I used to go down there when I was married."

"Ain't you married no more?" he said, wondering who'd marry her in the first place.

She shook her head and looked put out. "I quit him," she said. "What for?"

The girl removed a strand of dry hair from her cheek. "He cramped my style."

"Well, would you say that E-laine was about as far away from that BB-gun factory as I could get?"

She turned and stared up at the cinder-block restaurant a moment and faced him again.

"I'd say there's lots of places you could get farther away from that BB-gun plant than E-laine, Arkansas, though I doubt if you could find a worse one."

"I need me a place to be low and still get out to the plant when I need to."

"You ain't going to find you no lower place than that," she said.

"That'll do it," he said, and smiled at her, and the girl tapped the tray with her fingernail and walked away.

13

The River Road ferried out along the telephone lines into the marshed fields and pecan orchards eight miles, then angled back through the cypress and followed the shingle of the old river, a long shining horseshoe stoppered at both ends by green-and-orange shumard swamps.

The road twisted finally back into the fields, past standing cotton wagons and silver ammonia tanks on trailers, frosted in the sunshine. He surveyed the long grass levee, amber and flat, reaching away from the tip of the swamp down the margin of the true bottom, back of which was the dark invadable land the levee had been built to guard.

Elaine was a single plank grocery building at the highway, with the wetted fields sprawled against it. The ruined gin sat in the opposite weeds, the metal walls bent in and twisted, exposing the thick oxidized machinery and the cypress rafters that supported what was left. The store was a pale plain rectangle of bricks anchoring the end of a tractor lane that bore back into the boards and over the levee. A "Be Sure With Pure" circle was faintly stenciled on the wall facing north, and a shingle was strung to the eave saying GOODENOUGH'S.

Across the tractor path a light green '57 Oldsmobile was parked in the dirt with a white Servel refrigerator standing inside the trunk. The car had been backed up to the highway, and given a sign painted on the door that said NIGHT CRAWLERS $1 PAR CARTON FIREWORKS. Dark green stars had been put on the sign, and the doorhandles on the Servel had been sawed off and replaced with a big hasp lock.

The boys were squatted in the dust beside the refrigerator. He parked the truck by the store. One of the boys jumped up and waved and stood watching as he walked across the road.

"Yes suh," the boy said, rubbing his hands and smiling, uncovering a large empty space in his mouth where a lot of teeth had been. Both boys were white-headed and red-faced, and had their hair slicked and glistening in the sun. The boy standing was older, though the one sitting had eyes wide apart and a big mouth that made him look serious. The younger boy still had his teeth, and when he squinted they all showed at once. A tick-tack-toe game was scratched in the dirt, and the younger boy was eying the game, using a cotton twig to prod at the two squares that were empty.

"I'm trying to find a man named P. H. Gaspareau," he said, looking off down the tractor lane toward the levee.

The tall boy smiled and leaned around the edge of the icebox and pointed. "Take this here down the other side of the levee and stay on it, and you'll drive right straight through his house." He snapped a look at the tick-tack-toe to warn the other boy against cheating. "You come from California to go fishin?" the boy said, wincing at something inexpressible.

He looked back at the truck and couldn't see the license tag for the way the truck was parked against the store wall. "Where is it you fish?" he said.

The boy thumbed toward the levee. "It ain't no good. Bout wasted a trip."

"I'll find something to do," he said, looking at the tops of the shumards across the levee.

"Ain't nothin *to* do," the younger boy said without looking up. He marked a zero in one of the boxes, then blotted it out. "Bout have to go to New York City."

"He's ignorant," the bigger boy said, smiling.

"He might be smart," he said.

"I might fly to the moon tomorrow, too, but I ain't bought my wings yet," the older boy said.

The shorter boy whacked his brother with his twig, and the older boy scraped his foot straight through the tick-tack-toe game.

"You was winnin it, fool," the younger boy cackled.

"You ought to buy you a whole mess of crawlers," the older boy said, sniffing as if that was the signal to commence business.

"I ain't fishin," he said.

The smaller boy got up, dusted his pants, and got a big jelly glass of red liquid out of the refrigerator and took a drink. There were several white paper cartons inside the refrigerator, smudged with crumbled dirt, and a gray cardboard box marked "M-8os."

"You one of them people goes on the island?" the tall boy said indifferently.

"Which is that?" he said.

"The other side of the lake is a big island. It ain't even in Arkansas. It's in Mississippi."

"I don't know nothin about it," he said.

"There's a man owns it from Mississippi. He's old." The boy let his tongue dawdle in and out of the space where all the teeth had been. "He's always got some people going over there to hunt. I carried the Ole Miss football coach over there one time."

"You ain't done it," the younger boy said, and gave his brother another gouge with his cotton switch, and put the glass back inside the refrigerator.

"Shut up, igmo," his brother said, and kicked him a hard lick in the knee, which didn't seem to bother him. "I carried 'em when Gaspareau was having his throat cut at the Veterans Hospital in Memphis."

A Trailways bus came into sight up the road, its flasher blinking to turn.

"What's the man's name?" he said, having a look at the bus, then back at the boy standing in front of him.

"Lamb," the boy said, watching in the direction of the bus. "That old scoundrel's mean as ptomaine."

He let the name go through his mind and decided it didn't mean anything. The bus slowed, crossed over the highway, and grumbled under the flat eave of the store. The door shoved out and a big pale-faced man in a wool jacket and tennis shoes got down, shielding his eyes from the sun. As quick as he was out, the bus groaned back up on the highway and got lost beyond the gin. An old woman came out of the store and stood under the eave talking to the man who had gotten off.

"What come of your cotton?" he said, looking back out at the water reflecting little strips of sky all down the field rows.

"Wet," the older boy said confidentially. "Couldn't get no combines in in September. It ain't going to be no more cotton if the sun don't stay up." The boy glared at the sun as if he had threatened it.

"Then what'll you do?" he said.

The younger boy's slate eyes gleamed and he started pointing with his nubby thumb toward the Oldsmobile. "We'll git our ass in this here shit bucket and drive to New York City, and stop sitting in the dirt like a couple of fools."

The woman stepped around to the side of the store under the "Be Sure With Pure" sign and pointed out the levee. The man bent to listen, looking like he might have an interest in what was over on the other side.

"He's ignorant," the older boy said, smiling pitifully. "He thinks getting in that car'll fix everything."

It dawned on him that the man might be somebody going after the job, and that if he had any sense he better get down the road, since it would take the other man time to get there on foot in the heat. He trapped a big drop of perspiration against his temple.

The older boy walked back authoritatively, opened the icebox, took a big drink out of the glass, and shut the door. "You don't have to be growed up to know better'n that," he said.

"You ain't never going to be grown up," his brother said. "You might as well figure you know it all already even if you don't."

He started back across the road without speaking to the boys. He heard the woman say something about Gaspareau, and he gave the man a suspicious look. A hawk was riding the vapors out over the fields and for a moment he watched it fall back toward the river, climbing and growing smaller every second. The man didn't seem like somebody who wanted to guard somebody else's property. He looked more like somebody who worked in a bank. The man walked by the truck down the road, staying to the shoulder. He had taken off his coat and had his wet shirt unbuttoned so that his belly pushed over the belt loops.

He let the truck idle into the road until he was up even with the man. He opened the window and stared suspiciously at the man, who was sweating in the dusty sunlight. "Where you going?" he said.

The man put his elbow in the window and wiped his face with his coat. "Some goddamned island," he said.

"About that job?" he said, ready to hit the gas.

The man looked as if the sweat on his cheeks was giving him a lot of pain, and he answered by frowning. "I don't know anything about it," the man said, stepping back out from the window, ready to start walking again.

He tried to take a fair gauge on the man and what he might be doing out in the heat dressed like a banker, and couldn't. "Get in," he said shortly.

"What's that?" the man said.

"I'll carry you. Ain't no need to walk in the hot."

"You sure I'm not going to take your job?" the man said, opening the door but standing back shielding his eyes.

"No," he said, looking off across the fields dismally. "I'll run over you in this goddamned truck if you're lying."

"That's not the worst offer I've had today," he said, sliding onto the seat. "At least I know what to expect. Newel's my name." He stuck out his hand.

"Names don't make a shit," he said.

"Well, mine's Newel," the man said, using the same hand to wipe away more sweat, then letting it hang out the window.

"Hewes," he said softly, wishing he didn't have to say it. "You don't need to remember it. It won't mean nothin if I've got anything left to say about it."

PART II

Sam Newel

1

In the taxi he had started going over the first day one more time, reproving himself for every instance. He had found a room on Harper Avenue, pried out the dormer, stood up between the gables and let air pour, exchanging atmospheres, circulating around his bags and under the bedstead, while he leaned out, taking the climate, trying to fix on it and be cued to the city. He had satisfied himself before leaving Columbia that Chicago was a rare place to learn the law, mired in the middle of the country. The air smelled like piled newspapers and the city felt low-spirited and musty like an uncle. Next morning he had stumped down in the dark fog across Jackson Park to the long cement strand and calculated the midwestern sun bulking up beyond the buoys, baking the sky maize and copper and magenta, until the day was full up. And at the end, the time had seemed incantational, and the air had smelled like cooling bread circulating down the city lines, pressed into the fog. And he had gone back to bed feeling exalted, ready to begin. Which goes to show, he thought, the cab shooting down the Midway in the rain, that nothing good lasts very long.

At the depot the rain had begun to bump off the cobbles in sparklets. He went inside, bought his ticket, set his suitcase at the end of a row of benches, and walked outside under the marquee to stand in the air. A taxi slid in under, discharged a passenger, and shot out into the avenue. He walked the sidewalk in the shelter of the station until he could make out the chain of lights up Michigan, brightening above Randolph Street into the luminance of the Wrigley Building. He felt the old exhilaration that he wished he could devise some smart way of sustaining so as to make it unnecessary to go off into the night on a lunatic trip he couldn't even understand the good sense of. The whole prospect darkened on his mind, and he had an urge to call Beebe, and have her taxi to pick him up, which he knew would thrill her.

The wind listed back. The train was called, and he walked back through the foyer into the arcade to get his bag. A group of well-dressed Negroes was standing at the swinging doors to the trains, talking noisily and stacking packages onto a fat woman who was taking a trip. The men all wore red carnations. He came to the end of the last row of benches and found the bag was gone. A little boy with drooping eyelids, the child of one of the Negroes, was left on the bench where the bag had been, patting his hands idly.

The Negroes began talking more loudly and one man abruptly shouted something that sounded like "bakery goods" and they all began hugging the woman with the packages. The little boy rose and looked casually over his shoulder and pursed his lips and turned back, as if he had seen what he had expected. The Negroes began shuffling out the doors, their voices softened, then silenced, leaving the sound of a teletype clicking at the end of the arcade.

He came back around to where the child was and looked at him. "Where's the bag?" He glared up the long aisle. The boy regarded him as though he were invisible and repursed his lips. "Who took it?" he said, glowering over into the boy's face until he could see the little amber tincture in his sleepy eyes.

The little boy smiled and produced a strand of pink gum from between his teeth and let it dangle between them like the clapper of an invisible bell. "Po-lice done got it," he said.

He scanned the wide nave for some guilty sparkle of police shield in the shadows, but no one was visible except a redcap smoking a cigarette by the doors to the outside. A radio began playing at the end of the waiting room, and he looked back down to where he could see through the glass the rainy headlights of the taxis cruising underneath the awning, scouting fares. He felt desperate.

"Didn't you see where the fuck he went?"

"Naw," the boy said, and rolled the gum between his palms and returned it to his mouth.

He lurched off through the empty arcade, leaving the child, bursting out the swinging doors empty-handed. The Negroes were all getting wet, bawling and waving handkerchiefs at the steaming train. He avoided them, hustling down the platform and leaping up the silver steps into the vestibule. He shot an accusing look at the Negroes, standing in the rain crying. None of them was holding his bag. They slowly began milling back into the depot and he watched them grow smaller in the station until they were absorbed.

2

He sat gloomily in the recliner and watched the city slide in the rain, down the old wards he saw each commuter ride uptown to see Beebe. The car swayed smartly by 65th, gathering speed. He could make out a strip of timbers stenciled in the foreground, and farther back the dark Midway, headlights swimming into the rain on Hyde Park.

The train stopped at 103rd for no one to get off or on, and hissed and heaved out of the salmon lights, leaving the city in the underwater darkness.

"The city is put here to solve our problems," Beebe had said, letting her fingers play in the thread of sunlight.

"My father would've agreed with you," he said.

"Of course." She smiled and ran her finger back along the icy line of shadow and light. "It brought us back together nicely. I'm sure he would've approved of that."

He eased into the dark half of the bed, peering through the

window into the alley, thinking about nothing.

"I'd like you better today if you weren't so churlish," Beebe said.

"I know the law," he said. "I don't have time for the Committee for Social Thought or whatever you patronize."

"You might go," she said, breathing mist indifferently against the cold pane. "I heard Jane Jacobs. She thinks we'd all do well to live in the cities."

"You should try it on the south side before you make up your mind," he said.

"I'm here quite a lot," she said, scoring her fingernail through the mist. "I get along with the boogies just fine."

He was silent.

"What was it your father did?" she said.

"Sold starch."

"Were there a lot of jokes about starch salesmen having firm erections?"

"I don't know."

"I was changing the subject to something more amusing." She was quiet a moment, then said, "A man exposed himself to me at the airport this morning."

"What for?"

"I'm sure I don't know. It was a cabdriver in the queue at Pan Am. I leaned to tell him I wanted to go downtown and there was his lingam lying on his leg."

"Did he take you?"

"Of course not."

"Did you say anything to him?"

"I said, 'That looks a lot like a penis, only smaller.' He was reading *Time* magazine and covered himself and drove away. I'm sure it embarrassed him."

"The city just hasn't solved his problems yet. Or does it only lavish its attention on you?"

"You're certainly cynical, aren't you?" She looked annoyed. "Why did you start limping today? It was very strange. Who did you see?"

70

"Nobody." He watched up the alley, pressing his nose to the glass until the skin numbed.

"Then why did you start limping?"

"It provokes compassion from some people."

She craned her neck and tried to see what he was looking at in the failing light. "I'm afraid I don't believe that," she said.

"All right, goddamn it," he said, exasperated. "When I walked out of the A & P I saw a man who looked exactly like me, carrying his goddamned AWOL bag to the laundromat."

"So?"

"It scared me. He looked a hell of a lot better off than I do, a lot firmer in the belly. His eyes weren't murky, either. I made a point to look at that."

"Did you speak?"

"Hell, no. What am I supposed to say? What if he doesn't think he looks like me?"

"I don't know why you felt you had to start limping."

"I don't like goddamned Doppelgängers." He stalked across the floor and slapped the radiator rung, making it gong. "This goddamn thing isn't worth a shit for a shoeshine."

She reclined her head to the window ledge, the light silhouetting her face at the horizon of the frame. "You have a poor tolerance for ambiguity," she said, rubbing her nose softly with her finger and watching him skulk in the shadows.

"What the hell does that mean?"

"To continue what you're doing when nothing is very clearly defined," she said. "It's a source of spiritual stamina for scientists. I think it has pretty uses for other people, such as you, for instance."

"What the hell do *I* do?" he said.

"You make things terrible when they're only slightly confusing." She smiled at him cheerfully.

"Like what?" he said.

"Like whatever you've decided is so dreadful you suddenly have to start limping to signal your decline."

"Well, goddamn it, look at me." He waved his arms perpendicular to his shoulders, displaying his torso in the poor light. "I look Promethean," he said, and peered at his chest, wondering if she would agree to what he saw.

"I can see you well enough," she said.

"Well?"

"Well, what?"

"What is it I supposedly lack again?"

"This tolerance for ambiguity." She smiled.

He kept his arms outward like a giant bird soaring in the gloom. "Everything I think I know is ambiguous," he said. "I'm flying apart a mile a millisecond for that very reason, which you'd notice if your attention span were long enough."

"I don't think so," she said. "You do have dandruff things in your eyebrows." She gave him a disapproving look and began examining her cuticle.

He moved out of the dark and back in again, making the floor squeeze.

"You must be cold with no clothes on," she said. "Why don't you get in with me? I'll make you nice and toasty." She smiled and raised an arm, opening the spot he could occupy.

He frowned out of the shadows. "So what am I supposed to do with the stuff I can't tolerate?"

"Let things work themselves out," she said quietly.

"Like you," he said.

"I have some things put away," she said, turning on her back and letting her breasts subside. "If it were so wonderful down there I'd live there, wouldn't I?"

"If what were?"

"Mississippi, all that foolishness."

"I couldn't say."

"Of course I would," she said. "I love to live where it's wonderful. I'm whimsical and fey. I don't like to think ugly thoughts. You're very proud to live *here*, that's perfectly apparent."

"Of course," he said. "I've been waiting my entire life to live in this goddamn lazaret. It's wonderful here with the whores and the geeks and the murders and the filth."

"Does it ever seem to you that fucking me lets you get back sneakily at your past?"

"It crossed my mind," he said. "Except it's not good enough."

"I was only teasing," she said. "Whoever heard of such a thing?"

"Passions have to come in from someplace," he said.

"Then where do mine all come from?"

"I couldn't say," he said.

"I bid an Amsterdam flight tonight. Would you like it if I bought you a graduation suit? I can buy linen very cheaply."

"I'm not attending," he said.

"But you need a suit. Isn't your behind frozen?"

"Yes."

"Then come get warm." She spread the horse blanket until he could see her thighs in the shadows.

"I'm testing myself," he said.

"Against what, dear?"

"Against ambiguity. I'm testing my tolerance."

"Fine." She was silent. "But how will you know if you passed?" She put her hands behind her head and lay so that the ellipses of her underarms shone in the darkness.

"That's a good question, too."

"I really don't think it matters, though, do you?"

"Yes."

"Well, I don't. I couldn't care less. You're such a serious boy, Newel, and you're only twenty-eight." She reached her fingers back until they touched the chill window glass and her body shone luminously in the vacant moonlight.

3

In 1947 they had had a black Mercury and his father had a heart attack and couldn't call on his accounts alone in the summer months. So his mother drove them. And in the black hot summer they had gone into Louisiana and spent a July day across the river in Vidalia, the first day. And when they had worked as far as Ville Platte the Mercury broke down and they had stayed in the Menges Hotel that had ceiling fans and snake doctors in the rooms. He remembered walking out of the hotel into the still street at noon and going with his father to the agency building, and a woman behind the glass cashier's in a beaded dress and red lips and short hair, and then back to the room holding his father's hand. The ceiling had covered over with grease that came out of the still air, and over that a covering of fluffy dust like a sycamore leaf. And the whole time the nine days they were in Ville Platte, he was afraid of the snake doctors and believed they would sting him and kill him though his mother told him again and again that they wouldn't.

4

She lay against the window wall, moistening the hairs of his belly with her lips.

"You're very happy with yourself," he said.

"Of course," she hummed. "Aren't you pleased?" She turned on her stomach and smiled at him.

He was quiet.

"That's good enough," she said softly, examining his stomach more closely, as if she had discovered something unnatural. "It wouldn't damage you to be pleased. I don't punish myself with things I can't remember."

"What do you do?"

"I don't let myself become bothered." She smiled again over the horizon of his stomach. "You have a stevedore's chest, Newel. How did you make it so big? I admired it from afar when we were children." She piloted her finger along his ribs until his flesh drew.

"I'm cold," he said irritably.

"Of course you are." She laughed out loud. "You don't have any dirt on you. Get under the covers."

"I want to tell you a story."

"If you'll get warm. You need some dirt on you. I'm sorry, I don't tell jokes very well."

"Do you want to hear it?"

"Of course."

He sat up straighter and rolled his head against the invisible window. "I went out one time, when I was seventeen, rabbit hunting with Edgar Boynton, out the other side of Edwards, Mississippi, in a silage field he knew about. And we'd been out for about an hour and hadn't seen a rabbit, and I went off by myself walking down the back of a hedge fence, and just kept walking until I heard somebody shoot. And quick as I heard it, I ran back up and around the hedge fence to where he was. And he was standing there looking at something I couldn't see until I got close up to him. He wasn't saying anything, just standing gaping. And when I got to where he was, I looked down in the grass and there was a big barn owl, pushed back up in the silage weeds staring at me and Edgar with his big heart-shaped face and some kind of awful fear in his eyes, and his talons bared and his beak stretched open like he was about to claw us to bits. And Edgar never said a word, he just stared at the owl like the owl had a grip on him, though he had shot one wing off completely and it was lying on the ground between us and him, all white on the bottom without any blood showing. And he had such an awful look, I just stared at him and couldn't take my eyes off of him. I was being terrified and attracted at the same time. And I just couldn't move. And right then Edgar's dog came sniffing up and got a look at the owl and made a lunge at him and Edgar grabbed him by the ear and yanked him back, because the owl would've killed the dog if he hadn't, one wing or not. And I couldn't help, I was so dumbstruck. The dog was barking and Edgar was yelling at him, jerking him, and the owl began to shove back an inch or two in the silage and his eyes got big and dark, like he was gathering himself for a last burst. And all of a sudden Edgar just shot him full in the face with his shotgun and the owl disappeared, or at least anything that might've made you think it was an owl there, just went away in half a second and left a big mess of blood and feathers all matted and stuck together in a clump. And I just sort of got faint, I think, because one second I was looking at the owl, and one second I was looking straight down at something else that was different. Neither one of us knew what was coming until it was over, cause Edgar was behind me and was having a bad time with his dog, and just figured the owl was the easiest thing to get rid of since he'd already blown his wing off, and it was hopeless. But it all happened too fast for me and I guess I fainted, though I never did fall down. He just obliterated him. The owl lost everything in one instant."

He slid below the window glass.

"That's an awful story," she said in a bad temper. "I'm sorry you told it to me. It doesn't make any sense."

"What difference does it make?" she said.

She climbed out onto the bare floor.

"But you understand it, don't you?" he said.

"Of course. But I'm not responsible anymore. Neither are you."

She stepped out into the moonlight for a second, and disappeared.

5

Out the double window he could see smoke rising against the humped moon, flooding the Illinois sky with the soft luff of corn-plain haze, spreading east in the night, taking the rain off into the Wabash valley, leaving the sky clean and stiffening in the cold.

At four-thirty he woke in the dark. The train passed onto a long trestle. The palings drummed between himself and the distance. He could make out the mauve exhalations of a river, coiling like a ghost of itself in the gloom. The rest was dark.

He had sat on the bed watching her put on her uniform.

"This would be easier to do with the lights," she said, groping into her overnight case.

"I like you better in the dark," he said, studying his abdomen lolled between his thighs.

"Why *is* that, Newel?" she said, hunting another piece of clothing on the floor.

"I don't like watching women getting dressed," he said. "I used to watch my mother get dressed, and it embarrassed me. It seemed clinical to me, like talking to her about my penis."

"Did she let you watch her *un*dress?"

"Did Hollis wiggle his zub in your face when you were tee-ninecy? I'm sure he didn't."

"No," she said, flicking a comb through her hair, and stepping noisily in the darkness.

He arranged his feet crosswise under his thighs and spread the sheet over his legs.

"Tell me something," she said, dropping her brush in the bag and tipping the lid with her toe.

"I don't know anything. You're the world traveler—you tell me."

"There's no need to be boorish. I simply want to know about your father."

"You asked about him before, remember? When I told you he sold starch, you said you didn't really care."

"What happened to him?"

He rested on his elbows and let the sheet shift off his legs.

"He got killed in Bastrop, Louisiana, on his way to New Orleans. He got behind a big flat-haul and I guess he was going to pass, I don't know. He was a traveling salesman and never drove over sixty, never got close behind cars. But he was behind this truck for some reason, and all of a sudden a load of corrugated steel pipe came loose and slid off down in the front seat with him. Cut his head off. Left him sitting in the front seat. He could've kept on driving if he'd had a head. It didn't even bump the compass on the dash."

"For God's sake, Newel. Do you have to dress it up?"

"I have a son's right to embellish it."

"So how old were you?"

"You know goddamned well how old I was," he said, irritated.

"What difference does it make how old I was?"

"I'm simply trying to understand what's got you so exercised. Today you started walking with a limp in front of the A & P and turned pale as a paper, for no apparent reason. I was just wondering." She picked her blouse up off the floor.

"What do you think of Mississippi *now?* New York is someplace different. This place is certainly different from most places I've been in." She glanced at the walls and continued buttoning her blouse, pausing after each shiny pearl to reestimate the room's disposition.

"What is it you want to know?"

"If it's scared you," she said matter-of-factly. "Because your father died in that outlandish way."

"I see," he said, and stationed his head on the pane and pulled the sheet all the way up over his chest, exposing himself below the waist. "It's not any more threatening than it is out there." He pushed his finger at the door. "There's goddamn whores right in this building, right below us. When they're around things can get real *special,* you might say, especially if they're coons, which these ladies certainly are. There's plenty of everything right there, if you want to be scared. Some poor Pakistani managed to get his throat cut standing in the middle of Kenwood Avenue. That's fairly outrageous." He sank back onto the bed.

"Then what about the other?" she said.

"What other?"

"Your father getting killed."

"So? Does he need some sort of coda?"

"How do I know?" she said. "I'm just trying to get you out of this dismal place, through law school, and stop your walking circles around this room like sheep. Though you seem dedicated to rotting in pure filth."

She sat on the edge of the bed, waiting.

"Do you want me to say that happened to *him,* and I couldn't cope with my past because it was so awful?"

"Yes."

He fidgeted his brows. "Jesus. There's more important things than that. How he died was practically slapstick, for Christ sake, compared to how he lived."

"So tell me. I have to go."

"Does it occur to you ever that you fly to Belgium like other people go down the street for a goddamn knockwurst?"

"I like it that way," she said, and smiled. "It's the Netherlands. Amsterdam is not in Belgium. Someday I'll sit down and pay attention to all your theories, but I don't have time right now."

He reached his hand in under her shirttail and touched her arm and the curve of her shoulder.

"We don't have time for this, either," she said. "If you don't tell me, I'm leaving. I have to catch a bus at the Windermere, and catch a cab to catch the bus. It's complicated." She stood and walked to where her overnight case sat.

"It's not important," he said.

"You said it was more important than his dying," she said, pushing bottles down below the rim. She got on her knees and tried to see inside.

"Only to me," he said.

"Fine," she said, picking her jacket off the floor and buttoning it. "Then I'm off."

"Telling you doesn't make anything different, goddamn it," he said. "You're one of those people who thinks if you can just *say* something, it doesn't matter anymore. That's horse shit."

"Then I'll be marching off," she said pleasantly.

"But it's nothing," he said.

"So tell me," she said softly.

He struggled up and went and stood by the radiator, his body blue in the darkness.

"I'll just sit right here," she said, finding the bed.

He could see her silhouetted a moment in the window and then disappear. He could see sodium lights furring the walkways in the park. He tried to imagine how he would feel inside the room, in the first moment when she had gone, and he thought that it would be awful and later much worse.

"Newel," she said patiently. "Are you going to tell me?"

79

"Sure." He rubbed his chest. "I have to think how, though. It's making sense out of things that don't make much sense. My father isn't finally important. He's just adhesive for everything. I puzzle about him to have somebody to puzzle about. But I still end up thinking about just parts all the time. There's something easy about them I don't understand, and I can't hold them together well enough to figure out what it is. It's ridiculous."

"Quit mumbling and tell me what it is you're going to tell me, for God's sake."

He stood against the rungs and watched her shadow.

"He sold starch to wholesalers, I told you that. He'd go into Ville Platte, Louisiana, and I went with him when I was little in the summers to give my mother a rest. We'd drive to some big warehouse and he'd go inside and talk to a man and they'd drink coffee and in a little while he'd get out his order book and write up an order. Then he'd leave. Maybe he wouldn't sell anything. That was it. Then he'd go someplace else. One hundred fifty miles a day, seven states—Mississippi, Arkansas, Louisiana, Tennessee, Alabama, Florida, part of Texas. Port Arthur." He shoved up on the radiator and let his heels dangle between the rungs. "He did that twenty-six years. He worked for a company in St. Louis that's gone bankrupt. And he had scars after all those years doing the same thing. He had piles as big as my thumb that bled in his underwear. He had those for years. He'd have them cut out, and they'd come back. He had a spring cushion, but it didn't help. He had bad circulation in his legs from having the blood cut off at his waist. And for a long time Mercury made a car with a door that was easy to catch your hand in. The most logical place to grab the door was right where you couldn't get your hand out of fast enough, and you closed your hand in the door. The company bought Mercuries for the salesmen, and they were all slamming their hands in the doors. My father closed his up three times in one year, and finally had to have the finger nubbed—lost all the feeling in it. Then he got a corn on his foot from the clutch. I don't know how he did that. It was funny, and I'd see him sitting on the commode in the hotel slicing at his corn with a razor blade, and putting Dr. Scholl's on it. It always seemed to be funny, cause he was so goddamned big. Bigger than I am. Anyway, the corn got infected and got worse and worse, until he limped, and after a while he had to use a cane because the pain, I guess, was hideous. I think he cried sometimes. And my mother finally made him go have it removed surgically. But then he couldn't stop limping. It was as if he thought one of his legs was shorter than the other one, though it was just a corn. Does that seem at all funny?"

"No."

"It began to seem funny again to me for a second. It's funny because he was gigantic, and all the things that pestered him were little. You'd think he wasn't smart, wouldn't you?"

"Maybe," she said. "Aren't you tired of sitting on the radiator without your clothes on?"

"No."

She sighed.

"He had a heart murmur that kept him out of World War II. I don't know what would've happened to him. Nothing worse, I guess."

"I agree," she said.

"That's the thing, though," he said. "He loved it so much, I think, it seemed fun to him. And that wasn't the worst. The worst was sitting in all those goddamned rooms, in Hammond, Louisiana, and Tuscaloosa, with nothing at all in them, for *years*. Just come in late in the afternoon, have a drink of whiskey, go down and eat your dinner in some greasy fly-speck café, smoke a King Edward in the lobby, and go back to the *room*, and lie in bed listening to the plumbing fart, until it was late enough to go to sleep. And that was *all*. Five days a week, twenty-six years. Maybe he saw my mother two-sevenths of that time. They were married fifteen years before I was born, and they were friends. They loved each other. But he went off every Monday morning, smiling and whistling like Christmas, like it was fun, or he was just too ignorant to know what it *was* like." He thought of it awhile, listening to Beebe breathe.

81

"How do you know he didn't have a woman?"

"Don't say that." He moved opposite her where he could see her more precisely. "Why do you have to believe that? Why does everything come down to a fast fuck with you?"

"How do you know he didn't?" she said coolly. "Some little Choctaw up in Tupelo might've looked good, something else in Hammond, something else in Tuscaloosa? My father knew a man who worked for Gulf who was married to a woman in Mobile and had a whole other family back home. Something kept him alive. Two-sevenths just isn't enough. I don't care how much he loved her. There had to be something, even if he didn't care about it."

"That's wrong," he said.

"All right. What was it, then?"

He stalked back across the boards. "His pleasures somehow just got grafted on his pains. That's what happens to you if you don't look out. They grow together. That's what worries me."

"That's ridiculous," she said, tapping her fingernails on her overnight case. "It's just some idea you've concocted."

"What the hell do you think anything is? How the hell are you supposed to understand a fucking thing if you don't figure it out yourself?"

"It just doesn't make sense," she said.

"Nobody gets laid, that's what's the matter. He didn't know what the hell was going on. It was just something that happened. Who knows what might've happened to his brain otherwise. When I was little we had a flat tire right on the bridge at Vicksburg, and my mother grabbed me and held me so tight I couldn't breathe, until he had fixed the tire. She said she was afraid of something happening."

"She thought he was already crazy, right?"

"She already knew about those rooms."

"She was afraid he might decide to kill you all?"

"I don't think she knew it. But it's possible to decide some things are just that awful and not be crazy at all. She just knew the limits to things. He never found out because he adapted."

"That's very romantic, but what does it have to do with you?"

"It frightens the shit out of me." He tried to make out a look on her face but couldn't. "I don't *want* everything the same. Your past is supposed to give you some way of judging things. So it has to do with me because I say it does."

"There's no need answering you," she said.

"Shouldn't I have *something* besides the assurance that everything will eventually be the same? I ought to marry you, then, or kill myself like your old man. I'd get rid of a lot of worries either way."

"So?" she said, flipping the handle of her overnight case.

"I'm lonely, that's what's so."

"And what are you doing?"

"What do you mean, what am I doing?"

"To find out what you need to find out, whatever it might be. If it's so important, I'd think you'd do something about it."

"I'm worrying about it."

She lay back, her elbows against the sash, looking at the soft haloing lights. He could hear her breathing, the mist of breath on the pane, tiny circlets widening and withering. He felt his body sag as if his torso were slowly falling toward the floor. He felt like a fixture in the immobile darkness.

She stirred over the sheets, her toes touching the floor, her figure rising into the window frame. "I don't know what you're talking about," she said.

"It's complicated," he said, feeling sad.

"Go to the island," she said cheerfully, as if that had been an acceptable option all along, and she were just rehearsing it for the record.

"And do what?" he said irritably. "Run through the woods screaming while they shoot at me?"

"I don't know *what,*" she said. "But there isn't anyplace left for you to figure out whatever it is you seem jinxed into figuring out, all that dismal mess you were shrieking about. If you aren't prepared to move into a cleaner place, screw me and be pleasant —this is all I have to offer." She smiled.

"If you can't hump it, why bother?"

"It seems to me I've bothered," she said, "and all you've done is act insulting and indulge yourself. I'm tired of arguing with you."

She got up. He stared at her out of the shadows.

"What would I do?" he said.

"It's a very good place to go to compose yourself, or do whatever you'd like. It's Mississippi in its most baronial and ridiculous. You can go tonight if you want to; all I have to do is make a call to the boat camp." She set her case on the bed and snapped the clasps to search for the number.

"Stay off the phone!"

"Are you expecting a call?" she said, bothering through her case.

"Some asshole calls me all the time and asks me if I know where my wife is, then hangs up."

"I'll call tomorrow, then. I'll be back by then. I'll tell Popo you're coming but he shouldn't expect you until he sees you. That'll be nice."

"Nice for whom? Why don't you just say I'm presently in an institution for the morally unsure and won't be released for some time?"

She closed her case again and refastened the clasps. "You should call Mr. P. H. Gaspareau, in Elaine, Arkansas, and tell him who you are and that you would like him to tell Mr. Lamb you're coming at my invitation."

"Then what happens?"

She smiled, letting her case swing down.

"What the fuck do I do down there?" he said.

"Strive to come back in a better humor," she said. "You'll have to tell the bus driver to stop at Elaine, otherwise he'll go right by."

"Wait a minute!"

"Did you know," she said, looking abstracted, "in 1911, some poor people went to sleep in Arkansas and woke up in Mississippi. The river changed course at 3 A.M. and everyone was forced to make some adjustments. Popo's colored man insists he was in the river in a wood boat at the moment of the change, but I don't believe it."

"They won't know who the fuck I am."

"Of course not. But you should have a nice long talk with Popo and tell him who you are and go for several walks with him in the woods, and they'll both like you fine."

She came toward where he was standing and kissed him softly on the cheek. "I'm not trying to get you to screw me this time." She smiled. "I'm relying on other resources. I think they're not as good as my others, but I like to believe I'm adaptable. I would never have thought you would grow up to be so serious when we were children. Nothing is that serious. You should learn that, sooner or later, then everything will be wonderful."

"How do you know?" he said.

"Because," she said, confidently. "Everything is always splendid for me."

"What's the purpose of all this, if you don't mind my asking?"

"To bring a little frivolousness into your life. It's too gloomy in there now. Look at this room—it's awfully morbid in here."

"I like it," he said.

"Fine, but you must go to the island and act frivolously. Though I think sometimes, Sam, that if you were any more frivolous you'd be lost."

"To whom?"

"To me, of course," she said. "Who else is there?"

"Nobody."

"There's the answer," she said sweetly. "There's the answer right there."

The train shot through a country station, rattling the doors, and passing the vacant red flasher where there were no cars waiting. He tried, peering down into the lighted streets, to get a reading on the place, estimate if they were out of Kentucky now and into Tennessee, or only leaving Illinois with the hill country yet to go before daylight. But it was no use.

6

In Thibodaux there had been a man named Gallitoix who owned a wholesale warehouse for food. And his mother had parked the Mercury in the sun while his father walked up on the loading platform, his back bent, and into the man's office to sell a boxcar of starch. In the car he sat with his mother and watched the tractor trailers pull away from the high dock in the heat. The seat covers were blue and white and felt and smelled like old straw. She opened the windows and there was no cool breeze, except for the sweet smell of feed riding the hot air out of the warehouse and over the tiny bleached sea shells that covered the lot like gravel so that everything was white. His mother drew a pencil diagram of where the gears were on the steering column, and there, while they were suffocating, he learned to drive.

7

The train got to Memphis early with new light hung behind the capitals of the brokerage sheds. Two people got off and scurried down into the station. He looked the length of the platform for a phone, but the one booth at the end of the shelter was in use, and he decided to make his call later.

He walked down into the vestibule, and found the bus station in the converted depot transept that had been roped off and fitted with plastic chairs. He bought a ticket to Elaine and walked past a Trailways huffing at the depot doors and down Adams Avenue toward the river. The street passed for a time under the Arkansas bridge, and he could hear trucks slapping the girders, and see, across the thick, gravy-colored water, east Arkansas profiled at the bottom of the sky.

He crossed the boulevard and walked out on the brick apron

that paved the riverbank. He went down and squatted and let his hand dangle and felt the water draw through his fingers, and it occurred to him that for all the times he had crossed the river, riding in his father's old rattling Mercuries off into the opposite delta, and out of the little levee towns, he had never felt the river, never had it in his hand and let the water comb through his fingers to find out just what it was. It seemed now like a vast and imponderable disadvantage, and made him feel like he needed to know.

He took off his coat and surveyed up the boulevard in both directions. Two men were standing by a long tar-colored barge hove to the bank a hundred yards away, talking, the river panning out in an open Y behind them. Trucks were pounding across the bridge, but no one inside was able to see except whatever was far up the open river. He sat on the bricks, took off his tennis shoes, and stripped his shirt, exposing his belly to the light. He stared at the bridge, expecting to see someone peering over the railing observing him, but there was no one, only the pigeons wheeling out of the girders along the defiles of steel struts. With his pants at knee level, he made a brief inspection of his legs. They were white and billowy and speckled with tiny sores like ant bites. He shuddered and felt unpleasant, and the sudden prospect of going to physical ruin made him agitated. He hugged himself and hunched forward in the breeze. He took a step and tied his brows, and stared at the surface, looking for a reflection of himself and seeing only his shadow frozen on the current.

He recognized that he was now, for all purposes, risking self-annihilation without even willing it so, and that by all probability armies of people in the grip of doing away with themselves thought simply that they were taking an innocent swim in the river or the bay, or had merely concluded a window ledge was the only place to find necessary peace and quiet. It is only, he thought, afterward when the realities begin to percolate. He felt his toes wiggling. He looked downriver and saw the two men standing beside the barge were no longer talking but were staring at him. Somewhere he could hear a loud honking and turned and saw the

Trailways that had been at the terminal come to a halt at the foot of Adams Street. The door swung open and the driver, a short man in a khaki uniform and a campaign cap, jumped out and yelled something that sounded like "woncha-woncha-woncha." And he immediately dived in.

The impact took his breath away and he felt himself going uncontrolled and limp while his heart began whumping and his stomach burned like flames. He sensed he had hit the surface too severely.

The water was colder than he had expected, and below the surface an almost immediate numbing started in his feet, sending dull signals to the tips of his fingers, which were busy flittering to maintain his head above water.

Simultaneously he was confronted with two very unsettling facts. One was that in the time it had taken to get righted and regain a minimum amount of breath, he had moved a surprising distance from his clothes, which he could just see strewn in a circle twenty-five yards upstream. The other fact was that his shorts were now gone and he was floating with his privates adangle in the cold current, prey to any browsing fish.

The bargemen had begun walking up the gangplank, from all appearances in no hurry. The bus driver was standing at the curb, pointing out for the benefit of his passengers a man's head floating with the current.

Water trickled on his neck and he sensed he was becoming colder while maintaining a constant distance of ten feet from the bank, unable to touch any part of the bottom and unwilling to turn and look at the river, sensing the utter vastness would shock him and cause him to panic.

Though what surprised him was that on once claiming a breath, he felt relatively little fear while he faced the bank, and was suffering none of the gulping hysteria he feared he *might*. It was not difficult to stay afloat, the current buoying him as it moved him steadily, and he felt unusually relaxed, though cold and still strange that his parts had become potential forage for the fish.

88

He could see the bargemen bringing a long wooden boom from the invisible rear of the barge, dragging it in the water as if they were trying to pole against the current. He looked back up to where the bus was standing. Several children had begun running along the bank, though most of the other passengers were straggling back up to the bus.

The bargemen took up a position at the bow of the boat with the boom trailing in the water and stood watching him with idle interest. He estimated that to avoid slamming into the front of the barge and being dragged below by the current, he would need to orbit several feet out into the river, yet not orbit too far so as to be unreachable. The barge began to get larger, and he squirmed to get beyond its girth, kicking away from the bank with some vigor. He kicked until he saw where a true course would just miss the lead edge of the barge and bring him into line with the boom, and that with modest luck he could catch it as he went by. Though as he reached the forward bulwark of the barge, around which a large tuft of yellow fuzz had collected, the current eddied unnaturally and spun him out from the end of the pole which the bargemen had shoved in his direction, so that he was turned and facing the river, looking at Arkansas in the flat distance. He fished backward, and tried to relocate the pole. The barge was making a thick gurgling sound that he could feel vibrating below the surface. He breathed in a large tuft of the foam. One of the bargemen yelled something, and he felt the sawed end of the long boom scrape his back, causing him to flounce backward, grasping for whatever he could touch, and missing the pole entirely.

Panic occurred all at once. His ears felt as if someone very close by had turned up a radio on which there was nothing but loud static. He flailed in several directions. His head sank a moment, and he felt his feet enter a denser zone of cold water. His skin grabbed, and he stretched to get his nose up and have a look at the barge and the shore and the Memphis skyline before drowning. As he surged to get his head elevated, a heavy weight twisted along his neck, stopping his breath momentarily, so that he gagged and struck with his fist as if he were being assailed. He felt the current binding it into his skin. He accepted another enormous mouthful of water and felt himself sink. The current was pulling, and he tried to raise his head to see, but the current mounted water in his face and he perceived he couldn't see without allowing gallons of water to run directly up his nose.

He could feel himself beginning to be maneuvered sidewise to the current instead of simply dragging against it, and he got rigid, eyes shut, hoping for better treatment. And then the current all but ceased. He raised his head an inch above the water line and saw that he had been hawsered into the slack behind the barge. The surface was being boiled by the barge's diesel, and the water was slimy and thick and tasted metallic, but there was no more pull to the rope.

He let himself be hauled to the bank and gave up the rope and lulled in the gurgling wake, trying to get a whole breath. He burped up a portion of water, tried to see, and found that the men who had lassoed him were down off the barge now, watching him impassively. He tried to make them out, but the sun had rotated higher in the sky and was shining almost straight in his eyes.

"No wonder he liked to drowned," one of the men observed, "he's so fuckin big."

The other man began coiling the rope, dragging it across his shoulder. A heavy canvas life preserver bumped his ear and skittered across the bricks toward the man's feet.

"Whyn't you grab the ring?" the first man said irritably. "I made my all-time-best chunk and you grabbed the rope."

He belched up some gamy-tasting water.

"You like to strangled," the man said, sounding melancholy.

He squinted up into the sun and saw that the two men were twins, and were staring at him as if he were a one-of-a-kind fish they had landed and didn't know quite what to think.

"Is there a blanket?" he said.

"Loan a towel," the twin without the rope said, and walked back up to the barge.

He pulled himself a little farther onto the bricks. There was a big scaly burn mark on his shoulder and his ear felt like it had grown larger. Some of the numbness was departing his feet, and he was beginning to feel more of a piece.

He wanted to say something to the man with the life preserver. But the man simply stared at him quizzically, looking disappointed to have wasted a throw in behalf of what he had pulled in.

The twin returned dangling a crusty towel with "Peabody Hotel" stenciled on it. The towel was hardened with axle grease, and it smelled like diesel. The man tossed it and stood beside his brother as if he weren't sure what he might get to see next. He draped the towel over his abdomen, and tried quickly to outline what he wanted to say in appreciation and not waste too much of anybody's time. The men were out of their thirties and dressed in oily jeans and oily boots. The twin who had retrieved the towel had on a green cowboy shirt, but his brother wore an aquamarine T-shirt with the sleeves cut off and "UCLA Tennis Team" silkscreened on the front. He lay a few moments trying to think of something to say, letting his toes dangle in the water, and looking alternately at their long immovable faces.

"I'll bring you back the towel," he said, and stared down the stone beach. He tried to stand and felt his chest sag and his back begin to burn where the pole had gouged it. He looked at the men hopefully. The brother who had gone to get the towel smiled, but the other seemed to be scowling, holding the life buoy with one hand as if thought had abandoned him but he hadn't noticed the absence yet.

"Thanks for saving me," he said.

"I wouldn't do it again," the unsmiling brother said.

He tried to feel the point of the threat, then gave up and limped back across the bricks, holding the towel around his belly, the sun starting to draw on his shoulders.

Several muddy footprints were stamped into his pants, and one of his socks was kicked to the edge of the water. He scanned the beach and up the drive, where a few cars were visible. The bus was gone. A number of drivers stared at him and made inaudible remarks, and he began picking up his clothes.

A station wagon stopped at the curb, a blue Chevrolet with a plastic screen in front of the radiator. The passengers stared down at him behind sunglasses, making remarks and pointing politely. Suddenly the door swung open and a tiny girl with long red hair and a pink Sunday school dress popped out holding a tiny camera pressed against her stomach and took his picture and disappeared back inside the car. The passengers smiled and nodded, and sat a minute watching him dress, as if they were expecting some singular gesture in recognition. And when none was given they seemed satisfied and drove slowly back into the traffic.

He walked back up the hill to the bus station, feeling worn out. The ticket agent acknowledged him with a greasy smile and looked back over his shoulder at the Trailways clock and pointed to it meaningfully.

He settled his head against the back of the chair and stared at the old milk-colored skylight, trying to empty his brain. Somewhere at the train station a voice came on the loudspeaker and said something unintelligible, and in a minute he heard a train vibrate into the upstairs platform, stop for several minutes while he listened to the brake cylinders bleed off, then start again slowly and fade into the daylight sounds.

"I was in school," Beebe said, "with a girl from Belzoni. She married a Phi Delt from Meridian. She was a precious sweet thing with her mother's complexion and lovely breasts. She married this boy whose name was Morris Spaulding. And Morris took her to Meridian and graduated to his daddy's Dodge agency, and the first thing any of us knew, he had her doing some ghastly tent show across in Alabama while he was in the audience doing who knows what to himself. All because she was such a sweet little thing and let him make all the decisions for her. I'm afraid that's a little out of my line, Newel, though maybe not for you."

"I don't know what you're talking about," he said. "Who asked you that—who cares?"

8

In 1951 in the summer, they had driven in his father's Mercury from Jackson to Memphis, and on the first day he had sat with his mother in the Chief Chisca Hotel and looked out on Union Avenue and sighed, while his father went off in the heat to call on his accounts. And in the evening they went in the car as far on Union Avenue as there was a street to drive on and stopped at a white house with blue shutters where his father knew a man named Hershel Hoytt, who sold raisins. In the house, the man was there and wore golfing shorts and carried a golf club and wore thick black-rimmed glasses and had a face like a stork. They sat down at the round table in the kitchen and drank whiskey and laughed and sang and ate spaghetti with Vienna sausages, and he was shown to the bedroom, where there was a wide bed with a white chenille cover, and told that he could go to sleep. At two o'clock he was asleep with the light on in the ceiling, when the door opened and his mother and father came and stood beside the bed and looked at him and said he was pretty (though he was awake by then) and gently moved him onto the pillows and lay across the bed themselves and went to sleep. And he lay in the bed, the three of them lying crosswise in the tiny room with the fruit-salad globe in the light, still shining over them, and he smelled their breath and listened to them breathing and remembered their singing, and listened to the strange house become quiet until he began to cry, and left the house.

9

On Union Avenue he walked back to town, walked back until he came to the chalky red bricks that sloped straight toward the river, and when he walked farther down toward where the water

*was, there was a terrible stink like oil and old cabbage, and he went
back up the levee and over into town, and walked to the Peabody
Hotel, where his father had said the rich people stayed when they
came to Memphis. And in the upper lobby he went to sleep behind
the notary public's desk.*

*In the morning at seven o'clock he waked up and looked down
on the wide lobby from the mezzanine and saw people were standing at the circular fish pond in the middle of the wide room,
holding tiny boxes of crackers and staring at the bank of elevators
built into the wall with gilt mirrors for doors. And in a while the
elevator door opened and a Negro wearing a white waiter's jacket
came off followed by six mallard ducks, walking in a line behind
him. And when the Negro had walked to the pond and stood beside
it, the ducks all walked into the pond and began to float and quack
and eat the crackers the people were holding for them, until the
people were gone and there were small red and white cracker boxes
floating on the water with the ducks, which the Negro later took
away.*

*When he had found them again in the Chief Chisca waiting,
his father said that they would never drink again, and that each day
the Negro brought the ducks down precisely at seven o'clock, and
precisely at five o'clock he came again and stood beside the pond
and the ducks simply walked out and got on the elevator and rode
it to the roof and got off and sat in their nests of straw and waited
until he came again. Once, he said, a man from Arkansas came
and fed one duck one tiny crystal of cyanide. And when the duck
died, which wasn't very long, the others would not come down for
a month. The Negro would ride the elevator to the roof and stand
beside their nests and wait for them, but they wouldn't come. They
simply quacked and quacked at him, as if he were the man who
had betrayed them. Though after a month of quacking at the Negro
and sitting on their nests all day getting fatter and fatter, when the
Negro came with a different-colored coat and stood beside their
cages, they came along the way they always had. And before long,
his father told him, sitting looking out the window of the Chief*

94

Chisca down on Union Avenue, the man went back to wearing his white jacket and the ducks could not remember they had thought he had betrayed them.

10

"You remind me of somebody," Robard said, spitting out the window.

"Who?"

"I don't know, a movie star, somebody like that."

They drove up the levee and turned and went a hundred yards along the top on another tractor path to where the road bent over the other side. A red combine was bogged down in the field below the levee. Someone had attached a cable to it and tried to pull it out with a heavy Fordall tractor, but the tractor had foundered in the same row and both machines were sitting in the sun. The plants around them were all blackened and bent in broken rows with dried fibers clinging to the bolls. Someone had laid a plank walk over the mud and there were signs on the planks that people had been going to the levee and back. But neither machine seemed to have ever moved, and all the sticks and cardboard sheets and logs and blankets had finally been left under the wheels and the business abandoned.

"Why do they take machines in a field that muddy?" he said.

Robard let the truck wobble down the river side of the levee. "I guess they intended pickin it."

"They could just look at it, though. Why didn't they just say fuck it?"

"They might've strained their imaginations," Robard said thoughtfully. "They ain't got too much of that."

The road widened and cleaved back along the inner coast of the levee, then bent north across another cotton lot that was tilled and dry and waiting for planting. It struck into a grove of maples and sycamores behind which he could see the sheen of the lake and the first low buildings of the camp. The road straightened and passed under a banner plank that had DINKLE LAKE CAMP painted in red, beneath which were the cheesy remains of a hound, and sixty yards on, the camp, which was a bight of five cracker-box cottages with low, green-pitched roofs, the first looking like two of the smaller ones bradded together, with the rest left in a half coil reaching toward the lake, the last cabin up to its joists in backwater. Someone had put up a pipe bracket in front of the first cabin and hung a World War II whistle bomb off two chains and painted the whole architecture white. Back of the smaller cabins in the maples was a litter of turned-up sawbuck tables, two snail-back house trailers with curling roofs, and the husk of a yellow school bus set off its axles in the grass with burlap curtains strung along the glassless windows. The lake was a dark silver-black ankle lying to the north and south, with the island five hundred yards away, a dense revetment of shumards and willows reaching as far as he could see in either direction. It looked to him like a re-proach, and he felt that he ought to turn around and try to put the whole business behind him. "It isn't much," he said, looking at the lake.

"We ain't there yet," Robard said, letting the wheels straddle the remains of the dead dog.

Six more black-and-tan deerhounds fetched out from under-neath the first cabin and took up barking, and creating a lot of noise. Robard drove up into the grass and honked the horn, which made the hounds bark louder.

"Eat you alive," Robard said, staring expressionlessly at the hounds.

"Honk the horn again," he said. The boat dock was down the bank, a raft built out of oil drums and car tires with planks roped over the tops, floating behind the last swamped cottage. An alumi-num boat was moored to the dock, motionless in the water.

An old man appeared outside the corrugated-roof porch, carry-ing a double-barrel shotgun and a swivel ash cane. The dogs managed not to see him and kept barking and kicking dirt until he got behind them, looking put out by the noise, and gave the nearest dog a stripe across the ribs that dropped it off its feet. The others immediately clammed up and trotted back around the house while the wounded dog tried to crawl away without taking his eyes off the stick, though the old man managed to catch him again across the hind leg, sending him springing off into the sycamores.

The old man set his cane back on the ground, renewed his hold on the shotgun, and limped to the truck, looking in the bed first, then narrowly into the cab. The old man was bald and wore loose clean khakis, and had a thin chain around his neck fastened to a silver disk with a hole in the middle which was buried inside a plug in his throat. When he had satisfied himself with the contents of the truck, he set the cane against his hip and put his finger on the disk. "You boys?" he said, cradling the shotgun higher up in the crook of his elbow. His voice made a squeaky sound.

"I'm to see P. H. Gaspareau," Robard said.

"That's me, what about?" the man said, jabbing his finger on the disk so it picked up a flicker of light.

Robard held a newspaper to the window for the man to see where he was pointing.

The old man perused the paper, then stared up over it. "What's *he* want?" His eyes grew smaller as if the sun were on them.

"Have to ask him," Robard said. "I brought him from the store." He folded the paper back carefully.

"I want to go on the island," he said. "Beebe Henley was supposed to call you. My name's Newel."

"A goddamned month ago," Gaspareau croaked, and kept on glaring at him.

"I got detained."

"I told him you was coming, but that was four weeks ago."

"I'll pay you," he said. "Otherwise I'll jump in that goddamn lake and swim across."

Robard looked at him uncomfortably.

"Mr. Mark Lamb pays me, you don't." Gaspareau wheeled the barrel end of the shotgun in the general direction of the island. "You won't be doing no swimmin."

"What about the job?" Robard said, sucking his tooth.

"What's your name?"

"Hewes."

"Where you from? Them ain't no Arkansas tags, is they?" The old man bent back slightly as if he were trying to see around to the back of the truck without moving off the spot.

"California," Robard said, and settled his eyes at a point in front of the headlights. "I was raised up in Helena."

"You know anybody up there?" the old man said.

"Nope."

"Then why you want to come back?" Gaspareau said, his voice blowing and wheezing out the top of his throat.

"I used to switch on the Missouri Pacific."

"That's a goddamn good job," the old man said sourly. "How come you to quit that?"

Robard contemplated the steering wheel. "My wife liked California."

"She wants back, is that right?"

"Not exactly."

A smile cracked the old man's wet mouth so that his big busy tongue came into view. "Niggers is took over everywhere else," Gaspareau said.

He looked past Robard at Gaspareau's mouth and at the metal disk, where the skin was all pinched and eroded and looked like the foot of a volcano.

"I need that job," Robard said.

"She come with you?" Gaspareau said.

"No."

Gaspareau tightened his grip on the shotgun. "I'da left her ass sittin, too."

Robard put his eye on Gaspareau and smiled. "I come about your job," he said.

The old man lost his humor. "But you don't know nobody in town, do you?"

"I'll give you a man's name in Hazen," Robard said. "If that ain't enough, you can give it to Newel here."

Gaspareau looked deviled. "What's his name?"

"Rudolph," Robard said.

"You know how to use a pistol?" The old man put the shotgun against the side of the truck and grabbed his cane off his hip.

"Point it and pull the trigger," Robard said.

Gaspareau looked insulted. "Shoot your dick off that way," he said. "I ain't hiring you, though. He is. I know where to get somebody to shoot."

"Where's that?" he said, leaning across Robard and sticking his face in the window to annoy the old man.

Gaspareau smiled and shoved his finger to his throat. "Did you see them tow-headed boys sitting up at that big icebox?"

He couldn't remember seeing anybody at all, though Robard seemed to nod that he did.

The old man looked craftily at both of them and uncovered a few mahogany teeth. "That biggest boy there killed a man a year ago. A bastard broke loose of a road gang in Mississippi and tried to break in one of my cabins." The old man looked around at the cabin as if he wanted to be certain it was still there. "Shot him deader'n a toadstool with a twenty-two rifle. I sent him over with a letter pinned to his shirt, but the old man sent him back."

"Aren't you going to pick up your dead dog?" he said, trying to see around Robard's head.

Gaspareau quit grinning and picked up the shotgun and cradled it back in the crook of his arm.

"I ain't," he said slowly. "Been a month. If I was to go down and start shoveling him up, he'd just come to pieces. I'll let you borrow my shovel, if you got an interest in him."

"I don't like dogs," he said, and removed from the window.

"That one ain't going to bite you," Gaspareau snorted, then thought about something else. "Park back by the last cabin, and go on down." He jerked the barrel of the gun at the boat dock and went stumping off to his house.

Robard backed the truck under the willows between the last cabin and a maroon Continental with Mississippi plates.

"You still think I want your job?"

Robard looked at him gravely. "That mouth of yours about tore your ass," he said, reaching across and fumbling into the glove box. "Ought not to mouth a man like that. Bastard'll shoot you or put one of them boys up to it, and wouldn't nobody be the smarter."

"*You* would, wouldn't you?" he said.

Robard laid his hands on a big flat-bitted screwdriver with a transparent orange grip, climbed out, and went about unscrewing the license tag. "I'll tell you," he said, holding one screw in his hand and commencing the other one. "It suits me to stay out of the way of things. Bullets, anything like that, I'm glad to be out of the way." Robard looked up significantly.

"I'd like to go in something and never come out," he said, staring at the rusted holes in the bracket. "You know what I mean?"

"I don't," Robard said. "I always want to get out. It makes me itchy, like something was about to happen I didn't know about."

He watched Robard wrap the plate in a newspaper and lay it up under the seat.

"If you're smart you'll figure out the same thing." Robard smiled and walked off to the boat dock.

11

He stood listening to the clatter of maple leaves. He could just make out the imprint of a deer standing motionless outside the barrier of shumards and cypress spires across the lake. He moved his eyes up the bank for some clear break where Gaspareau could make the boat in, but the trees seemed to grow in a compact wall down the long twist of lake, and he couldn't fashion how a boat could penetrate and break back into the bank.

Robard sat on his heels by the painter cleat smoking and tapping ashes in his pants cuff.

The screen slammed and Gaspareau came rolling across the

yard without his shotgun, but with a little silver revolver strapped to his belt in a walnut holster. He was wearing a big straw hat with a wide green plastic brim in the front, pulled down so his face was visible only from the nose down. Robard gave a significant look, passed his eyes over Gaspareau's pistol, and gazed expressionlessly back on the lake.

Gaspareau stumped out onto the dock, stepped down in the boat, and started jabbing intensely at the gas bulb with his toe. "Anybody need to piss?" he said, his face contorting and a peculiar scraping sound originating somewhere below his throat.

"You ready for me to untie it?" Robard said, standing at the cleat.

"Quick as this other gentleman gets in."

"Get in, Newel," Robard snapped.

"Where?" he said, staring at the boat blankly.

Gaspareau shoved his entire fist up to his neck and his voice seemed almost able to come out his mouth. "Just get your ass in!" he said, glaring furiously.

"Going or staying?" Robard said, and pulled the burnt end of the painter until the boat listed away from the dock, the old man sunk in the stern.

"Leave the son-of-a-bitch!" Gaspareau hollered, stropping the starter and setting the water boiling. Gaspareau fumbled into his pocket, dragged out a pair of old rubber aviator's goggles, fitted them on his head, and set his hat back on top of them.

"Newel!" Robard yelled.

"Going." He stepped off into the sun-warm water and squirmed over the gunwale directly in front of Gaspareau, who was revving the noise as loud as he could.

"Turn me loose, Hewes!" Gaspareau's voice was barely distinguishable over the whine of the motor. "Turn me loose, goddamn it!"

Robard towed the boat alongside the dock and jumped in, and they took off furiously into the lake toward the wall of motionless trees.

12

Robard sat bent in the front of the boat, hunched toward the gunwale protecting his cigarette. Gaspareau twisted open the throttle and let himself slump against the motor, the pistol situated in front of his stomach, the barrel pointed between his legs. He sat gloomily in the middle, watching the deer he had seen browsing outside the trees. When the motor had begun to whine, the deer had stared a moment, then disappeared up into the timber. But when the boat departed and succeeded into the lake, the deer had reappeared, nose poised toward the boat, and trotted out into the lake, its head barely clearing the surface, striking for the other side. He watched the deer make way through the water with difficulty, keeping its head firmly up, rising and sinking regularly as if it was trying to leap toward safety. Gaspareau gave him a kick in the back and pointed at the head with his cane, gurgling something through the hole in his neck. He thought for a moment the old man was proposing they have a run at the deer, and he turned and shook his head, which only made Gaspareau repoint his cane and frown as if he wasn't being understood. Gaspareau conned the boat closer toward the opposite bank into the corridor of water between the deer and the trees, and he decided the old man had not been intending to have after the deer, but just to point it out to the both of them. He gave Gaspareau a conciliatory look and peered back at the deer. It had swum almost to the middle of the lake, its rises and descents more regular and articulated, as if it had begun to feel out of reach of whatever had driven it off the shore. Robard pointed his flat finger at the deer, and for a time they watched it silently while the boat buzzed and buffeted, closing toward the bank well back of the deer. Until suddenly the deer disappeared. At the height of one regular ascent the deer seemed to be jerked off the surface, as if whatever had found it had moved with such awful force there hadn't been time to breathe before going under, or as though the force had been so irresistible it had given up without a spasm, leaving the surface where it had been glistening and almost tranquil but for the soft weals of water traveling backward across the lake.

Gaspareau never stopped. He turned toward the unbroken line of trees and screwed his hat closer to his goggles and looked away.

He stared back past Gaspareau to where the deer had been swimming, as if he expected it to thrash up out of the tentacles of some beast and be dragged back, its head stretched toward the sky. But there was nothing, and as he scanned the water he began to feel uncertain where the deer had been in relation to the dock, which was now downlake and only a stitch against the bank. He worked his eyes regularly backward from the place he thought he recognized to someplace beyond it, compensating for the speed of the boat, but he could see nothing or recognize nothing about the lake. He turned and stared past Robard, who seemed unmoved, huddled in the anchor well striking a match against his belt buckle out of the wind.

Gaspareau killed the throttle and swung the bow straight toward the trees and let the wake boost the boat through the outstobs and cypress points until Robard could manage one of the tree trunks and arm the boat in. Gaspareau shut down the motor and jacked it out of the water, took a paddle off the floor, and began poling the boat one-handed. He could just detect a vaguely marked passage through the trees and farther could see the transom of another Arkansas Traveler marooned on the bank, chained to a tree stump painted red. The bank had been hacked out of the trees and extended ten yards to the foot of a low bluff, on top of which he could just see the windshield of an open jeep, backed by the woods.

Gaspareau poled the boat and Robard guided until the stern began trawling sand and Gaspareau jabbed him in the ribs with the paddle blade. "Tow us in there, Newman—you're wet anyway. It won't kill you."

He climbed into the water, which was colder and deeper than

it had been the other side, and led the boat forward until it caught the shoal.

"That's enough!" Gaspareau squalled. "I've got to get out of here." The old man skinned off his goggles and leered at him. "What happened to that deer?" Gaspareau said. "That was somethin, wasn't it?" He kneaded his eyes with his knuckles.

"What *did* happen?"

Gaspareau smiled. "Gar," he said. "Alligator gar come along and sucked him. I've seen it before."

"Not in his mouth," he said incredulously. "He didn't get him in his mouth, did he?"

"No, not *in* his mouth, *with* his mouth!" Gaspareau said. "His mouth ain't *that* big. He just grabbed him by a forepaw and went to the bottom, like a bass and a tadpole. That's why them deer don't like to swim in there."

He tried to think about a fish big enough to drag down a 150-pound buck like he was a tadpole, and couldn't do it.

"When the river switched," Gaspareau said, still grinding at his eyes, "left all them fish stranded, and the big 'uns got bigger than they ought to. People quit putting out trotlines and none of the gars got caught, and they went to eating catfish, and pretty soon they was some goddamned big gars."

"But a deer?" he said, unable to see it at all.

"I've seen 'em turn over boats and do all kinds of plunder," Gaspareau snorted. "A deer ain't nothin."

He stared at Gaspareau, trying to read his face for the truth.

"See that there jeep?" Gaspareau said, directing his cane up the bluff.

He looked skeptically around toward the jeep.

"That's the old man's. The key's in it. If you can start it, you can drive it to the house. If you can't, you can walk three miles. Hewes, you tell Mr. Lamb you're the last man I'm sending. He can just as well take you." Robard nodded. "I don't know what *you*'re going to tell him, Newman," Gaspareau said distastefully.

"Newel," he said.

"Whatever the shit. He's particular who comes on the place and when they come."

"If he doesn't like me he can run my ass off," he said, feeling like he'd be happy to kick Gaspareau in the mouth. "Why don't you sputter on across your pond?"

Gaspareau let his hand fall on the handle of the pistol and grinned.

He started walking up toward the jeep away from the old man.

"Get me out of here, Hewes," Gaspareau yelled.

Robard pushed the boat free with his foot and sent the old man sliding backward, rearranging his goggles under his hat brim. The motor fired and Gaspareau backed the boat out past the last stobs and whipped it a loop and plunged out into the lake facing the sun.

From the jeep, he watched the boat's bow pop out of the water with the old man's weight settled in the stern.

Robard sat down and looked at him, rubbing his hand back through his hair. "I'll tell you," Robard said wearily, setting his sack of clothes in the boot. "You get an old fart like that mad at you, and he'll kill you."

He glared at the old man skating off like a bug, the motor whining out in the distance. "He acted like I was a goddamned parvenu."

"I don't know what that is," Robard said, tampering with the ignition and waggling at the starter pedal at the same time. "When the shooting starts, though, I'd as soon be some distance from where you're at. I wouldn't act quite right if I was dead."

"So stay away. I don't give a fuck," he said.

"I'll do it," Robard said. "I'll do that very thing."

13

The jeep path followed out of the willows into a saw-grass pasture, the other side of which was another belt of softwoods. The road had been wet-rutted and the tires skidded the sides and pitched the jeep sideways. The haze had burned off and the sky was white and watery, loose clouds crowding and the sun diminished and telescoped behind the trees.

Robard draped his arms over the wheel and stared across the straw field toward the woods. "I seen a thing like that deer once," he said. "I was stood out by a lake in Lee Vining watching the fish, just standing there holding my pole, me and this other fellow. And we stood there for a while trying to figure whether to fish or not and not seeing anything working. And there wasn't any reason in the world for the fish not to be tearing up. So old Ralph reached in his sack and took out a slice of Wonder Bread and sailed it out there and let it float. And pretty soon you could see some little fish rise to it and nibble the crust, just enough to perturb the water. And we just sat there watching because them little fish wasn't big enough to hook, and we were waiting on a big fish. Little ones get interested before the big ones do, that's why so many little ones get caught and so few big ones. The big ones are smarter. We stood there and watched and watched. And pretty soon an osprey come over and made a little pass on the bread, just looking at it. Then he flew around again and looked at it again. Then he flew way up and just dropped with his claws all stuck out in front of him headed right for that bread. And just the second he got there, whoosh! here was this great big rainbow struck up and took that slice out of sight in one gulp. And the osprey hit him with everything he had and got both his claws in his back and got a good hold, and that bird just went right out of sight. Cause that was a big fish."

"You ever get anybody to believe that story?"

"Well," Robard said, watching the woods. "I *seen* it. That's about as much satisfaction as I need. Though I wouldn't call it really satisfaction; it's just a recollection I feel satisfied with. The situations aren't really equal anyway. That osprey just chose more than he could chew. That little buck didn't look to me like he had much to choose. You might say he was a victim."

"Of what?" he muttered, grabbing onto the frame of the windshield to steady himself.

"Hisself." Robard smiled.

"What kind of sense can you make out of a story like that?"

Robard took his arms from around the steering wheel and shoved back until they were stretched straight in front of him. "I don't know," he said deliberately. "It was something that happened, so I suppose I made sense out of it already."

He turned around so as to be face to face. "Does that help you?"

"Do what?" Robard said unhappily.

"Make your mind up about anything."

"Like what?" Robard said, steering the jeep into the field to avoid a chuck hole. "I have a hard time remembering what it was exactly I did yesterday," he said, trying to see up over the hood and get back in the gauge.

"I don't believe that," he said. "You let on you're not smart so you can get the edge on people. But I know better."

"Newel, I think we done talked enough today."

"I don't know," he said, facing front again, feeling exhilarated. "You're crafty."

"Well, let's just put it to you in these terms, then," Robard said. "If I'm so goddamned smart, why am I chauffeuring you around in this jeep in the middle of someplace I hadn't got any business being?"

"I could ask the same question," he said.

"Then why don't you," Robard said, "and leave me to peace?"

"Because," he said, "you might be my chance."

"There's lots of people in the world would run jump in the river if they thought I was their chance at anything. Sometimes I think I'm one of them."

14

The road slipped out of the little grass prairie into bush poplars and pine yearlings, back into another pasture. The sun was low, sparkling through the poplars, turning the weeds gold and splintering the shadows through the woods. North of the road, a section of grass had been mowed and a trapezoid lined out in surveyor's sticks and red bicycle reflectors. On the near side an iron stanchion was holding a gray windsock that twitched in the breeze, and at the end of the strip a lean-to shed had been built and the grass allowed to grow up around it. Crows began making a racket when the jeep broke out of the woods, and one by one they flapped out of the tall grass into the trees.

Back of the airstrip the woods opened to a more important oak break in the back shade of which was a long green-plank barracks house with a shake roof and square windows run end to end. The house was raised a man's height off the ground on pyramided concrete spilings, with wood steps leading off either end. Three outbuildings were set off from the house; one he could make out easily as an outhouse, by itself twenty yards from the north steps. The other two were less distinguishable, though he surmised one to be a living quarters with a small breeze porch and propane tank, and the other, a corrugated metal enclosure with a lean-to ceiling, looked like a toolshed.

The road split, with one arm making a hemisphere to the left, and the other keeping straight then switching back so that both arms met beside the south steps of the house. Robard took the way that allowed him to go straight, then braked as the path turned toward the house, and let the motor idle as quietly as possible.

The sun had almost died. The pale light showed olive through the woods, with only a final narrow filament catching the house in its salient and turning the planks bright green. He felt an almost insufferable calm, as though the sun passing off had stranded the house and everything else in lush neutrality in which nothing could move until dark.

Robard shut off the jeep and filled his cheeks. "I'll let you announce us," he said, expelling the air.

"I'm a fucking month late," he said. "You think that's a good credit letter? You've got business. I'm just a goddamn parvenu."

"Go on, for Jesus' sake. You act like a fool."

He gave Robard a grieved look and climbed out. A voice, bent on expressing extreme displeasure, came all at once from somewhere back of the house. Several waxwings began taunting a blue jay up in the sycamores and went fluttering out behind the house.

"No, T.V.A.," the voice cried imploringly. "Goddamn it, son, don't turn the thing *that* way. Turn it the way I say."

He looked over at Robard reproachfully and waited to hear a reply from whoever was doing the turning.

"Go on around there and see," Robard said crossly, lighting a cigarette and flipping the match on the floor.

He nosed past the foot of the stairs and stopped beneath the piling and looked back into the dooryard.

A small turkey-necked old man wearing duck trousers and a yellow pajama top was standing hands on his sides beside a Negro in overalls, who was bent on all fours over a thick iron pipe protruding several inches out of the ground. Beside them, an orange and white pointer puppy was watching. The colored man had an enormous black pipe wrench he was applying to the pipe at ground level, taking it off each time he turned it half a rotation, refitting it, and twisting it again, while the old man stood supervising the whole operation. He could see that each of them was dedicating a terrific quotient of concentration to the winding process, so that each time the colored man removed the wrench to reapply it, the white man insensibly muttered "Good," and crowded a quarter inch closer.

The dog was the first to ratify anyone else's presence. He picked his head up and stared momentarily, flogged his tail once, then went back to observing the operations on the pipe.

He felt that he'd like to disappear altogether, but continued standing by soundlessly as the colored man grappled with the enormous wrench and the white man redeployed himself to the other side as though he wanted to beat the Negro to seeing down the hole as soon as it was opened. When the wrench was finally brought off with the entire four-foot length of pipe fastened to it like a magnet, the old man quickly dipped to his knees, pushed his face right into the hole, and held it there for several seconds while the Negro backed away a few feet and gave the goings-on a grave look.

"Goddamn it," the old man bellowed, lifting his head and wiping his nose with his sleeve and pushing his face back down to the hole for another test. He seemed to want to get part of his head inside the hole, but the hole was apparently too stingy. He sat back on his haunches abruptly, wiped his face again, and shook his head piteously.

"What do it smell like?" the colored man said. He was standing over the old man now with the entire pipe-and-wrench conjunction dangling in one hand like a watch fob and delving the other hand into his thick hair.

"Shit," the old man said. "There's shit in my well water, by God. Mrs. Lamb knows what she's talking about."

The colored man shook his head ruefully and stood over the hole, staring at it as if it were a grave.

"I bragged on it," the old man said, still levered back on his haunches.

"Yes suh," the colored man said.

"Don't *ever* brag on nothin you own, son."

"Yes suh," the colored man agreed.

"It queers everything. I told Gaspareau a month ago what a goddamn good well I had, been good since 1922, and the first thing I know the privy goes and infects it. That was a jinx, and I'm to cause."

"I wouldn't know," the colored man admitted.

"Well, I know, by God," he said. "It's like feeling piss down your pants leg. You know you done acted hasty."

The colored man turned and glanced at the house and saw him standing there and gave him an anguished look that suggested that if he looked again he didn't want to see anybody still there. He flicked his eyes at Mr. Lamb, then back at the house, then fixed him with a purely baleful look.

"We got somebody," the colored man said.

"What?" the old man snapped.

"Somebody done come on. . . ."

"Mr. Lamb," he shouted, propelling himself away from the house, regretting to have to speak at all.

"Who is it?" the old man grunted, twisting his face around so he could see.

"This *here* him," the colored man said, pointing down at the old man, who was still on his knees in the grass, looking up with his entire forehead enraveled behind his glasses.

"I'm him," the old man said loudly, batting his eyes and struggling to get on his feet. "That's me right here."

"I'm Sam Newel." His voice stopped inexplicably.

"Who is it?" the old man said, staring at the colored man with the same bewilderment he'd centered on the pump.

"Newel," he said with greater difficulty. "Beebe Henley called you, I believe."

"The sound's out of this ear," the old man said, batting his right ear as though he were swatting a mosquito. "What did he say, T.V.A.?"

"He say he a friend of Miss Beebe's," the colored man shouted directly into the old man's good ear.

"He is?" the old man said irascibly. "Newel?"

"Yes sir?"

"You sure are a *big* pile of shit," he said, finally hoisting himself with the colored man's help, and taking a great handful of his trousers and staring at him with a hot intensity, as though he were only going along with a joke that was about to come quickly to an end, at which point he intended to claim the last laugh. "We thought you was coming a month ago." His eyes flicked up and down. "You're the lawyer, aren't you?"

"Yes sir," he said, trying to clear up the trouble with his voice.

"Well, everybody needs a goddamn lawyer sometime. My will's made, though." The old man peeped up under the house, and saw Robard sitting smoking placidly in the jeep. "Who in the hell'd you bring with you?"

"That's a Mr. Hewes," he said, trying to aim his answer directly into the old man's working ear.

"It is, aye? Well, who the hell is he? Not another goddamned lawyer, I hope." The old man took a faster grip on his duck trousers and jerked them up until the cuffs were several inches above the lasts of his bedroom slippers.

"No," he said uneasily, trying to look under the house again and finding he couldn't see underneath as easily as the old man could. "He's here about some job, I think."

"Let's see the bastard, then," the old man said, lurching off hoisting his trousers with both hands.

He stood looking hopefully at the colored man for some sign of affiliation, but the colored man avoided his eyes and went trailing behind Mr. Lamb.

When they started to the jeep, Robard jostled out, mashed his cigarette in the grass, and started muttering something inaudible.

"Look here," the old man said, batting his eyes in several directions for emphasis, as if he'd already given Robard fair warning. "If you expect to talk to me today, you're going to have to talk at that ear, or you might as well not talk."

"Gaspareau sent me," Robard shouted, staring at him behind the old man as if he suspected he'd been betrayed on the other side of the house.

"What the hell about?" Mr. Lamb said.

"About the guard job you had in the paper," Robard yelled.

The old man looked at him accusingly. "You ain't no murderer, are you?"

Robard grimaced. "No, I ain't."

"Gaspareau sent a *murderer* over here last week, and I run the son-of-a-bitch off. He killed some poor con-vict over there last year without the bastard even looking around."

Mr. Lamb suddenly took all his teeth out of his mouth and worked them together, as if he were trying to iron out an irritating defect. "I don't want no goddamn murderers shooting up my island," Mr. Lamb gummed, giving his teeth close inspection. "That boy won't live to be twenty-one, I'll guarantee that, the little shitass."

Robard said nothing and stared back at him painfully over the old man's bony shoulder.

The colored man went sneaking off toward the house, set the pipe and the wrench against one of the pilings, then leaned against it himself, lit a cigarette, and took up watching the proceedings from a more comfortable distance. He scowled at the Negro and waited for the old man to finish examining his teeth.

"These things," he said ruefully, referring to the pink and porcelain teeth. "I wouldn't give a nickel for a hundred of 'em. Used to, when I had my teeth, I could get WRBC on my second molar after 10 P.M. at night." Mr. Lamb's eyes flashed by Robard and quickly found the colored man, who turned his face and cackled.

Robard smiled weakly.

"What's your name?" the old man said.

Robard pronounced his name as if he hated to hear it.

"Well, I'll tell you, Hewes," the old man said, finally reinstating his teeth in his mouth and smacking them up and down fiercely. "The job I got pays twelve dollars a day just for one week of turkey season starting tomorrow and going till Thursday, plus your food and your place to stay. It ain't but a week's work, and I want you on the job six to six unless you and me arrange different." The old man gave Robard an odd look as if he were trying to talk him out of it. "I'll give you a cap gun I got in there, but I don't want you even to take it out. I want you to have it cause some of those farmers over there like to get funny with you sometimes if they think they can get away with it. Gaspareau lets 'em come in here. There ain't nothing I can do about it." He stopped suddenly and stared at Robard. "You ain't no kin to Gaspareau, are you?"

"I hadn't ever seen him before a hour ago," Robard said, and looked away.

"You sure about that?" Mr. Lamb said, his eyes moving rapidly back and forth across Robard's face, examining every feature thoroughly.

"That's what I said," Robard snapped.

"All right, then," Mr. Lamb said.

"One thing, though. I got to get to Helena some nights."

"What the hell for?" the old man shouted, cocking his usable ear so as to hear the excuse free from interference.

Robard looked out at the woods, which were almost dark. "Some business," he said quietly.

"Is that so?"

"Yes sir."

"Well, Hewes. I'm going to call you Hewes. That's what I call my employees. You tend to your business. But when the sun ups, you tend to mine."

"All right."

"Use the boat, but don't let it get empty of gasoline. People are going to come in here to hunt turkeys, and I don't want you poopin out the gas with your *business trips.*"

"All right," Robard said, and started to walk away.

The puppy came twisting up behind the old man from where he'd been lounging in the grass, and sat down at his foot and stared at Robard.

"This here's my huntin dog," the old man said, admiring the dog and giving its ear a friendly jerk. "She's my long-casted pointer. I need me a long-casted dog since I can't walk anymore from the bed to the pisspot."

The colored man began chuckling again and disappeared around the house with the pipe and wrench in his hand.

"You see my huntin dog, Newel?"

"Yes sir," he said, moving forward a little, thinking about the hound flattened out in Gaspareau's road.

"Say, 'My name's Elinor,' " the old man instructed the dog, bending down and picking up a fat patch of flesh behind its head and grinning. The veins in his face fattened up dangerously as he bent, monkeying with the dog's skull. "You got any gear?" the old man said to Robard, glancing at the back of the jeep.

"What's in my sack," Robard said.

"What about you, Newel?"

"No sir," he said, thinking dismally about his suitcase strewn open like debris in a train wreck. It made him feel like he needed a bath.

114

"You're just a couple of goddamned derelicts," the old man shouted, standing straight up and hoisting his pants a little higher. "Beebe Henley didn't say you were a goddamned derelict."

"Somebody stole my bag in Chicago," he muttered.

"The hell they did?" the old man said. "You oughtn't never live in a place like that. The bastards'll steal everything you got."

"A policeman took it," he said.

The old man looked at him, temporarily astounded.

"Well, put yourselfs in the Gin Den there. That's where the men sleep, except me. Me and the ladies all sleep in the house, so there won't be any unauthorized screwin go on." The old man's eyes brightened considerably. "Hewes, you'll start tomorrow."

"Yes sir," Robard said, turning toward the jeep again.

"We'll eat supper in a little while and I'll tell you what I want you to do. Newel, what the hell are you going to do?" The old man frowned at him through the tops of his spectacles. "You haven't come to hunt turkeys, have you? You don't look like much of a hunter to me."

"No," he said, trying to think up something believable.

"I didn't think so," the old man said crisply. "I'll tell you, though, Newel." And he paused. "I don't care what you do. Beebe says to let you do what you want, and I will so long as you don't get me shot. Is that agreeable to you?"

"Yes sir," he said, happy not to have to say anything else.

"Good," the old man said. "I don't like people around here who aren't satisfied, except me, and I can be any goddamned thing I please. The bathroom's over there." He pointed down under the house to where he alone could see the bottom few boards of the outhouse. "You'll just have to walk a little if you have to piss, or else use God's privy." The old man leaned forward and peered up under the house. "Did you ever hear the story about the two farmers sittin on the two-holer?" the old man said, pleased with the thought of another joke.

Robard shook his head somberly and stopped what he was doing in the jeep.

The old man looked at them both cautiously. "Well," he said, "there's these two old farmers sittin side by side in the privy, and one old farmer stands up and starts to grab his braces and all his change falls out down the hole. And right quick he reaches down in his pocket, pulls out his wallet, and throws a twenty-dollar bill right in there after it. And the other old farmer says, 'Why, Walter, what in the world did you do that for?' And the first old farmer says, 'Wilbur, if you think I'm going down in that hole for thirty-five cents, you're crazy as hell.' Haw haw haw haw." The old man bellied over so hard the puppy backed off several feet.

He did the best he could to ignite a smile, but Robard seemed to think the joke was funny and laughed.

The old man took off his glasses, wiped his eyes with his sleeve, and looked up at him thoughtfully, holding his pants loose around his waist. "You know," the old man said, "you don't look so good. Could be you need a purgative. Mrs. Lamb's got some Black-Draught. You look like you could use a good reamin."

"I couldn't say," he said, feeling embarrassed to be there.

"Well, *I* could!" the old man shouted. "Just be careful you don't wake Hewes up trotting across the yard. That man's got to work tomorrow."

He wondered if there wasn't right then some convenient way to get back over the lake before another bus ran. He looked back across the field. The olive light had completely died, and hanging up over the horizon were leaded clouds, and through the woods gloom was massing up. He tried to imagine the air at Meigs Field at that very moment. Far out on the lake, beyond the reflection, you could see the tiny pinchpoint running lights of the ore boats farther up into the darkness than you were, at some moment when the air was a sweet liquid enveloping you and making you feel like walking on the polished lakefront before coming in out of the dark. He felt raw now. And he had never thought until this very moment that he could long for it, want whatever erroneous comfort it had, making him invisible. And for a moment, in the natural order of things, he felt large and frail and brought down out of place into a painful light that made him want to hulk away back in the dark.

The old man stared at him with an odd solicitude.

"I believe we done exercised Newel," Mr. Lamb said to Robard. "Don't get peeved, Newel. We don't take ourselves serious down here like you do up there, do we, Hewes?"

"I guess," Robard said, looking at him a moment, then turning toward the metal shed the old man had designated.

"I've got to cap off that goddamned well before it gets pitch dark or Mrs. Lamb will step in it and break her leg. Did you hear that, Hewes? The privy queered my well. I got to sink a new one."

"I heard it," Robard said, starting to the tin house.

"T. V. A. Landrieu'll ring dinner in a little bit, and we'll all eat and try to cheer up old sourpuss here. Or we'll throw his fat ass in the river."

The old man straggled up toward the house, clutching a fistful of his pants and hollering for the colored man to come after him.

From the door of the metal house, Robard watched him come down from the jeep. "You heard it," Robard said, letting the screen wag back between his fingers.

"The old turd," he said. "I'll go out in his asshole woods in the morning and yank a few trees up by the roots and drive every rational animal right in the lake. Let them take their chances with the gars or whatever that was out there."

Robard looked amused and stood in the doorway watching the killed light, while he sank back on the bed. "If I see you I'll run the other way."

"Tell me something." He hung his feet over the cot latch.

"It ain't some more what I make my memories out of, or whatever that was you said, is it?"

"No," he said, arranging his arms in back of his head.

Robard lit a cigarette and let the smoke feather through his nose and get drawn through the screen. He lifted his cheeks toward his eye sockets as if someone were shining a light in his face. "Don't you ever get tired and want to think just whatever comes in your head?"

"I've got to ask somebody besides me," he said. "You've probably got better answers anyway." He watched Robard, trying to calculate the sense he was making out of it.

"I don't know shit from a shoeshine," Robard mumbled, looking away again.

"Just tell me about your family," he said.

Robard picked a fleck of tobacco off his tongue and looked around in the gloom as if he were considering walking outside. "My daddy's dead," he said abruptly. "He got drowned, and my mother married an Indian in Sallisaw, Oklahoma. They live down at Anadarko. What else?" He sucked his tooth.

"Why'd she marry an Indian?"

"She's a half," Robard said. "Her daddy was one of them oil-well Osages. Bought him a big Maxwell automobile, and they had to drive it in the woods one day clear to Arkansas to get it away from the Oklahoma creditors."

Katydids were zuzzing out in the yard. He tried to think of something to say but couldn't.

"I got an old picture of them," Robard said, "set up in a wagon with a mule, after they had sold the car. She stayed up in north Arkansas after that, up till the time my own father died, till I hired out on the railroad, as a matter of fact. She worked in a brassiere plant in Fort Smith. And quick as I left she married this Indian that had a dry-cleaning business in Anadarko." Robard looked at his toes as though he could see what he was saying in the darkness separating him from the ground.

"Your father wasn't Indian, was he?"

"He was a German," Robard said, letting his heels grind the cigarette butt. "In fact, they wanted to stick him in prison up in Cane Hill during the war, put him with a bunch of Japs they had at Fort Chaffee."

"And don't you keep in touch with your mother at all?"

"I'll tell you," Robard said, looking at his heels awhile. He had become a silhouette in the open screen. "She had her little piece of business to attend to, and I had my little bit. She's sweet." He smacked his lips. "I think it would make her nervous if I showed up, cause I couldn't fit in nothin. It might make me unhappy, and

I don't need that. I like to keep my business manageable." Robard turned around and walked back into the shed. "How come I get to answer the questions?"

"So we can start off even," he said. "I'm the only person who'll take me seriously.

"You'd think that'd teach you something," Robard said quietly. "Though I'm afraid nobody ever took me serious in their life."

15

Mr. Lamb sat brooding at the head of a short deal table, scowling at Landrieu through the kitchen door and fingering a glass of whiskey. The screen porch gave directly into a small dark kitchen that smelled like crowder peas boiled in molasses. The colored man was inside frowning at various flickering portholes on a large wood cook stove, exchanging pots and skillets rapidly and keeping an eye on Mr. Lamb, who sat lowering over his whiskey. Farther on the length of the house through a pair of open clear-paned gallery doors was a large pine-floor sitting room with a high hearth fireplace, beside which Mrs. Lamb was seated manipulating the knobs on a big silver radio, staring at the lighted dials as though she were seeing the horizon of a faraway country behind each tiny window.

Mr. Lamb's eyes snapped up and a smile cracked on his face. He had put on a red flannel shirt with sleeves that came down over his hands and a hand-painted picture of a mallard duck about to land on each collar point. He had buttoned on a pair of red and yellow striped suspenders and combed his straggly hair wet against his head, so that he looked like the guest of honor at a birthday party.

The instant impression the old man gave was that he had shrunk to half the size he had seemed an hour before. His face was sunken at the temples and his eyes looked fragile and sallow.

"Sit down, for God's sake," the old man said loudly toward the kitchen. "Bring two more glasses in here, T.V.A."

Mrs. Lamb frowned up from her radio knobs and gave them both a disapproving look. She was a big woman with scarlet hair, a large expandable mouth, and dusky skin she accentuated with dark lipstick, which made her look Latin and obstinate. He tried to smile at her through the gallery door. Mrs. Lamb was listening to Eddie Arnold sing "Cattle Call," and a large queenly smile froze over her big mouth as if she were reliving a moment when the tune had expressed some unexpressible felicity. He wondered vaguely if she wasn't some old doxy Mr. Lamb had corralled someplace and kept out on the island to amuse him, and for whom he had provided the gigantic radio to help her maintain audio contact with the rest of the world.

The colored man, who was now wearing a white porter's tunic with "Illinois Central Railroad" stitched on the pocket and several gold hatches glorifying each cuff, appeared from the kitchen with two cut-glass tumblers, set them on the table, and removed himself out of sight back to the pantry.

Mr. Lamb picked a quart bottle of Wild Turkey off the floor and set it down decisively in front of Robard. "Mrs. Lamb makes me keep my whiskey under the sink," he complained, smirking and ducking his head as if anticipating a lick.

"With the other abrasives," Mrs. Lamb interjected from the opposite end of the house.

"She won't tolerate having it on the table, either," the old man said, still smirking.

Robard poured out some whiskey in his glass and set the bottle across the table. He poured a nice line in his own glass and set the bottle on the floor beside Mr. Lamb's foot.

"That's good," Mr. Lamb said, satisfied with everyone's glass including his own, which was half full. "I think we ought to all of us get drunk."

The colored man snickered in the kitchen.

"That's Mark's only toast," Mrs. Lamb said. He felt she was aiming her remark directly at him.

"Ma'am?" he said.

She smiled at him regally and turned down the radio. " 'Let's all get drunk' is the only toast Mark knows."

Mr. Lamb's face brightened. He swiveled around in his chair and gave her the benefit, and took a generous drink of whiskey.

"Mrs. Lamb is a dear, gentle woman," the old man said to the two of them, his face red and his little eyes humid with the whiskey. He smacked his lips distastefully as though he'd just drunk piss. "I've had her for fifty years, and we've never had an argument. I wish she'd come in here," he said, shouting over his own voice.

"I wish you'd let me listen to my program," she said irritably.

"I'd like you to meet these two gentlemen, Mr. Hewes and Mr. Newel. Mr. Newel is your granddaughter's spark, ain't you?" he said.

"Her friend," he said, letting the whiskey drain through his throat.

"Friend, then. He says he's her friend. Haw. I wish you'd come to be introduced."

She glared at her husband and almost simultaneously smiled at him and Robard and turned up her radio to hear the last straining notes of "Cattle Call."

"I bought Mrs. Lamb that radio ten Christmases ago," Mr. Lamb said gloomily, bracketing his hands beside his glass. "We don't have a phone, and she used to get lonesome with just men around, drinking and telling lies. So I bought her that there we're all listening to, and now I can't prise her loose. She'll start listening to the Memphis police calls in a minute. She hears the goddamnedest things. I don't know what goes on in Memphis—everybody's raping and killing and robbing everybody else. I used to know it when Crump was mayor, and *none* of that went on."

"That's not true," he said, his throat becoming anesthetized with the whiskey. "It was just good business to keep quiet about it."

"The hell it's not," Mr. Lamb snapped. "I say it *is.*" The old man scowled at him and thickened his brows, his spectacles catching light in directions. "What'd you say you was, a lawyer?"

"Yes sir."

"You talk like a goddamned lawyer, don't he, Hewes?"

"I don't know nothing about lawyers," Robard said, paring his thumb down the ridge of his jaw and staring back coolly.

"Neither does he," Mr. Lamb said, and smirked. "He just talks like he does. I used to go to the King Cotton Hotel every October for the Ole Miss and Arkansas game, and there was never a bit of unpleasantry took place. Memphis was a *wonderful* city, and I've been in it more times than you've pissed your britches."

"May be," he said.

"Is he nuts?" the old man said, looking at Robard.

Robard shook his head uncomprehendingly.

"Shit," the old man said. "I don't need nobody to tell me nothin." He drank off the last ounce of whiskey and scrutinized the kitchen door. "What the hell, T.V.A. Have you took up your residence in our dinner?"

"I can't cook it no faster than the stove," the Negro replied, and stuck his head around the door sill and gave the old man a hateful look.

Mr. Lamb picked up the bottle, awarded himself another portion of whiskey, and set the bottle on the floor. "A lawyer." He snorted as though it put him in mind of a dirty joke.

"Almost," he said.

The old man eyed him belligerently. "Well, almost, what the hell do you know about the law? I'm a stupid old asshole, don't know nothing about anything. Me and Hewes is just alike. We're ignorant as two coons."

He measured some whiskey, took a breath, and looked Mr. Lamb in the face. "I guess the law has always been a good alternative to strangling everybody's youngest son," he said.

"Any nitwit knows that," Mr. Lamb snorted. "That's not the law. That's Moses, for goddamned sake. If you want to read the Bible, go sit on the privy. I've got a copy on the wall with a piece of twine, so you won't haul it off. I know the Bible, by God."

He let another tiny drop of whiskey slide by his tongue and

looked placidly into the old man's face, which seemed to him to have sunk nearer the tabletop, as if the old man were on his knees.

"What else do you know, moron? You ain't told me nothin I didn't already know myself," the old man said.

Mrs. Lamb all at once sat around and gave the antenna on her radio a severe twisting. The radio responded by broadcasting a fine, high-pitched crackling noise that sounded like cellophane being crumpled up in somebody's fist. Two short bursts of an unintelligible male voice were followed by more crackling, and then another man's voice, then more static.

"Shit!" the old man boomed, gyrating so he could see backward. "Can't you find something else than that? Isn't that just the goddamned Clarksdale taxicab?"

"I'm looking for the police," she said, unperturbed, frowning at the little lighted dials and twisting a fat chrome knob back and forth without making any noticeable improvement. "They aren't on the air. I can't account for it."

"I can't either," he said, "but I want you to turn it off before I come adjust it my own way."

She snapped the radio off and rocked back in her chair and stared impassively at the unlighted box. All there was to hear now was the sound of whatever was frying on the stove and T.V.A. scuffling his feet.

"All right," Mr. Lamb said, looming forward again, his eyes red and unsteady. "What else?"

"The law of inches," he said. "That has to do with the crime of sodomy."

Mr. Lamb's face became quickly ashen.

"It states that penile and oral copulation between two men, or between a man and a woman, is absolutely out." He paid the old man an arrogating look. "But oral copulation between two women is not a crime due to the lack of the penetration of the sexual organ. . . ."

"That's all I care to hear about it," the old man said, rearing up in his chair and pounding his hard little fist on the table, glaring at everything at once. "That's against nature, by God."

"In ancient church law men were stoned to death for doing it," he said. "But women only got whipped, which is a serious inequity. What's sauce for the goose, so to say, ought to be good for the gander. I'm sure you agree."

"The hell," the old man fumed. "This is my table, I'll decide what I agree with. T.V.A., bring in the goddamn food or I'll come out there and put you in the pan and we'll all eat better."

Landrieu instantly emerged with a crock platter of braised squirrels, several bowls containing new potatoes, peas, and okra, a gravy boat, and an amber pitcher of tea. Mr. Lamb grimly contemplated the food's arrival as if he were searching out some petty delinquency he could hold everyone but himself responsible for. Mrs. Lamb arrived and sat at the opposite end of the table, while they all stood. Landrieu came back with four glasses of ice, then watched while Mrs. Lamb scrutinized the table and slowly nodded, whereupon Landrieu disappeared promptly back into the kitchen.

"Where do you come from?" Mrs. Lamb said, redirecting conversation toward Robard.

He watched Robard with pleasure. Robard set down his fork, allowed himself time to swallow, then sat thinking about some possible answer. Mrs. Lamb smelled like spoiled lilacs.

"Hewes ain't a talker," Mr. Lamb spurted with his mouth filled up with peas and potatoes. "This one is, though," motioning with his fork.

"From Cane Hill, Arkansas," Robard said, and looked around suspiciously.

"What'd he say," Mr. Lamb shouted. "This side is my bad ear." He gave his ear a good whack and turned his working ear toward the conversation.

"If you wouldn't pound your ear like that, Mark, you'd hear better," Mrs. Lamb said.

"The sound's out of it," the old man said, and looked perplexed. "We had a cyclone two years ago, blew off two of Gaspareau's little shotgun houses. Blowed so hard I had to crawl up under the Willys to keep from blowing away. And when it was over the sound was gone out of this ear." He pointed at his ear as something he would never fathom.

"I believe," Mrs. Lamb said authoritatively, loading peas on her plate, "Mark poked things in his ear all his life until he ruined it. There's no reason a strong wind should make you deaf."

"Unless it does, goddamn it." Mr. Lamb frowned and clattered his teeth. "You and Newel ought to sit together in church."

T.V.A. appeared, collected the whiskey glasses, and carted them away to the kitchen.

"You know what?" Mr. Lamb said, leaning up over his food.

"No," he said, watching the old man seethe.

"In Arkansas, over there"—Mr. Lamb gestured with his thumb —"to get to be a lawyer, you know what you got to do?"

"No," he said, spooning sugar into his tea glass, and watching it sift down among the ice cubes.

A grin stole over the old man's rubbery mouth and he pulled closer to the table, as if to enlist a privacy between the two of them. "They make you spend two days in the in-sane asylum before they let you join. Haw haw haw." The old man's mouth split open, his face reddened up until his eyes dampened, and he had to take up the edge of his napkin to dry them. "Didn't you know that?"

He took a bite of the squirrel and chewed it. "Why do they do that?" he said.

"Shit!" the old man said. "Cause they figure it'll do 'em good, I reckon. They must think you all need it or they wouldn't do it."

Mrs. Lamb looked painfully at Mr. Lamb. "The bar examination *is* given in the lunatics' asylum in Little Rock," she said quietly.

"With all them monkeys outside screamin and ravin like nature intended them to," Mr. Lamb gloated. "It ought to be a law that every lawyer spends a year in the in-sane asylum before starting, just to be on the safe side. What do you think about that, Newel?"

"I think it'd be a good idea," he said. "We'd be able to let some of the sane people out then and start putting the crazy ones in there where they belong."

125

The old man smiled roguishly. "I think me and Newel have finally reached agreement on somethin," he said, and scrutinized everyone to see if they agreed. "Where'd you say you was from, Hewes?" he said.

"Arkansas," Robard said deliberately.

"Hewes is my trespass man," Mr. Lamb said to Mrs. Lamb, who promptly regarded Robard skeptically. "He ain't a murderer, either," he said. "We found *that* out."

Robard gave Mr. Lamb a rum look.

"Hewes, now listen here," Mr. Lamb commenced, leaning back in his chair until the struts popped and the chair gave evidence that it might just fly apart. "All you got to do is get in your jeep and drive the roads that's on this island. It don't make no difference which ones you take, or where you start, just so you watch where you're going and don't shoot nobody, or let anybody shoot you, or let none of them sons of bitches from over there slip over here and shoot my turkeys. All them roads eventually comes right back here."

Robard kept his eyes fastened on his plate, watching everyone out the corners as if he didn't like taking orders in front of people. "All right," he said.

"Though if you can get a clear shot at old Gaspareau you might ought to take it." Mr. Lamb's eyes flashed. "Mrs. Lamb would never stop thanking you enough."

"That's fine, Mark," Mrs. Lamb said. "We all appreciate Mr. Gaspareau's service."

"Mrs. Lamb wouldn't mind having a short season on Gaspareaus, if the Game and Fish would let her do it." Mr. Lamb quaked silently.

He tried to feature what style of vileness Gaspareau might have committed to pass him to the dark end of Mrs. Lamb's affection. It seemed, though, like almost any one of Gaspareau's private habits might have antagonized her, though it also seemed like Mr. Lamb could probably match Gaspareau habit for habit.

"I'll acquaint you to whoever comes in here with my permission," Mr. Lamb continued authoritatively, "so you won't be running *them* off. Otherwise, if you hear an outboard, go where you hear it, cause it'll be some of them shitasses slippin in over here to get 'em a turkey without me knowing it. Do you know where the river is?"

Robard skinnied his eyes until his face looked like a razor. "No," he said, fingering the haft of his dinner knife.

"That way," the old man said loudly, jabbing his left arm toward the back of the house and the other side of the island from where they had come in. "If anybody comes, outside of Gaspareau and one of them murderers of his, they'll come from the river. That's where I want you to spend half your time."

"All right," Robard said.

Mrs. Lamb finished her plate and rang a tiny table bell, and T.V.A. created a fierce racket getting on his feet and out of the kitchen. He appeared in the doorway, a napkin in his collar and his mouth full of squirrel, some of which was still marooned in the corner of his lip. He gave the table a half-vexed look, though neither Mr. Lamb nor Mrs. Lamb noticed. He picked up Mrs. Lamb's plate and handed it back inside the kitchen.

"See them maps?" the old man said, marshaling everyone's attention toward the wall behind him and leaning arrogantly back into his chair.

Everyone, excluding Mrs. Lamb, stared dully at two maps nailed to the wall board. One was a grayed-in aerial photo of a giant blurred teardrop mass, with the round lobe of the drop crimped inward. The other was a cartographer's job, displaying a section of the river opposite the town of Elaine, showing the river running straight as a plumb line past the site of the town, represented by two concentric red circles on the map, but without designating any esker of land or earthwork that might represent the island. The river carried straight by Elaine without a jog one way or the other. The map was drawn by the Army Corps of Engineers, whose little colophon sat at the right-hand lower corner.

"See anything queer?" the old man snorted.

Robard cradled his chin in his hand.

"What about you, smart aleck?" Mr. Lamb said. "You don't see nothin queer, do you?"

"Nothing except this island doesn't exist on the map where the aerial picture shows."

The old man looked at him venomously and went on as if he hadn't heard. "This island ain't on the goddamned engineers' map," he boasted, a rakish smile organizing his old wrinkled face. Mrs. Lamb rose demurely and went off into the sitting room and took a seat by her radio. She sat a moment staring at the fire in the stone fireplace, then switched on the cold tubes. Mr. Lamb looked at her strangely, changed his expression and went on with what he was dying to say. "Them goddamned Army bastards think they're so smart going around noodling with everything, building a dam in every ditch with an ounce of water in it till you have to ask the sons of bitches for water to take a bath in. Well, I fixed them, by God." His eyes snapped wildly back between the two of them, waiting for one to ask the question, but nobody said anything. "I was down there on the river one day must've been ten years ago, nosing around down there not doing anything in particular, when I seen this couple of big fat does go up over a little knoll and head for the river, and I went in after them cause I wanted to see what it was they was going to do over there. So I commenced running up over the hill—that's back when I could plant one foot in front of the other one without falling on my face —and right away real quick I heard this *boom-boom-boom* out where the deers had run. And I hit the goddamned dirt, because you can't never tell what might be going on over there. And I laid there for a minute or two, and didn't hear nothing else, no shooting nor yellin nor nothin. And I just kindly eased up the hill there till I could see down to the river, and here was these two jokers in a motorboat about to touch bank. They had the motor hauled up and was poling in on the slack water. One of them was holding two rifles—two of them stubby little Army guns—and the other was poling the boat with a long-handle paddle. Both of them was Army guys, I could see that, because they had uniform jackets on, the ignorant sons of bitches. And of course right there

128

on the bank was them two does, dead as hammers, shot right through the neck, though they had shot one twict. And I could see just exactly what was going on, and quick as they stepped out of the boat and got ahold of a deer each, I come roaring over the hill with my deer rifle, got them both for trespassing, hunting deer from a boat, hunting deer with an unauthorized gun, hunting without a license, shooting illegal deer, shooting another illegal deer, and hunting out of season. I had them sons of bitches dead to it, too, cause they started shitting pickles as quick as I listed off their offenses. Both of them was majors, had their uniforms on, so it might have been a whole long list of other crimes, too, that could've been added on to the ones I knew. So I lawed the bastards. I told them they was on their way to jail, and the shitasses turned white as paste and started looking at one another like they was trying to figure some way to appease me, and one of them said was there anything they could do to get me to let them loose without turning them over to the sheriff? And I said, 'Well, I don't know.' Turns out that they were down there from Memphis, doing the float work for drawing up a new map of the river, cause the Corps of Engineers keeps a check on the river since there ain't no war to keep 'em busy building. And when they asked me if they couldn't do me some kind of favor to make up for all them crimes they'd committed right in my presence, I said, 'Hell, yes. You can erase this island off your damn map, and make it hard to find for anybody who ain't supposed to be looking.' And those sorry bastards said sure they'd do it, since it didn't make no difference to a asshole bunch like the Corps of Engineers what went on the map and what got left off, since they're all so god-damned crooked they have to wind themselves into bed every evening anyway, and half of them are on the take from the state in the first place. So that's how come we come to be off that map. And that's how come it ain't easy to find this place, cause that's the way I like it. When I come over here I don't want a bunch of nitwits running all over the place shooting up the country and killing my deer and turkeys and whatever else I got out here."

"What happened to the deer?" he said.

"What deer?"

"The deer the majors shot. Did you let them take the deer, since they did you the favor?"

"Hell, no. What the hell do you think *I* was doing out there at six o'clock in the morning? I wanted them does myself. I had me a salt lick set out there. Where do you think them does was headed when those morons potted them? They was headed to my lick, that's where."

"I thought you said it was out of season for deer," he said.

The old man looked at him malignantly. "It's *my* land. It's open season on anything I take a notion to shoot. Piss on deer season and every other season. I'll shoot what I want to shoot. I got a covey of pet quail right out between the house and my airfield this very minute." He stabbed his finger toward the closest window. "I'll take Elinor and walk right out there and shoot me two quails and eat them for dinner, if I want to. I don't need nobody to tell me it ain't quail season, cause it *is*. Them quails is always in season—*my* season."

"Just curious."

"Well, then, there's your answer, Curious. This here is *my* island and I don't care about nobody but myself, by God, and I don't care if I do, either. I can't help it if there ain't no deer or no quail or nothin else wild around here on these poor bastards' farms. I protect what I got. I got Hewes hired to keep the assholes off. They done screwed the works on their own land, now they want to screw the same works on mine. But they ain't. Hewes here'll see to that, won't you, son?"

Robard looked up from his plate, sucked his tooth, and declined to participate. The old man leaned back and eyed them both arrogantly. He had worked his way to the edge of his chair telling the story, and now he pushed his fingers under his suspenders and gave both of them a proprietary look, as though he was challenging anyone to contradict one single word he'd uttered.

Mrs. Lamb began adjusting the knobs through a hail of static.

"Get the news, Fidelia," Mr. Lamb said matter-of-factly, squirming until he could see to the next room.

"I want the weather," she said, staring at the little shining panels and plugging in a set of ancient wire PBX headphones that shorted the sound and left the house quiet except for the colored man skating around the kitchen.

"Mrs. Lamb goes according to the weather," Mr. Lamb said, turning back slightly bewildered. "She don't care what time it is, just so long as she knows what the weather's doing."

"At least she doesn't worry about getting older," he said.

"Who the hell does?" the old man snapped, pushing backward in his chair and creating a fierce bracking noise on the floor. "You worry about getting old, T.V.A.?"

"No suh," T.V.A. said invisibly from the kitchen. He could make out the spattered toes of the colored man's shoes where he had taken a seat around the doorway.

"Why not?" the old man said.

"Suh?" T.V.A. said.

"Why don't you worry about getting old, son? Newel here is worried about getting old. We ain't, are we?"

"No suh."

"Why not?" the old man demanded impatiently, turning his ear up to hear exactly what was to be said.

"Cause if I wasn't getting no older, I'd be dead."

"Haw haw haw haw haw." The old man broke up in more gasps of strangled laughter. T.V.A. never moved from behind the door. Mr. Lamb banged the table with his fist and all the glasses convulsed, and tea frothed both sides of the pitcher. "You'd be dead, Newel, if you didn't get no older," the old man wheezed, just able to get a word free. "You, too, Hewes, you'd be dead. We'd *all* be dead."

Mr. Lamb once more removed his teeth from his mouth, dipped them in his iced tea glass, wiggled them with his fingers, then let them sink quietly to the bottom. He looked up with his cheeks sucked in over his gums and his mouth flapping like the nozzle of a collapsed pink balloon, making himself look more like an old woman than an old man.

"I'll tell you something that *you* don't know, Newman," the old man said indistinctly, folding his hands neatly in front of him. "Was used to be," he mumbled, his teeth idling uselessly at the bottom of his tea glass, "that when a man got put in the penitentiary, the big experts on the subject come in and pulled out all his teeth, cause they had 'em a theory then that bad teeth was to blame for all the crimes. It wasn't your childhood or whether your mother was scared by a goat, or what kind of neighborhood you lived in, or if your mother dressed you up like a girl—none of that baloney. It was your *teeth*. If you had bad teeth, you was a criminal. So they went in all the jails and started yanking out prisoners' teeth, and turning them loose right and left. Now, I think that's a pretty good idea, don't you? I bet you didn't know that."

He watched the old man's mouth work unconsciously gum to gum. "Is that where you got all yours pulled out?"

The old man smiled a dark smile, leaving his hands anchored to the table. "No, I got mine pulled out in Memphis," he said.

"Have you committed any crimes since then?"

"Just one," the old man said.

"What was that?"

The old man's eyes darted and he swiped his lips with his sleeve and uncovered a big empty grin. "I had to kick the shit out of a wise-ass one day. But he was the only one I knew and I haven't had to do it since." Mr. Lamb's blue eyes flickered dangerously, and he fixed him in a long intense smile. "Did you ever hear the joke about the nigger caught stealing ax handles that got called up before the judge?" Mr. Lamb stood up from the table and steadied himself on the back of his chair. "The judge looked at the nigger real careful and said, 'Rufus, have you ever been up before me before?' And the nigger looked at the judge real serious and said, 'Well, I don't rightly know, Judge. What time does you get up?'" The old man's eyes danced back and forth, waiting for a response. T.V.A. started giggling, banging metal against metal. The old man looked at them both a second longer until the smile completely vanished. "You bastards lack *one* necessary," he said confoundedly. "A sense of humor. Every goddamned one of you young people don't know what in the fuck's funny and what ain't. I asked some little asshole in Helena last week, just to be a-talking to him, without nothing to gain on it, just bein friendly, I said, 'Where the hell do all you kids come from?' And the bastard looked at me like I was a pail of shit and said, 'You tell me. You're the ones been having us the last thirty years.' " The old man glowered flatly and stumped away into the other room.

16

He stood looking out the screen at the woods where the moon had ignited a thin sheeny mist through the treetops. He heard the colored man come down the steps, tramp across the dooryard, and enter the other cabin. He could hear the light switch on inside, but couldn't see the house or the light through the doorway, though he could hear the colored man's feet on the bare pine floor. Past the haze the sky was clear. A few brief specks of cloud were drawn in against the face of the moon. He could hear Elinor making a final investigation of the perimeter of the yard, snorting in the wet leaves and pawing in the grass before passing on, her leash tinkling lightly.

He breathed through the screen and let his chest empty until he felt himself at ease. He had stood days at the gauzy window and watched the park as the evening floated up like a mist, trying to be at ease. And late in the night the miseries commenced, his eyes smarting, his tendons fibrillating. All of it caused by necessary impulses, like a box of bees whirling to come out.

Robard, who had come down ahead of him and gone immediately to bed, turned in his sleep and exhaled a long sigh, letting his hand scrape the rippled wall.

He stood at the screen, imprinted against the moonglow, hulking in his undershorts, took a deep exhaustive breath and let it out through the matrix wires, allowing the emptiness to inhabit him and for an airy moment release his mind to everything.

17

In the summer, in the tiny tourist cabin in Angola, he had sat with his father and stared out the door toward the prison, a wide barbed-wire compound, visible by day and only a ring of tiny lights at night. The day before, a brown panel truck had come down from Shreveport with the electric chair and driven through the center of town, making everyone stop in the sun and look. The state owned a single electric chair and delivered it wherever it was needed, from courthouse to courthouse all across the state to where there was someone to electrocute. At midnight everyone in the town turned on their lights and stood at their windows and waited, and when the chair was turned on, all the lights in town went dim for a time, and all the glimmering lights at the prison went dim, and in the motel room with his father he lay in the bed and watched the ceiling fan turn slower and slower until it stopped. And in the morning he had gone with his father in his old Mercury to the gate of the prison, and through and along the well-paved macadam to the compound of long white barracks that looked like chicken houses. And in the lot his father had gotten out and gone inside to a man's office to sell him starch for the prisoners' laundry, and he had sat still in the car in the moistened heat of early morning and stared down the long rows of chalk barracks and wondered where the dead man was, wondered if he and the dead man, an unforgiving murderer named Walter L. Magee, were locked up there together, or if in the night they had taken him secretly out of the chair and carted him into town and left him in a room overnight to cool.

PART III

Robard Hewes

1

In the morning he woke before light with rain on the shed. Newel lay like a mountain on his cot, breathing roughly, his nose against the corrugated wall. He stared awhile, drifting in and out of sleep, not able to gauge time. He rose once and stepped out in the rain and craned his head around at Landrieu's shack and up to the house. But it was all dark. A spotlight was shining at the top of the steps and rain darted through the steamy light. He went back inside.

"Look here," the old man had said, lowering his chin into the wattles of his neck, whiskey still in his eyes. "Blinded pigs can dig acorns." The old man's eyes widened as he handed over the gun.

"Yes sir," he said.

"You know what that means?" The old man angled his head down to get a better look.

"I guess," he said, wondering.

Mr. Lamb stood back and leveled his shoulders. "I don't think you do," he said, and acted as if he was about to walk away, but stopped. "It means any shitass that's got a gun can figure out a way to shoot somebody." The old man's eyes rewidened as if he were searching out a weakness that would let him not have to part with the pistol. "I don't want you shooting that gun, you understand?"

"Yes sir," he said, putting his toe to his instep and looking away.

"By God, this here is a symbol of *my* authority," the old man announced. "You're just carrying it for me, cause I'm too damn old to boss people off my land by myself. Even if I wasn't, though, I wouldn't go around shooting people, you understand?"

"Yes sir," he said. He stared at the old man's toes swaddled in his duck trousers.

"So, Hewes," the old man growled, "you treat this gun like it was your pecker and keep it in your pants."

He lay on the damp sheets and listened to the rain pepper the roof. Newel spoke a word in his sleep and raised his fist in the air and clinched it as if threatening some intruder in his dream, then opened it like a flower and drew it back.

2

He woke up again in blue light, the old man flailing at the porch bell, and the dread of W.W. hanging like another big bell without a clapper. He lay still and listened to the old man curse. Newel lay under the sheet, deep in some wretched dream.

There would have to be considerable cautions taken now. He couldn't simply drive to wherever she lived, beep the horn, and have off with her locked in the cranny of his arm without everybody in fifty miles yanking out the phone lines to tell W.W. that some swarthy man in a pickup had just collected his wife and driven her off to God knows where, with her nosing out the inside of his arm like a worm seeking drier air. He'd have to come up with something better or W. might seize on drastic measures.

The old man started punishing the bell again. He heard Landrieu's screen slap and Landrieu's feet on the wet steps, and the old man roaring.

Newel rolled on his back and stared at the spiderwebs, letting the cover slide off on the floor. Newel's body was white as an aspirin, and one arm was like two of his. His own stomach was hard as a cord of wood and Newel's was a big mass of hair and chest and belly piled on the sheet like dough.

Newel squirmed over on his side and stared at him. "You're sure fit as a goddamned fiddle, aren't you?" he moaned. "You should've been abusive to yourself like I have. We'd have something to talk about then."

He stood and stared at Newel with nothing to say, and began putting on his pants. Newel dragged the covers up to his chin and straightened his legs and seemed to go back to sleep.

The thing would be to call her as quick as he could, arrange a rendezvous where he could sneak her in the truck and nobody notice anything else but a pickup going down the highway to nowhere anybody gave a shit about. Except time felt against him now. He looked at Newel suspiciously as if he were lying there figuring out a way to interfere.

The old man suddenly raged out onto the porch and slammed the old bell again as hard as he could. "Goddamn it, Hewes," he fumed. "You working for me or in business for yourself, you son-of-a-bitch?" A long silence opened up, then the old man slashed the bell again and barged back inside the house, unable to stand silence another moment.

Newel sat up against the cold wall, poking at his eyes. "Tell me one thing," he said.

"How's that?" he said, ready to go out.

"What in the hell are you doing down here? I laid up trying to figure that out. A smart guy wouldn't waste time doing what you're doing if it wasn't important."

"Didn't nobody say it wasn't." He couldn't quite see Newel's face in the gloom.

"All right," Newel said, running his finger around in his nose and sinking back on the bed. "I hope it's not just some hot young nooky you got farmed out so you have to slip around and take your license plate off to get ahold of."

"Why is that?" he said.

"There's more important things in the world."

"Name me one," he said.

Newel's flesh brightened in the light. "There isn't any use my telling you."

"Shit." He caught the latch nail in his fingers. "I was hoping you were going to say 'Another one.' "

"Another what?"

"Another piece," he said. "That's all I know's more important than a piece of tail. I was hoping you'd say that, then we *would* have something to talk about. I'd of thought a lot more of you than I do now."

"I bet you wished *you* believed that," Newel said.

"You know I believe it," he said, and laughed. "You better hurry and get smart, boy. You ain't got that much time."

3

Mr. Lamb was sitting in his place at the end of the table when he came in out of the rain. The colored man was wearing a dented chintz chef's hat and an apron up around his armpits, and wouldn't look at him as he went through the kitchen. The room smelled like hot oatmeal.

He sat down and took up his napkin while Mr. Lamb glared at him silently for a long time. The old man had on the same red and yellow suspenders and canvas pants he'd had on the night before, worn up over a yellow pajama shirt that was buttoned to his neck.

"If it wasn't raining, I'd run your ass off here," the old man said, making his eyes into tiny slits behind his spectacles.

"Why is that?" he said.

"The sun's up," Mr. Lamb said, and shot a look at the window to make sure everybody knew he knew it was raining. "Any bastard wanted to sneak up to this island has already done it time you get your ass out of bed. If it wasn't raining I'd put you right in the boat."

"If it wasn't raining I'd let you do it," he said calmly.

The old man frowned and thumbed the bowl of his spoon. "Bring him some oatmeal!" he shouted, and put several quick loads in his mouth and began chewing vigorously. "Where's Newel at?" he said.

"In the bed."

"Son-of-a-bitch," the old man gurgled, drinking a little coffee out of his saucer and spilling some more in.

"I'll need to go in town this evening," he said.

The old man's face was stricken. "Don't you want to do *any* work?" he said. "You don't arrive in here till after six o'clock, and you're already thinking about taking off again. Shit."

"I said I was going to have to go some," he said.

"What the hell for?"

"Business."

The old man looked at him resentfully for not being let in on the secret. "What kind of business?"

"We already discussed that," he said, and washed some grounds around the bottom of his mouth.

"Have we?" the old man said loudly. "You ain't plottin no armed robbery up there in Helena, are you?"

"No sir." He tried to get the oatmeal to stir and found out it wouldn't.

The old man took another big bite and eyed him up and down. "You got people in Helena?"

"They all moved off," he said.

"I don't know *nobody* in Helena," the old man said. "I'm from Marks, Mississippi, and if it didn't happen I had to come over across that Helena Bridge to get over to this island, I wouldn't come over there at all. I hate it. This island resides in the state of Mississippi. I don't have no business in Arkansas at all. There ain't nothin but nitwits and criminals in Arkansas, like that old piss ant lives across the lake. If you want to go rob that little Bank of Dixie in Helena, go right ahead, cause I ain't got a cent in it."

"All right," he said, ready to leave.

"What do you think about Newel?" the old man said aggravatedly.

141

"He asks a lot of questions."

"I don't think he'd have sense to pour piss out of tall boot, do you?" The old man grinned and his teeth subsided slowly away from his soft gums.

He thought about Newel lying in the cool, half awake and half asleep, while he had to cozy up to the old man just to beg one night off, and Newel seemed right then to have things in a good deal better hands than he did. "He'll make a lawyer."

"Shit," the old man snorted. "Them bastards is crooked as corkscrews, every one. I let 'em make out my will, but that's all, by merciful God, that I'll have to do with them." The old man's face became studious. "You done made your will out?"

"I hadn't thought about it."

"You ought to," the old man said, lowering his chin confidentially. "I got mine made and feel a whole lot better about everything." He regarded his fingers as if the benefits were spelled out right there. "Ain't no telling when you might plop over like a hoe handle. You're married, ain't you?"

"I guess," he said.

"Well, then," the old man said, and rocked back in his chair and let his lips loosen in the corners. "You know why the birdies wake up singing, don't you?"

He let his head come up to the old man's eye level, and tried remembering a bird singing in the wet limbs, and couldn't remember anything but the drone of the rain and the specter of W. standing in the trees.

"No sir," he said.

The old man's lips twisted into a little tricky smile. "Because," he said, "they're happy to be alive one more day. You can't count on that, Hewes. Them little birdies know it, too. That's why they're out there singing all the time. They're trying to tell us something. 'Tweet, tweet, you're alive, you ignorant asshole.' " His eyes rounded and he croaked up a rough laugh and got up on his feet. "T.V.A."

Landrieu appeared in the doorway.

"Go out to the castle and warm up the throne."

The colored man went off across the porch and down the steps.

"I can't stand to sit on a cold seat," the old man said, thumbing his supenders off his shoulders.

He looked into the sitting room to see if Mrs. Lamb was there, but the room was empty, and the house felt tranquilized. The rain had left off, and he could hear the water hitting the puddles underneath the eaves. He listened for a bird in the trees and thought about Newel in the cool bed and W. staring curiously at the hollow chamber of some air rifle wondering why he wasn't throwing baseballs, not signing autographs, not being the toast of somebody's town instead of doing what he was doing. And it all made him feel peculiar, like he was missing something going on close to him he couldn't see on account of some defect. He listened for the sweet sound of the birds, but there was nothing except the water sliding off the shakes in slow irregular drops, and somewhere in the distance the sound of the spring on the privy door drawing shut.

"Get your ass out of here and go to work," the old man shouted from the double doors. He had his zipper down, holding his pants by the empty belt loops. "If you see Mr. Newel out there some-where, tell him he's missed his breakfast." The old man went hustling out.

He stepped out onto the screen porch and breathed the cold rain fragrance and listened, but heard nothing but the door to the outhouse slamming, and the great trees dripping water into the grass.

4

At five o'clock he drove the jeep across to the lake and took the boat back to Gaspareau's. The light was fanned out in bands whitening in the haze toward Helena.

Two of Gaspareau's hounds strolled out into the dirt and stood blinking while he fastened the boat and made his way under the hackberries. Neither one offered to bark, as if they felt someone coming off the lake was not someone to bother with, and in a moment they walked back up under the house. He waited for a sign of Gaspareau, but there wasn't one. Mr. Lamb's Continental sat where it had, collecting hackberries washed down by the rain. Katydids hummed in the trees up the lake, and repose hung over the camp and the bight of cabins stretched into the water. Gaspareau's whistle bomb was holding the last direct tincture of sunlight.

He drove up the tractor lane and across the levee into the watered field. The water was still and reflecting black and white in the furrow rows, like silver arrows mirroring the crusts of the sky.

He stopped in at Goodenough's. Mrs. Goodenough was standing behind the mail cage in a green visor, watching the sun lower into the windbreak, leaving the sky purple at the horizon.

He wedged behind the baked goods, took the paper out of his shoe, and dialed.

"It's me," he said, holding the receiver below his shoulder so the sound couldn't get away.

"You bastard," she said, her voice low down.

"What's the matter?"

"Why didn't you come?"

"I told you," he whispered, and filched a look down the aisle at Mrs. Goodenough, who had gone to sorting letters, examining each one from several angles, then inserting it in a canvas bag on the counter.

"I'm on my way," he said, keeping his mouth walled in by the receiver.

A long silence came on the line. "All right," she said.

"Don't you want me to?"

"Yes," she said coldly. "I wanted you *last* night."

"I'm coming tonight," he said.

"All right."

"Where do I get you?" he said, and flatted the receiver to his chest.

144

"Pick me up here," she said nonchalantly.

"I ain't going to last a minute if somebody sees me."

"Then come get me back of the post office."

"Won't somebody see you?"

"No. And it don't make any difference if they did. I don't have to be good for nobody."

"Where's *he* at?"

"Where do you think? Playing baseball in Humnoke. W.'s done turned hisself into a baseball. Where you at?"

"At E-laine."

"Ain't nothing but snakes and mosquitoes down there, is there? Not that I'm down there too often."

"I'm coming on," he said.

"Not on this phone you're not," she said. "You told me I couldn't, so you can't."

He looked at Mrs. Goodenough, who had taken to staring at the sunset again. He could see the sympathetic line of brow beneath her visor, silhouetted against the window glass. He felt in a frenzy, and she seemed locked away in a solace nothing would ever disturb. She turned her head and looked at him and smiled.

"Where we going?" Beuna said noisily.

"Where there ain't nobody," he said, trying to keep from looking at Mrs. Goodenough.

"We going to get a motel?"

"You go on to the post office," he said.

And she hung up.

He walked to the door feeling upset. Mrs. Goodenough smiled and twisted a frond of her hair back beneath the band of her visor. "Going to town?" she said.

"Hope so," he said. "If I haven't slipped up someplace."

She looked at him sympathetically as if she knew exactly what he meant. "Oh, well"—she smiled—"we make mistakes, but we're still here."

There was no other sound in the store but their breathing, separated by odd cadences. They waited for her words to catch someplace or drift away.

"Yes, ma'am," he said. "I just hope I'm here tomorrow."

She picked up a letter and examined it carelessly, and he stepped out into the evening, looking up the straight River Road toward Helena, whose lights were a shabby taint to the sky.

5

The post office was a buff brick structure across the train yards. He drove up the unpaved part of the street that bounded the yards, by where Beuna's father's house had been, and found that the house was gone and the lot had been turned into a depot for fireplugs. The plugs were sitting by themselves inside a cyclone enclosure, tilted every way they could be, in a cone-shaped pile at the back corner of the fence, behind which were some chinaberry trees he remembered. The town was back of the lot, facing the highway, so that the post office was on the dark farm edge of town, almost in the bean rows.

He switched across the rails by the yardmaster's house, a light burning behind the shade. He could feel diesel on his lips and on the air. He turned back parallel toward the post office, and felt little fingers itching inside his stomach.

He stopped on the shoulder and tried to think. He wanted to draw himself together now so that at the moment of setting eyes on her he would have reduced to such a compact item that he could completely command himself, so that no limbs or parts were out of control.

He got still and stared down into the yards, watching the hard little red and green foot lanterns and the flatcars loaded with pine timber, listening to the engines heave in the darkness, regulating his breath, setting his mind on one thing and nothing else.

In the yardmaster's house, where the yardmaster sat and read the Memphis paper, there was a tiny dark inner office with painted windows and a great black banquet of red and yellow and green lights, darting and flashing before a man in a straw hat and perforated cotton shirt, who pressed buttons and flipped toggles and talked to trains out on the line, using a slow drawling voice over a two-way radio. He sat in the room undisturbed for seven-hour stretches and ruled every train and every crew in and out of the rails between Memphis and Lake Village, everything dependent on him to keep from spilling into one another, and keeping the one passenger train that used the line from shooting off into dead spurs at seventy miles an hour and collapsing like a string of garbage cans. Late at night he had slipped in the room and watched the man, whose name was Wheeler, studied him, his white shirt pink and chartreuse in the tiny reflected lights, puzzling at how when the lights started snapping and flashing and trains started heading toward one another at awful speeds, and conductors were howling threats on the two-way, Wheeler could always speak to them in the same mild country voice, adjusting the brim of his hat and flipping a switch to open a rail that was a green light on the banquet, and never making a remark to whoever was sitting behind him, since there was always somebody there watching in total amazement, always keeping his business to himself. He had sat a long time, and despaired over sitting alone in the dark with all the trains and all the switches and the engineers and the conductors and the passengers facing you through one tiny light after another, until the pressure was too great, and you'd fall to the temptation, one night, of letting it all run together, of opening every switch and watching lights converge in a slow series of blinks and snaps, until they all were together and there was nothing left to dispatch.

He had waited in the morning on the settle beside the yardmaster's house until the daylight dispatcher came and Wheeler came out in the open air, his hat in his hand and a St. Louis Cardinals cap on his head, blinking in the steely light. He stood up quickly and looked at Wheeler, who for all the hours they'd spent together watching lights blink on the dark, silent board had never once seen him, and said out loud, "How can you run that all night, in that teensy place, and not ever drive it all together?"

And Wheeler looked at him as if he had asked himself the

question a thousand times and was not amazed to hear it from somebody else. "Mind like a moon," he said easily, taking off his Cardinals cap and stroking his fine sparse hair. "If you stare at the moon a long time, all you'll see is the moon, and all you'll want to see is the moon. I can do it."

He sat in the truck and stared at the yardmaster's house in the mirror, a yellow light above the cramped casements, and the panel of painted glass all the way to the end. The moon had risen so that it stood up above the post office, drifting back into some gauzy smoke. Here it all was, he felt, the time when there wasn't any holding out, the one true last time, and he didn't want to do it halfway, since halfway was as good as nothing.

He throttled the truck and broke out straight down the narrow truck corridor the wrong way between the post office and the cotton broker's shed. At the end, the pavement blind-switched left directly into the rear alley of the post office. The truck barely missed taking the corner of the building and leaped on into the alley, losing purchase and fading rearward toward the back wall. He fought the wheel, surprised to have got going so fast in so short a space, then suddenly Beuna was in the headlights and he was pounding the pedals to keep from barging right out over her and carrying on into the street.

And Beuna never twitched. When the truck bucked the back corner full tilt, sliding and seizing two directions at once, she stood up unperturbed in the lights, lifted one hip an inch above the other, and smiled as though she had fallen heir to a power that pickup trucks couldn't impede.

The truck halted and he blinked at her through the fly-specked glass, his heart lunging like an engine ripped off its mounts. She was wearing tiny terry-cloth shorts that had shrunk up in her crotch and made her thighs look bigger than they could be and made him feel strangled, bound up, as if he wanted to be both in the truck and out of it someplace way away all at the same time. She had worried her hair up in little pencil curls that haloed her head and gave her face a round shape. She turned slightly in the light and smiled at him or toward wherever she thought he was

148

in the truck, and rounded her eyes and unbuttoned her little sleeveless blouse until it sagged open and a big quarter of her breast nosed between the parting.

He felt like there wasn't enough air to breathe, and the only movement he could school himself to make was to kick on the high beams and shoot her in a hot wash of crackling lights. Her features instantly turned inward and twisted in a mean way. Her hips contracting as if she was trying to withdraw from the light, she raised her bare arm to her eyes so that both her breasts broke out of the shirt, and with her body bent at the waist, wagged over the tops of her shorts.

"Goddamn!" she yelled, ducking lower under her arm. She writhed, trying with both arms to stop the light. He tried to move, but couldn't work his arms. "Robard!" she screamed.

He all at once stamped the light pull with his heel and sank back in the seat, hearing his name going off through the dark.

And the alley disappeared. There was a pause when he couldn't see anything, then Beuna's face popped up in the window, glaring through the dark air.

"Asshole!" she said, burying her chin on her collarbone so she could see which button matched which hole. "What piss-willy trick you call that?"

"I screwed it up," he said, shaking his head, but keeping an eye out on the mouth of the alley to make sure somebody wasn't heading around to see what the noise was.

"You sure as *hell* screwed up," she said, minding her buttons, but suddenly snapping her chin up at him angrily. "You just about blinded me with my attainments hung out for all the world."

"Git in," he said. "You're going to have the law out here."

"I give a shit if I do, too," she said, slapping at the buttons, flinging the door open and flouncing in.

She wore the same sweet flower smell he had waked up in the night at Bishop and smelled on everything, some little fragrance off the desert he couldn't keep from giving himself to, imagining her somewhere miles away from where he was at that moment. He touched the finish of her blouse where he could feel the

149

weight of her breast, and she slapped his hand and crossed her arms.

"Leave them alone!" she said.

"I done come three thousand miles for them," he said in amazement. "You want me to turn 'em loose?"

"That's right," she said. "I ain't going to have you pawing me."

"Shit," he said, trying to see her in the dark. "How come you stand out there wagging them around like a puppy show?"

"My business," she said, setting her chin so the soft flesh on the underside disappeared.

"Well, I'm making it mine," he said, grabbing her by the elbow, waggling his hand inside her blouse and popping off one button after another.

"Robard?" she said, her legs stiff as stones.

"What," he said, roaming over her breast.

"I want you to tear me up," she said, her little blue eyes flat as pebbles.

"I will," he said, his breath all gone.

"I don't want there to be nothin left when you get finished."

"There won't be," he said.

"Robard?"

"What?"

"I want to do it in the back of the truck in the dirt and the rocks and the filthiness."

He dislodged his hand and felt suddenly like a man in a tornado. "We will, hon," he said, "we will."

He drove up the rise to Main and turned out of town toward Memphis. He passed a drive-in theater, the fluorescent lights shining in the glass office, then two motels, the long fenced-in limits of the BB-gun factory, and a beer bar at the limits of the fields. Then the town disappeared, and the road took west and north into the delta.

Beuna arranged herself under his arm and stared at the highway, hugging her knees. "You know what I did when I was in high school?" she said, looking up at him as if she were apologizing in advance.

150

"I couldn't guess," he said.

She stared back at the highway. "Well," she said, pulling at her ear lobe. "We had this teacher in school named Mr. Fisher. M. B. Fisher. He was just a little puny thing, had headaches all the time that liked to killed him. I used to go over to his house on the pre-tense of working on the school newspaper, and he'd get out his little Polaroid and I'd get on the rug naked and spread out, and he'd take pictures." She looked at him to gauge how he was liking it. "And we'd get them pictures back in a minute or two and sit on the floor and laugh and laugh. I used to say to him, 'Mr. Fisher, I thought them cameras was only supposed to take pictures of land.' And he'd laugh and laugh. We had us a good time." She let her eyes wander on the highway.

"How come you and him never got past the picture-taking stage?"

"We did," she said. "But that wasn't as funny."

"I guess not," he said, thinking about a motel.

"I don't see nothing funny about fuckin," she said seriously. "Do you?"

"I guess not."

"Where're we going?" she said.

"Get us a room."

"I don't want it!" she said.

He looked at her to see if she had gotten mad without his knowing it. "Why not?"

"It's like every day," she said, turning her head away and sitting straight up in the seat. "Get in the bed, turn on the TV, fuck, then go back to watching and hope you ain't missed nothin."

"We don't have to turn on no TV," he said.

"I done told you, Robard," she said. "I want to roll in the dirt and the sand and the whatever you got back there and fuck you till you're blue. You understand that?" She thrust her hand in his trousers and got a fierce grip on him.

"All right," he said. "What about Memphis?"

"That's a exception. I want to go up there and have me and you get in one of them showers and get my little bag out. I'm dying to."

"What's that about?" he said.

"I'm not telling," she said. "If I did you might decide you didn't want to. But if I can get you up there in one of them ritzy twenty-dollar rooms with them shower baths and get ahold of you, you'll do any damn thing I tell you to." She squeezed to let him know she could do it. "It chills you, don't it?"

All his blood was headed down, leaving everything else afloat. He slid onto the shoulder and down onto a macadam road perpendicular to the highway. Beuna started grappling his belt as soon as the headlights illuminated the road.

"What'd you tell Jackie you was doing?" she said.

"I didn't tell her nothin."

"You know what I made W.W. do?"

"What's that?"

"Have a vastectopy, one of them operations," she said.

"Why'd you do that?" he said, thinking about W. being forced into something else he didn't want to do.

"Cause that boy ought not to *have* children," she said. "They wouldn't none of them be nothin but baseballs. I don't need no kids anyway."

He let the truck ride to a stop in the field. He could smell Folex in the air, mingled with the sweet smell of Beuna.

"Why not?" he said.

"Cause I don't," she said. "You think I ought to raise some kid up like me? I'll just have me a good time and let the next bunch take care of theirselves without adding to the misery." She stared out the window and went back, cradling her knees. "Tell me something," she said.

He inspected the mirror for some sign of headlights back up on the highway, a mile off. "All right."

"What kind of tube is your Fallopian tube?" She sharpened her eyes to warn against making a joke.

"It's inside you," he said, and rubbed at his stomach. "That's where your eggs get hatched."

"I thought it was one of them little tubes in your ear."

"Something the matter with yours?" he said.

152

"I was reading about it in a birth control magazine they give W. It said I could of got mine tied instead of him getting his cut, but I would of had to go in the hospital, and all he had to do was come in the doctor's office without eating nothing, go to bed early *one* night, and keep from using his thing for two weeks. He never did know what the thing was for anyway."

"That's too bad," he said, shoving down in the seat and getting his face in her breasts.

"You like my attainments, don't you?" she said, opening her blouse and pushing her chin up in the darkness so her breasts got firmed.

"You'da thought I never seen any before," he said, tasting the salty bottoms of them and pushing in between them.

"Let's get in the back," she said.

He elbowed the door open and held her hand while she climbed out. The road had turned into moist clay and grass that smelled like dust. On the highway headlights were leading north toward Memphis, the cars hissing away in the night. An odor of rotting plants rose on the breeze and held back the smell all over Beuna. He tried to see out in the moonlight to where the water was standing, but could see nothing but the sallow glow of Helena on the sky.

She climbed up in the truck and stood in the bed and took off her blouse and stretched her arms, her body bulky and pale. She faced across the fields with the light to her back, and he could see the failing whorl of hair along her backbone.

"Robard?" she said.

"What?"

"I told W. if I hadn't of married him I would've married you." She looked at him gravely. "Now I want you to get up on here," she said, releasing the snap on her shorts and wiggling them out of her crotch and looking at the little curlicues of hair on her belly as if she thought they might not be there this time.

He looked at her and thought maybe the best thing to do was to get back in the truck and out of there right then, and not waste another minute. Except that whatever it was she had, badness or disappointment or meanness, was the thing that was indispensable now, and he wanted to draw in to her and glide off in infinitude and just let loose of everything.

He sat on the side panel and unbuttoned his pants and let the letter fall out of his shoe without caring. She got him quick between her thumb and her first finger like a string on a bow and held his neck and pulled him off the side of the truck. She chivvied him, the corners of her mouth frozen, her breasts clutching his ribs, straining her jaw, pressing his feet with hers, gouging as if she were trying to wear away the bone. Sweat came all at once and he got his pulse in his throat and couldn't get a breath. He took a hold up on her thighs and felt his body winding up and spread his feet trying to get purchase somewhere. There was a soughing sound, and his back got quavery and the air across his neck chilled, and she began to rock him with her legs, and he could feel her throat vibrating against his lips, the sound out of his ear slipping into the air. He let her rock him, her feet standing his like stirrups, with each traction sliding on her knees as if a gravity were drawing him backward and a new contraction would trickle up his spine until she drew him again and supported him again in the fork of her legs. And in a while she let him fall off on the bed, and went limp, let her feet splay and raised her arms behind her and fingered the post of the jack below the window and made a little humming sound and got quiet, breathing almost not at all, her arms cool and dry.

He moved his hands, which had been driven in the gravel, and sat on his heels and looked at her staring in the shadow of the cab, her belly moist and her breasts sunk into her rib cage. He licked his knuckles and wiped the sweat where it had gotten trapped, and let the breeze dry his forehead. He felt like he'd been pushed through a cave of flashbulbs but couldn't see any of the pictures.

She drummed her fingers against the jack and stared at him down the length of her body. The wings of some large bird flapped up into the night as though it were using a great effort to pound its body into flight.

"What's that?" she said, looking around over her head.

"Somebody's soul done took flight."

"Shit," she snorted. "What the hell is it?"

"A hawk," he said.

"Doing what for?"

"Flying off, I don't know," he said, staring at the air.

"Uooom," she said, and crossed her arms and let her head lie back so she was staring up. "I got scratches all over me."

"You didn't need to have," he said softly, wishing he were somewhere else. "We coulda got a motel in Marianna, or someplace."

"I didn't want none," she said. "I wanted all them scars."

"What're you going to tell W.?"

"Tell him I been sleeping on a bed of nails. He wouldn't know the difference, he's so dick dumb." She took a little bite at her thumbnail.

"Whatever happened about his baseball?"

"I didn't like it," she said. "I didn't like all that batting around we was doing. I come back here and rented me a little trailer. And the end of August when he got done up there in Tacoma he come on back and went to work at the BB. They sent him a contract after Christmas, and I told him I wasn't going to no Tulare, California, or to no Tacoma, Washington, and he just tore it up, that's the last I heard about it. Some fella called him from Arizona and asked him why he wasn't out there, two months ago, and he said he wasn't coming. And he ain't heard no more from them. He's done had his baseball career. He'd been trying to get brought up six years, and flubbed his one chance he got."

"You think that makes him happy?"

"Makes *me* happy," she said. "That's who I watch out for. Let him worry about W.W."

A breeze picked up off the fields and dragged through the weeds and raised the flesh on his arm.

"What're you doing at E-laine?" she said.

"Running folks off an old man's island. It ain't much."

"How long you thinking about?"

"Turkey season. A week."

"You done had it with Jackie?"

"I don't know," he said, thinking about it. "I don't think so."

"You're just like me, Robard," she said, smiling as though a perfect picture of something had formed in her mind.

"What's that?" he said.

She laughed and pushed back so that her bare spine was against the wale of the truck and she could see him straight. "You want to screw who you want to screw. But there's a difference, too."

"What's that?"

"It don't bother me," she said.

"How come you think it bothers me?"

"Cause you got a dead-dog look, like you was afraid of something," she said, and smiled.

"I ain't bothered about nothing," he said, feeling aggravated.

"There's something," she said. "I could tell on the phone, and I'll tell you something else, too."

"What's that?"

"I don't give a shit." Her face got taut, as though something had frozen it in stone. Though as she was frowning, it began to leach away and her lips drifted forward a little and she sighed against the breeze. "Robard," she said in a small voice.

"What?"

"It wouldn't take nothin else for me to be happy."

"What else is there?" he said.

She slid on her hands and knees until her head was laid against his leg and her body curved around his feet. "Get me a divorce," she said, lifting her eyes and smiling until she looked pretty.

"Look here," he said.

"It don't matter." She reached and grabbed him and pulled. "When can we go to Memphis?"

"When I get done working."

"All right," she said, beginning to kiss the muscle up his thighs. "I love it, Robard, I love this so much."

Somewhere in the air the hawk made a dipping turn toward the defile of trees at the border of the field, where the air was thicker, and cried, and Beuna looked up, as though she were hung on the fine edge of disappearing.

156

6

He drove back after midnight, parked the truck, and took the boat across. A long grainy strand of mist hung above the water and the boat slid smoothly into the hidden space beneath it. At the island he beached the boat, turned it on its top, and stood out on the shingle looking back through the willows into the mist. He could hear one of Gaspareau's hounds strike a rabbit in the woods and get joined by all the others, until they were all silenced by a sharp *blat* sound and then quiet eased out on the long bend of water and captured everything and held it suspended.

He tried to fathom what had ruined her. It seemed like she could rule her life to the point of perfect control, which was the point of purest despair, and after that she had lost it all and suffered as if something indispensable had been grabbed away so quick she didn't know she had had it or ever could have controlled it. And that ruined her.

He didn't like the idea that whatever had turned her life into a hurricane had turned his the same way and made a part of his own existence sag out of control down into the sink of unmanageables. Because if nothing else was clear, he thought now, that much *was*. Either by diligence or intuition or just good luck he had brought his life to order. And it satisfied him that doing it hadn't called on anything more than his own good instincts.

She had had him drive the road to Marvell, toward Little Rock, and pointed to the side of the road at a little gravel spin-out that dipped into the trees, and had him stop. At the bottom of a path leading off in the dark he could see a pine lean-to opened to the highway. She said she wanted a quarter, and got out and went down and stood up under the shelter, and he heard the coin drop inside a tin can and she materialized out of the trees.

"What was it?" he said when she got back inside.

"The Gospel Nook," she said as if she thought he ought to know what it was.

"What the hell is that?"

"Where you go pray for whatever you want," she said. "Whenever you want. That's why they put it out in the open."

"What'd *you* pray for?" he said, amused by the whole business. He took another look and saw the shape looked like an outside toilet.

"My soul," she said.

"What's wrong with it?" He pulled the truck around back onto the road and aimed it toward town.

"Nothin," she said. "But if I got one, I want it took care of right."

"Why didn't you pray for Robard?" he said, feeling good and skinning his hand up the soft inside of her legs.

"I prayed for him," she said. "I give a quarter to St. Jude."

"Who's he?" he said.

"The one for the lost causes," she said. "They got a list of saints stuck to the wall. I don't know nothin about them. What difference does it make to you?"

"It don't make one in the world," he said.

"That there's why I done it," she said.

PART IV

Sam Newel

1

He heard Robard go down the steps, walk to the Gin Den, pick up the gun and the box of bullets, and leave. Somewhere back of the house Mr. Lamb started yelling for the colored man to start the other jeep, and in a few minutes he heard Robard head back up the road in a hurry.

He lay listening to drops pilch outside the shed. In a little while the other jeep went banging around the house, the old man yelling something at Landrieu which Landrieu didn't answer back. When the jeep got even with the shed the old man pulled up and sat a time in silence then finally fumed, "Goddamn it, get your fat ass out of the bed before I start Landrieu digging a grave for you." Mr. Lamb fired the jeep and barged off toward the lake. And he lay in bed staring up in the metallic light, thinking about Robard and about nothing. In a while he heard Robard drive slowly back through the yard and go off in the other direction, the jeep hitting every third stroke. Elinor came to the door and stopped and looked in and sniffed, then passed by. And he lay silently, satisfied to collaborate with everything by sounds, lying bare in the cool without gawking into Mr. Lamb's blistered old eye sockets, justifying himself a mile a minute.

Robard had caked his blankets back on his cot as carefully as if he thought he was something else besides cash help, and the idea that Robard miscalculated his circumstances pestered him and made him think that locked up behind Robard's stingy mouth was a little fugitive terror that wanted everything just so and couldn't keep still till he had it that way. And he couldn't stop himself from thinking Robard was going to let him down sometime on account of it, on account, he thought, of just being fastidious. Though he admired him for that very thing, for keeping a kind of life apart and private, something he himself had never been lucky enough to cultivate, so that everything he thought he ended up having to say out loud.

Landrieu suddenly appeared in the doorway and batted the tin with his spatula, squinting to see inside without actually opening the door. "You better get up," he shouted, twisting his face into a scowl. He had on his chintz chef's hat.

"Who says?" He stayed out on the sheet just to antagonize Landrieu.

"She in there waitin," Landrieu said, and disappeared. He could hear Landrieu pounding back up the steps.

He felt gratified at the prospect of sitting down to eat without the old man there to fence at him. He got off the bed onto the scaly concrete and stood looking out toward the trees where the morning light was waxy through the trees. He wondered about just how it would be when Robard let him down, and whether it would ever make any difference to either of them, in any way whatsoever.

He got dressed and hopped across the wet yard and up the steps into the house. Landrieu was in the kitchen overseeing four strips of bacon in an enormous skillet of grease, and refused to look up.

Mrs. Lamb was installed at the low end of the table wearing a man's red plaid shirt that disagreed with the red in her hair. She glanced up at him and took off a pair of half bifocals fastened to a piece of string around her neck. She was reading a *Farmer's Almanac*, her back to the kitchen.

"Predicts rain today," she said smugly, as though she had found an amusing flaw in the book's accuracy. She gave off a fresh lilac scent and had an old brown sachet sack stuffed down the front of her hunting shirt.

"Can't fault it too much," he said, smiling and trying to appear amiable.

Landrieu entered with a tulip glass of orange juice, set it in front of him and left.

"It also remarks," she said, redeploying her glasses over her nose, "that it rained this day one hundred years ago, and that the rain caused a sinister flooding to occur in Mississippi—where this island is located—and that two hundred croppers washed out of their houses." She pushed her glasses higher up onto her nose and peered at him over the rims, as if there were a gravity involved in what she'd said that anyone in a hundred miles should be able to grasp.

Mrs. Lamb's right eye, though the same yellowish hazel color as the left, was not, he could see, a working eye in the ordinary sense, and owned a slightly mesmerized cast.

"Do you suppose history runs to cycles?" she said, observing him with the same interest he'd seen Mr. Lamb bestow on the infected well.

"No."

"Neither do I," she said imperiously. "Gone is gone to me. Mark Lamb has a difficult time believing it."

"Anything you're attached to is hard to give up," he said.

Mrs. Lamb frowned at the almanac again as if it were the bearer of faulty information.

"Where's Mr. Lamb gone?" he said.

"He's taken his Willys and gone across," she said, her large rouged mouth turning down as though the remotest thought of Gaspareau had just awakened in her mind. "People were supposed to come this morning to hunt turkeys, but no one's arrived. Mark thinks they aren't coming. He thinks it's terribly hard to *find* the island," she said gravely, setting her almanac down. "He worries when people don't come when they're supposed to, so he's over there calling Oxford, afraid they've all gotten lost. He conceives of Arkansas as another country where people need his special guidance to find their way."

"I didn't think he wanted people to find it," he said.

"No," she said deliberately. Landrieu installed a plate of scrambled eggs and two biscuits in front of her and an oval platter containing the bacon in the center of the table. "Mark doesn't want the *wrong* people to find it. He *does* want Coach Wright to find it, and he does want Julius Henley, your friend Beebe's uncle, to find it. He has it in his mind because it doesn't appear on the Corps of Engineers' map, it has ceased to exist for the rest of the world."

T.V.A. entered with another plate of eggs and biscuits, put it down, and stood while Mrs. Lamb scrutinized the table for any signs of misrule, nodded, and returned him to the kitchen.

The house was quiet, and he could hear the tinkle of Mrs. Lamb's fork against her plate.

"Do you approve of it down here, Mr. Newel?" she said.

"Yes ma'am," he said.

She picked up a biscuit and examined its sticky interior as if she expected to dislodge something hidden. She looked up thoughtfully. "What are your plans, Mr. Newel?" she said.

"Which plans?"

"You're a man with several plans, then," she said, inclining her head gently toward him.

He smiled, trying to guess if she was going to be sympathetic. "All divergent," he said.

She sighed. "Everyone's plans are diverging now. There's no reason yours should be different. Beebe Henley's diverge to the slightest mention of them." She set her biscuit back on her plate. "You're in the law?"

"Next month, I hope."

She nodded, sliced a strip of fat off the rind of bacon, and put it in her mouth. "What are your plans for Beebe Henley?" she said in the same unmolesting tone.

"I don't know," he said, and wondered just what plans he did have. "There's some chance I don't have any." He looked up uncomfortably.

Mrs. Lamb began carefully aligning her clean silverware at the edge of the table, swallowed the last morsel of bacon fat, and settled her gaze on him. "What are you doing here on my island?" she said coldly.

164

He remembered the old lady's tough juridical frown freezing every available molecule between himself and Robard like they were two rarees about to sell Mr. Lamb an interest in the Helena Bridge. Mrs. Lamb's good hazel eye grew considerably smaller and darker, and she levered her chin on the tip of her thumb and stared at him until he began to feel a flapping need of something else to attach his *own* eyes to. His gaze rose upward, then fell fugitively onto the two maps, showing the island from the air, and not showing it at all.

"People come down here, customarily," she said casually, "to hunt or to fish or to rusticate. Some come down here just to visit with the Lambs." She paused. "Under which category ought I to entertain you?" She kept her chin balanced on the tip of her thumb, not moving a flicker.

"It's difficult to express," he said, trying to separate his gaze from the maps and order it back down into the old lady's immediate presence. "It would take a lot of patience," he said.

He could hear the little jeep slamming into the yard behind a terrible fury.

"I have great reservoirs," she said, looking annoyed. "When I was forty-five years old, Mark and I were living on this island, and I developed tuberculosis on account of the dampness, and had to be taken to Memphis in rather a hurry. And the way doctors treated tuberculosis at that time was to fill the afflicted lung with glass marbles and leave you stay a few months until the lung simply regenerated itself by forbearance."

"Yes ma'am," he said.

"It was awkward," she said coldly. "But I developed great patience. And I think I have adequate patience to listen to anything you could ever tell me in your entire life." She regarded him in an unfriendly way.

Someone's feet began pounding the outside stairs and kicking every door on the way. Mrs. Lamb's eyebrows rose to an aristocratic peak, and she raised her chin slightly and inclined her head in anticipation of an abrupt entry. He got his eyes solidly stationed on his plate and began eating eggs with as much application as he could rouse.

Mr. Lamb suddenly burst through the pantry door, red as a tomato, continued through the room straight into the sitting room, and disappeared around the corner without a word. He was wearing rubber boots that came to below his knees and a long canvas coat that reached the tops of the boots, giving him the appearance of a small bell with a long clapper. "Shit!" he yelled where no one could see him. "Son-of-a-bitch."

Mrs. Lamb's eyebrows re-arched themselves firmly, and she thrust her lower lip over her upper and set her hands on the table, waiting for Mr. Lamb to emerge from wherever he was fuming and cursing and banging. He felt at that moment like he would like nothing in the world as much as he would like to leave, and just hoped the old man hadn't seen him on his way through. Mrs. Lamb, however, ruled everything with silence and with the expectation that Mr. Lamb was about to return and wouldn't like it if anything had changed from when he'd seen it before. He set down his fork as unobtrusively as possible, drew in his legs, and let his hands come to rest in his lap.

"Sons of bitches, sons of bitches," Mr. Lamb gurgled, appearing starkly around the corner in his sock feet, without the coat, and wearing a pair of gallused canvas pants and the same red shirt with the mallards on the collar. He glared at both of them and took a strangle grip on the back slat of his chair, his face overcome by red.

"What has happened, Mark?" Mrs. Lamb said patiently.

"The bastards ain't coming," the old man seethed. "I called both of them. And both of them said they weren't coming. Said they was too goddamned tied up working or some stupid business like that. Julius said he had to be in court and Lonnie Wright said he had to fly to Pennsylvania to pay some nigger to play at Ole Miss. If that don't beat anything I ever heard of. Neither one of them said a *thing* beforehand. Sons of bitches didn't even intend to call me." His face blackened.

"Did they say they were coming?" Mrs. Lamb said.

"Hell, yes. They come every year, don't they?" Mr. Lamb glared at her as if he'd sensed betrayal. "They don't have to say they're comin, they just damn well are. Except the bastards ain't, goddamn it." The old man's eyes snapped at him unexpectedly as if he were unquestionably to blame for everything, but was simply too despicable to look at for more than an instant at a time.

"Well, Mark, sit down," Mrs. Lamb said softly.

"What the hell for?" the old man snarled. "Where has common decency gone to? I'd like to know that." He glowered around the room as if decency were there someplace but wouldn't let itself be seen. "What the hell business has work got coming into strife with turkey season? I'd like to know that, too." Two tiny wads of white spit sproated in the crannies of Mr. Lamb's mouth, threatening to rupture.

"Wipe your mouth, Mark," Mrs. Lamb said.

The old man sawed his shirt sleeve across his mouth and plunked himself at the head of the table and eyed the two of them accusingly. His hair was tufted into two unruly swipes that gave him a wild look, lowering at the end of the table like a thwarted demon.

The room got very quiet suddenly, and he thought maybe this was the time. But the old man was holding everybody captive and was not about to commute a sentence without having a terrible penalty first.

Mrs. Lamb sighed and looked sympathetically at her husband, while Mr. Lamb gradually sank into a profounder gloom. The old man bit off a sizable chunk of his thumbnail and crunched it between his teeth.

"Mark," Mrs. Lamb said, "you ought not gnaw your nails. All those little nails collect in your appendix and then you have to have it removed. When they took mine out it was chock full of little crescent slivers, and I haven't bitten mine since."

"I don't know why," he growled. "You ain't got no appendix to worry about, you might as well gnaw what you please."

She looked at Mr. Lamb casually and the old man seemed to take a certain pleasure in mocking her, though it quickly vanished and he sank back into his evil. Landrieu, who was sitting in the kitchen slicing boiled eggs, made a firm entry into the wall of an egg and plopped the white and the yolk into two crockery bowls.

"I just don't know," the old man said, jamming his little hands together and starting one thumb into orbit around the other, becoming momentarily engrossed as though it was no small task to keep them both going at once. "First my well goes queer, which it had never been known to do in fifty years. Then the turkey season fouls up, then the goddamn lease is coming up." The old man squinted at him as if he were considering including him as a fourth calamity. "There's something's wrong, ain't it, Newel?"

"I don't know," he said, hoping he wouldn't have to say it again.

"Well, I know," Mr. Lamb fumed. "Cept I don't know what the hell it is wrong. Things have just gone sour as hell."

The old man sank lower into his chair until his face was six inches above the top of the table, and the entire house was still, except the eaves dripping and Landrieu's chair squeezing as he crept closer to his bowls. The air was warm and weighted and pressed on everything with a powerful force.

Mrs. Lamb got up, switched off the overhead, and strolled into the sitting room, leaving them in a gray light. She moved her chair beside the radio and began fanning herself with a cardboard church fan decorated with a sepia picture of Niagara Falls. He felt a hot drop of sweat on his temple, while the old man stared morosely into space.

"I didn't know you leased it," he said, unable to stay quiet.

"I *ought* not," Mr. Lamb lamented. Mrs. Lamb fanned herself, smoothing the flecks of hair away from her forehead. "I ought to own the goddamned place," he said. "I've had it fifty years this August. I give it to Mrs. Lamb"—he sprung his thumb back at her—"for her birthday and a wedding present both. I didn't think I'd live fifty years, nor her either one."

"Who owns it?"

The old man pinched his mouth with his fingers and let his eyes almost close. "Chicago Pulp and Paper owns the deed," he said quickly.

"But won't they renew?"

"I suppose they will," the old man said sternly.

"So they're not going to make you leave."

"I suppose not." Mr. Lamb sat staring abstractedly at the open kitchen door. Landrieu seemed to feel himself being watched and backed his chair out of sight.

"So it's not so bad," he said.

The old man batted his eyes hotly. "I'm the one says what's bad and what ain't. I don't like them greasy dagos coming down here in their sorry-ass airplane, making me haul them around like I was a bus driver. It's demeaning." His eyes flamed again. "They come flying down here every five years, pissin around, messing in my business, marking my trees like I hadn't been here fifty years. Not one of them was there when I took the land out, they're all new. And I've got just about a good mind to plow up that airstrip they built and let them land their plane in the woods and be rid of them." The old man ground his hands together as if they were two warty slabs of bark.

"It seems more important, though, that you keep it," he said, trying to seem reasonable. "You could get a lawyer and have him show it to them, and you and Mrs. Lamb wouldn't have to even be here."

"A lawyer," he said indignantly. "I said I done made my will. You're trying to drum you up a little advance, are you, Newel?"

"I'm not a lawyer," he said.

"The hell you're not," the old man said, and gaveled the table with his fist, his voice elevating with each succeeding word, so that the spider veins in his face thickened and turned blue. "But I'll tell you this much. I'll be there when them dagos step out of that airplane, and I won't need a paid-to-talk mouth to cloud up my issues, either."

"That's fine," he said, standing and starting toward the kitchen.

Mr. Lamb leered at him. "You don't understand that, do you, Newel?" he said. "Why I don't like them wops coming in here in their airplane piss-nosing around on my land, even if it's them that owns it?"

"I think I do," he said, stopping in the pantry door.

"No, you don't!" the old man shouted. "It's an in-dignity to suffer their presence on this island, like this was some part of De-troit or one of them other hellish places. It's an in-dignity to stand it. That's something they don't teach you anymore. You don't know nothing about dignity. I'm just afraid you don't."

"I was just trying to talk about priorities," he said quietly. "But maybe you're right."

"Priorities be goddamned," Mr. Lamb shouted, slamming both his fists on the oilcloth and glaring out of an enraged fury. "Piss on priorities and all that other horse shit. We're talking about dignity and about Mrs. Lamb's wedding present, by holy God."

"I misunderstood," he said, and disappeared out the door.

"I guess you did," the old man shouted. "I guess you did, too."

2

When he was twelve he had gone with his father and his mother to Biloxi, and they had stayed on the beach at a large white hotel called the Buena Vista that had deep shady verandas and rows of white cottages in the back under the banana trees. His father went away in the day and came back in the evening, until Saturday when they went to visit a man his father had known in New Orleans, named Peewee McMorris, who had worked on oil derricks until another man had dropped an orange on his head accidentally from the top of the derrick, and after that he never worked again and was permanently stiff in his left leg and stayed in bed in his shabby pink cottage in the palmettos behind Keesler Air Force Base near the VA. His wife's name was Josephine, and when they arrived she made them all take tall drinks and took them out to visit Peewee, who was sitting on a nylon chaise in the back yard, putting down sprigs of St. Augustine grass from his chair, out of a peach basket he had beside him. Peewee was a small knuckly man with a long Italian jaw and was very glad to have a drink in the hot afternoon.

When he had taken his first long sip of whiskey, he smiled at him and asked him if he wanted to see a trick. When he said yes, he would, Peewee jimmied himself off the chaise longue and put his hand on the boy's shoulder and walked stiff-legged to the corner of the house to where Josephine had planted azaleas and hydrangeas to hide the water meter. Inside the largest azalea bush, which was blooming with violent pink petals, Peewee found a large wasp nest and pointed for him to see. He was afraid of wasps and did not like it, if that was to be the trick, and stood back. Peewee laughed, and when the last wasp had landed on the broad crusty hive and none were left flying around that he could see, he carefully put his hand into the nest and let the wasps light on him and walk around on his knuckly skin and try their stingers on his flesh, until it seemed they would reach the bone. Peewee, without shaking, began to laugh and laugh, and said that since the man had dropped the orange on his head he had not been able to feel pain in many parts of his body, and that his hand was one of the parts, and that a wasp could sting him until he was blue in the face and that it would not hurt. He drew back his hand with one wasp still clinging to his middle finger, his stinger sunk in Peewee's flesh. And Peewee laughed and flicked the wasp away like he would a match and left the stinger in place inside his hand. When he had looked at Peewee's hand for a long time, dangling beside his highball glass on the thick mat of St. Augustine, he told his mother he would like to go for a swim in the gulf before he went to bed. And when he had stood in the brown brackish gulf water for a long time and looked out along the hotel's whitewashed pier at the old men dipping crab nets down toward the shallow water, he could see the blue man of wars floating in on the tide, riding the lazy surf toward the beach, and he wondered if they would sting him if he mingled his legs among their straggling tentacles.

3

He spent the day in bed in a surly temper contemplating Beebe's father, who had been the lawyer for the city of Jackson, and who had begun drinking whiskey in genuine earnest the moment destiny locked him onto a course straight for the state supreme court, and afterward expended a great deal of energy appearing drunk in courtrooms, submitting clownish briefs, making ill-considered statements, and ultimately bringing general odium on himself at the expense of judges and juries all over the state of Mississippi.

He could perfectly think of sitting in the sun porch of Beebe's old yellow colonial with a remuda of Impalas and Town Wagons in the drive, while Hollis paced back and forth contrasting the law of Mississippi with the Napoleonic Code of Louisiana and trying to epitomize precisely what it was like to lawyer in the state of Mississippi.

Hollis was a short volatile man with jet hair and small arms, who at certain extravagant moments favored Senator Theodore G. Bilbo. In the course of talking, Hollis would stride out of the sun porch into the living room, speaking all the time, make a circuit through the room, pick up some petty table article and conduct it back to the sun porch cradled in his hand, eventually returning it during the next circuit, when he would appear with something else, a lighter, or a shell figurine, a framed photograph of someone, anything he could conveniently fondle and still talk. He had recognized this as Hollis's ultimate courtroom stratagem, an intrigue for diverting the jurors' attention from what he was saying to whatever singular object he was hoisting around, lulling them into only an addled interest in what he was saying by manufacturing a more thralling interest in what he was holding, and thereby implanting the conviction that he must be saying something worth listening to or they wouldn't be paying such close attention.

At Ole Miss Hollis had come under the sufferance of an agitating nervous tic. At the conclusion of every lengthy sentence, which ended, by design, in a burst of hard short consonantal sounds culminating in an upward trill of voice as if a question were being asked when it was not, Hollis would thrust the left corner of his mouth down and wildly to the side, jarring his body as though he'd been stamped by a horse, and in a way that suggested he might be trying to scratch his shoulder with his chin. Immediately, he would spin heel and toe and stride off in the direction the tic had driven him, so that if the listener was not watching closely, or was watching something else, the speed of the agitation and the evasiveness of the turn might cloak the tic completely, and the listener, already perhaps in thrall to whatever Hollis was holding, would see nothing, yet be convinced something heartbreaking had been said, even though he himself had not heard it.

Hollis had begun the afternoon toting around a small porcelain bird that resembled a stylized replica of a frigate bird, transporting it periodically to the living room, yet returning each time with the same bird webbed in his fingers, as if his point swelled to greater and greater pertinence each time he reunited it with the bird.

His comparison had fulcrumed on the point that in Louisiana deeds and all legal instruments were not collected in a central archive, but were maintained among the papers of the parish magistrates, who exacted unregulated fees to authorize copies and institute searches, and by that fief, oversaw a large pork barrel, the spoils of which were pared in favor of themselves and the governor. The creative case in point had been that of Governor Long, who granted appointments in exchange for whatever obstructions and embarrassments the appointees could promote against the governor's enemies, such as leaking accusations that well-known legislators were partners in Bossier City whorehouses, then being out of the parish when attorneys arrived to certify the deeds.

"In Mississippi," Hollis declared in a rounding voice, taking a sober look at the frigate bird as if it deserved an immense amount of specific attention, "it is a far simpler system, often too simple for my lights. Litigation is sometimes too available. Yet our deeds and public records are housed in the capitol"—and he pointed the bird in the general direction of the capitol building, several miles back into town—"and legal action is not subject to the canton system, which sponsors so much subornment across the river." He frowned and looked perplexed in the direction of Louisiana and ended in an upward trill in his voice followed by the trick in his mouth that sent him striding into the living room, but quickly returned holding the bird with an abstracted look as if his exemplum had somehow failed. "It isn't my intention," he said balefully, "to aver that law practice in Mississippi is interesting or even mildly diverting, which is why I do my practicing before the NLRB and the ICC, which is where the money is, though not the celebrity." He took a glance into the living room, which was backed up with overstuffed wing chairs, stinking floral antimacassars and mismatched end tables, the sole remainders of his wife's dowry. "The state court of Mississippi is an informal affair requiring an attorney loving humanity somewhat more than the law, affections I lack in favor of loving money." And he strode promptly out, made a turn in the living room, took a peek into the dining area as if he was contemplating a future trip there, and returned again with the bird.

He himself had since sunk deep into the couch mesmerized by the bird, nodding only when Hollis's voice crescendoed in the manner of a question that didn't desire an answer.

"I believe I can make the point this way," Hollis said, lifting the bird as if he were about to let it speak for itself. "When I was the prosecutor I was called once to try three Negroes charged with stealing a house off another man's land. We were never able to discover how they actually managed to *remove* the house, but they did it nevertheless, in the space of a few hours. So a little while before their case was to be brought up, they were all three led into the court, just as another case was being concluded. There, the jury had been dismissed, and the attorneys were talking, and the space at the defense table was still cluttered with papers and documents, and the bailiff simply led them to the jury box, sat them down, handcuffed them to the balustrade, and left the room entirely. The men had already entered a plea of not guilty to the charge of conversion," he said, "and were there to be placed in actual trial without a jury. So time passed and the other attorneys left, and my assistant and I and the attorney for the Negroes entered, with various of the witnesses, and finally the judge and clerk. The bailiff never did come back. And all of us sat down and I noticed that the three Negroes were all sitting together in the jury box by themselves, looking around as if they knew what they were doing. And the old judge took his seat and looked at the defense and said, 'Is the defense ready?' And they announced that they were. 'And is the prosecution ready?' And I said we were ready. And the judge's eyes strayed over to the jury box, where the three Negroes were sitting there like they owned all the chairs. 'And who are you?' the judge said, somewhat stoutly, since Negroes were not allowed on juries then. And the one tall shovel-jawed nigger jumped up, snatched off his cap, grabbed the balustrade, and said, 'Why, we's the thieves.' "

Hollis stopped and stared at him significantly, as if taking account of his deep fascination with the bird. "So there you are," Hollis said very disgustedly. "A mistrial was immediately motioned, granted, and all three of them got off, though I later put one in Parchman for stabbing the poor bastard who confessed." His mouth snapped toward his shoulder and he went lurching off to the living room and never returned.

And it had stayed in his mind that law in Mississippi would probably be a blend of imbecility and gentle fastidiousness that didn't allow you any recourse but to get drunk and remain that way.

One day three years later, Hollis drove his Cadillac to New Orleans to try a case before a Labor Relations Board referee, and at the noon recess, drove out onto the Huey P. Long Bridge, got out, and jumped in the river. The people who stopped to get a glimpse of whoever it was floundering around in the dishy water said that by a stroke of famous bad luck Hollis had missed the river and landed like a sack of nails on top of the concrete piling. Though, they said, with effort he had managed to crawl off into the water before anyone could skinny the ladder and hold him back, and had gone out of sight immediately.

Beebe said everyone could figure what got him off the bridge. Some people had actually been wondering what had taken him so long. But no one, she said, could understand what got him off the concrete.

And he had sat in his apartment on 118th Street above Columbia and decided that nothing less than two thousand miles would be safe enough to keep him off the bridge. Or worse, that he might just make all the necessary adjustments to imbecility and boredom and unreasonable gentility that everybody there seemed to make, but that nobody seemed to care much about.

4

Early in the evening Robard arrived, changed to his green rodeo shirt, and left, mumbling about business. He sat on the side of the bed and asked after the nature of the business, and Robard smiled and disappeared out the door.

He lay up and thought about his plans for Beebe since he'd told Mrs. Lamb he didn't have any, and tried to come to what was true. He thought about the pleasure of taking the IC up in the afternoon, getting off at Randolph, and riding a bus to Goethe, then walking the two blocks. At midnight she'd take off to Tokyo or Addis Ababa, and he wouldn't think about her anymore and would take the train home. It made him feel fulfilled.

She had once had a boy named Ray Blier she was in love with, and who had gone to Annapolis. She had spent almost every college spring in expectation of spending nights with Ray Blier whenever there was an opportunity, flying off to New York, amusing herself in the way some women amused themselves sufficient to carry them to their graves. And it seemed strange to him that she would let it go. She said Ray Blier was holding down a pencil in the War College and champing to get back to Ole Miss Law

School, where he'd feel safe. And she said it was venomous and she didn't want it. There were times when she came and didn't call. And there were times when he heard the phone and decided it was her and didn't answer. And none of it was ever charged. Everything was based on a nonchalance that didn't include *plans* in any customary sense. Though there was something to it all that made him feel dreary, and that made him believe it would lead to something bitter, and that it would all sweep over him one day without his knowing it was happening.

5

"Have you wondered about my eye?" Mrs. Lamb said, setting her cup on the oilcloth, regarding him through a denser aroma of lilacs than usual. She had explained that Mr. Lamb was feverish and had gotten in bed, put his good ear to the pillow, and gone straight to sleep. He felt a vague contrition for having been the catalyst that sent the old man to bed in a snit, and the thought occurred to him that the best thing to do would be to catch the bus after dinner and make the morning train to Chicago.

"I'm sorry," he said, denying any notice of the eyeball.

"My left eye is a prosthetic one," she said, concentrating on lining her silverware again along the edge of the table and making no effort to demonstrate the eye in any way. "In 1919, before Mark and I were married," she said, smiling to herself, "I had a job in a broom factory in Clarksdale, Mississippi. Mark was trying to make a start farming and I was merely marking time until we could get married. It was long before the child labor laws, at least in Mississippi, and I felt it would be nice if I took a job to support myself. My father was considerably older than he should have been to have had a daughter fifteen in 1919. And he worked only now and again, as a cotton estimator, and did well considering the little time he spent at it. So I went to Clarksdale patently against his wishes and took a job in the Choctaw Broom Works, binding broom ends with red twine. And one day as I was walking out to go sit in the shade, a broom handle went flying out of a circular saw and hit me right in the eye, and I subsequently lost it."

She smiled and he tried to seize on something sympathetic to say, but had to work to keep himself from looking point-blank at the eye.

"I was vastly afraid Mark would see me with my little glass eye and be reviled," she mused, toying with her cup handle, "shrink from marrying me. And so I went for some time without seeing him."

"But he didn't care, though, did he?" he said, denying himself another look at the eye.

"No," she said. "It didn't bother him. Mark was a very enthusiastic farmer then. He had several hundred acres to farm when he was twenty-two years old. So it wasn't actually until we were married four years that he looked at me one afternoon, sitting in the breezeway of our house in Marks, snapping beans, and said, 'Fidelia, have you got something in your eye?' I said, 'No, Mark, I have not.' My terror had considerably subsided, as you might imagine. And he said, 'I think so.' And it was then I told him about the broom."

"What did he say?"

"He said . . . let's see if I can remember. He said, 'Well, that's one less eye to keep on me.' He fancied himself a ladies' man then, but I always thought he was too short."

"He might've made it up in spirit," he said.

"I expect he might have," she said, and brushed at her eyebrows.

The outside light was smeared into the trees, the last of the daylight. Landrieu came in and cleared the table, and went back to the kitchen and began pouring water from a metal bucket into a dishpan.

"The first spring we came," she said, staring dreamily at the lintel over the gallery door as though the season were represented by a frieze, "the river flooded, and Mark and I had to stand on the porch killing water moccasins with hoes as they came up out of the water. We were afraid the whole house would break loose and drown us both. I was pregnant with Lydia, and Mark was afraid something awful was going to happen to her on account of my having to kill all the snakes. But I said I wasn't afraid of snakes, and there was nothing to injure the baby, as long as I wasn't bitten, and that seemed to satisfy Mark, who simply wanted somebody to tell him he was wrong. And as it turned out, Lydia was never afraid of snakes, although she is deathly afraid of the river for some silly reason."

"I think I understand," he said grimly.

She looked at him curiously and composed her hands on the edge of the oilcloth. "We're very much tied to the river stages here," she said scrupulously. "Much more than to the clock and the calendar. Though the river doesn't change so often since they've finished the T.V.A. and stopped the Tennessee adding its part."

Landrieu popped his head around the corner, looked strangely, and disappeared.

"Mark put the house on concrete so we wouldn't have to worry with being washed away, but the ground is porous and very moist. I wouldn't be surprised if the pilings were beginning to deteriorate, nineteen and a quarter feet in the ground, fat end down."

He lifted his eyes to the old woman's shiny face. Her eyes seemed larger and darker, reading his face vigorously.

He wanted to render a private gesture of recognition and absolute submission, but the old lady unexpectedly got on her feet.

"It's hedonistic of us to suppose we should perplex the world by lasting on it forever—don't you think that's a true fact?" She tended her smile forthrightly.

"Yes ma'am," he whispered.

"Good," she said, and walked straight out the gallery door, pausing a moment at the window to inspect her radio, then disappearing into the dark where Mr. Lamb was sleeping.

6

He wandered out through the kitchen and down the steps, past Landrieu straddling a nail keg savoring a cigarette. The sky still looked as if it might turn and rain. The moon was visible very high, but there were scabs of ash cloud sliding by it, growing denser as they went, as though they had detached from some large, lightless vault out over Arkansas.

Elinor uncoiled under the steps, slapping her tail on the risers, and trotted off into the dark, where he could hear her collar tink in the stillness.

He touched the closest column that held up the house, and made a flat echoless slap on the girth. He shoved up into the dingy shadows where the air got colder and limey all at once. He could see strung to the joists several cane poles, a few broken and rusting garden implements, and something that filled half the length of one entire joist board, and looked in the oily darkness like small three-finger garden trowels, but on better looking turned out to be small cartilaginous birds' feet, turkey feet, he guessed, maybe a hundred nailed to the wood with roof studs, hardly noticeable above the darkness. He reached through the cobwebs and fingered one set of toes so that it cracked against the rafter and threatened to break loose in his hand. It seemed perfectly plausible for these feet to be *here*, bolted to the house, waiting for their bodies to come pluck them off and go hurrying back down in the woods. He couldn't quite sense the necromancy, but he thought highly of the idea and felt certified somehow just by standing in the province.

He heard Landrieu step down the steps unaware of him and walk out across the wet yard toward his house, the glow of his cigarette marking him down into the dark. The lime smell seemed to be growing intenser toward the middle of the house, and he thought quickly about breaking down one foot for himself and having off with it, but the idea seemed like some vague mistake, and he bent over instead and backed out of the cold shadows, trying to stay clear of the pipe courses and keep from getting gashed. He stood up clear in the moonlight, and watched the door go closed to Landrieu's house and the light paint over the shade. A queasy light was still burning in the Gin Den, seeped between the joints, making the shed its own skeleton in the dark. Elinor moseyed back across the dooryard and looked at him sullenly and disappeared back under the steps. He thought wistfully that if he could just arrange a good enough subject he could go present himself to Landrieu and make the evening out to talk. Except he couldn't arrange anything Landrieu was likely to want to talk over as much as he wanted just to be left alone, and he gave up the thought.

A number of paths similar to the one they'd driven in on all converged on the house, and in a complicated way, through several shunting tracks, reconnected and provided a transport to anyplace on the island. He had traced during breakfast an itinerary to the river using the aerial map, tracking the roads as they coiled back toward the house, and intersected other lanes that led nearer and nearer the outside of the island. He traced what seemed like the simplest path, and with it in mind struck out past Landrieu's house through the oak, across a queer patch of burnt ground he hadn't seen before, and made to the edge of the woods, where he could smell the sweet milfoil and the privet deep down in the brake.

He could see a gray dog trail down into the dark, leading east away from the house clearing. He felt confident he was walking faithful to the river.

When he had walked fifty yards, the bush path ended in one of the two-track jeep roads, and he took that toward what seemed south. He looked back up toward the clearing where the three buildings had blossomed in lights, and there was nothing now but the gray path eclipsed into the privets and cotton bush.

Water stood in both axle paths, and he walked on the hump, where it was soft but less saturated. He could see in the trees shadows where the land appeared to back low into larger oaks and separate clusters of shrubbery and briers, though nothing past that. He supposed there were bays trapped parallel to the river, and past that a raised sand barren, and then the river. The road, according to the estimate, canted closer to the river as it swung round the first thick lobe of the island, and passed finally within twenty yards of the main river channel, necessitating no pathway through the bottom. He thought he was almost where Mr. Lamb had stood his salt lick.

The crickets had begun and the clouds that had been threatening had dissipated. The moon hung out at the end of the road so that the light illuminated the path and into the first trees on both sides.

He thought he felt fitter than he had since August, when he and Beebe had taken the ferry across from Waukegan and spent Labor Day on the dunes. He remembered feeling dazzling. Beebe had gone to Bangkok, and he had taken her apartment and gone off to school twice a week and hung around the *Law Review* basement reading headlines in the *Washington Post.* In the evenings he ate dinner out and strolled up the cement beach to North Avenue and finished the day watching television.

In a month classes began and he moved back on Kenwood with strangers trafficking through the park all night, and things began to get suspicious. At Halloween his knee ligatures had begun to crepitate, and little launching pains began popping around his ear and burying themselves in his head. All that had seemed nicely parsed out began muddling into obsessions about starting the future with the past completely settled.

By Christmas he had an inventory of afflictions, and spent a lot of time worrying about them, forgetting his essay for the *Review,* which was late. He made conciliatory phone calls to the editor, who accused him of sitting in the lounge drinking coffee and skimming prestige while the staff burrowed in the stacks running down case notes they hoped would land them a job clerking on somebody's court. He eventually developed a dislike for the editor, a Jew from Ohio named Ira Lubitsch, and made loud inflaming remarks over the phone, agreeing to finish the article by May. In February the afflictions divided and became virulent. He detected a yellowing in the sclera of both eyes, though there were no conforming symptoms. His ligaments were tight. In March he stopped going to school and spent every day glowering out the window at the Negro women walking children in the park and the winos pissing in the bushes. At the end of the month he had an uproar with Mrs. Antonopoulos, who accosted him on the stairwell with two nephews lingering around the newel post like shoplifters. She said she had not received the rent for February and that if he did not remit she would not be responsible for the consequences. She cast a long and darkly prophetic look at her nephews. The next day he found a cloth bag of carpenter's tools in the hall and screw holes in the door and tiny mounds of sawdust on the carpet. The carpenters had gone down to the deli, where he had seen them drinking milk and eating cheese blintzes. He entered the room, locked the door, and when the carpenters arrived, flung it open and threatened to call the police and charge them with detainment. The carpenters were bewildered, packed their drills, and left. He had closed the door then and not come out for a month, pestered by a return of the little pinching pains behind his ear, a stiffening in his knees, and an inability to yawn properly, as though a governor had been gauged to his yawning mechanism, leaving him with a growing anxiety like wanting to sneeze but lacking the pent-up strength to bring it off.

The median path bent perpendicularly to the left, and a new dog trail drove straight into the cluster of weeds beyond which was a break of scrubs that seemed completely to absorb the track. He heard the crickets behind him in the direction of the house, and in the opposite direction a sound like a low deep-mouthed hissing, more like the absence of sounds than the emanation, as though the hissing were a constriction in his mind to account for the silence. It was like the sound of wind, though not the wind, but the sound a great empty place makes in the distance. He concluded it was the river, beyond the next tier of trees and over the hummock where the sand would give out onto a clay shingle that sloped straight to the water, and he would be there.

He stepped into the path toward the hissing, the ground becoming quavery as if it were suspended over jelly. His feet made a sucking percussion back into the swamp. With one hand to guard his eyes, he poked into the grove, which seemed to be beech saplings and plum bush, until in front of him he could no longer see how the trail parted the brush, and he could smell the sweet plums, and his next step was a long one down into the water.

The breath caught in his throat and no sound got out. He realized he was sinking and sprawled forward in the direction of his momentum toward the closest tree trunk, so that he floundered farther into the water to keep from going under. He hugged the tree while the cold water waffled around his waist and trickled by his stomach, tugging at him stiffly. He let one gasp free, trapped another one and held it, and smelled the sweet fertile river aroma on his tongue. His weight seemed not to affect the tree, and he had the thought that he was not going to drown at that instant. The fact that he had been floating on the same water thirty-six hours ago fetched up and seemed mildly irrelevant since the situation now was all out of control and there was no one there to see if he stayed down for good.

He gripped more tightly to the beech bark, and with his foot felt along the bottom roots. He experimented letting go of the tree by degrees and extending one foot in the direction of what seemed like the ground, but the water persuaded his foot easily downstream, and he had a bad sense about the depth of the water a foot below where he was holding on.

His teeth began to chatter and he tried to see upstream. There seemed to be other trees between himself and the step-off, and he felt maybe that by reaching trunk-to-trunk and root-to-root in a cumbersome, Tarzan-like way, he could tack back up the river and get nearer to land.

He realigned his hands on the bark and faced precariously against the river. The stinking water sagged against him, and he began to feel giddy and not in complete control of what he might do.

From the first beech trunk he made a roundabout extension to the next closest upstream grip, which was an oak husk that he had to slip past, standing on roots, toward where trees were more thickly disposed, and where he could bend out more in the direction of the bank. A little at a time, he waded in the tufts of foam over the roots and disintegrating bottom to the semiknee of land he had stepped off several yards down the stream.

He bellied out of the water, and somewhere up the bank he heard the water whacked loudly, and the commotion of something frothing in the water, then the sound of limbs popping and sediment rolling onto the surface, and the lesser noise of some beast wheezing and snorting and trotting into the break. He wondered, shivering with his legs caved under him and his shoes full of silt and draining, whether some animal had swum the river, and if so, which didn't seem likely, what could have driven it. He filled his cheeks and let it slowly out and thought about Beebe's theory that animals remained faithful to their own wretched unpromising territory—past when the food had depleted and they were impoverished and falling over to predators. "It's the strongest urge they have," she said, nibbling a piece of her thumb in the manner he'd seen her grandfather munch his own after breakfast. "And the stupidest," she said.

7

In New Orleans his mother took the train to Jackson, and he went with his father up Canal Street in the sun to the Monteleone, where they had oysters and root beer and took a long nap in the shady room. At six o'clock his father was asleep, and he dressed in the shadows and put on his shoes and took a walk down the long silent hallway that smelled like hot bread and clean laundry. At the end of the hall underneath the exit triangle he stood and looked down into the deep well of Royal Street, where the people looked small and silent, until the breeze through the long green corridor blew ajar the door beside him and he could see two women on the bed side by side smiling into the narrow angle of the doorway. They were lying on the fresh white sheets, naked, with a pint of whiskey half finished between them, and their hair wet and dripping as if they had just come out of the tub and chosen the bed as a place to dry off. He stood looking at the women for a long time, while they looked at him and made smiling buzzing remarks that he could not hear. In a little while a fat man came with white hair and a shiny blue suit, and looked in the open room and saw the women and told them to go back where they belonged because he was going to call someone. He went back to his room, where his father was still asleep. And after a while he got in the bed and slept until it was dark. When his father woke up he said he had seen two women naked in their bed drinking whiskey. His father said he would ask, and in the lobby he approached the fat man and asked about the women, and the fat man said they were women whose husbands owned plantations east of Baton Rouge, and who had sons in the state legislature and daughters who were state debutantes, and who had reputations to consider where they lived. He said that the women had come to the city to buy clothes for a trip to Los Angeles, and after spending one day in Godchaux's had spent the next two getting drunk and raising cain, and that he had been sorry but had called the police just the same and had them taken away to the station on Broad Street.

He went with his father for a walk down to the ferryboat across to Algiers, and asked him why the women would do such a thing as that. And his father said that now and then things get away from you and you couldn't control events anymore, and that though the ladies had probably seemed like trash to him, they probably were not, or else they wouldn't have raised sons to the state legislature.

PART V

Robard Hewes

———————

1

He parked back in the willows, folded the pistol in his handkerchief, put it under the seat, and took the Traveler over to the camp and drove in to Goodenough's.

The two tow-headed farm boys were at the junction, resting in the shade of the Servel scathing the dirt with their heels. They gazed at him and didn't seem to remember. He caught the one boy in the corner of his eye as he turned in the store, the tall boy with rangy arms and narrow turquoise eyes. He stopped and tried to act like a man who'd forgotten something while he watched the boy scrape his heel across the dirt as though he were covering something up. He watched the boy's wide good-natured face move in the shade of the icebox, while his brother spoke something that made him laugh, and he wondered if they were some kin of Gaspareau's.

"Where you at?" Beuna said, as though she'd been out searching and given up in exasperation.

"At E-laine. I got to go back," he said secretly.

"I got all swelled up," she said. Her voice seemed to be coming out a long strip of narrow pipe. "I thought you'd come up here today."

"I got to work!" he said. "If the old man caught me over here he'd bust a seam."

The store was lighted by one sallow tube bracketed to the ceiling, and the light died before it could find the floor and left the store in long rectangular shadows. Mrs. Goodenough was sweeping out back, singing in a tiny high-pitched voice.

"You better not come in here tonight," Beuna said threateningly.

"Why is that?"

"W.W.'s gonna *be* here," she said. "He works late and can't go out cattin like he likes to, so he thinks he's coming on in and cat with me. Cept I got news for him."

He wondered if W. might not come home frisky, snatch her up behind, and look right at a whole Rand McNally of scratches and bites. The idea plunged him in a black mood.

"Robard?"

"What?"

"We going to Memphis, ain't we?"

"I guess," he said, staring at the shelf of glazed doughnuts, trying to put W. out of everything.

"What do you mean, you guess?"

"I mean I guess we are going," he said.

"You ain't got some whore with you, have you?"

"No," he said, wishing it were over with.

"What's wrong with you, then?"

"Nothing's wrong with me that keeping him from seeing your ass won't help."

"Aw, shit."

"I'm serious."

"I got all the bruises to prove it, too." She dropped the receiver and made the bell chime. "Look here," she said, starting a long way off, then almost shouting at him. "Ain't no way he's waking up to nothin less I tell him to, and I ain't tellin him nothin cause I been waiting on this about as long as I can."

"I want this to go right," he said, "without nobody getting in dutch."

"Like who?"

"Like me," he said.

There was silence and he could hear her drumming her finger on the mouthpiece. "Something ain't right, I can tell it," she said.

"Isn't nothing the matter," he said.

"Something don't smell right to you, does it?" He could hear the sneer in her voice. Somehow she was managing to drum her fingers on the phone and continue to talk.

"Look now," he said. "The only thing that wouldn't be right is for him to find out. I don't want him plundering into nothing and screwing the works. He stays out, I'm happy as a bird."

There was another silence, during which his ear started to hurt.

"You ain't ashamed of me, are you, cause you feel bad about making a fool out of W.?"

"I ain't made a fool out of W.," he said. "A man makes a fool out of himself. It don't take nobody else." He pushed the phone into the other ear until something clicked inside and made his ear feel like it was made of metal.

"Robard?"

"What?"

"When can I see you?" Her voice had become childish.

"Tomorrow evening?"

Mrs. Goodenough came in carrying a broom and gave a startled look at the corner where he was hunched up hiding the receiver. She masked one hand over her right ear and disappeared back into her quarters.

"Can't tomorrow," she said. "We eat at his daddy's once a month, and Thursday's it. His daddy wouldn't look at me if I was a hand mirror."

"Why?" he said, thinking that he already knew.

"He thinks I ruined W.'s playing baseball career, but W. gets more fun playing at Forrest City than he did in Tacoma, Washington. I told him so and he just looked at W. and left the table. W. keeps making me go over there, but none of them can't hardly chew and look at me."

"Friday, then," he said.

"He's going to Jonesboro, Saturday both. We can stay out all night and half the day doing it. Ain't that cute?"

"What time?" he said coldly.

"He's leaving at nine. Come get me at one minute after."

"We got to get us a new place," he said, thinking anybody that saw Beuna slipping off from in back of the post office at nine o'clock would get to the phone before they even got their mail.

"I'll tell you," she said, whispering. "Drive up Main at ten o'clock and keep looking right. You'll see me."

"You might just as well let me pick you up on first base in Jonesboro," he said.

"No!" she said. "Pick me up. I like that. You ain't gonna meet nobody commoner than I am anyway. You might as well pretend you ain't never seen me before, and got a look at me standing there and decided to give me a poke."

It didn't sound any smarter after she'd explained it, but he felt like now was the time to stay to the good, since it was two days before he'd be to get her, and it might be smart not to give her any reason to get herself used up, and just keep her mind on whatever she had mapped out about being picked up like somebody's whore.

"All right," he said faintly. "Don't make no production number out of getting in the truck. Just when you see me, get your ass in."

He glanced through the store to see if Mrs. Goodenough was anywhere in earshot. He could see her shadow moving back and forth around behind the green bead portiere and hear her singing in her little fine voice.

"Robard?"

"What?"

"We are going to Memphis, ain't we? You ain't just going to carry me to Clarksdale or some little nasty punk place, are you?"

"No, hon," he said. "I said we were going."

"Then I can't wait," she said, getting giddy. "I can't wait to see the Peabody and them shower baths."

"Just don't dawdle," he said.

"I won't do no dawdling," she said, letting her voice fall. "Though I might do some diddling." And she hung up.

He stepped down the aisle, his ear aching so that he couldn't touch it, hoping all the time he could get out without seeing Mrs. Goodenough. But she appeared the moment he hung up, wiping her hands on her apron and smelling like cucumbers.

"Phone's done got mean to your ear just lately," she said sympathetically, as though she were embarrassed it had acted that way.

"It'll quit," he said, touching the doorknob.

"Do you want to buy you a postcard?" she said, smiling and making a fragile show of salesmanship.

He took a look outside and gave the knob a useless turn.

"I guess," he said, looking out the glass.

Mrs. Goodenough skittered behind the metal cage and forced up the metal window.

"We're in the post office here," she said, and produced a Roi Tan box from under the counter and set it between them. She flipped the lid and tendered the box, poking a few near cards with her finger.

The cards smelled as if she had been keeping them in a well. Mrs. Goodenough frowned and the stale aroma passed off into the room.

"I can fix the wrote ones with epoxy," she said, sorting through her end of the box, removing an occasional card and admiring it.

He flipped through, passing over a picture of President Truman and one of President Hoover, digging until his finger scratched bottom, wishing he could leave. He took a large stack and sorted through them quickly.

"There's lot of presidents," Mrs. Goodenough remarked, watching cards flipping by, her chin balanced on the heels of both hands. A portrait of Franklin Roosevelt seated before a fireplace holding a dog went past. Mrs. Goodenough looked perplexed. "There's people say it wasn't the States' War ruined the country, it was the cripple man."

"I don't know what done it," he said.

"One man never is to blame for anything," she said committedly.

"Yes, ma'am," he said.

A photograph passed his eye, a tired man standing in the middle of a dirt field holding a hoe and a straw sodbuster. The man was wearing muddy overalls and caked brogans. His hair was slicked and he wore a big smile on his mouth. The photograph had been tinted to look old, and along the border at the bottom were printed the words "Outstanding in His Field." He stared at the card a long time, and took it out of the box and set it on top of a picture of the Liberty Bell.

"That'un," he said.

Mrs. Goodenough tried to peer over the top of the card, holding her stack of favorites between her fingers.

He flashed the card. "This here," he said.

Her smile dwindled and she offered the stack in her hand. "Those *are* funny ones," she agreed, trying to retrieve the fugitives. "You might like these."

He inspected the back of the card for the space for writing. "I like this one," he said. "Looks like he had him a day."

"Looks *like* it," Mrs. Goodenough said stiffly. She patted her own choices affectionately. "I call them *novelties,*" she said.

"They *are* novel," he said, and turned the card and looked at the man again, a cheerful face. The smile and the weariness were both put-ons, he figured, and the second the picture got snapped, the fellow threw down his hoe, got inside some car, and drove off with whoever owned the camera and got drunk in some bar, laughing about selling cards, once they doctored it to look genuine, like a man who knew something about what the pose was trying to put on.

"How much?" he said, fingering change in his palm.

"Fifteen for the card," Mrs. Goodenough said glumly, gloomy about his decision. "Six if you want a stamp."

He put a quarter on top of the box.

"Would you like a commemorative?" she said, forgetting she was disappointed and fumbling into another concealed box. "I've got an A & P Anniversary and a Financial Patriots."

"Anything," he said.

He took the A & P Anniversary she gave him and stuck it on

the blank side and put the card in his shirt pocket.

"Ain't you going to write it?" she said, returning four cents and looking disappointed again.

"I'll write it tomorrow," he said.

She put her hands on the smooth counter and smiled and said nothing, as if something had just ended.

He went out just as the bus with Memphis marquee went past. The driver honked, and through the windowpane he could see Mrs. Goodenough lift her hand off the counter and wave, still smiling thinly in the gloom, as the bus passed into the field.

2

The boys gave him a fishy look when he drove back up the road toward the camp, as if they had finally recognized who he was out of the haze of their past, and weren't amused to see him still around.

The sky had resolved into a flat panel of grayish blue disappearing into Mississippi. Up behind him, heavy white clouds were sagging around the sun as if they were falling with it toward the horizon. He figured for no rain now and that maybe the weather would snap and the fields would leach dry in time to plow.

When he drove past Gaspareau's, the old man stumped out the busted screen door in his wide-brim hat with the green visor and stood looking at him while he backed up beside Mr. Lamb's Lincoln, got down in the boat, and started noisily back across the lake. The air on the lake was cooler than the air in the camp, and the wind came from out of the west, riffling the water in little wavelets that urged the boat more quickly in the direction he was taking it. Half across, he looked back, but Gaspareau was gone from the stoop of the house and the camp had begun to drop in the trees.

He beached the boat, set it on its top, and chain-looped it to the stump Mr. Lamb had painted red for that purpose. The old man refused to keep anything under lock, so he could motor all around in his jeep and have access to everything without having to carry a wad of keys.

He crawled up the bank to where the willows had turned the light down the path jade. At the jeep he saw Newel's head leaned against one of the tires, his shoes kicked off. A flicker dropped out of the willows and dipped down the clearing path fifty yards, and struck the woods.

"Old man passed by," Newel said. "I told him you'd gone on your coffee break. He said he was happy for you to knock off whenever you felt like it since you worked your fingers to the bone anyway."

He scraped his instep across the sill of the jeep. "That's good," he said. He lifted the mud off the sill with his finger, and sat and looked into the willows, back of which hung the lake, still lightly perturbed by the breeze.

"You run anybody off yet?" Newel looked in the same direction, as if they'd both seen something in the water.

"Not hardly."

"Mr. Lamb said nobody was coming," Newel said.

"It don't surprise me," he said. "I ain't seen the first turkey." He eased himself on the sill. "I've made it twenty-five times around, and every once in a while I'll stop and make a little cluck and listen, cause you can hear 'em strutting around trying to get into something. And I ain't heard nothin yet. There *ain't* no turkeys or else they're all got smart and hid out with their voices kept down, which ain't likely."

"That's too bad," Newel said. "If he thinks he's got turkeys and there aren't any."

"Can't nobody poach what you ain't got," he said, smiling. "You can't have fun with a coon that's gone."

Newel stared awhile at the lake and worried his forehead into a little ruck. "I want you to tell me something," he said, and sighed.

He could hear the flicker *kee-oo*ing out in the shumards. "What would that be?" he said.

Newel drew himself up a little closer. "If you like things so goddamned manageable, just what're you doing down here?"

The bird kept up its racket. He could hear its wings fluttering in the high leafy branches. "If I'da wanted you to know, I'da done told you, don't you s'pose?"

Newel's eyes looked like they had grown smaller. "There's something not right, though," he said, "or you wouldn't be back down here. You'd be back there with your wife in California, or wherever you live, managing everything. Instead you look like somebody going to a funeral for a fellow you didn't know."

It made him irritated. He squirmed to the edge of the fender so he was looking straight down at Newel. "Maybe I wouldn't look that way if you weren't aggravating me." He grabbed onto the chamfer and gave it a good squeeze.

Newel got up, dusted his pants, and stepped a ways off to look at the lake, as if he were expecting to see something rise off the surface. The sun was barely visible past the boat camp, an orangy liquid, shapeless at the tip of the levee.

"I don't see why I have to waste my time with you when I could be having me a big time driving circles around this island." He climbed off the fender and sat in the driver's seat.

"You got some woman you're fucking up there in Helena or wherever it is that's running you crazy," Newel said loudly, turning around and staring. "You look like a criminal every time I see you, so it just must be something cheap-ass."

He drummed his fingers on the steering wheel, took a breath, and let it go out slowly, staring at his feet as if he were looking in a well of fast-flourishing disasters. "All right," he said, and laid his hands in his lap and let his elbows tap his ribs. "It don't prove nothing. I'd bet you nine out of ten things a man does outside of the ordinary would trace to some woman he's got hid out, or like to have hid."

"That doesn't matter," Newel said, and looked off as if he might be angry. "If you just wanted to cadge a little pussy you didn't have to drive three thousand miles. You could just go *home,* or down the road, or next door. You didn't have to come where you don't even like it. And if you're just scared of getting caught with your dick out you wouldn't look like you *do* look, like somebody grieved about something."

"You done got me tired now, Newel," he said.

"Just so you know it, though," Newel said angrily, looking at the lake one more time and turning back.

He started the jeep, got his pistol out from under the seat, and put it down in his belt wrapped in the handkerchief. The woods were at the moment of turning brown. "How come you even care about it?" he said softly, to nothing.

"I don't," Newel said, and climbed in the jeep, rubbing his arms as if a cold had penetrated into his bones. "I just want you to know I'm not full of shit."

"I guess I'll have to hold off on that," he said, and drove away.

3

Mr. Lamb sat dumped behind the end of the table, frowning over an assemblage of patent medicines, peering out between the vials and tins as if they were a city whose streets he didn't know. Landrieu was huffing through the kitchen, consigning pots to and from stove plates, frowning sternly at whoever came in the house.

The old man looked up at them curiously. Mrs. Lamb was in the sitting room listening to the radio through her headphones. He sat down quietly across from Newel and tried to cause as little disturbance as he could while the old man, from all looks in a poisonous temper, menaced the array of bottles crowded in front of him on the tabletop.

The old man had assembled a big chalk-blue bottle of Phillips, a tiny vial of liver pills, a bottle of Hadacol in which the liquid had separated into amber and black strata, a black bottle of hemorrhoid pills, a tin of headache powders, a bottle of Black-Draught laxative, two different-shaped bottles of calamine lotion, each with a druggist's paper label, a clear bottle of brown liquid with a handwritten label that said Gordona Specific, and in back of everything a small paper box of d-Con.

Mr. Lamb gave Newel an unfriendly look, then turned his eye around back onto him so that his face felt cold and hot all at once.

The old man drew up on one of his skinny elbows and started looking at several directions simultaneously. "You threatening my life, Hewes?" he said.

He gave a quick look down at the d-Con and tried to tell if the old man had somehow roped his name in with the roach poison. "No," he said, and gave Newel a queer look.

"You sure?" the old man said, and leaned out over the tiny sea of bottles until all the ruckles stretched out of his neck.

"Yessir," he said, nervous.

"How come you come to dinner carrying a pistol, then?" the old man croaked.

He looked down and saw the black rubber butt of the old man's revolver still wrapped in the handkerchief and stuck out the top of his pants like a snake gone half in its hole. The old man glowered, his eyes flashing as if he wanted to keep both face and gun butt trapped in the same field of vision so he wouldn't miss anything that happened to each.

He grabbed at the handkerchief, groped the gun instead, and jerked it out of his pants, the handkerchief a-cling. He stood up and flourished the gun in front of him.

"Look out, Newel," the old man shrieked, and lurched backward in his chair, a grimace fixing on his face, his hands thrown at the ceiling. "He's gonna blast us."

Newel's face got caught in an odd smile and he appeared to be completely paralyzed.

"Good Jesus," the old man gurgled, and pursed his lips as if he were just before receiving a terrible blow. Mr. Lamb suddenly whipped his face about and looked forlornly at Mrs. Lamb, who was still intent on her radio, her back silently to the rest of the house.

He slammed back from the table, tipping his chair, barreled the muzzle toward the floor and bolted out, the gun ferried in front of him like a dowser, down the steps and across the yard.

He got inside the Gin Den, turned on the overhead bulb, and shoved the gun under the mattress, breathing quickly, his heart squeezing the bottom of his windpipe. It seemed unaccountable, he thought, for life to transport you this way, to where you'd never thought of going nor wanted to go nor even knew to exist. It made him feel giddy and out of control. He had planned it for Friday, for slipping away afterward, but there wasn't any planning it finally. He saw it all at once. It was all right to plot it, but you had to be ready to glide in the wake of fate sooner or later, and not be surprised when things surprised you.

He turned out the light and stood in the door, watching the house gone darker than the sky behind it, the windows oranged and faintly shining. Landrieu's silhouette passed in the window like a grasshopper, a kettle hung from a bar, then in a moment, in his chef's hat, disappeared into the far room with arms full of bowls. He lit a cigarette and blew the smoke in the air and felt chilled in the dew. He thought of sitting on the porch in Cane Hill when the air was purpled and velvet before the sun completely died, watching his father's cat loll on the step, its lemon eyes drowsy, its tail switching upward and back. His father had come out and stood behind him and looked at the cat as though he could read its mind, and all at once had stood down and grabbed the cat by its back hackles and spun it so that everything was reverse, and the cat's fat tail switched off the other end of the step in the vervains. And his father stood up again and looked at the cat strangely as if he couldn't read its mind anymore. And the cat never missed a heartbeat, its eyes falling the way they had, its paws grasping out toward invisible creatures in its dream.

"Ain't it queer," his father said, and whipped a handkerchief out of his pocket and wiped his nose vigorously and snorted. "I turned old Mine cattywumpus and he never so much as blinked."

"I don't think Mine cares," he said.

And his father looked at him as if somehow he were part of the cat they were both wondering about, and stuffed his handkerchief in his pocket and went back inside.

He watched the house take better shape in the night and felt satisfied with his old man's memory, since his father was a planner and a conniver and thought the way he set the world up was the way it should go, even though it was wrong. The porch light was still off, and the night was sweet then and like velvet. He felt in his pocket and took out the card he'd bought in the afternoon and tried to make it out in the skimpy moon's light and couldn't and went back inside the Gin Den to sleep.

PART VI

Sam Newel

1

Mr. Lamb sat reconnoitering the sea of bottles as if he had come on them unexpectedly and was perplexed as to how to get to the other side. He elevated the Hadacol so he could read the label against the light, and grunted when he had digested what the bottle had to say, and set it down and reappraised the remainders. He suddenly snaked out his arm, plucked up the box of d-Con, and brought it straight up into his skinny field of vision. He pondered the label, turned the box over, and squinted at the tiny red printing until he slowly began to frown and his entire face contracted into a scowl of grave condemnation.

"What the shit is this here?" the old man said. At that Mrs. Lamb sat back in her chair, bent her chin around to look at Mr. Lamb, and returned to her radio, the PBX wires swooping out her ear directly into the dark back panel of the box. "Somebody's trying to assassinate me," Mr. Lamb bellowed. He shoved the box of d-Con out away from his face as if it were a hateful mirror. "What the hell does that say?" the old man said brashly, thrusting the box at him with the crucial panel already rotated. Mr. Lamb's pink mouth opened as if he planned to receive the important information orally.

He studied the box, then began to read it out loud. " 'Warning: Do not swallow. May be fatal if taken internally. Keep out of the reach of children. Call a physician at once if ingested.' "

"That's enough," the old man said peremptorily, whacking his knuckles on the table so that all the bottles moved a little sideways and the vial of liver pills rollicked and rolled off the edge. "Landroo!" he shouted.

Landrieu hooked his head around the jamb and looked in suspiciously.

Mr. Lamb's fierceness altered instantly to a tone of obsequious affability. "Are you trying to kill me, son?" He motioned to the box congenially with his thumb.

"No suh," Landrieu said, as if it were an idea he'd simply never thought of, and disappeared out of the doorframe, his voice trailing off into the kitchen, where he seemed to be assiduously stirring something in a pan. "I ain't tried to kill you today," he said.

Mr. Lamb kept talking to the doorway as if Landrieu's head were still in it. "Well, *somebody* put this roach powder amongst my nostrums," he said thoughtfully, eying the box back and forth.

"I don't know nothin about d-Con," Landrieu said, invisible to everyone.

Mr. Lamb sighed and carefully reorbited his thumbs, working them slowly until he got the proper cadence, then spinning them at a vigorous pace. "Well, it says there not to in-gest none of it, and somebody musta had a notion I was planning to in-gest one of these cures when he brought them out here to me."

Landrieu declined an answer.

Mrs. Lamb sat forward, unjacked the headset, and let the radio lash forth a fierce voice speaking Spanish at a terrible rate. She regarded them both boldly as though to indicate she was understanding it as well as any Mexican. The man kept yelling, *"E-u-ro-pa in-cre-í-ble! E-u-ro-pa in-cre-í-ble!"* and Mrs. Lamb continued promoting it all with a triumphant smile.

"I didn't ask you to bring me no roach poison," Mr. Lamb mumbled underneath the sound of the radio, his thumbs filing past each other at a faster and faster pace.

"I just brung what you said," Landrieu said irritably through the open door. "Whatever's laying on the window ledge's what you said. That's what I brung. I didn't pay no attention to no roach medicine."

"That's two people tried to murder me inside of five minutes," Mr. Lamb said dolefully.

"I ain't tried to murder nobody," Landrieu mumbled.

Mrs. Lamb's radio began to sound brittle, filling every squinch in the house. The old man suddenly wheeled in his chair and fired a half-vengeful, half-supplicating look at Mrs. Lamb, who was enjoying having everyone listen at top volume. He wondered furtively if Mrs. Lamb might not be of Catalonian lineage.

"Would you turn that down, Fidelia," Mr. Lamb said patiently, audible to no one but himself. Nevertheless, Mrs. Lamb shoved the jack back in the terminal and the sound disappeared like an invisible curtain snapped across the room, leaving a discomforting quiet. Landrieu was cooking ham in the frying pan, and the hot ham scent tainted the room with a queer nauseating sensation.

Mr. Lamb abstractedly appraised the army of bottles and tablet vials.

"Are you sick?" he said to the old man, wanting to quell the sick feeling in his own stomach.

Mr. Lamb looked up at him queerly and stuffed his hands together so that his thumbs had to stop rotating. "The golden age is gone," he said morosely, and squeezed his knuckles in a tiny gesture of frustration.

"Maybe you just didn't sleep well?" he said, smiling and hoping the old man was not about to make him the culprit of another plot.

"There's never rest for the wicked, Newel," the old man said, a vague larcenous flame in his eye.

"Why don't you see a doctor?"

The old man cocked his head to get his ear back into alignment with the sound. "What's that?" he said.

"See a doctor?" he said, feeling less confident.

Mr. Lamb stared at him keenly as though he'd just received an insult he didn't intend to ignore. "Because I goddamn don't want to, that's why," he said, his eyes tightening into hard little twigs. "Bastards swarm you like ants on a cupcake," he said indignantly. "When they're done sticking and cutting there ain't nothin left to carry home. That's why, by God." The old man clenched his teeth and pressed his fists against the table as if he were intending to levitate himself.

"I agree," he said.

"What's that?" Mr. Lamb gave his defective ear a good whack with the heel of his hand.

He shook his head. "I don't like doctors either." His stomach felt somewhat better.

The old man glared at him as if he suspected a plot were knitting and he was the intended victim. "You don't?"

"No."

"Why don't you?" The old man inclined his head toward his shoulder at a severe angle as if he thought he could hear a lot better that way.

"All they get to see is disease," he said, "so that's all they recognize." He brought his hands out of his lap and laid them on the table in a way that modeled the old man's. "When they don't see it at first, they keep looking. They're not trained to see health, and I don't like them."

The old man's teeth dangled slightly in his mouth and he slapped them up with his tongue. "Is that right?"

"Yes."

Mr. Lamb let his eyes drift slowly down onto the army of bottles as if he expected them to say something, and when they didn't, pushed them all off the table straight onto the floor in one careless sweep of his arm. And the clatter was immense. Landrieu sprang into the room, and Mr. Lamb gave him a victimized look.

"What'd you do that for?" Landrieu shouted.

"What?"

"Push them off and scare me like that?" Landrieu made a jerky motion with the back of his hand to indicate all the bottles and vials newly arrived to the floor.

Mr. Lamb's innocent expression transformed into a pale malevolence which signified Landrieu had just improvidently overdrawn his account. He swiveled slowly in his chair and let his gaze settle on Mrs. Lamb, who had not responded to the clatter at all. She was seated with her back to everyone, gazing out the window into the dark, still listening, he supposed, to more Mexican travel advertisements.

Mr. Lamb turned his gaze back around as if he had just spoken with Mrs. Lamb and heard Landrieu implicated in a scurrilous falsehood. "She ain't heard nothin," he announced scornfully. "I ain't. This fella here ain't." He batted his eyes hotly. "You the only one heard anything."

Landrieu's face got significantly harder. "I ain't pickin up what nobody ain't heard," he said, and was gone.

The old man fingered his napkin, twisted one of the corners up into a firm projectile, and rammed it in his good ear, giving the ear a generous reaming. He turned one corner of his mouth up into an idiotic smile and forgot all about Landrieu. "You don't like them gut plumbers, huh?" he said, twisting vigorously and hoisting his lip higher as if he were trying to hear through the reaming sounds going on inside his head.

"No sir," he said, feeling vaguely guilty about Landrieu.

"Me neither," the old man said, withdrawing the napkin and the waxy prong as if it were a nugget. "I feel worse every time I get close to one."

Mr. Lamb rebalanced himself in his chair, leaned forward, and drew right up in his face. The old man's feet accidentally disturbed some of the bottles and sent them rolling over the floorboards, and he quickly drew his mouth down into a dark conspiratorial frown, so that his eyebrows hung heavily over his little burnt-out eyes. "I'll tell you something," Mr. Lamb said, grabbing his wrist tightly. He could smell a brash antiseptic odor coming from the old man's mouth. "I wouldn't want to be a doctor on account of all the death," he whispered, as if he'd broached an unspeakable subject. "I think when *they* get old, all the death comes back on 'em, and they can't think of nothing but dying and bodies rotting and breaking apart the way they've seen people do all their lives." He smiled craftily.

"Yes sir," he said, wishing he could rescue his wrist. Mr.

Lamb's skull was visible beneath the jointure of two jaws, and from that advantage he looked like an animated skeleton.

"Mrs. Lamb's nephew, little Ber-trand," Mr. Lamb said privately, angling so he could eye his wife before going on, "he had him a job in Washington, D.C., examining titties and nothing else, as far as I can make out." The old man's eyes got hot, and he drew himself up so as to exhale more antiseptic breath directly in his face. "He worked for the government in the physicals department. Now, that's a doctorin job I'd take to. Haw haw haw haw." Mr. Lamb's face became radish red and the veins in his temples fattened up like roots.

Landrieu paraded into the room, arms paved with dishes, wearing his apron and chef's hat, but with eyes broadcasting indignation at everything in sight.

Mrs. Lamb spied him, switched off her radio, and made a way in through the bottles just as Landrieu was deploying the entrées out over the table. He swept back to the kitchen, returned with the tea pitcher, stood back reproachfully while Mrs. Lamb certified the table and nodded, then disappeared, letting the pantry door swing closed behind him.

"Me and Newel's going fishing tomorrow," Mr. Lamb announced, shoveling cream corn into his mouth as fast as he could work the spoon.

Mrs. Lamb regarded him sternly, as though to mark the fact that something had finally been uncovered for him to do.

"Ain't that right, Newel?" the old man said, chewing furiously.

"Sounds wonderful," he said, since it seemed superior to fighting all morning, then spending the rest of the day sulking in the Gin Den out of sight.

"Good," Mr. Lamb reveled, paring off a piece of ham and dropping it directly into the corn. Mrs. Lamb was having one biscuit with drippings and another one with molasses poured in a big puddle on her plate mixed with butter so the mixture became a thick yellow paste. Mr. Lamb retrieved his ham, and went on smothering whatever was not already covered with cream corn.

"Mrs. Lamb's a light eater," the old man said, chewing. "Soon as it gets light, she starts eatin.'"

Mrs. Lamb bent one elbow on the table and watched the old man while she chewed, as if he were an old clown that no longer amused her. Which caused the old man to waltz around in his chair and roam his eyes all over the walls.

He thought he might just change subjects and give the old man a relief. "What caused that burnt spot out behind the house?" He peered at them both at once.

"Haw!" the old man brayed, and looked supremely pleased to hear this particular subject brought up.

Mrs. Lamb gave her husband a poisonous look and rared forward over her plate as if he were about to utter a perfidy she was deadly set on suppressing.

He thought right away of renouncing the subject and going on to something less controversial, except he had somehow lost control of everything and simply had to sit while whoever *did* have control decided how to exercise it. There was something queer, he saw, about the old man whinnying the very moment the burnt patch was mentioned, as if the subject were a scandal to Mrs. Lamb and therefore absolutely risible to him.

Mr. Lamb squeezed tightly back in his chair, scuttled his shoes noisily against the table feet, and stiffed his arms on the apron of the table as if he meant to catapult himself onto the tabletop by means of an invisible spring attached to his seat. "That burnt spot," he snorted, *"was a house."* He eyed Mrs. Lamb cagily, his eyes sharpened. He relaxed his arms and sank back in his seat.

"My cousin used to live there," Mrs. Lamb said loftily, as though she'd been bullied into the admission. She very carefully set down her fork, situated both hands behind her plate, and regarded Mr. Lamb coldly.

"Her cousin, John," Mr. Lamb announced, smiling villainously, "was a comical old prune, to say the least." He snuffed his nose like a man trying to work back a sneeze. "He had some queer habits."

He wished someone would bring out another subject.

Mrs. Lamb was in the process of staring a hole in Mr. Lamb's forehead, but the old man seemed to be steadily freeing himself of all outside influences, and smiling and working his teeth up and down against his gums.

"Ol John used to have him a little wood boat out on the lee hip— The devil lived here forty-five years," the old man interrupted himself. "And before there was all the nigger trouble, when the water got down he used to get in his boat and putt-putt over to Mississippi and go to the baseball. The niggers had 'em a sandlot over at Stovall. In fact, T.V.A. Landrieu was one of their famous stars till he got too damn old." The old man let his eyes roam to the pantry, gave Mrs. Lamb another taunting look, and curled his upper lip a little more, his eyelashes a-flutter. "Anyway, he'd go over in the evening and sit up in the grandstand and yell the awfulest nastiest blasphemies he could think of, at anybody that was on the field. He'd just give 'em all a terrible time and be drunker'n Cooter Brown by the middle of the first inning. And every time one of them devils would go to throw the ball, he'd yell, 'Peee-uuuuuu, you stink,' and start fanning the air with his little umpire's cap like there was something smelled bad where he was. And sometimes they'd just have to quit, because John was up there making such a ruckus. He had a wood leg, you see, and whenever they'd send some big powerful bluegum up there to shush him, he'd pull out his old pig bleeder and stob it right in that leg and grin like he was so unmindful of stobbing things that he'd just stob himself, and the niggers all went shy of him after that. And I can't say as I blame them, either. They didn't feel too good about nobody that went around stobbing theirselves. They didn't figure that was quite natural." Mr. Lamb beamed and right away started drumming his fingers as if he was hoping somebody would ask him another question so he could give another enthralling answer.

Mrs. Lamb rose quietly and walked back into the kitchen and began speaking mutedly to Landrieu about going to Helena the next day.

"See now, I'll tell you," the old man whispered, grinning at him evilly as soon as Mrs. Lamb had let the door swing to, craning over the table in a craven conspirator's posture and grasping at some part of his available anatomy and getting hold of a wrist before he could snake it away. "Johnny Carter was a half-wit," Mr. Lamb said in a stage whisper he knew Mrs. Lamb could hear through twenty doors, which made him get itchy in his seat. The old man got a faster hold on his wrist. "Another one of his nitwit tricks was to walk in somebody's store, pull a little bullfrog out of his pocket, and eat it. Right in front of ladies and little girls, just pop it in his mouth like a charm and chew it up, then bust out laughing. And of course," the old man said, becoming magisterial, "all them women delivered their what-fors to *me*, cause they knew he was Fidelia's kin and knew he lived out here, though that's all they knew. But it wasn't nothing I could do about, cause he wasn't crazy enough to send to Whitfield, and I think if I'da ever tried, he would've killed me and everybody else he could of got his hands on, the same way he killed them Choctaws." The old man relaxed his wrist and sank into a sober expression, as if at the bottom of all the foolery there lay still something altogether enigmatic and hard. Mr. Lamb's mouth gapped open a quarter inch and his eyes got momentarily abstracted.

"How come he stayed so long?" he said, hoping the old man would say something about the Choctaws without his having to ask it directly.

The old man's eyes stayed gazing at some point on the white pantry door as if he were envisioning something he absolutely could not reason with.

"Well," the old man said lamentably. "He had him some difficulties. He married a little Choctaw gal up in Pontotoc County in 1925, and the wench died giving birth. And before he could do anything, a bunch of her people come and run off with the baby, which was healthy, and took it to where they was living in Rough Edge, Mississippi, amongst a bunch of lowlifes, and let it be said they wasn't going to give it up, cause they didn't care too much for John and blamed him for the gal's dying. So he went up there to where they were, right in the town of Rough Edge, and stood on the front step, and said he'd come to get his baby, since it *was* his. And they said for him to go jump in the pond, that he wasn't even going to get to see the baby. And I guess" —Mr. Lamb's eyes seemed to be trying to see the past—"he must have just sheered a bolt, cause he went back down to Pontotoc and got his shotgun and come back and shot four of them dead as a Indian could ever expect to be, right out on the porch, took that baby and delivered it back to his daddy's house in Pontotoc, and the next thing I knew he was out on this porch. And I just let him stay on, cause there wasn't nothing else he could do. I figured he wasn't too dangerous as long as he wasn't around no Indians. And he stayed forty-five years, right there in that little house."

"What about the law?" he said, not seeing any way he could be accused of soliciting if old John was already dead. "Didn't anybody come and look for him?"

Mr. Lamb looked at him curiously as if he'd never thought about that. He pushed his little hands together in front of him, shoving his plate back, and seemed to get lost in his thoughts again. "Well," he said, bemused, "I don't know. Didn't nobody ever come looking. He told me what happened right off, and I thought, 'Shit, I'da done the same damn thing,' and he seemed satisfied to stay out here and help around. He built that cabin, and I just didn't never ask about no law. I expect they *was* after him up in Pontotoc, but I never did get private with him on the subject."

"He *did* kill four people, though," he said, trying to argue in whispers without drawing Mrs. Lamb back out of the kitchen. "Didn't he admit it?"

"Yes," the old man said indignantly.

"He *could* have got his baby some other way," he said. "A Mississippi court wouldn't give a half-white baby to a bunch of Choctaws."

"We didn't worry about no courts," the old man said, trying to rein in his temper, his cheeks coloring a little pink.

He had a fast-failing mental picture of Hollis hitting the concrete. "Why the hell not?" he said. "Four people get blown up because some psychopath cousin wants his old man to take care of his baby, and you deprive the law the chance to settle with him."

"All right," the old man said patiently. "But wouldn't you of put up your own wife's cousin if he'd done it and it didn't put you out any?"

"No!" he said.

"Well, goddamn it, Newel," the old man whispered furiously. "You *ought* to. It's family!" Mr. Lamb glared at him, his nubby little fists pressed on the tabletop as if he'd decided to attempt a handstand.

"But it's against the law," he said.

"Fuck the law, goddamn it." The old man almost strangled himself keeping his voice inside the foot of space that separated them. His spectacles slid down onto the soft skin of his nose, and he gave the table a good shaking that made the whole room vibrate. "I didn't like the son-of-a-bitch no better than you did. He poisoned three of my pups with thermometer mercury and stole every bottle of whore water I ever kept out here and filtered it through a biscuit so he could get hooched. He was nuttier'n a pet coon, but I didn't law him, by God. He was Mrs. Lamb's cousin."

Mrs. Lamb's face appeared unexpectedly in the gap of the pantry door, casting ominous looks over both of them, her upper lip drawn into a tight little pucker of disdain. She let the door shut abruptly and the old man got caught between his rage and his guilt.

"Fidelia," the old man bellowed, whacking his fists on the tabletop.

No sound came from the kitchen. He pictured Mrs. Lamb and Landrieu sitting in the cooling darkness, silent, while the two of them floundered in their own conspiratorial baseness.

The old man snapped toward him, ready for another affront. "What *would* you have done?" he demanded, abandoning whispering altogether.

He sighed, realizing he just wasn't up to the old man's ferocity. Whatever the old man had stored in never-ceasing abundance was exactly what he lacked. And he wondered when his had been siphoned off, or if he ever even had it, and if he had, where it had gone. It occurred to him that if he did indeed have it, it was certainly all directed inward now, while all the old man's fury was pointed out like ordnance at the armies of contravention and deceit that had him under constant siege. "I'd have gotten him a good lawyer, if there was one," he said soberly, "had him plead dementia praecox, put him on the stand, and told him to act crazy."

"What the hell's the difference in that and what I did?" the old man said. "I saved a lie by telling one." The old man looked at him as if it were as clear as anything he'd ever said in his life and he should see the wisdom in it and give in. "You got to have a lawyer before you can fart, don't you, Newel?"

"Four people got killed," he said wearily.

"Choctaws," the old man said contemptuously. "They absconded with his baby and run him off when he come to claim it."

"I know," he said.

"The hell," Mr. Lamb said. "You're a fish, Newel, by God. You belong back up in Lake Michigan where it's cold and wet, not down here where people's got blood." He thrust himself backward into his chair as if someone had smacked him on the chin.

"What happened to him?" he said.

Mr. Lamb squinted as if he were surprised he was still able to speak. "Who?" he said.

"John."

"He died, that's what happened to him."

"Did the house just burn down by itself?"

The old man pinched the edge of the table between his thumb and his index finger as if he were trying to crack off a piece. "I *burnt* it down," he said loudly. "I went in and I piled up all his old shit in the middle of the floor, including his umpire's hat, and set the torch to it, by God. And that's what's the cause of that skint spot." His eyes quit snapping and he seemed to lose his energy all at once, as if the recollection of the house going up had burnt off all his anger. "You know what?" the old man said, glassy-eyed.

"No."

"Him and Mrs. Lamb wrote the state song." The old man licked his lips and smacked them as if he could appreciate the feat. "Mrs. Lamb wrote the lyrics and John Carter made the tune. They sent it to the contest in Jackson in 1938, and won five hundred dollars and a picture of Senator Bilbo and J. K. Vardaman holding the sheet up in front of the U.S. Capitol. I told them they ought to send back the picture of Bilbo cause that little bastard was a dictator, but he pasted 'em both up on the wall in his house, and said he wondered what old J. K. Vardaman and Bilbo would have thought if they knew he had their picture up on his wall and had been hiding from the law thirteen years. And I said, 'Them two's been hiding from the law longer'n that.' I would ask Mrs. Lamb to come in and sing it for you if you wanted me to."

"You don't have to bother," he said.

"No, no. Fidelia." The old man spoke softly.

The pantry door swung open and Mrs. Lamb appeared again on the sill, regarding them both with contempt. The kitchen was black. "What, Mark?" she said.

"Newel here would like you to sing 'The Magnolia State,' a cappella." The old man had on his most beatific smile, his body erect in the anticipation that the idea would succeed.

"Well, I will not," she snapped. "You have a lovely voice—you sing it for him yourself." She strode around the other side of the table from the bottles and disappeared into the bedroom.

"It's all right," he said.

Mr. Lamb's face sank dismally. "I'd sing it, but I ain't got the music," he said.

The floor squeaked in the bedroom. Outside it was dirt dark, and the light from the chandelier shimmered in the flimsy panes.

"What happened to the five hundred dollars?"

"She give it to him. She hoped he'd take it and go off to California and start a life. But the bastard stayed right there in his house, and when I went to pile all his stuff, I found four hundred-dollar bills. I don't know what he done with the other one. Everything he ate he killed. I never seen him spend a nickel. I sent them four to the Blind Made Brooms in Jackson with his name wrote on it. What the hell. It was a paradise down here for him he wouldn't of ever had if he hadn'ta killed them Indians. What's the good of sending him to Parchman?"

"I understand," he said. He felt as if he wanted to go to sleep, though he didn't want to strand the old man, sinking lower and lower.

"You know," Mr. Lamb said softly, his eyes shining, "I used to roam all over this island, all times of the day or night, and it didn't make any difference where it was I went or when, I'd always see him. He'd be down at the dead lake, or squatting in the road, or I'd see him off in the trees, see his little miner's light he had on his cap, barging around back in the sumacs doing what, I don't know. And it used to make me mad as hell that I couldn't go without seeing his painful presence everyplace. But after a while I got used to seeing the old prune, and sometimes I'd see him standing down at the river looking and looking over at the Mississippi side like he was trying to make out something, and then turn around and go running back off without ever having seen me, just laughing like hell. And by God, when he died"— the old man shook his head as if it were a mystery of unfathomable complexity—"I took a fear of going out in the woods after dark. I know I ain't going to see him. And I didn't even like the son-of-a-bitch, and me and Mrs. Lamb sat up nights conniving against him, talking about how crazy he was, eatin them frogs. I must be a fool, ain't I, Newel, afraid of the dark?" The old man peered at him as if he were hoping to find out he wasn't a fool at all and could declare as much to Mrs. Lamb and win back her heart before she went to sleep.

"I don't think so," he said.

Mr. Lamb bolted back across the floor with a loud bracking and stood up. "We going fishing tomorrow?" the old man said, light revived in his eyes.

"Yessir," he said.

Mr. Lamb began walking out before he answered, moving squat-legged into the gallery doors without turning. "I can fish and you can row," he said. He clicked off the light in the sitting room, where Mrs. Lamb had left it on, and disappeared as she had back into the darkness.

He sat at the table, the chandelier glossy in the cheap window, showing him back his own features wide and angled, his shoulders concave as if a wind had blown them and bent them around his chest. He could hear the old man scuffling in the bedroom, his voice low and appealing. The dishes were unmoved. He stooped and began to pick up the old man's bottles and remount them on the table the way they had been. There had been a look in Mr. Lamb's face as if he just felt the ballast of his life going off, and couldn't stop it, and an abstraction had come on him for the first time ever and scared him and made him go after cures, which he knew in advance wouldn't work, since he knew there wasn't any way in the world to end it now. Since everything you were lonely for was gone, and everything you were afraid of was all around you.

The old man, he thought, had fifty years jump and was just now tearing apart, warring every inch, a war he felt he lacked the outrage to make, since it didn't seem the least bit crucial to win it or lose it. He felt like a man wandering in a department store with no money and no attraction to anything under glass, but with a dilettante's need to acquire. And it scared him. And back in some long night precinct of his mind there was a rising to get out and get on the train fast and get back before his own ballast went off and he was in the fix for good.

2

The year his father died he went in a car to Vicksburg with a boy named Roscoe Sampson, who liked to dance. In Vicksburg they took one quick drive down the red brick streets to the bottom of the hill the Confederates had defended for months, and drove along the riverfront past the bootleggers, and stared in the darkness out across the river into Louisiana, where tiny specks of houseboat lights were bobbing snugly against the other side. And when they had finished driving, Roscoe Sampson said he wanted to dance, and they bought a bottle of whiskey and a Seven-Up and went to dance in a Masonic hall where the lights were high up in the vaulted ceiling set in reflectors with wire mesh across their mouths. Roscoe found a girl and went and danced with her until the collar of his shirt was wringing wet and the red was high in his cheeks and he looked frantic. He came and told him that they would both take the girl for a drive in the car over to Louisiana into the cotton fields and that the girl would do it for both of them, because she was a typical Vicksburg girl and liked nothing better. But when Roscoe asked the girl if that would be fine with her, she said it wouldn't and made a serious threat against him, and Roscoe came and told him he was ready to leave. In the car they drove back down toward the river, down the dark, murmuring brick streets to the bottom of the hill. And when they had driven around the same block twice, Roscoe rolled the car slowly past one house where there was a Christmas tree in the window that had nothing but tiny blue lights, and whistled out into the night and stopped. In a moment a Negro man came to the screen and whistled, and they parked the car and went in. In the house the air smelled like disinfectant and was hot, though it was cool in the street. Roscoe said that between the two of them they had one dollar and sixty-eight cents and would like to know what that would call to mind for the man. The man gave them a shabby smile and said they were lucky to be alive carrying that much money, and that as far as he was concerned it wouldn't buy them safe passage out the front door, but that they should take it up with the woman in the room. When they got in the room, there were pictures of Jesus stuck to a vanity mirror and a narrow bed with a chenille counterpane, and it was hot. The woman, who was nice and reminded him of a lot of ladies he had seen waiting for buses on Northwest Street, said that while a dollar sixty-eight was not much, she was not busy, so that she simply pulled up her dress and laid the change on the night table, and first he did, and then he sat in the captain's chair at the end of the bed while Roscoe Sampson did, Roscoe's testicles bouncing against the woman like peas in a collander. And at the end the woman got up out of the bed and went to the corner behind the door and squatted over a dishpan and cleaned herself with a strong pine-scented disinfectant and a yellow sponge that smelled like the floors, and said it was the best there was when you got used to the sting and to the funny feeling it gave you way up in your stomach.

3

The morning got exploded by shotgun fire coming five feet from the Gin Den door. Robard had gotten up before light, dressed, and disappeared into the darkness. He had been waked by Robard's jeep cranking and sputtering, and for an hour the house was still. Then somebody started firing a shotgun outside the door and whooping and making noises like the Fourth of July. He pulled himself up, holding his blanket, and looked out, leaning against the door facing. The sun hurt his eyes. It was working light down through the low limbs, making it painful to see more than a foot. Beyond the trees the airstrip was yellow and burning like wheat. A haze hung a foot over the bear flowers. The bicycle reflectors were twitching and snapping back to the far line of trees, and the whole business made seeing an ordeal.

Mr. Lamb was twenty yards from the door, facing the other direction down in the scrub brush between the larger trees and the airstrip apron, stalking down into the crosshatch of chokeberries, a shotgun at order arms, wearing his old canvas coat and woodsman's cap with red flaps tied over the crown. Ahead of Mr. Lamb he could see Elinor's skinny tail curved up and around, quavering above the clutch of weeds, the rest of her body out of sight. Behind the old man, who was accosting Elinor with an awesome caution as if he expected a Cape buffalo to come swaying out of the thicket, stood Landrieu, apparently reconciled, standing nonchalantly in a pair of overalls smoking a limp cigarette, and balancing a big steel-gray double-barrel so that the barrel end rested on the flat of his foot.

He wondered how the old man and Landrieu had so promptly made up their differences, and decided it was because each one thought the other had picked up all the bottles, but didn't dare say anything about it.

Mr. Lamb began to croon, "Clooose, clooose, now, El'nr," as if he were casting a spell over the ground in front of him. Elinor was getting more and more jittery with the old man closing on her with his shotgun, and was probably, he thought, watching whatever she was supposed to be watching and at the same time mapping out a quick place to hole up when the shooting started.

Landrieu took a last drag on his cigarette, snapped the stub in the grass, spit, and all at once everything commenced. Two birds went up out of the chokeberries, wing to wing, directly into a spear of light, and got by the old man's face with an unimpeded whir. The old man never had a chance and had to swing his gun up just to protect himself from the birds, who split at the very last second and fired by him in different directions, while the old man yelled, "Wuuuup, wuuuup," at the dog, who had started barking. Six more birds rose then and went fanning through the trees in a line ahead of the old man, and he managed to get the stock to his shoulder and bust off two shots, which didn't draw a feather. Landrieu carefully got his big two-barrel to his shoulder in case any more of the covey started back toward him, and one promptly did, getting up behind Mr. Lamb's feet, heading in the opposite direction, and Landrieu let go at the bird head-on and hit it in a way that reminded him of atomic attacks on sturdy brick houses. First the bird was there in flight, brown and black and white and crop-winged and intent on a lucky escape, then its physiognomy got changed and none of the original features were intact. It was as if Landrieu had thrown a mottled dishrag in the air and blown a knot in it.

"Da-umn," Landrieu said, lowering the barrels and frowning at the welter of feathers that hung in the air without seeming to move.

Mr. Lamb gave him a pathetic look and went back to scrutinizing Elinor, who clearly believed there were more quail in the brush and hadn't much moved from where she'd been, though she had barked several times while the first birds were starting up and displeased Mr. Lamb considerably. He began crooning again and frowning at Elinor as if he thought she was stubbing at the birds and encouraging them to take flight before he was ready for them. He got behind her again, and almost even with her head, then began thrashing the brush with his foot and holding his gun up with the barrel pointed out from his waist in the direction he intended the birds should go when they went. All at once a single came up out of the cover and beat out toward the airstrip, its neck stretched and its wings reaching as far into the empty air as they could. The bird had chosen the ideal direction, and with incalculable calm the old man raised the muzzle in one smooth, articulated motion, sighted down the single barrel, paused a second while some ideal distance was attained, then squeezed off a shot that overtook the bird without seeming to displace a feather, dropping him on the skin edge of the airfield. The old man never bothered to see if Landrieu had observed the shot. He moved forward in a fell, workmanlike stride toward where the bird had hit, calling "Dead" to Elinor, who bounded out ahead of him, head high in the weeds, until she reached the short grass and pounced on the quail with her forepaws and began rending it wing from neck, anchoring it with her feet and drawing the flesh away with her strong puppy's teeth. The old man hastened a step, arriving at the bird two seconds after Elinor, and delivered her an immense kick in the ribs that sent her head over forepaws back into the grass, losing all grip on the bird, and trying to force out a yelp at the same time she was trying to win enough air back into her lungs to keep from suffocating.

"Shitass!" the old man grumbled, inspecting the sagging bird briefly before stuffing it in his coat and starting back. "Tried to savage my bird," he said up through the trees, making his way to where Landrieu was standing, balefully fingering what was left of the bird he'd mangled.

"Yassuh," Landrieu said glumly. "This'un a little tore up hisself."

"You use that goddamned Peter Stuyvesant gun," the old man complained, coming and standing beside Landrieu as if they were waiting to have their pictures taken. The light had become more generalized, and the yard took on a waxy appearance. Elinor crept blackly up from the bushes, made a berth of the hunters, and slunk back to her loll under the steps. She paid the old man a sorry look and disappeared out of his sight. "If you'd get you a little twenty like this here gun," Mr. Lamb continued in a fatherly manner, looking at Landrieu's bird, then hefting his little Remington and giving it a commanding look, "you wouldn't blow your birds apart like you do, and you wouldn't wear yourself out portaging it around." Landrieu's gun was lying on the ground in front of the two, and Mr. Lamb gave it a tap with his toe as if it were a serpent he had personally scourged.

"Yassuh," Landrieu agreed, still looking lamentably at the bung of feathers in his hand.

Mr. Lamb stared down at the devastated bird another moment, then started back to the house, talking to Landrieu as if he were still beside him.

He walked back inside the Gin Den and relaxed on the edge of the cot and listened to the two men stamping up the stairs into the house, talking loudly. The door shut and he was left in the cool of the shed, staring at his toes and thinking how to work the day. It was the day to leave, without doubt. Get the bus to Memphis and be on the late train, and sometime tomorrow find a place to stay, since Beebe wouldn't be home and he didn't have a key. And later he could take the IC down to school and get signed up for the cram course, and get started in the way he felt fated, if for no other reason than that was the only way left. There was a squeamish serenity in that, of choosing the only thing left, when everything else was eliminated and not by any act, but just by the time and place. It was the compromise satisfaction a person got, he thought, when he is washed up on the beach of some country after spending weeks floating around on a tree limb, too far from home ever to hope to be deposited *there*, and satisfied to be on land, no matter really which land it happened to be.

The only impediment to leaving was going fishing. He felt obligated to cater to Mr. Lamb, except the idea of hazarding a boat with him seemed treacherous, since the old man liked to launch around and jump to his feet the moment things didn't go to suit him and would probably be just as given to it in a boat as elsewhere.

He dressed and slipped out in the direction of the closest woods, keeping so that the hulk of the Gin Den stayed between him and the porch.

At the boundary of the trees he stepped in two dozen yards, so that the house was visible to him, but he was not visible from the house. He watched Landrieu come to the edge of the porch, sling off a pan of water, and disappear inside. He thought maybe the old man had decided on a nap and would forget fishing, and after a while he could just come in and say goodbye, and have himself ferried back across to the bus.

He walked parallel to the road, staying in the denser woods to the end of the airfield, where he switched back to the road out of sight of the house, and struck toward the lake. The sun had moved beneath some blotchy, dark-bellied clouds, and the imprints slid over the road, disclosing the sun directly, but quickly secluding it again. Beyond the woods was another open croft hemmed by trees, the coarse grass crowded by purple thistles that sprouted the tops of the weeds and swayed noisily, though there seemed to be no breeze. He thought he heard Robard's jeep and listened, but the sound died, and he could only hear a faint windless sibilance in the woods. He looked toward the house, saw nothing on the road, and went ahead. In the next trace of timber a block of pink salt was roped to a wood feeder crib. The area was trampled and bark was scabbed off the trees, and the low branches nipped and munched at, though there were no animals to be seen.

He walked until he could smell the warm fishy smell of the lake, and reached the hump of overlook where the jeep had been, found a sandy patch and sat, prepared to stay as long as he could stand it.

He mooned across the lake at the camp five hundred yards away behind another tier of willows, identical to where he sat watching, though sparser. He could see movement in the lot, two figures unrecognizable, three-quarters of the way between the dock and Gaspareau's business cottage. One of them he supposed was Gaspareau, and he made a guess which it was, having it be the broader figure in the light shirt who seemed to be pointing the other man in the direction of the island, more or less to where he was sitting, which produced a prickly feeling in him as though both the figures were talking over what they were going to do if they could ever get their hands on him. He thought about Gaspareau's little red-crust speaking hole burping out sounds when he mashed on the little metal life preserver, and wondered what he was saying and to whom, and wondered if old man Lamb's company had finally arrived a day late. The two figures came down onto the dock and walked out as if they were going to get in one of the boats. He made out that the man he had guessed to be Gaspareau *was* Gaspareau. He was pointing in the direction of the mud landing, waving his cane as a pointer, indicating for the other figure, who was taller and slightly slumped, precisely where he would have to go if he was going to the island. He wondered, then, if Gaspareau wasn't directing a poacher to the island as the old man suspicioned all along, and in arrogance of all his specific proscriptions and threats. And it was comical to think of the old

226

man having to employ one man to watch over another who was getting paid better. After a few moments, both figures walked back off the dock and disappeared toward Gaspareau's cottage, where he lost them in the willow mesh.

In a while he saw a dark-colored car go back over the levee ahead of a funnel of dust, and disappear into the fields. In the camp activity halted. The bight of cottages and scatter of beached rowboats lay in the sun and in the creases of dingy shade looking defunct, the possibility of new movement remote. He wondered what sorts of squalid enterprises Gaspareau could master from the boat camp, stumping around with a big nickel pistol strapped to his belly and some sinister adolescent on his payroll.

Two mallards scooted up and out of the flats below the camp, winging smartly out over the reach of open water, scanning the lambent surface as they flew, each a vigil on his own quadrant of flight. As they angled up the corridor of the lake they seemed to lose lower and lower, as though they were searching for something specific that lay along the perimeter of the willows. As they reached even with the landing cut, they suddenly veered sharply in formation, as if they had spotted where they were going and intended to bend back and drop straight in onto the stobs and cleared timber. But at the unsuspected sight of his face alone and still, gazing up white and enthralled, they wheeled and broke up and to the right, backdrafting as if they were seeking to outdistance his very sight, tripling the space between them in a matter of microseconds, and scatting in opposite directions back up the open water, the steely pinging of their wings barely breaking the silence, making him feel like shrinking back into the woods and hiding.

Robard bumped down the road from the direction of the house with a cigarette sunk in his mouth, looking wizened. He steered the jeep out of the rut, up over the willow roots, and stopped, letting the motor idle.

"I just watched Gaspareau point us out to some guy," he said. Robard looked at the dock, a stitch at the water line. "One of them football coaches," he said, looking at his cigarette to see if it was burning. "What'd he look like?"

"Taller than Gaspareau," he said.

"That wouldn't be too hard."

"Whoever it was went back over the levee," he said, taking a look at the long levee revetment.

The jeep motor choked out and Robard watched the lake stippling light up through the willows. "I got something I want to ask *you*, Newel," he said. He snapped his cigarette in the grass, produced another one, packed it against the steering wheel, and laid it on the side of his mouth. "What is it *you*'re doing down here?" Robard pushed his thumb knuckle in his eye socket and gave his eye a good kneading.

"I'm forgetting all about that," he said, and got up and stood around to the front of the jeep, feeling ready to go back.

"Life ain't *that* difficult." Robard took a match from behind his ear and scratched it off his zipper.

"I just have to adopt a plainer view of things," he said.

"That's me." Robard puffed luxuriously.

"I had all these ideas I couldn't make sense of." He came and slid over onto the back bench of the jeep and let his feet dangle. "People's names, a lot of things at random."

"But ain't that just your memory?" Robard said.

"Yeah, but it started giving me the creeps! I couldn't remember anything else, except what had happened the day before, and some little bits of law school. Didn't that ever happen to you?"

"No," Robard said, touching the ash with the nail of his little finger. "I ain't been to law school."

He frowned at Robard, who was admiring his cigarette. "Anyway, goddamn it, I got obsessed with what the hell I knew, and all I knew was just those things—bits of time, pictures of people in my mind, little places, my old man. You can't attach yourself to a bunch of crap like that. I sat in my apartment a solid month trying to stitch it together into some reasonable train of thought, and none of it worked."

"How come?" Robard said, turning around as if he really wanted to know the answer.

"I don't know."

"How come you to leave in the first place?" Robard twisted his legs so they stretched out across the seat next to him. The air off the lake turned a vaguely fishy smell that seemed to come from the boat camp.

"It was boring as shit in Mississippi. I would've stayed otherwise."

"Wasn't your mother there?"

"I didn't think about that," he said, and stared off. "She died one day. That's the only time I've been there."

Robard sighed as if he were looking at everything philosophically. "All right," he said.

"I was just going nuts up there trying to figure out if that jumble amounted to enough to say I ought to go back and pick it up again."

"You like Chicago better now, do you?"

"I don't care," he said.

"You come all the way down here and you're going back without having done nothin?"

He tapped his heels, watching the dust settle on the grass. "I figured one thing out," he said.

"And who's that—me?" Robard said.

"I don't give a shit anymore," he said precisely, listening to the air wash up through the willows. "The old man cares more than I do. It's right up in his face all the time."

"And he's got both feet in the grave," Robard said, and let his chin rest on his knuckles. A strippet of the wind raised his hair against the part. "What did you think you was doing down here in the first place?" His eyes seemed to get wider.

"It feels like I remember the South being," he said. "It seemed like a good place."

"But ain't you the same up there as you are right here?"

"Yeah, but I was at the end of the fuckin rope with it." He felt morose. "I thought if I could come down here and be part of something happening, not something I remembered, that would help."

Robard stared at him as if he had crossed over a line beyond sanity. "What'd you have in mind?"

"Anything! Shit! I thought the old man would tell me something, except he's crazy. I thought I might know if I could just get it all into the world."

"And what happened?" Robard said.

"I'm sick of it," he said gloomily. "And I'm getting the hell out. Every day I think of something new that's exactly the same. If I could fly across that water right now, I would."

Robard cleared his throat as if he were beginning to speak, then looked at the lake.

"I thought you might be in the same kind of fix," he said.

Robard rocked his head slowly side to side. "I ain't in no kind of fix at all," he said slowly, "though if I was to try to pin together my past and make something intelligent out of it I'd damn sure be in one then. I'd either get bored to tears or scared to death." He looked up significantly, as if he considered he'd said something worth repeating. He pinched his mouth. "Except as far as I'm concerned, things just happen. One minute don't learn the next one nothin."

"I don't like that," he said, beginning to be sulky.

"Shit! If the only thing you can bear is just coming back to this little cut-off tit of nothing, somebody ought to tell you something, then." Robard raised his eyebrows to signify he was going to be the one to do it. "If you *did* really want to come down here to live, somewhere, you wouldn't choose this place, cause everything's trapped right here, and I'm positive you wouldn't recognize nothin else. Down in Jackson there ain't nothing but a bunch of empty lots and people flying around in Piper Comanches looking for some way to make theirselves rich. It wouldn't feel like nothin at all anymore, to *you.* Just cause you think up some question don't mean there's an answer."

"I heard that before," he said, trying to prise himself out of the jeep.

"You ought to have paid better attention, then," Robard said, and grabbed his arm and pushed him up and out.

"The old man's granddaughter says I ought to get in bed with her and fuck everything else." He walked a few feet down toward the lake.

"I ain't got no delusions about that myself," Robard said, and sucked his tooth. "You might just get accustomed to it. I never did think it was so bad, though."

"Don't you take some loss, then?"

"I don't know," Robard said. "I agree to cull what ain't possible and take what's left." He fingered a match out from behind his ear and, snapping off the head, gave him a quizzical look.

"So are you taking your own advice?" he said.

Robard pulled on his ear and pushed around in it with the match and threw the stump away. "I always do that," he said, and smiled. "I got somebody to kick then when it all turns to shit on me." Robard pushed the snake pedal and let the jeep jerk and kick over with a grunt and motioned him to crawl back in.

4

In the summer they were in Lake Charles, and in the lobby of the Bentley Hotel his mother took him to the fish pond and told him that in 1923 General Pershing had come and given a speech standing on the gold mosaic border of the pond, with men teeming in the lobby, smoking dark cigars. And in the street, troopers from Camp Polk had formed up in their lines to listen and be led by him back down the highway to the camp limits. The general spoke for a long time, his words being carried outside by loudspeakers, and when he walked out under the porte-cochere to assume his command, the men were mostly passed out from the heat, and some were sitting on the hot asphalt crying because they had let him down, and because they were sick to be at home.

5

On the sea wall at New Orleans there was a picture that his father took of him sitting with his mother on the white concrete wall, with Lake Pontchartrain behind them. And when the picture was taken his father came up, and they all sat on the wall facing the water and ate pralines. He had worn his brown tennis shoes and when he began to take them off to wade in the water, one of them fell in and went out of sight immediately. And his mother got him and held him so tight in the hot sun that he thought he would stop breathing.

6

When they got to the house Landrieu was just before setting foot onto the seat of an old wire-back drugstore chair planted below one of the concrete pillars that held the house up. He was clutching a spindled *Commercial Appeal* in one hand and what looked like a silver cigarette lighter in the other. Mr. Lamb was taking in the entire enterprise from a considerable distance, standing behind the hood of the little Willys, so that there was plenty of metal and space between him and whatever Landrieu was doing.

When he noticed Robard's jeep, the old man started waving his hands frantically. Robard cut it off and they got out and walked around until they could see Landrieu's face rising into the air with a look of profound uncertainty forging big clefts into the middle of his forehead. Mr. Lamb, ramparted behind the little Willys, was focusing his intensest interest on Landrieu, murmuring something unintelligible for being practically inaudible. Elinor was sitting in the seat of the Willys watching Landrieu silently.

Suddenly Landrieu achieved his full height on the chair seat, gave the lighter wheel a nervous flick, producing a large yellow flame which he aimed into the spindle of newspapers, and promptly rammed the quick-catching torch into the crux between the house and the pylon that held it up.

And all at once a great flurry of activity got centered on the area of the torch. In foisting his baton so ruthlessly into the hole, which no one could precisely see, Landrieu managed to disrupt his balance and propel himself backward off the chair, directly onto the ground, making an ugly *whump* sound like a bundle of newspapers dropped off the gate of a truck. And just as quickly the air around the joining got thick with flying insects, dropping out of various secondary holes and buzzing angrily, looking for the cause of all the heat. Mr. Lamb started yelling for Landrieu to clear out before the insects connected him with the fire and lit on him with a vengeance, but Landrieu was momentarily incapacitated. He had hit square on his tail bone and was lying with his arms stretched palms down, staring straight at the sky as if he were waiting for someone to ask him how he felt. Almost as many wasps were tumbling out of the area of the flames as were zizzing the air, and it seemed like considerable clumps were falling directly on Landrieu's stomach. One fat rust-colored wasp took a low pass by his face, but Landrieu seemed not to see him and the wasp flew back into the higher atmosphere.

Mr. Lamb had begun yelling, shouting profanities and threats at Landrieu as if he thought that could devil Landrieu into recovering faster. Above him, the burning paper torch was still creviced between the house and the piling. A small feather of flame had blossomed on the wood facing, and several small curls of gray smoke began to cloud through the worm holes, making more wasps fall out.

Landrieu apparently discovered the wasps on his stomach at the very moment of partially reclaiming his senses, and scrambled up and began slapping his chest, grabbing his neck, and punching in his hair as if he had discovered stinging wasps everywhere and couldn't get in touch with any of them.

"Looka there, son," Mr. Lamb said, removing his attention from Landrieu and pointing out the little scroll of smoke. "You done set my house afire."

Landrieu stopped slapping himself and stared upward at the involved portion of the house, as if he knew it was impossible for the house to be burning.

Mr. Lamb, however, was satisfied. He leaned against the fender of the Willys, twiddling with the latch on the hood, taking in the progress of the fire.

Robard suddenly appeared, sprinting down the steps of the house hauling Landrieu's metal pail, slopping water in fat gouts. He rushed past, eyes intent on the smoke, arrived at the bottom of the piling, drew back the bucket, and threw it in the middle of the flames, engrossing everything in a great sizzling expenditure of green smoke. Water began trickling back immediately and raining drops off the bottom of the house, and Robard stood back and scrutinized the nexus of smoke for any flames that might survive, and for a moment everyone was held in thrall.

All at once all attention was drawn irresistibly upward from the segment of blacked siding to the square window just above it, where Mrs. Lamb stood, frowning. She watched them all a moment, her PBX set clamped to her head like a medieval caliper compass, focusing immense private displeasure squarely on Mr. Lamb, who was utterly stunned. And then she was gone, as unpredictably as she'd appeared, and the window was returned to the dull, murky green color that showed a fragile, watery reflection of the trees.

"I'll be goddamned," Mr. Lamb observed, a childish smile broadening his face. "We almost burnt up *Mrs. Lamb.*"

Robard started around the house looking disagreeable. He set the bucket on the bottom step and started to the Gin Den. Landrieu commenced dragging his chair toward his little house, walking in a broken side-thrown limp understood to be the result of the fall. Mr. Lamb stood beside the jeep, observing everything, his little hands nested on the fender, the same witless smile on his lips as though there was something funny happening but he couldn't tell what it was.

Mr. Lamb turned the little smile around, and he knew the old man was just before bringing up the fishing trip. He took a fast look at the Gin Den, but Robard had disappeared, and the old man had him trapped. He wanted to let the moment slip away. He walked over beside Elinor, seated in the passenger's seat, gave her a tap on the head, and looked up at the still-smoking facet of outside wallboard.

"Landroo, you know," Mr. Lamb said thoughtfully, gazing at the ruined hoardings and sighing, "Landroo's the kind of man'd stand in a storm with a teaspoon to get a drink of water."

"I don't much like wasps myself," he said, keeping his eyes someplace else.

"Hell, no," the old man argued. "Nobody does in their right brain. But most of us can keep from getting stung without rupturing ourselves."

Mr. Lamb was counting Landrieu's misfortune as an incalculable pleasure, fostering a real withered admiration for Landrieu, who in all the years of slandering and threats had been tricky enough to stay put. It was a measure of his intelligence that he was still there to accept the abuse, since it wasn't so much abuse as an inverted form of sympathy, which Landrieu was savvy enough to recognize. And he himself didn't feel at all sure that he owned an intelligence half equal to it.

"Look here," Mr. Lamb said, very businesslike. "Ain't you and me supposed to go fishin?" His face was very alert, and full of purposes all having to do with the business of fishing.

It caught him off guard. The old man knew very well he didn't want to go and had tricked him and sprung it on him just at the moment he was thinking he wouldn't have to.

"I guess so," he said, turning back to the Willys.

"Then get your big ass in. If you can't go huntin turkeys, then you might as well catch a fish."

The old man started working the snake pedal with his toe until the motor concussed and the jeep broke forward abruptly without ever seeming to actually start, but just to be in motion spontaneously.

He flung his arm at Elinor, who climbed out, and he wedged

himself in the skimpy little iron seat while the jeep was moving, and got his legs stuffed inside the well.

"What about poles?" he said, looking wretchedly toward the underside of the house, where the poles were strung.

"The what?" the old man bellowed, the motor whanging intensely.

"Poles!"

"Shit on poles," the old man shouted, careening off toward the outhouse, getting both hands on either side of the wheel and seeming to lose control.

He grabbed onto the frame of the windshield to keep from being jarred loose.

"I like to telephone the fish," the old man said craftily, and motioned with his thumb to the back of the jeep at a little black metal box with a smooth wood-handled crank and two long half-stripped copper leads fastened to gold thumbscrews at either end.

"What is that?" he said. The road had reached the line of ashes and was quickly diving off the bank over a series of long narrow rain defiles that reached down a short bluff into a bottom. The jeep was pitching violently and the old man's eyes were intent.

"That there's my telephone," the old man yelled, and broke out in a raucous laugh, and the jeep almost went over on its side and he could actually feel the wheels leave the ground. The old man looked at him wide-eyed and laughed again.

The jeep ducked below the rim of the bank, and he looked back disconsolately at the house and saw Robard kneeling out in the dooryard to the Gin Den, changed into his green whipcord pants and his silk shirt with the arrow pockets, nuzzling Elinor's head and holding her collar to prevent her from running after the jeep. He had a feeling that when he got back from wherever he was going, some inexplicable place where you caught fish by telephone, Robard would be long gone, and it made him feel queer and almost angry. And he had the sudden insignificant urge to signal him somehow, to wave his hand up, but the jeep straggled down beneath the flat marly rim of the bluff, and he was gone, and there was no time even to get his hand off the frame of the glass and into the air.

At the foot of the bluff the road commenced out through a tall shadowy bottom where most of the big trees were dead or in a state of corruption, except for sprigs of green isolated in the barren crowns where the sunlight kept them alive. The roots had elbowed through the oaty ground, and the trunks had a pale brownish veneer banding the bark three feet off the ground, and there were no limbs on the larger trees nearer than thirty feet from the ground.

There was, too, an unanticipated air change in the bottom, a cool insularity and practically a solemnity, he felt, the high interlock of dead branches and higher foliage tangled and interwoven and causing the underneath to be protected and sequestered from the island proper.

The road the old man took was a road only in the sense that several other sets of cleated tires had passed on the ground and worked triangular gauge troughs in the mud, bearing straight off through the woods out farther than he could see at any one place.

The jeep was producing a lot of smoke and terrible strangling sounds that filled the bottom, and Mr. Lamb had retreated into the clamor and begun to look a little debilitated. In the mossy light his skin was pale and the blood pounded the artery in his forehead, percolating hotly back into his brain. His frame was bent over the wheel and his suspenders had luffed forward away from his chest as if nothing were inside them to hold on to.

All at once the old man hacked up a pocket of phlegm and spat it and gave him a tricky look as if something were tempting him to speak but he was intent on keeping it a secret until precisely the right moment when he'd spring it and startle everybody.

A woodpecker swooped out on one of the oaks and went walloping down the glimmer of trail, having a difficult time keeping its fat body aloft. Mr. Lamb watched the bird keenly as if he were making a mental note of it, then glanced at him again craftily as though there had been some import to the bird's flying the way it had that shouldn't have been missed. He went back to staring at the tracks when he got no response.

"Did you ever hear the story of the slaughterhouse goat?" Mr.

Lamb said, as if he were tired of his own moodiness and wanted to supplant it with some sort of scurrility.

"No," he said, wondering if there was some indignity waiting to be sprung on him in the old man's upcoming account.

The old man looked at him suspiciously to see if he could detect a trace of insincerity in his attitude toward the story he proposed to unfurl. He smiled back with as much earnestness as he could, and the old man lolled forward and seemed satisfied.

"This is true," the old man assured him over the gurgling of the jeep. He brought up another freightload of spit and loosed it out the side. "There was this here goat, you see, a handsome big billy with a fat white chinny beard." The old man motioned toward his own chin. "And they kept this old goat, you see, at the abattoir, to lead the sheeps and cows down the chutes to where they had stationed a big burly nigger with a sledge to hit 'em on the head and knock the shit out of them." He regarded him again keenly, his old wet eyes glistening in the flicker of sunlight, to see if he was appreciating everything the way it should be appreciated. "Sometimes, you see," he said, "one old sheep would commence to be suspicious when he started down the chute and take a notion he wasn't going. Maybe he had an inkling what was waiting for him. So right away the whole damn chute would pig up with a lot of noisy sheep or Hereford cows, and everything would be topsy-turvy, and somebody'd have to wade down in there amongst them to get 'em straightened out and flowing again. But if they had that goat there a-leading them, then everything just went out smooth as shit through a tin funnel, and sheep commenced dropping like ducks at a shooting gallery, and everybody was happy, including the goat, cause just before he got to the spot where the nigger did the braining, a little Houdini gate opened up on the side and the goat trotted off one direction, and the gate closed back real quick, and the sheep just went on another couple steps, and *boom!* the lights went out all over town. And the goat went back around to the garbage and had him a couple of soup cans before he had to be to work again. And you see, he was a feisty goat," the old man said. "He'd hike up on his

238

hind legs and eat the phone directory right off the stock manager's desk, eat up his fountain pens and his Dictaphone wires, paper clips, and everything. And then he'd turn right around and go lead another bunch of sheep down the chute to get poleaxed."

The character of the woods had gradually begun to shift lower, allowing some speckles of undiverted light to accumulate. The dead trees had begun to disappear and shumard saplings were clustered together, tightening the trail. He smelled the aroma of stagnation from no one place, though out ahead, where he couldn't see among the mesh of branches.

"So," the old man said, "it got to where there was some at the abattoir didn't particularly care for the goat, whose name was *Newel,* coincidentally." Mr. Lamb stole a mutinous look at him and quickly returned his eyes to the road. "Some thought that ole Newel was considerably too big for his britches by the way he acted, eating and chewing everything his eye fell on, then turning right around as calm as you please, and leading a whole passel of friendly sheep—who was, in some ways, kin to him in God's eye —to their eventual doom at the hands of that unerring nigger. So they gave some thought to letting him go on through the chute one day and having that colored gentleman poleax him along with the rest of the disposable livestock, figuring it would teach him a lesson he wouldn't forget. Except they couldn't get around the fact that they sorely needed the old bastard and didn't want to have to go to the pain of training up another goat to do what this goat already did fine—if he hadn't been so disagreeable." Two tiny wads of spit had begun waging a war for space in the corners of the old man's mouth, and had begun to interfere some with the way he opened his mouth. "So," he said, "they decided they'd play a trick on old Newel, thinking that that would cure him of being so uppity. So they went and got him and set him down in the chute in front of a whole big drove of sheep and opened the gate, and there, of course, old Newel went, with them sheep took in following him, like Moses leading the Jews. Except that when they all got to the little Houdini gate that usually opened up so old Newel could weasel out at the last minute, the little gate didn't open, and the force of them sheep coming down the incline shoved old Newel right into the face of that big sweaty nigger holding the bleeding sledge hammer. And quick as a flash he raised up that hammer and made like he was going to poleax Newel the same as he was any other sheep, and what do you think happened?" The old man's voice was hoarse from shouting and he peered out with his lips everted and his eyes illuminated while the jeep wallowed on out into the full sunlight.

"I don't know," he said, trying not to think about it at all, since he already knew it would have him as the brunt of it.

The old man looked at him intently, suds forming two prominent white anchors in the wedges of his mouth. "He had a heart attack and died," he shouted, a great sweeping grin overcoming his face and showcasing his teeth, waggling precariously out of his gums like a cracked porch beam. "Haw haw haw haw." The old man couldn't restrain himself any longer.

The jeep had suddenly lumbered out of the shumard saplings into the clear, and the old man had to stand straight up on the brake pedal to keep them from driving right on out into the water that opened all at once in either direction for a quarter of a mile, and stretched two hundred yards across into a plain of dead timber where the water simply phased out into the woods and spatterdocks, rather than coming to an end at the edge of an identifiable dirt bank.

Mr. Lamb looked completely bewildered. He was breathing forcefully and staring over the heeled nose of the Willys, his skinny brows clamped together, trying to factor out how it was he had almost run his jeep right into his own water and drowned himself in the process. For some reason, when he had started to drive, Mr. Lamb had removed his spectacles, and his eyes now looked flat and watery, and the little blisters where the pincers had fastened on his nose looked vile and scarlet as if he'd finally had to remove the glasses at the behest of a gigantic pain.

He looked and could see the old man's mind backtracking systematically toward whatever it was he had been involved in recounting before both of them were almost pitched off in the water for good.

"Oh, yeah," the old man said, the smile reviving. "So what do you think the morale of that story is about the goat named Newel?"

"I don't know," he said gloomily, resenting the old man for the whole story.

"The morale is," Mr. Lamb said, transforming his eyes into tiny peepholes of unrivaled significance, "a smart goat will always outrun a dead one." The old man's eyes suddenly snapped wide open, in imitation of the response he expected to see but didn't get. He just gazed at the old man expressionlessly to record his disapproval, and Mr. Lamb began to look suspicious and flare his nostrils hotly, irritated at not being congratulated for having brought his story to an instructive end.

"Grab the box," the old man snapped suddenly, clambering out the side of the jeep and marching off down the shingle toward where a green Traveler was beached on the baked dirt, harnessed to another red stump up from the edge of the water.

The sun, which was just sinking below a thick cusp of cloud, banked the surface of the lake and caught light in the fine spiderwebs hung on the water beyond where the old man was headed. The lake smelled hot and sweet, and there was no movement at all on the water, only the sound of a woodpecker back up the path, an empty *plock* that carried over the lake and dissipated into the floating woods beyond it.

He got down and lifted the black box which Mr. Lamb somehow planned to use as his telephone, and found it was very heavy, as though it contained unalloyed lead. He set it down, bound the loose copper leads around it once, grabbed it up, and shuffled toward the boat, which Mr. Lamb had managed to seesaw onto its side, letting the water slag off into the lake. The smell of the water seemed intensest when the wind was low, and each time the sun moved from behind the cloud and burned on the surface. The lake was long and cigar-shaped, and the water was the color of liver and looked thick and creamy. It was making him feel light-headed just to be there.

"Help me now, son," the old man said, letting the upended gunwale rock down and starting to give it a stern hoist toward the lake. His face instantly purpled and the artery in his forehead bulged like a snake. He had a panic, right then, that the old man might just explode if something wasn't put in his way fast.

"Lemme," he said, setting the box on the mud and quickly giving the gunwale one menacing jerk that wrenched it out of the mud and the old man's grasp and flung it halfway into the water.

Mr. Lamb simply stood back and looked at the boat and the distance it had cleared in one short flight, and muttered, "You gotta family to raise, son," and then hustled around and grabbed up the black box and made for the boat. "Now I'll get in and you push us off," the old man said, tiptoeing out over the seats and throning himself backward in the bow end so that his pants cuffs gapped six inches above his skinny ankles, while he pondered the effects of his tussle with the boat. "Get in, get in, Newel, god-damn it!" he shouted.

He dropped the painter rope in the well behind the seat, gave the boat another, less conspicuous heave, and the Traveler sagged out through the weeds and stobs of the shallows and coasted serenely into the open water, where the reflection of the sun dulled the surface and seemed to locate the light somewhere in the water itself.

Mr. Lamb straddled around on his seat and began making a meticulous survey of the west arm of the lake, a hand on his black box and another shading his eyes against the sun. He began to worry about just what the old man was going to do once he picked out whatever it was he was hunting for, and he wondered if it was going to be the cause for some more ranting and gyrating. He slumped silently in the weighted end of the boat, fingering the loom of the paddle and waiting for the old man to say what to do.

Mr. Lamb sat another minute in the shade of his hand without speaking and perused the bank as if he were waiting for something to identify itself and deliver up a potent sign.

Ahead, in the dreamy shallows on the north boundary of the lake, he could see a family of mud turtles sunning themselves along the high side of a half-submerged oak log, unperturbed by the commotion on the water. The woodpecker struck another *plock* back of where the boat had been fastened, and he sat motionless in the sunshine, fingering the warm tongue of the paddle, watching the old man's face twitching up and down the length of the slough, the boat drifting aimlessly west, pushed by the movement of stale air out of the woods. Mr. Lamb sat another minute, watching, for all he himself could tell, nothing at all. The old man had put on his spectacles and was staring intently along the bosky sides of the lake, until all at once he snapped his head around with a venomous leer and pointed toward where a hummock of mud and sticks had been heaped out of the water to make a fat gluey mound. "Row me right over to there," he said in a loud whisper.

"Where the mound is?" he said, attempting to point out the mound with the blade of the paddle.

The old man looked at him impatiently. "That there's a beaver house," he whispered, and fell into unwinding the copper wires from around the box and pressuring the little gold thumbscrews more securely into their terminals.

He began to try, as he shouldered the boat across toward the beaver mound, to feature what quirk of the cut-off process had caused the formation of the lake, which was probably, he felt, a twelfth the size of the lake they had come across with Gaspareau, and apparently completely stagnant. From the appearance of the water, the slough was kept active entirely by rain and by the floods that eddied up once a year, then receded, leaving the lake replenished with trapped water. He tried to recall if he had seen evidence of a lake on the aerial map, but could only remember the contour of the island, a large blotchy teardrop imprint, bounded by the river, but nothing else. It seemed possible that the picture had been taken when the lake was dry and the ground mossed over, though it seemed equally feasible that the old man had schemed and cajoled and managed to delete the lake from the picture by design, the same way he had scourged the entire island from the official map of the Corps of Engineers.

A few yards above the beaver house, he could make out a

number of white plastic jugs of the character used to contain antifreeze, floating bottom-up in a more or less circular pattern around another jug, which appeared to be impaled on a stob a foot and a half out of the water, the whole arrangement situated fifteen yards from the marshy beginnings of the woods.

"Right there," the old man whispered, pointing at the impaled jug and the four others circling it. "Row me to that boy there."

Mr. Lamb raised the box and resituated it on the well between his feet and smiled at him over his shoulder.

"What is that?" he said, jiving the paddle until he could feel the bottom seize on the blade.

"Huh?" the old man said, not hearing him right and directing his good ear around into better line with the sound.

"What is all that?" he said.

"That's Landroo's fish feeder," the old man said, snorting as if the idea of a fish feeder were perfectly ludicrous.

"What does it do?" he said, worrying some of the cold marl off the blade with his fingers and getting a potent smell of the bottom, which was foul and smoking and made his stomach heave. He pushed the paddle back quickly and splashed his fingers in the eddies.

"You see," Mr. Lamb whispered, "Landroo's a cane-pole fisherman, like any upstanding nigger would be. And back up behind his little house, he's got him what appears to be a toolbox built, with a hinged door over the top of it. Except it ain't a toolbox at all." He stopped and studied the white jugs as they slid toward him, as though he felt he'd explained the feeder as much as it needed explaining.

"But what the hell is it?" he said, hauling up another annoying bolus of blue smoking gunk and slapping it back in the water stoutly.

"What?" the old man said, frowning, having forgotten the conversation entirely and become reengrossed in stealthing up on the jugs.

"The box," he said, raising his voice. "The hinge box at Landrieu's house."

"That thing," the old man said, as if it were a perennial joke.

244

"That's his worm farm and his cricket farm and his roach farm, and his everywhateverelse kind of farm." He snorted. "That's one reason Landroo never cared much for John Carter, that and all the Cain Johnny raised over there in Stovall at their baseball. John was always getting Landroo's crickets and throwing them in the fire, and Landroo didn't like that cause he bought them crickets in Helena and paid money for the buggers, then old Johnny would come along and toss a bunch in the fire and sit there and listen at them pop, and that'd be old Landroo's money poppin. And it made Landroo mad as hell, don't think it didn't." The old man began tampering with the box as if he were planning to spring it into action momentarily and wanted to have it in a state of absolute readiness. The boat was making a way imperiously, closer in to the bank now than to the jugs or the beaver lodge. "Anyway," Mr. Lamb said, distracted momentarily by his box, to which he administered a tentative crank with the wooden handle on its side. "Anyway, anyway, Landroo likes to fish with all his worms and roaches and doodads, except he don't like to spend all day out in the hot sun. So he went out and got him a regular lath peach crate and filled it up with sweet hay and tied it up with baling wire, and took it all and tied him some sash weights to it and hauled it out here and dropped it where that middlest boy is, and rigged him up floats out of them Prestone jugs, and glommed a bunch of worms and roaches and crickets on a treble hook and knotted one to each of them jugs and set 'em out beside his hay bale, and them fish can't hardly wait to get hooked up. And he'll come out here every two or three days and paddle over here and check his 'trotlines'—that's what he calls them, though they ain't true trotlines in any sense."

He began to think that if there were already fish hooked and waiting to be pulled up on Landrieu's fish trap, why was it necessary to do anything more than get them out and go home, and forget about doing any telephoning, whatever that was. He looked at the back of the old man's head for a long moment.

"Why can't we just borrow a couple of Landrieu's fish?" he said, frowning up at the floating jugs.

"Cause they ain't ours," the old man snapped, and bent his

head around and looked at him in surprise. "I'll tell you, though," he said, smiling strangely, "Landroo's a comical old coon. When he comes out here, he won't go right to where them jugs are at. He'll rig him up a cane pole and take a bunch of whatever he likes that day, worms or roaches or whatever's he got in his 'farm,' and start down there in them dead falls and nigger all the way up to here." The old man grinned at him in amazement as if Landrieu were a living mystery to match all mysteries, never divining Landrieu might take some considerable pleasure in the leisurely divertissement of fishing, before he got down to the actual business of taking in the fish. "He likes to go down there and just sit a long time, watching them spatterdocks," the old man said, grinning to prove he faithfully liked Landrieu, but was entitled to exercise his private jurisdiction as Landrieu's chief critic and adviser. He got himself almost completely turned around, his eyes big and round and his face turned red. "And he says to me, 'And all at onct then, Mr. Mark, them crappies commences to hist straight up in the air snatching them little skeeters off them pads and making all kinds of noise, ah-sha-sha-sha-ah-sha-sha-sha, boiling that water like two hogs on a mudhole.' And I said to him, 'Well, what did you do then, Landroo?' And he said, real sheepish, 'Oh, Mr. Mark, I just eased on in there real sweet with my boat and laid my little gob of worms on top of one of them pads and one of them big suckers snatched that hook off there like God snatching back a palsied baby.' " The old man was thoroughly regaled by his own story. "But I'll tell you," he wheezed, "Landroo might be a real fisherman, but I had to carry him to Helena one evening with a treble hook in his forehead, bout stuck clear to his brain. One of them big crappies took a swipe at his worm on one of them lily pads, and Landroo got excited and jerked the thing back too quick and it hit him in the head like a roofing nail. And the son-of-a-bitch wouldn't let me touch it. I said, 'Landroo, I'll get a pair of needle-nose pliers and have it out in two shakes.' And he said, 'No, suh, take me to the emergency room.' " Mr. Lamb looked at him, gravely questioning Landrieu's far-reaching concept of an emergency. The old man turned and eyed the beaver house as it slid by the boat.

As soon as the boat slipped past the beaver house, Mr. Lamb held his finger to his lips and waved his other hand to signify he ought to quit paddling now and let the boat propel itself toward the jugs.

He watched the beaver house ease by, wondering if there were beavers sitting around inside or if they had heard the howling and shouting and made a fast exit. He scanned up the vestige of submerged bank, thinking he'd see a big beaver hurrying off into the denser woods, but he saw only a fat sparrow twitting and sputtering in a jungle of dead boxberries, creating a racket with his wings as though he had gotten inside the bush by misadventure and now frantically couldn't figure how to get out.

Mr. Lamb gave the sparrow a grieved look and swiveled on his seat and drew the black box closer between his legs, holding both lead wires in one hand, and deliberately began cranking the handle. The boat began to sidle slightly, taking more of a broadside approach to the jugs than a nose-first approach. All the turtles lined along the limb of the deadfall began craning their necks to find out what was going on, though none of them seemed to think enough of the commotion to move from where they were. One finally became uneasy and wobbled to the opposite end of the log, but Mr. Lamb didn't notice and none of the turtles seemed to want to leave for the bottom just yet. He stayed as still as he could in the back of the boat, the sun shining on the crown of his head, and let the paddle lie across his thighs so that it dripped back into the slough.

Mr. Lamb gave the box several more rigorous cranks, then separated the twin wires to each hand, holding each by its rubber sleeve that had been stripped ten inches from the tip.

When the boat finally drifted by the first of the encircling jugs and sliced into the middle water, Mr. Lamb turned and gave an inflamed look and in a loud stage whisper that made the one nervous turtle dive for the bottom, said, "I'm just going to make a local call." The old man's eyes squeezed together as if he could barely keep back the heaves, and he promptly jammed both wire ends over the side and into the water like an old picador administering the pic to a motionless bull.

And the total effect was nothing.

Both of them peered at the water, anticipating something unforeseen to happen, but nothing did. He expected the current traversing the plus-to-minus terminals to get shorted through the boat and deal them both a sound shock. But instead he felt nothing, though he experienced a strange thrill when he saw the old man's eyes and had tightened his ass in case the box was wound up a lot tighter than he thought.

Mr. Lamb, however, had clearly reckoned on something formidable. He glared at the water, the two discharged wires dangling from his hands, searching the surface fiercely as if he expected the surface to get suddenly thick with stunned fish. But the water stayed the same. The turtle came climbing slowly out and strained along the spine of the log and found itself a suitable location and began to take in whatever else was going on.

The old man turned and scowled back at him, as if he were personally responsible for the sabotaging, then jabbed the cords back in the water and waggled them as if he were hoping to attract whatever fish were in the area of the hay crate near the surface so he could spear them. "Shit," the old man said, again employing the stage whisper and staring at the ends of the wires. "It ain't a good day to fish." He turned and gave him another belligerent look and started cranking at the box again, the two inert leads squeezed side by side in his left fist.

This time Mr. Lamb cranked a much longer time. The boat sidled in until it gently tapped the impaled jug, then sat silently in the slack water. He kept his paddle across his thighs and patted his warming crown, and watched the old man get redder behind the ears the longer he cranked the telephone. Mr. Lamb turned and fired back another irritated look while whirring the crank, and he recognized the look then as the face of dead-out desperation, frozen on the old man's face as a fierce grimace which would not relent. Mr. Lamb looked at him with the expression of a man trying to pump air into a blown-out tire while staring enigmatically into the face of someone holding an ice pick. It was, he thought, the look of unrecognized betrayal.

The boat, with the old man's increasing gyrations to perturb it, began to waffle precariously and send lap waves heaving under the jugs, causing them to strain against their string anchors, and making him get a grip on the gunwales and begin inspecting the timber for a place to cling when the boat eventually swamped. Waves were licking up into the trees and rising under the deadfall where the turtles were sitting silently, staring back at the boat. He felt now he should do something to save them.

All at once Mr. Lamb stopped cranking, his ears grown scarlet, and sweat thickening the collar of his flannel shirt. The old man turned and gave him a defiant look, then grabbed for the wires in his other hand as if someone else were holding them out to him and had placed them just an inch out of his reach, so that by some miscalculation he grabbed onto both spiky ends at once and discharged the entire stored-up quotient of telephonic electricity directly into his body.

"Oops," the old man said in an obvious surprise, and threw up both his hands, dropping the cords into the water and pitching straight over backward into the middle of the boat, making a loud whumping sound on the chinky curvature of his spine, his eyes wide open as if he were about to instigate another imitation of Landrieu but had somehow gotten sidetracked. He did not hit his head. The rocker effect of his spinal curve mediated the blow so that his head only lightly touched the slatted bottom of the boat the way an acrobat's head passingly touches the mat at the start of a somersault. His skinny ankles stayed draped over the front of the forward seat on either side of the box, and his arms flailed out to the sides partially over the gunwales. He stared at the old man for a moment, his paddle still laddered over his thighs, expecting him to jump up and start cursing. But once down, the old man didn't move again.

He crouched forward on his knees, losing the paddle, and sending the boat into even greater flailing gyrations. He pressed both his hands against the old man's cheeks, which were warm and sentient, though his eyes were open and unblinking and his chest was relaxed. He stared into the old man's face, welled in between his thighs, and yelled at him so that a tiny flower of spittle sprouted on the old man's cheek and began to slide toward his ear.

"Mr. Lamb!" he yelled, his voice careening through the rank woods and disappearing. "Mr. Lamb!" he shouted, as if the old man were at the opposite end of the lake and could not hear him.

The old man's blurry eyes turned pale and glaucous and his face became famished, the color of the sky. He sat back and stared at the face, shaded in the thick well of his thighs, until the adroitness of the old man's death refrigerated his own insides and left him with a very businesslike feeling of needing to act efficiently and without excess of energy, and to become as unquestioningly useful as he could to anyone within a hundred miles. He pressed his hands again onto the old man's cheeks and found that they were warm, but less warm than before, which seemed to him more or less correct. The idea crept into his thinking that perhaps in the fraction of a second between the time the old man had completed the circuit of the telephone and the time his eyes had frozen open staring straight up at the sky, his face becoming white as sugar, then gray, *he* could have done something, could have sealed his mouth over Mr. Lamb's and blown for all he was worth and inflated his cavernous old lungs and started his heart to thumping by the simple gale force of all his own lung power concentrated inside the old man. But then, he felt assuredly, there simply hadn't been the time. A year ago he had sat in Beebe's apartment on Astor Place and watched a football player die of heart failure, draped over the thirty-five-yard line, and later the announcers declared the player was dead before he hit the ground, maybe even in the locker room hours before. If this was so, he supposed, the boat still teetering under him causing the old man's face to wag back and forth against his knees, then this old man was dead before he even got in the boat, since nothing could've worked such a devastation on him in so short a time, unless it had gotten started some time earlier. And without divine prescience of whatever it was starting, he had been helpless to assist the old man at all.

His back began to tighten and his knees began to strain against the ribs of the boat. He sat back and rubbed the furrow in his forehead for a long time and gauged his own breathing. The old man looked thin as paper, his temples sunken considerably, and absolutely ridiculous lying in the floor with the mallards flying off his collar and his yellow suspenders gapped above his shoulders as if they had been made for a much taller man. He reached down between his legs and mashed his eyelids down and noticed how simple and unspectacular a matter it was to do that, since the lids closed willingly and stayed shut without the slightest effort, as if there were no difference in being closed and open. Though the old man looked unmistakably dead now, and the businesslike impulse rose in him again, and he reached for the stob where Landrieu had impaled the white jug, threw the jug off, and pulled the boat over to where the paddle had floated. With the paddle he piloted the boat over to a patch of quavery ground, got out and towed the boat up partially, took off his shirt and draped it over the old man's face. He scanned the cluttered end of the lake and saw nothing. The turtles had departed the deadfall, and the lake was empty and somnolent. The sun was forty-five degrees off the top of the woods, shining out from behind a long peninsula of crusted clouds. There was the smell of rain mingled with the rank scent of the water, and with his shirt off he felt the breeze slide against his stomach, causing his flesh to run up into the hollow of his ribs, and he rubbed himself and turned toward the sun and tried to let it warm him, but it wouldn't.

He pulled the old man's arms off the gunwales and fixed them at his sides. He lifted his skinny ankles off the bow seat, folded his legs in such a fashion that his knees listed against the sides, and put the black box by his feet for support. He grabbed the bow handle of the boat and pushed off back into the lake, letting the boat scrape through the shallow grasses, perched on the narrow bow on his knees, poling the boat farther and farther into the lake until he could no longer touch the marly bottom with the blade and until the boat, with the old man down in the broad flat end, rose out of the water like a gondola cruising some still and rancid waterway, and he the fat and efficient and shirtless gondolier.

7

In Jackson, Mississippi, in 1953, his father brought him downtown and left him in the lobby of the King Edward Hotel while he went away to the mezzanine to talk to a man about selling starch in Alabama. His mother was home in bed and too sick to watch him, so he sat in the lobby and watched the men standing against the fat pillars smoking cigars and shaking hands for minutes at a time. In a little while a midget came into the lobby wearing cowboy boots and a Texas hat, and attracted everyone's attention as he signed his name to the register and gave the bellboy a tip before he ever touched a bag. When he was ready to go to his room, the midget turned and looked around the pillared lobby into the alcoves and foyers as if he were looking for someone to meet him. And when he saw the boy sitting on the long couch, he came across in his midget's gait that made him look as if he were wearing diapers, and told the boy that his name was Tex Arkana, and that he was in the movies and had been the midget in Samson and Delilah *and had been one of the Philistines that Samson had killed with the jawbone of a mule. He said he had seen the movie and remembered the midget fairly well. The midget said that in his bags he had all his movie photos and a long scrapbook with his newspaper clippings which he would be glad to show him if he cared to see. Most of the men in the lobby were watching the two of them sitting on the couch talking, and the midget kept watching them and talking faster. When the boy said he would care to see the scrapbook and the photos, too, the midget got up and the two of them got on the elevator with the bellboy and went to the midget's new room, which faced the street. When the bellboy had left, the midget took off his shirt and sat on the floor in his undershirt and opened the suitcase and went jerking through the clothes looking for the book while the boy sat on the chair and watched. In a little while the midget found the broad wooden-sided book and jumped on the bed, his cowboy boots dangling against the skirts, and showed the boy pictures of himself in* Samson and Delilah *and in* Never Too Soon *and in a movie with* John Garfield *and* Fred Astaire. *There were pictures of the midget in the circus riding elephants and sitting on top of tigers and standing beside tall men under tents and in the laps of several different fat women who were all laughing. When they had looked at all the pictures and all the clippings, the midget said that he was sleepy after a long plane ride from the west coast and that the boy would have to go so he could go to sleep. The boy shook hands with the midget and the midget gave him an autographed picture of himself standing on a jeweled chariot with a long whip, being pulled by a team of normal-sized men. And the boy left.*

When he came back to the lobby his father was waiting for him, smoking a cigar, and he showed him the picture of the midget in the chariot, and his father became upset and tore up the picture, and went to the glassed-in office beside the front desk and had a long talk with the manager while the boy waited outside. In a while his father came out and the two of them went home where his mother was sick. And late in the night he could hear his mother and father talking about the picture and about the midget with the cowboy boots on, and he heard his father say that the manager had refused to have the midget thrown out of the hotel, and in a little while he could hear his mother crying.

PART VII

Robard Hewes

1

He stood between the house and the Gin Den viewing the sky skeptically. Long purple flathead clouds were sizing up and the air had moistened and cooled and felt electric. There was the sense now, though not the sound, of thunder and it unsettled the air and made him feel that he wasn't going to get across before it all broke down. There was silence on the island, and for a while he wandered back between the shed and the house steps, anticipating the old man and Newel, watching the sky.

He needed to get her shunted off to some motel since there wasn't any way he could take the time to go to Memphis now. Just get in the room, he thought, with the lights off, and get her to work her trick and be done with it without ever leaving town.

And it wasn't only that. He took a seat on the low rise of the step and watched the chalky sun being scrubbed out by the storm. The color of the sky was being altered on the minute, becoming more bruised and complicated every time he looked up. But the wind was low, and he figured the rain would hold off and come in when the wind was ready.

The real snake was two-headed. One, that any more time spent going through the motions with Beuna might be just enough to push it all over with Jackie, so that he'd arrive at an empty house without so much as a pencil pointed in the right direction—which would be ruinous, pure and simple, though he'd estimated that disaster, or thought he had, before he took the chance, and couldn't complain if that's what he picked.

The other head was that he didn't feel so good about Newel claiming to see whatever he saw, though it was only a word in a million, and it might be anything, but probably was something, since he had little premonitions for it. It made him itchy.

Mrs. Lamb stepped to the edge of the steps and consulted the thermometer-barometer nailed to the porch stud. She held her glasses forward with her hand and peered up through them, then stared at the sky as if corroborating the opinion of the gauges. He looked up and saw her hair was flatted against her head and her eyes looked unrested. He stood up to walk back to the Gin Den.

"It's smotherin," she said, as if she had just seen the center of the turmoil and could do nothing about it.

"Yes ma'am," he said.

"He loves smotherin days," she said calmly. "He'll just stay to dark if it don't rain, if the other man don't turn the boat over."

He looked at his jeep as though it had just arrived, then looked down the car path to where it disappeared into the bottom. "Hope he don't," he said.

"Decamping?" she said.

"Yes'm."

"And where is it you're going again?"

"California," he said, standing out in the grass. "My wife's out there."

"What are you going to do?" she said, passing time.

"Go to work," he said. "Construction. That kind."

"You're not going to bring her back?"

"No'm," he said, resting his toe against the step, watching her.

Mrs. Lamb elevated her chin as if she were catching some scent on the air and was diverted from the conversation. "Well," she said, "come and go."

"Yes ma'am," he said.

She regarded him a moment majestically, then went back inside.

It occurred to him just as she was letting the door to that he could have asked her to pay him, gotten off the island while there was light and no rain, and made it to Helena before it was dark, where he'd feel better. But she closed the door and there was no chance now of reopening the conversation on the subject of wages, even though he knew she was in charge of disbursals, and once the old man arrived he would just have to go back and get it from wherever she had it squirreled away.

He walked across the yard to the Gin Den. Landrieu had limped into his house and not emerged. The puppy had sprung after the little jeep, but in a little while come back and gone to sleep under the steps. And there had been nothing since then but waiting. He took out the postcard and gave it a reappraisal. The laughing man in the sepia glimmer of daylight amused him. If he had a pencil, he thought, he'd write, "Be to home—Robard," and stick it in the first chute he came to. And that might keep her until he got home again, some kind of promise.

The wind began to post off the lake. He could see the sock sprung out in the airfield, the funnel showing east. The clouds had blackened and were revolving fast and moving the air in different directions through the trees and under the house. Elinor woke, winded, and relocated herself behind one of the pilings.

In the woods he began to hear the sputter of the Willys, and walked out behind the Gin Den to watch for them, the wind flooding his satin shirt, making it cold down his back.

All he could see at first were Newel's bare shoulders buckled over the wheel as if he were forcing the jeep toward the house with the strength in his arms. As they came nearer he could see Newel's face fixed in an odd, exasperated expression he hadn't seen before, as if Newel had left the old man in disgust and come in by himself. Though finally he could make out the old man's feet, nylon socks rolled over his ankles, hung side by side across the gate like two sides to a stepladder. And there wasn't any urgency. Newel drove the jeep to where he stood, gave him the same exasperated look, and slumped backward in the seat.

He looked over the sill and saw Newel's blue shirt draped over the old man's face. Mr. Lamb's body seemed skinny, his wrists and ankles turned blue in the time it took to cart him back to the house. He had a keen urge to take a look, but looked up instead at the window and saw the glass was the color of swamp water and couldn't be sure Mrs. Lamb wasn't looking and would see the old man before she was ready.

The wind whipped under the jeep and tumbled out on the yard, making Newel grimace and get goose-pimply.

"What the hell happened to him?" he said.

"The old fart electrocuted himself," Newel said, and rubbed his hands together under the wheel. "Monkeying with his god-damned box and the first thing I knew he'd grabbed the wires and knocked over. He said oops."

"Said what?"

"Ooops." Newel smiled pathetically.

He took an unhappy look at the window. "I'll get the nigger. Get him behind the shed."

He trotted with the wind behind him to Landrieu's house and went straight inside. Landrieu was perched on the edge of his bed watching an enormous television set, and gave him a look of irreconcilable outrage, as if it were beyond all his comprehension anyone should tread into his one good safe place.

"Whatchyouwant?" Landrieu said, clenching the corners of the bedspread as if he wanted to pull the bed in on top of him. Over the bed was a large photograph of Landrieu, much younger, wearing a baseball uniform and smiling.

"He's dead," he said loudly, stepping out of the wind, getting a whiff of Landrieu's room, which was warm and smelled like rancid bacon grease. The television was on too loud.

"Who is?" Landrieu stood erectly and tried to see past him through the door.

"Mr. Lamb," he said over the TV, breathing the unhealthy air. "You gotta catch the old lady before she has a hissy fit." The wind kicked the door out of his hand and slammed it against the wall.

Landrieu got very grave. His left eye closed and his cheeks thickened. "Where he at?" he said, still trying to lean toward the door.

"In the goddamn jeep." He stepped out of the way so Landrieu could see where Newel had pulled the jeep around the Gin Den. Landrieu took a careful step to the door, looked out, saw nothing, then marched straight into the yard, stuffing his shirt down in his coveralls and sniffing. He walked across to the back of the jeep, reached in, and yanked the shirt off Mr. Lamb's head as if he expected the old man to pop up howling and was just going to go along with the foolishness. But the moment he saw the old man's face, his nostrils flared and he stood back and looked gray. The wind came up stiffly. Landrieu's hair shifted to the side of his head like a hunk of sponge, and he took another step backward and almost fell over his feet.

"What done happened to him?" Landrieu smiled queerly as if still not positive it wasn't a joke. His big television was blasting out into the yard.

"He took a collect call," Newel said irritably, and jerked the shirt out of Landrieu's hand and put it back on the old man's face. "Get on inside and tell Mrs. Lamb. We'll carry him in quick as you tell her."

Landrieu eyed them both, then the old man and the black box, which Newel had put in the back beside him, and tried to figure out just how duties were being assigned. "*Who* gon' tell her?"

"You," he said, wishing Landrieu would just go on. "*We* can't tell her."

Landrieu glared at him, hiked up his coveralls, and started legging it toward the house without another word, limping stiffly on his right leg. Halfway up the stairs, he stopped and looked back at them, then disappeared.

Newel leaned against the jeep, crossed his arms over his bare chest, and rubbed at his eyes, his flesh rigid in the wind.

Across the airstrip it was raining, like smoke creeping out of the woods. Behind it, the greenish sunlight narrowed the gap against the curve of the earth. The air smelled strong. He wondered just how long it was going to take the rain to cross the field and reach them.

He looked at Newel, then thought a moment. "What was it you said about my eyes? Something ignorant, I remember."

"I forgot," Newel said, looking away.

"No you didn't neither," he said. He bit up a tiny piece of his lip.

"You gettin worried?" Newel smiled at him.

"Screw yourself," he said, and stalked inside the Gin Den and let the door spring out in the wind. He sat on the edge of the bed and watched Newel through the open door and wished he'd never seen him.

Newel walked inside the doorway and leaned against the jamb and looked out. "I said there was something grieved about you." The wind had begun to keen in the joints, and the tin seemed to expand as if it wanted to explode. "Grieved might not be the right word," Newel said, wagging the back of his head against the chase. "Heartbroken might be."

"Nothin ain't broke my heart," he said, staring at the points of his boots, wishing Newel would disappear.

"I don't know," Newel said. "You know more about it than I do." He walked off from the doorway.

"I sure as hell do," he said loudly, trying to decipher just what there could be to break his heart.

Landrieu limped down off the porch, eyes big as buttons, arriving out of breath, hiking at his coveralls and looking up at the house nervously. "She comin," he said, and immediately made for the other side of the jeep and established himself so he could watch the screen door and the old man's body at the same time.

Mrs. Lamb came down into the wind wrapped in a black afghan, her hair strewn around her head and her mouth bent into a look of anger. She strode across the yard, acknowledging no one, and walked to the edge of the jeep and peered down. She looked at Mr. Lamb from one end to the other, studying him as if she wanted to be sure all his parts were there. When she wanted to look at his face she motioned to Landrieu, and he lifted the shirt off and the old lady regarded her husband even more carefully, without speaking to anyone. Her complexion seemed slowly to be losing its olive color, and the set of her mouth hardened as though interior shifts were taking place she herself didn't know about but which had already corrected her outlook toward the rest of the world.

She stood back, girding herself in the afghan, appearing dark and immense, so he wasn't sure if under different circumstances he could have ever identified her as a woman. She eyed both him and Newel, as if for a moment she couldn't tell who was who, then settled her eyes on Newel, who was standing half naked in the wind.

"What has happened to Mark?" she said, a tremble in her voice that he thought sounded more like anger than anything else. The wind was blowing sticks and field debris across the yard and dislodging her hair more and more.

"I think," Newel said, shifting off one foot to the other and keeping his bare chest covered with his arms, "he electrocuted himself." He tilted his head faintly toward the old man's telephone.

She regarded the box indignantly, then back at Newel. "And you were there?" she said.

"Yes ma'am," Newel said. "In the boat, and, ah, Mr. Lamb had the box up front and he just grabbed two wire ends by accident and fell backward. I don't think he took a breath." Newel lowered his head and looked out the tops of his eyebrows.

Mrs. Lamb pinched her mouth and considered that awhile. "So he didn't say a word?"

"No ma'am," Newel said. "Wasn't time for him to." He snapped his fingers softly.

The trees in the belt of gumwoods where the old man had been hunting were woven together, bending toward the house. Branches were breaking off and dragging across the dooryard. The charge of rain set up in his nostrils and he could hear the thunder, like buildings falling in.

"And he said nothing at all?"

"No ma'am," Newel said, rubbing his arms.

Landrieu secretly relaid the shirt on Mr. Lamb's face and tucked it under his head and backed off.

"T.V.A.," Mrs. Lamb said, glancing at him before he'd even gotten reestablished. "Bring in Mr. Lamb, go and call Rupert Knox in Helena, say Mr. Lamb has passed away suddenly, then come back to me."

She turned aside, paused, and regarded them both, the Gin Den bracking and buckling in the wind. "You men may go along," she said imperiously, and was gone, rebinding her shoulders in the tails of her afghan, bending her head into the gale.

Landrieu frowned at the cold remains of Mr. Lamb, then frowned at the distance between himself and the first thicket of catalpa woods he would have to cross in order to reach the lake, and set his mind to working on a way out.

Landrieu watched Mrs. Lamb into the house, then turned his attention to him and Newel. "How I supposed to get him in that house, then me across that lake with all this?" Landrieu said, his eyes roaming grievously into the storm, then back at the two of them, awaiting an answer.

"Come on," he said, and grabbed Mr. Lamb's heels and waited for Landrieu to take hold of his shoulders. Newel shoveled in under the old man's back, and the three of them put him up and ran with him across the yard and up the stairs just as the first drops hit the grass and popped the Gin Den roof.

They angled the old man through the kitchen, straight to the back, where the room was dark and warm. Mrs. Lamb had set up a vigilance in a chair beside the two-poster bed and had spread the afghan on top of the covers for the old man to lie on.

When they had him situated, there was a moment in the room when they all stood still and looked at nothing but Mr. Lamb as though they were surprised to find him in that state and wished the world he would relent and get up. He felt like the three of them were filling up every available inch of the room, breathing and squeezing the boards, straining the plaster on the walls. And he wanted out.

"Landrieu," Mrs. Lamb said, and shut her eyes.

Landrieu's mouth gaped as if he was scandalized to be discovered anywhere near where he was. "Yes'm," he said, casting an evil eye at him and Newel and a quick one at the old man.

"Call Rupert Knox now."

"Yes'm," Landrieu grunted. He took a long backward stride and was gone, Newel behind him.

"Mr. Hewes," she said with the same lasting patience, her face back out of the light.

Mr. Lamb's mouth came open several inches and stopped.

"Ma'am," he said.

"Your wages are put on the supper table. Mark would've been grateful for your loyalty. Leave his pistol in the Gin Den."

"Yes'm," he whispered, and could see her face then in her own darkness. "Mrs. Lamb, I'm sorry about him," he said. He could hear Newel and Landrieu tromping down the porch steps into the heart of the storm.

"He slept on the right end of the bed last night," she said, bemused.

"Yes ma'am."

"When it got spring, Mark always slept with his head to the foot. He thought it equalized his body's pressures. And when I woke up this morning he was sleeping with his head next to mine, and I said, 'Mark, why are you sleeping to my end?' And he said, 'Because I went to bed thinking I was going to die, and I didn't want to be turned around like a fool. I had a feeling my heart was going to stop.' And I suppose it did. I've spent the day getting myself ready, and now I am."

"Yes ma'am," he said, looking around into the shadows, unable to make out the wallpaper. "I'm sorry about him," he said.

"Not as much as I am, Mr. Hewes," she said.

And he had to go that instant. He took a step through the dining room, grabbed up the money envelope, stapled and neatly written on in pencil, and headed out into the rain, thinking about situations that draw you in and wring you like a rag, and let you go in the rain when the use was out of you and you weren't good for anything.

265

2

Landrieu limped to the Gin Den wearing his yellow raincoat, inside of which his face looked cold as the night. He poked his head in the doorway and announced he was ready to go.

He got his gun from under the seat, laid it in the middle of the bed, put on his slicker, and stood in the door while Newel dredged up an old paint tarpaulin and draped it over his shoulders, then the three of them took off in the jeep with Landrieu driving and Newel humped in the front, scowling.

When they got to the overlook, Landrieu paid the lake a menacing look. The water was swelling and the camp was invisible, and through the rain he could see only indentations of shore willows.

Landrieu untied the Traveler, and the two of them sledded it into the water. Landrieu hauled the little All State out of the brush from under an anhydrous ammonia sack, and screwed it on the transom. He then started pinching the bubble and spinning the crank, and staring at the lake as if he were watching a vision of his own calamity.

"Push 'em off," Landrieu shouted meanly, installing himself in the bow. And they heaved until the boat rode out of the mud and came under power. Newel hulked in under his canvas at the middle of the boat, rain skating his cheeks and wetting his pants. They both faced Landrieu, who kept looking at them malignantly, as if they were undercutting his ability to pilot the boat by simply being there, and when the bow slipped clear of the timber, he whipped the rudder bar to the side and spun the boat into the wind, knocking Newel flat off onto the floor.

"What about the old lady!" Newel shouted when he'd gotten back on the bench. The slap of the water was getting fierce, like metal tearing on the boat's underside.

"I'd rather leave her as leave me!" he shouted, and Newel made

266

a sour mouth and disappeared in the canvas.

When they got where the dock was visible, the boat had collected two inches of active water and was low enough in the channel that the motor scudded bottom and kicked out suddenly with a whang that shocked Landrieu and almost rocketed him off his seat. He looked puzzled a moment, then motioned Newel out of the boat to wade. Newel crouched lower, shook his head, and pointed on to the dock. Landrieu looked reviled and whipped off down the lake sixty yards and veered back in and approached the dock from upchannel, easing the boat expertly against the swell, baffling the truck tires and cutting the motor.

He got out, tied the painter, and with Landrieu limping out ahead, started toward Gaspareau's, where there was a light in the front room.

He let Landrieu struggle on while he slid inside the truck and got a cigarette. Newel got in beside him, letting the tarpaulin stand in the rain.

"Where're you going?" Newel said, gumming his face with his hands and wiping them on his tweed jacket.

He blew smoke at the windshield and watched it hang on the glass. "Motel," he said.

"Going to see your sweetie?" Newel said, leering.

"Man." He let the cigarette dangle off his lip while he wrestled his slicker off and stuffed it behind the seat. "Why don't you turn me loose?" He felt in his pocket to be sure the card hadn't gotten soaked, then sat back and hitched his knees against the dash.

"I've got a feeling you're fucking up," Newel said, widening his eyes to see better.

"Where're you going?" he said.

"Chicago."

"I ain't going that far. I'll carry you to the store."

Newel nodded and looked wretched.

"You going to be one of them big-time shysters makes a lot of money?" He fished his key out and put it in the truck.

"That's about it."

"If I had the money I'd buy me a new truck."

"You going to put on your license plate?" Newel said.

"One'll hold me," he said.

"It's none of my business," Newel said.

"Maybe we can get to the highway without you changin your mind." He cranked the truck and watched the gauges climb.

"One thing," Newel said earnestly. "You don't really think the best way to solve a problem is just forget about it, do you?" Newel peered at him, his face shiny and smooth.

Rain hammered the truck. He turned on the wipers and cleared out a path where he could just see Gaspareau standing on the porch conversing with Landrieu, who was out in the rain in his yellows. He looked at Newel. "If you're to where there ain't nothing else, it is," he said.

"Is that where I am?"

"Where?"

"At the end of my rope?"

"Sure," he said, smiling. "I figure you were at it a long time ago."

Newel chewed his cheek and faced forward.

He let the truck idle out from beside Mr. Lamb's Continental, toward where Gaspareau was listening to Landrieu, jamming his finger at his disk every time he wanted to talk. When the old man saw the truck come up even with the house, he waved his cane and started out, leaving Landrieu standing in the rain.

Gaspareau stumped out to the side of his whistle bomb and poked his face in the window, obliging Newel with a sour look. He had on his hat with the green visor in the brim, and rain was loading it up and guttering off the back.

"Looky here," Gaspareau said in a strangled voice, having a look at Landrieu before he spoke. "Feller come this afternoon, give your truck a good going over. Got in it and looked around. I told him you was over with the old man, and he had me point to where you was."

"Must've wanted to buy my truck."

"May-be," Gaspareau said, his eyes flickering.

"What else did he say?"

268

"Wanted to know who you was. I told him I didn't know who you was. I said you worked on the island and didn't ask my permission to breathe."

"What else?" He stared through the windshield at the rain.

"That was all. Just looked at the truck—that was before I could get around and tell him to leave it be. Me and him went out on the dock and he had me point where it was you put the boat in over there."

"You catch his name?" It was raining on Newel's arm.

"Didn't say nothing about it." The old man's face was streaming. The rain was loud.

He gave the motor a little toe nudge. "I wouldn't mind selling it if I could get out what I put in."

"Why sure," Gaspareau said, smiling widely.

"What'd you say he looked like?"

"Regular boy, long kindly arms."

"I don't know no regular boys," he said, and throttled the engine loudly. "Except Newel here."

"What do I hear about old man Lamb?" Gaspareau said, smiling as if something were funny, his ears dripping rain.

"He died. That's funny, isn't it?" Newel said right in Gaspareau's face.

Gaspareau stepped back and scowled, his cheeks rising. A circlet of rain slid down his neck across the silver disk that fitted his throat, and disappeared in the hole. Newel put his hand on the window crank and looked at him, his legs getting wetter.

"Police might want to talk to you," Gaspareau said, swaying on his cane. "Where'll I tell them you're at?"

"Chicago, Illinois," Newel snapped, and raised the window halfway.

"I'll be somewhere," he said, letting his eyes roam. "I'll get in cahoots with them."

"What if that feller comes looking for you?" Gaspareau said, looking at Landrieu again, who had sheltered himself under the eave and was looking disconsolate.

"Tell him I'm sorry to miss him," he said.

"He'll be sorry he missed *you,*" Gaspareau said. He stood back, and looked at his soaked feet, loosening a stream of water that shot off the brim of his hat and covered his shoes. Gaspareau grinned as if he had done it on purpose, and he suddenly gunned the truck and left the old man grinning at nothing.

The truck rumbled down over the hound's carcass and up the side of the levee. Beyond it the rain was fierce, and the field rows toward Helena were blurred out. Goodenough's was half visible and both the tractor and the combine mired in the field were past their hubs in blinking water. A single crag of blue sky was just apparent where the rain had passed and left the air clean. The sun was below the plane of the fields, refracting a bright peach light behind the rain. He let the truck swagger down the side of the levee into the fields and onto the bed that was draining water off the high middle.

"Who was it looking?" Newel said.

He kept his eyes to the road. "Couldn't tell you."

"Don't you wonder?"

"Not a whole lot."

"You said you didn't like to advertise, didn't you?" Newel said.

"I might have said it."

"If you don't advertise, who was it looking? You must've put an ad someplace."

"I don't know nothin about it," he said. He tried to make out the outline of the store in the rain, and could only see the shadow above the dumpy profile of the land. He tried to put whatever it was Newel was trying to stir up straight out of his mind and concentrate on when everything would be over with.

"Wasn't your gal's husband, was it?" Newel said.

He kept watching for the store. "Let me go, would you do that?" He felt himself itching, concentrating on the dark little square emerging shade by shade out of the storm.

"A man diddling another man's wife in the state of Arkansas is fair game if he's caught in flagrante delicto," Newel said.

"You have to talk English to me," he said.

"My granddad knew a man in Little Rock named Jimmy

270

Scales, who shot his wife in bed with another man. The fellow jumped up and climbed out the window and went running all hell down the street and ran in Walgreen's to call a cab, and when the cab came the guy walked outside in his underwear and Jimmy Scales shot him in the eye. And when he came up, the jury found him guilty of murder two for shooting the man in a fit of rage. They didn't even press charges for the wife. The judge suspended and gave him a lecture about being quick on the trigger. That man's a urine tester at the Hot Springs race track right now, if he hasn't died with everybody else."

"Is that what you're going to do when you get to be a big-time lawyer—amuse them judges about how they practice the law in Arkansas? I think you better figure out something else to do."

Newel folded his arms behind his head and leaned back in the seat. "I thought you might be interested."

"Why, Newel, won't you just let it go, goddamn it? If I want to sly around, why won't you just let me do it?"

"Because you're so goddamned stupid, dicking around after some fellow's wife until you get him out hunting for you. Don't you know that's the one thing that's *not* supposed to happen? Except if you believe the whole world just boils down to a piece of mysterious nooky, I guess that's the one thing that's always going to happen. I'd just hate to see anything happen to you, Robard, cause it'd take you so long to know it you'd be dead."

"You won't," he said, watching the store arrive finally on the roadside.

"Won't what?"

"Won't see nothing happen to me," he said, "cause you'll be on your train, and won't be thinking about *me*. And I sure as hell won't be thinking about you." He pulled off and idled in under the awning between the gas pumps and the building. Mrs. Goodenough stood in the double doors smiling as if she had plans for both of them. He held out his hand for Newel to shake. "Now, Newel, I want you to save everybody up there, you hear?"

Newel took his hand and pinned it to the seat as if he were keeping himself from leaving. "Screw yourself," Newel said, and yanked his hand back and jumped beyond the protection of the awning into the rain, then hurried inside the store without looking back.

He reached across and pulled the door to, took a breath, and watched Mrs. Goodenough close the door, then idled out from under the awning and made a turn back into the rain toward Helena.

3

At the first town buildings the rain was already fading. Lights were turned on under the awning of the drive-in where he'd eaten. Cars were pulled up under, their parking lights blinking slowly.

The uncertainty made him edgy now, kept him watching the streets as if something were almost ready to barge out on top of him. And if it was W.W. out scouting the country, where, he tried to figure it, would he least likely hunt, if he wasn't going on the island, which he might after all be intending? And if that was so, then *he* could just forget W., since he'd end up out on the island with no explanation for being there, among a throng of people he didn't know coming and going, undertakers, lawyers, sheriffs, deputies, and could spend the next day explaining why he showed up on private property the day old man Lamb had picked out to die, and all so close to turkey season on top of it. He could be down the road, he figured, by the time W. cleared customs.

But that was part of the uncertainty, since W.W. was never one to stay at a thing longer than it took somebody, like Gaspareau, to convince him to do something else. He might just have mooned at the island awhile, surmised there wasn't any use going over, satisfied himself on one inspection of the truck and all its contents, getting a good enough look so he'd remember it if he ever saw it again, and gone home and stationed himself where,

when he saw the same truck slip out of some alley, he could let
go with whatever artillery he had to let go with.

Which brought up the prize question. Just how was it W. got
caught on in the first place? It wasn't likely anybody had been at
the post office to see the goings-on, and less likely around when
he brought her back, since he'd have heard about it by now from
Beuna herself. And there was no reason he could figure Gaspareau
to be suspicious, at least not enough to hold his own private
investigation and come up with precisely the right man and bring
him to the camp, then go to all the trouble to stand right up in
the rain and concoct a bald-headed lie about some "stranger" he'd
caught, since that would just alert him and give him the chance
to get out of town. And as foul a soul as lived in Gaspareau, the
bastard just wouldn't have gone to the trouble, and he knew it.

Which only left her. Which wasn't smart either, since it was
her wanted a trip to Memphis, a shower bath in the Peabody
Hotel, and a chance to show her trick. And he figured she
wouldn't ruin that just before she got to spring it, since it seemed
like the climax to something everlastingly important to her whole
life.

He drove up the hill to West Helena. The hill was grown up
in Kudzu. The road took a short pass below the lip of the bluff
before turning up onto it, and he could see back on the town,
darkening, the rain glossing the dusk, little furry lights socketed
into the train yards, a necklace of vapor lights draped through the
heart of things. In the jade sky the rain hung out darkly over the
bottoms, a smear of storm and thunderhead sweeping into Mississippi, the bridge in the distance catching the spangles of low
sunlight. He made the gloomy turn into West Helena wondering
if the getting would get any gooder than it was right now.

The town was only a couple of poorly lit streets. Each ran a
short way in opposite directions and quit. There was a brick
millinery, a drugstore, a domino room, and the Razorback Theater, which looked like it might be going. The other fronts that
weren't boarded looked empty. A John Deere was closed on the
corner. He thought there had been some people with French

names back along the bevel of the hill away from town, and some rows of houses on the west edge where the Negroes lived who worked in the fields toward Sappho, and who rode to work in the trucks that came up from Helena.

Two motels were set out past the shanties on the highway beyond the Kold Freez, one for colored, where there were plenty of lights and a lot of long cars with Illinois and New Jersey plates in front of some loud-colored cinder-block rooms. And a quarter mile down, four cabins were strung off the road behind a moving green neon on the shoulder showing two mallard ducks batting the air in three separate figurations of flight.

The man in the office was drunk. He appeared from behind a bead portiere with a plastic cocktail glass and went searching under the counter for a card without saying a word. He finally just shoved out a key, tried to straighten his shoulders, breathing whiskey into the room, and sauntered back through the portiere, where a television was on and a woman's voice was talking softly.

He compared the key to the first door, and found his way to the last cabin, where the weeds were rooted in the sidewalk, and the little building was dark blue and nearly invisible. Bullbats were cutting the air after mosquitoes, croaking up in the night. He could hear their little membranous wings flutter above the burble of the motel sign, get a glimpse of them wheeling close to the ground. When he had worked for Rudolph and had lived in the shack on the sluice gate and listened to the radio at night, he had liked to walk out in the dusk with his shotgun, step across the bridge over the barrow pit, and stand on the old man's levee and shoot bullbats against the orange twilight, where they showed up like razors, gauging shots to hit two birds crossing and spin them into the moss-trussed reservoir like elm seeds, slapping the surface with their wings until they drowned. And in the morning, he went across the pit and down the levee to close the pumps, and he would look out into the strumpy water and see nothing but black turtles stretched along the deadfalls, sunning themselves in the milky light, and hear the grasshoppers buzz in the grass, and there would be no sign of the bullbats, though they always came in the evenings in greater numbers than before.

274

He got in the truck and drove back to the Negro motel, where he had seen a cold-drink machine on the outside. He bought a root beer and a package of Nabs, and stood in the drink-machine light listening to music and voices sliding out of the rooms. Parked in front of each door was a dark automobile with an out-of-state plate, the rear ends weighted almost to the gravel with whatever was in the trunk. He remembered seeing heavy cars on the road to Los Angeles, full of black babies and mean-mouthed in-laws packed in the back seats, gawking at the desert as if it were all part of a long dream. And down the road two miles you'd find the cars crippled on the shoulder, one fender hoisted, the wives and in-laws and babies standing off from the roadway fanning themselves while some skinny husband wrestled with a tire, his pink shirt black with perspiration, listening to the radio as the cars whipped by. It was always a joke. They had enough credit for the car, but not enough to finance the tires. So they took a chance. And those big Buicks and Lincolns broke down all the way across the country for lack of tread rubber, which was the last thing a nigger wanted to think about when he got the notion to take off.

He ate the last cracker and bent and fingered the tread on the car nearest the truck. It was thick and warm and deep enough to lose a nickel in. He took a drink of his root beer and tapped the tire with his toe and went back.

He backed the truck up to the cabin door and let himself in. The room was damp and smelled hot like the room they had put the old man in. The ceiling fixture gave out a grainy light. He opened the bathroom, inspected the shower, and pulled up the casement to let a breeze circulate the mildew air out of the room. He washed his face, turned the light off, and stood in the window, letting his skin dry. No cars were running the road. The lot was empty. The ducks' wings were buzzing in a soft green haze of light, and someone had turned on the red NO sign. He took off his shirt, lay on the bedspread, and let the breeze settle on his stomach and soothe his legs.

He could rent a big Pontiac, he thought. He could get a big room at Manhattan Beach, have a swim and see the movies, and come back while she was excited and love her like he hadn't been off, make her forget it, say how everything comes down to choice. One day you think you never even made a choice and then you have to make one, even a wrong one, just so you're sure you're still able. And once that's over, you can go back and be happy again with what you were before you started worrying. Though she'd say it wasn't like that at all, he thought, since women tied themselves to men like men wanted to tie themselves to the world. But if he could make her see that, he could still make her happy, on account of choosing her after he had already *had* her when there wasn't any reason to have her now except he wanted to. He lit a cigarette and smudged it and blew the smoke up and watched it sag off in the breeze. He could hear the duck sign buzzing outside. There was some mystery to Beuna still, some force that drew him, made him want to find her out, like a man plundering a place he knows he shouldn't be but can't help but be for the one important thing he might find. Something pulled him, over the squeezing and weltering that he thought he could just as easily dispense with now and *would* if there were some other way to get that close to her. Except that that was all she allowed and cared about and would just as soon for her own pleasures dispense with all that he wanted to save. W.W. came in his mind with the idea that she wanted to punish him and punish herself with one more thing she couldn't have. Then he forgot it. His eyes closed and he slid backward in the breeze, and heard one fast car hiss through his mind and disappear down the road, and then he let it all go.

4

The radiator began to tick and whomp at three o'clock, and when he woke up it was daylight and his head was cottony as though the heat were a drug he'd taken to sleep. He put on his shirt and walked out in the lot. Clouds had pushed out ahead of the wind, and the sky was plush, delving over into itself creating a stiff wool of low mist. He thought it would rain.

He walked to the office to ask the time. The clerk's face looked withered. His hair was stood up in back, and he had to close one eye as if he couldn't focus them both but still needed to be able to see. He told the clerk he was leaving for a while and coming back and would be another night. The office smelled like hot coffee.

"If it had come up cool last night, you would've been *hollerin* for that heat," the man said, fingering a styrofoam cup and looking sad.

"Don't matter," he said.

"If you like the weather this time a year, you just wait ten minutes," the man said, and displayed a wound that had enlarged one side of his mouth and made it gap wide open when he smiled. "It's gonna rain on us today," he said, as if he understood it hadn't rained in weeks.

He wished he had some coffee.

"What part of California you from?" the man said, sniffing. His shirt was unbuttoned to his belly and a little bleached-out Indian chief was tattooed into the flabby portion of his chest.

"Bishop."

"I went out December '47, in the Navy," the clerk said, gravely staring down at his cup. "Stayed till"—he stopped to count it up —"four years ago. Come back and bought this." He looked around the little office, admiring it. The man bent over the counter farther and cradled his cup in both hands. "I ain't getting rich and I ain't kissin ass." He raised his eyebrows significantly. "Had me a putt-putt up in Oceanside. But she never liked it in San Diego cause of the spics."

He tried to steal a look behind the portiere to see the man's wife, who might, he figured, know Beuna, and be somebody who practiced recognizing the backs of people's heads just as they disappeared through motel room doors, and grabbed the phone the second she saw something the least bit interesting. "How's she like it?" he said, trying to get a good look in through the beads.

The man ran his hand through his slick hair. "She's gone to

Little Rock to visit her sister," he said, and concocted a wry little smile on his ruined mouth and let his eyes roam the ceiling. "I'm ex-Navy." The left corner of his mouth looked red and embarrassing.

"Yeah," he said. He pulled out his postcard, laid it on top of the glass, beneath which were a lot of other postcards, picked up the motel's plastic pen and scratched a note that said: "Be to home Tuesday."

The man opened a drawer, tore off a stamp, and pushed it across the counter. "I stuck all them under there from people who's stayed here," he said proudly. "They come in and spend the night, a couple of weeks later I get a card from Delray Beach, saying how nice it was in the Two Ducks." He finished his coffee and wiggled his cup in his hand and looked up in a comradely way. "I'm made hopeful," he said.

"Yeah," he said. He stuck the extra postage to the card, thinking it would get there before he could get there himself, and stuffed it in his pocket. "What time you got?"

The man consulted his wrist watch. "Four to." He smiled and the corner of his mouth flapped down like the entrance to a bad place.

He drove off the hill and onto the little gravel streets of white mill houses with board-step porches and pink hydrangeas to hide the water meters. The street was bothered a distance by some young failing mimosas, but across the business spur the trees had been hacked down and a Red Ball store put up, and after that it was business to Main Street.

He turned a block before Main and drove to the south end, to a row of feed warehouses and the Phillips County Co-op, where the street ended in a weed lot, then turned up to Main and drove back the direction he'd come.

The street made him nervous right away. He knew the townspeople had gotten the forecast and got their business over and gone home, leaving him out by himself. The sky was higher, but the town seemed sunk and gray, only thin veins of light leaking into the air. He tried not to look sideways until he saw the old man's maroon Continental angled into a row of pickups, with Landrieu slumped in the driver's seat trying to stay out of sight. The car was stopped in front of an old two-story glass and granite building that had "R. M. Knox" stenciled on several of the windowpanes. Just as he passed he tried to see inside, but couldn't make out anything but a high metal desk and a secretary walking around in a skinny skirt holding a flower vase. She disappeared into where the glass was darkened, and he wondered what finalities Mrs. Lamb was making for the old man, whether she already had him moved off the island back to Mississippi, or whether there were laws against hauling bodies across the line, which was why she needed R. M. Knox. It all seemed like someplace he hadn't ever been but knew about, something away from his life altogether now.

Two men outside the bank regarded him casually and he raised a hand, and one of them waved and smiled and went back to talking.

He started watching the other side of the block, where there was a Pure station, the Red Ball storefront, and a cotton broker. The street was almost deserted. A Negro man was stopped looking at the sky and a pregnant white girl walked inside the Red Ball pushing a stroller.

And then he saw Beuna, past the corner, standing outside a lawn mower store, one foot on the curb and one square in the mouth of the gutter, looking like a white peony blossom.

Beuna was got up in a white gauze dress with a sateen boat top that looped down on top of her breasts. The dress then belled out to make a gauze skirt with lacy flounces down to her knees. She had on a pair of red shoes and a wide red belt that almost matched, and that was cinched so he wondered if she could breathe or had simply been standing at the curb all morning with her breath inside her trying not to turn blue. The dress had tiny straps holding it up, and she was carrying a big white patent purse. Her hair was down on her shoulders and bunched under, and she was smiling a big rougy smile as if she thought somebody was standing ready to take her picture.

He let the truck creep across the intersection, checking the mirror and aiming straight down the gutter to where she had her foot. He popped the door as he got clear of the cross street, and she had to get back to miss being smacked.

She sweetened her big airport smile so he could see her teeth were frowzed with lipstick.

"How am I?" She spread her legs so he could see through the gauze and make out everything.

"Like a har-lot," he said, feeling angry.

She licked her lips. "Don't I look like a kid?"

"You look like a whore," he said. He took another look at the mirror.

"Don't I look like a young girl, Robard?"

"Goddamn it, get your ass in or I'm leaving you for them hard dicks to pick over." He flashed at the mirror, expecting to see four or five men charging up the street.

Her head declined and she quit swinging her purse, and he could see a weal of flesh appear under her chin. She got in the truck and closed the door. "What was it you said I looked like?"

He could smell a sweet gardenia perfume over everything. "A harlot." He nudged the truck off from the curb, catching a glimpse of the spectators in front of the bank. They seemed not to be paying attention to anything but a blue and white state police car passing along the street.

"What's a harlot?" she said.

"A slut," he snapped, watching the police car intently while he slipped through the next crossing.

"Oh," she said, and slumped her purse in her lap and poked her hands through the strap. "I thought I'd look like I looked when you and me knew one another at Willard's."

"What come of Willard?" he said. He turned off Main in the direction of the bluff. The trooper cruised by toward Memphis. The street changed back to low-porch bungalows with old Chevies in the yard and motors hung up on chain pulleys.

"Him and her went," she said, nibbling a fleck of lipstick and spreading it over another tooth. "He took empyzema or some such and went to Tucson." She looked dissatisfied. "I don't write 'em nothin. I just write you." She pushed her lower lip out and made a face.

He started looking for a drop box on the street. He turned back to the street he had come in on, then up toward the hill. At the first corner, he aimed the truck across, slid in under the spout, and dropped the card in the slot.

"What the hell was that about?" she said.

"Jackie."

"Saying what about?"

"I was coming."

"Huh," she snorted.

He pulled back onto the road.

"You and me's going to Memphis, Tennessee, tonight, buster," she said. "I got me some plans that'll keep you out of circulation tonight." She looked cagey.

"We'll see," he said.

"What do you mean, 'We'll see'?" she said. "I'm going to be in the Peabody Ho-tel tonight looking out the window at the Union Planters Bank, or by God I ain't going to be no place at all." She glared, hiked her skirt, and crossed her legs.

The truck went a ways along a slip fault in the bluff, and the cotton fields began to be visible, opening away to the river toward the south. From the distance it was impossible to tell the fields were flooded and gummed, and everything looked dark and tilled, ready for planting.

"I got to pick up some stuff," he said.

She faced front, her cheeks pale as if in looking out at the river bottom she had seen something that made her unhappy.

The road made a turn over the bluff into West Helena. An old man on a ladder was changing the letters on the Razorback marquee and had put the word BLOW into place, hunting in a cardboard box for the members of some other word. The bottom line said OPEN SAT MAT.

One or two people were on the street, hurrying to and from the Skelley station. The sky made it seem like the aftermath of some public alarm.

"I hate it up here," she said, looping her purse around her wrist and glowering out the window. He was silent. "They's a Kold Freez up here," she said. "Pull in, I want me one."

He drove past the motel where the cars had been the night before, everything all gone, and the light in the soda machine was off, and the motel looked as if it had been shut up.

"That there's the gambling joint," she said, staring disinterestedly at the motel. "Niggers cut one another up there and pay off the sheriff."

The Kold Freez was off on the left, in the middle of a rectangular lot that let the cars drive all the way around.

"Gimme a quarter," she said, throwing open the door.

He fished out a quarter and she sauntered up to the window. A sign above the window said DOGS • BOATS • SLUSHES. One of the girls inside shoved up the screen slide and stuck her head in the opening to see out. Beuna spoke, and the girl stood up and stared at him through both wide panes of glass, then turned around and filled a paper cup from a big silver machine and delivered it to the window-way, where Beuna was leaning, staring up the road and fanning herself with her hand. The girl stood and looked at him again, brushing back a strand of strawberry hair out of her eyes, then disappearing behind the machinery into the private rooms of the building.

Beuna shoveled down in her seat with her knees on the dashboard, drinking something out of the cup with a striped straw. "Wasn't no change," she said.

He drove to the motel, backed into the last cabin, and cut off the motor.

"Is this the dump you're stayin in?" Beuna said, surveying the lot over the window sill, having another sip on her straw.

"Come on in for a minute."

"My ass, too." She threw the cup of ice out the window.

"I don't want nobody to see us," he said.

"This here's a goddamned cathouse," she said loudly, and shot out her lip. "Brashears don't give a shit if you take a goddamn sheep in here. He *knows*. You paid for a double."

"I ain't paid it," he said softly, and looked up at the office.

A truck of Negroes passed, headed for Marvell, men all standing against the side slats peering out like convicts. One of them yelled at the truckdriver and waved his hat, and he could hear the rest of them laughing, and the driver honked the horn and some of the others took up whooping.

Beuna looked through the side window, her head turned so her chin looked like part of her breasts. He grabbed her arm suddenly and pulled her over and kissed her on the mouth, but she kept her arms unbent and her neck stiff, and when he looked at her she was staring at him, a smile trying to figure on her lips. He ran his tongue behind his teeth. "What the hell's got the matter with you?" he said. He took another grip on her arm until he could see white radiating away from his fingers.

Her eyes got big and her pupils flattened and welled up, and she started to tremble and moaned. "I don't know you," she said, losing her breath, tears pearling off her face, disappearing between her breasts.

"Yes you do," he said. "You know me, sugar."

She gulped. "I thought we was going, and we ain't," she said, and covered her face with her hands. "We're just going in that room."

He pushed his thumb up through his eyebrows and stared at the floor. "Everything didn't work out just right."

"Why can't we?" she moaned.

"I can't be running off now to no Memphis," he said.

"*I* can," she bawled, another gout of tears breaking loose, flooding her cheeks.

"I want to, sugar, but it's just some things can't be."

"You little bastard," she said. "You ruin everything for me, tearing up my hopes."

"Come inside," he said softly, looking back up at Brashears' office, turning the door catch behind him.

He led her in where it was cool and green shadows. The bed was jumbled and his sack of clothes was dumped on the chair. The light in the bathroom was on and Beuna went in and shut the door.

He took off his boots and listened to her rattling things in the sink and running the toilet. He looked for a radio but there wasn't one. He wished he had some coffee and a sandwich, and decided that after a little while they could drive out to Marvell and get groceries and bring them back. He peeked out the curtain and saw his truck alone in the cool rain breeze. The sky was smoky, and the sun had inched higher into the clouds. A black Cadillac passed toward town and disappeared beyond the two ducks.

Beuna emerged, her lips swollen from crying and her dress flapping in the back. She had left the light burning and stopped so it was behind her and he could make out the silhouettes.

"I ain't mad at you," she said, and sniffed. "It don't make no difference about no Peabody. I wanted to look like a young girl to you, to take to Memphis with you. But it don't matter."

He watched her legs shift and twitch behind the gauze dress, and felt everything floating.

"Come here," she said. She pulled one hand from behind her, holding a little bag in her fingers.

He came to where she was and she clenched her hands behind his head and kissed him on the mouth and forced his lips back against his teeth so that his ears whirred. He got a hand at the bottom of her spine and moved her legs and she held his head and squeezed.

"You come in," she said, breathing in big gulps. She led him into the fluorescent bathroom light and turned on the shower and held her hand in until it was warm and steam started spreading.

"What is it?" he said, looking around at the moist plaster.

"Skin off," she said, and let her dress slide forward off her breasts.

He unbuckled his pants and let them down while she unbuttoned his shirt and pushed it off his shoulders.

The room was full of warm steam crowding out of the tub around his chin, though the floor tiles were cold and hard. It made him feel faint. He wiped the mirror and saw sweat sprouting on his forehead, his eyes pale and unfocused, and he wished he could get outside.

Beuna stood in the tub kneeling on the porcelain, water bouncing off her head, soaking her hair and beading up around her knees.

"C'mere," she said in a voice that reverberated on the tiles.

He took a step up to where she was holding the plastic sandwich bag and reaching out. "What is all this?" he said, trying to smile.

". . . this in my mouth," she said, waggling the bag in the circulating water. "And I want you to go."

"To what?" he said, straining to see her in the steam and not comprehending what it was she was getting set to do.

"You know," she said, letting the softened bag empty of water.

He took a step back and got hold of the round of the sink to keep from falling on his back. "What's the matter with you?" he said.

"I want to, Robard!" she shouted.

"Want to, shit!" He backed another step until his bare behind got out into the cool air circulating off the sleeping room, and almost made him turn around.

"Yes, yes, yes!" she screamed. "You have to!" She shook her hair and closed her eyes.

He got around and out the door while she began doing something he couldn't think to watch.

5

He lay staring at the amber fruit bowl on the ceiling, thinking about getting out.

Beuna stood fitting herself back into her white dress. "I used to sit sometimes, conjure I married you instead of him," she said, her voice straining from drawing on the zipper. "He's so *goddamned* dull, you know. I thought, if I just hadn't married *him*, me and Robard mighta lived no telling where. Up in Memphis maybe. Oklahoma City, someplace besides a goddamn mobile home." She shook out her hair. "I had *that* wrong. I'da ended up out in some goddamn tacky desert living in some tacky little house that ain't fit for nothin. That's cause you ain't nothin, Robard." She looked at him contemptuously, got a fresh hold of the zipper, and ran it up.

He lay staring at the globe, trying to keep her out.

"I told him you was here." She pulled the strap of her shoe over her heel.

He raised off the pillow. "What was it?"

"I told him you was at E-laine," she said absently. "I said you worked at E-laine, and I seen you, and you said hi."

He stood up and went to the window and took a look out where he could see the truck, the first fat splots of rain just hitting the hood. He gazed at her in the low shadows. "What the shit did you do that for?"

She kept working her shoe strap up and down. "So he'd hate it," she said, "worry I had me something he couldn't do nothin about. I thought we was going to Memphis anyway."

He peered out the window again, expecting to see W.W. standing in the rain. "What'd he do about it?" he said.

She walked to the edge of the fluorescent light. "Nothin," she said, "except make me go out to that beer bar with him and get drunk and act mean. I don't like it."

"Get your goddamn clothes on," he said.

"They are on." She picked up her purse and stood beside the bathroom.

"Then come on." He grabbed up the sack of clothes, opened the door, and stuck his head out in the rain.

Inside the truck, big gray drops were smacking the roof. He took a look up the road and around the lot on either side. He looked suspiciously in at Brashears' office. "Is he playing ball?" he said.

She looked at her nails and brushed the crystals of water out of her hair. "Less they got rained on," she said.

He backed the truck around and started out on the highway.

It didn't seem right that this ought to happen, that he ought to be still worried about getting caught so close to going. It should have been a nice couple of hours and been over with. He wished there had been time to eat.

"You know what the bastard done to me last night?" Beuna said, forgetting everything.

He kept his eyes on the road, which was slick and black in the rain. The row of pink cinder-blocks shot by and he watched at the corner of the last cabin, but no one was there, and he pushed the truck a little, as the first of the dumpy buildings came closer.

Beuna pulled her skirt over her knees and crossed her legs sideways. "He made me go with him to that damned Blue Goose out there where he works, made me sit out there and drink Falstaff beer while he loused around with his nitwit friends till twelve o'clock. And you know what else?"

He couldn't talk to her. The man on the movie marquee had given up in the rain and had left the west side blank, except for the OPEN SAT MAT in the right corner out over the street.

"What kind of car you got?"

"Shit-old Plymouth," she said. "They give it to him when he played baseball. I wanted an Impala, but he wouldn't say nothin."

"What color?" The road twisted down the face of the bluff, went straight a ways, then angled south along the face of the grade. The Kudzu looked almost black in the heavy light.

"Dark green. Grunt green. Let me tell you, though, what the bastard done to me. Him and his big buddy Ronald commenced playing pool while I was sitting over in the corner minding my business pretending to drink that horse piss. And course they both got piss drunk and started missing the balls and laughing and pouring it on one another. Then all to once they seen another friend of theirs named Tooky Dyre, and he come in and sat at the bar and watched 'em like they was twin monkeys. And W. went over to where he was and whispered something in his ear. And in a little while Tooky come over where I was, and I don't hardly even know him, cause he is a whole lot younger than me. He come up and reached in his pocket and took out a quarter and laid it on the table right in front of me, and just looked over at W. and said, 'I'll be next on this table.' And they all just died, like I was a damned pool table they all played on." She looked disgusted. "You think I'm a pool table, Robard?"

"I don't know what you are."

"That's sweet," she said. She opened her purse, took out a book, and started reading. The book had a photograph of a naked girl on the cover, swinging on a trapeze above a bunch of men in clown costumes.

He wanted just to let her out where there wouldn't be anybody to pay attention, and get out of town as quick as he could. The hill road wound down into the same muddy streets with the little postage-stamp lots and one-step weed porches that ran all the way back to the middle of town. At every crossing he looked down the street to see if he could see W.'s Plymouth, but there wasn't anything to see down any of them. He had his old picture of W. framed up in his mind again, inside the little pink bungalow in Tulare, wandering room to room in his white and orange uniform like he had a quince in his mouth and couldn't get it spit out. He had left out the back screen in the middle of the night and driven back to Bishop without a minute's sleep.

"Where'm I taking you to?"

"Turn right," she said.

"Where we going?"

"I'll show you," she said, flipping a page in her book and biting off a sliver of fingernail.

He went down a block, and encountered a street exactly like the one they'd been on, low-roofed wood houses with cars in the yards, leading to town. He could see the docks at the Piggly Wiggly and didn't see anything was unusual, except a queasy feeling in his chest like a sound he couldn't hear setting up vibrations in various of his organs. His heart had begun to bump the wall of his ribs. He wished now he had hung on to the old man's pistol instead of laying it in the Gin Den, since it might do him some good if things all of a sudden got hot.

In the next block the street got bad, and the old houses changed into little farms, with stumpy Bermuda lots ending in woods, and chickens and goats penned inside little square-wire fences. The rain had made the small animals go back inside the pens. A goat was standing in the rain, grazing nonchalantly, staring at nothing. The road slipped into a clump of gum trees and he could see where the first driveway opened right, though couldn't see any more buildings for the gum trees.

"Where we going?" he said, watching the mirror and seeing nothing but pillowy clouds shielding the light.

"Home," she said, closing the book and dropping it in her bag and giving him a big red smile.

The truck cruised to the end of a red dirt drive and he could see a trailer up amongst the stumps of the gum trees, set on cinder blocks with a propane tank at one end. W.W.'s Plymouth sat empty at the corner nearest the woods. There seemed to be a lot of sawdust on the ground from the cutting.

It made him furious. "Get the fuck out!" he shouted, reaching past her and shoving the door open, letting in the rain.

"I wasn't going to walk in no rain," she said, picking up the red pump she had let dangle off her toe. He raised his foot over the seat and kicked her in the shoulder and drove her straight out, sprawling onto the wet clay, her purse strewn over the seat and littering on the ground. Her red shoe was still inside, and he grabbed it and threw it out where she was just getting turned around in the mud, her hair smudged against her forehead and her gauze skirt up over her waist, showing her bare behind to the rain.

He revved the engine. She had one hand in the purse, pressing it down onto the mud, and the other fouled in several plastic sandwich bags that had spilled out. Mud clung to her eyebrows and under her chin. "You shit lick!"

"It ain't me!" he yelled. "It's *you*, goddamn it, that had to do it." He hit the gas again.

Out the end of the trailer came W., dressed in a bright orange and blue baseball suit, his hair cropped like an onion, his long arms supporting a short little rifle that looked half the size of any gun he'd ever seen before.

He watched the rifle through the open door as W. came thrashing, trying to make out just exactly what it was, and deciding it was a BB gun. He gave W. an interested look, and pulled the truck slowly down into first. W.W. suddenly dropped to one knee, fitted the gun to his shoulder, and fired one loud round that broke in the passenger's ventilator and went out his own window, filling the cab with a fine spray of glass, leaving both windows with ugly pucker-shaped holes and the rest of the panes intact. Beuna started shrieking, "Shoot him, shoot him," and he let the clutch snap off his shoe and pinned down the accelerator until the floorboard began giving way under his feet, and the truck started bucking like a buffalo, and him shoveling himself in the corner ducking another shot, glass sprouting out the side of his cheek like tiny trees in a forest.

A dozen yards by the trailer the road offered one alternative to going back, and he twisted off to the left and went careening back in the direction of town. He took a fast look back and saw W.W.'s green Plymouth wallowing out the drive, exhaust furring the ground, the gun barrel stuck at an angle out the driver's window. He could just glimpse Beuna, who had simply crawled to one side of the driveway to let the car get by, still sprawled in the wreckage of her white dress, looking as if she had dropped there out of the sky.

The roadbed ran out through another patch of gums, past a second sector of farm lots and rained-over houses that weren't meant to be farms, with the goats and low-roofed chicken houses alone in the little scratches of stumpy acreage.

In the mirror, W.W. came skidding, the Plymouth flailing in the wet clay, already losing distance.

He tried to think in a clear-headed way what to do. He had an intuition the road would merge south with the River Road, and that it would be a peril to go back in town and risk getting pulled over by the sheriff and detained long enough for W. to start blazing away again at close enough range where it would be hard to miss anything not moving. The little prick wounds began to bleed down his cheek, and he raised up until he could see his face in the mirror and see where blood was popping out of several little vents along his jaw. Splinters were bristling on his neck but there wasn't blood there yet, though there would be, he thought.

He shot down the row of scrub farms, the wind whistling between the twin bullet holes, and straight into the drizzly distance. A cab-over diesel was burning out of Helena heading for the bridge cutoff, smoke flagging in a long gray streamer.

He was disgusted for not thinking any respectable boy would keep a 30-06 behind the door on the chance some old buck might lose his bearings and decide to browse the front yard, in which case you were entitled to a shot just to protect your property from depredation. He picked a little sliver out of his cheek and pinched it through the glass pucker and took another look at the Plymouth, which was nothing but a hump in the dirt spray. Water had risen higher now than last year's rows and just the woody plants were visible above the surface.

When he pulled up at the junction he could barely see W. barreling down the straight stretch of road a mile and a quarter in the field.

He turned right into the force of the rain and beat the accelerator and got the truck hissing back down the phone lines toward Elaine.

He knew already from the old man's map that 185 just quit, kicked out into a rat's nest of farm roads and hog trails that he knew nothing about and that W. stood a better chance of knowing about and using to an advantage. He figured he could go on into Mississippi, but that there was just the chance somebody would be manning the boll weevil quarantine at the other end, and he'd get tied up on account of his plates, and W. would come off the ramp shooting every direction and killing people. And then, too, if he got across, there wasn't anyplace to go where he knew anything.

It would be best of all, he figured, if he could just open enough distance between him and W. to get back onto the island, and hold him off from the shore with the old man's pistol, and hope in a while he'd forget about it and go on home.

He could see W. lagging back, still bracking down the farm

lane in a mud fury, like a tornado dragging the tailpipe. At eighty-five the chassis began agitating, and wind funneled in the holes and stirred up more glass, and he let it back to eighty, considering the small good it would do to slide off in a ditch and have W.W. pot him like a sparrow in a birdbath. Which made him think for the first time how much serious peril there was of getting swept off exactly like his old man. And after he'd already decided he'd made it out, by staying clear of the evil Beuna wanted to get him into, as a way of convincing him that inasmuch as they were in the same bad way they might as well enjoy it. Because he'd seen the trap already. If he refused whatever included her little plastic bag, then he refused that he and she were in the same boat. And that was what had made her lead him right to W.W., a desire to end the dispute by cutting the knot. She was just determined that if she had to live with herself, she was going to let everybody else see how their lives had brought them as low. And in his case she was ready to have him see it just as he drew his last breath with her sitting in the mud shrieking.

He lit a cigarette. The blood dried on his temples and he could feel his skin crusty. When he passed the turnoff for Mississippi he couldn't see W.W. anymore. The highway bent around the course of the old river, then wound back toward the west, obliterating his view of the road and making him feel apprehensive since he couldn't gauge the distance and couldn't gauge his chance of getting across before W. could start pounding away at the lake.

The road sprung back east, passed over a cypress bayou, then fell along the straight open stretch of highway toward Elaine, where he could see the store bumped in the low distance above the cotton fields.

He tossed the cigarette and got a look at the road behind him, and saw nothing in the drizzle. To the west were long latitudinal flecks of waxy light at the rear of the storm, which still grayed the sky for miles. He thought the day would turn warm and be clear by nightfall.

He turned down off by Goodenough's and glimpsed the window where the old lady stood and watched the sky develop, but no one was there, and he aimed straight out toward the levee.

It bothered him about Newel and he wished he hadn't remembered it, inasmuch as there wasn't anything. At one time it might have been Beuna, though she hadn't ever had a real hold on him and couldn't have wormed inside enough to break his heart.

He passed the two foundered machines. A car was just out of the cypress, a pillar of rain behind it, but he couldn't make out who it was. He wiped the glass, but couldn't see.

He set off down the lee side of the levee, getting a little anxious about taking a boat without asking. The road flattened through the sycamores and crossed the gap. There were no lights in Gaspareau's little house and none of the dogs was out, and the row of cabins seemed as empty as they had been. He drove up under the willows and stared quickly at the last of the cabins, where he thought he saw some motion and color behind one of the torn screens, though it didn't materialize.

Mr. Lamb's Traveler was hitched at the end of the dock, the All State still fastened to the transom, dipping in the rain. He put on his jacket, stashed his clothes behind the seat, and got out.

He listened for the wheeze of W.'s Plymouth, but he could hear only the sough of the rain and the pearls of water dropping off the sycamore leaves.

He went down and surveyed the bottom of the boat and decided he'd have to go without bailing. He untied the painter, stepped in, and kicked away from the dock into the water. The boat began to drift backward in the breeze, and he balanced in the back, gave the motor a jerk, and let it flood out. He looked back at the row of cabins and whipped it again, and it bawled and kicked up smoke and lake bottom and rose partway out before he could catch the throttle and push the cowling down.

He wheeled and started down the lake the way Landrieu had approached free of the shallows, admitting that much more space between him and W., if W. arrived while he was half across and decided to go ahead and start shooting right away.

He took a look, expecting to see back up through the willows to the levee top, and instead saw someone who was not W.W. and was not Gaspareau, and didn't seem to be anyone he'd ever seen before on earth. He came clear of the shallows and piloted toward the middle of the lake and opened the throttle. The rain had started again full stream, and the boat slipped out over the tiny white wavelets that were headed toward the shore four hundred yards away.

He looked at the figure on the dock. The man was tall and built slenderly and wore only a T-shirt and pants and no provision for the weather. He held a long slender rifle he was just fitting to his shoulder with a fat bulb-ended scope bolted to the receiver. He stared at the man, wondering what he might be doing and who he was, and had it break on him it was the boy from the road sale, the boy Gaspareau had sent over for the old man's guarding job. It seemed clear he was left to guard the camp, and was probably right now under the impression he was stealing a boat to get over, since the island was as vacant as the camp appeared to be, and open season for whoever could get across and create mayhem.

The boy stood for a long time with the gun to his shoulder, sighting in the scope as the boat slid farther and farther out onto the lake. He scowled at the boy, trying to figure out measures to take, without having to turn around and go back and risk getting cornered by W. before he could make it clear he wasn't converting anything and get back on the water.

The boat passed the quarter way in the lake, and the size of the boy was diminishing, making him feel better. Though he could still see the boy clearly, sighting the scope, dropping the barrel periodically and looking out on the lake with just his eyes as if he were estimating the real distance to what he could actually see in the glass. He looked up the levee but couldn't see anything, and it made him uncomfortable again.

All at once he turned the boat out sideways so that it was pointed down the long curve of the lake, cut the throttle, and offered the boy a perfect broadside of the boat. He stood up in the bottom, faced the dock, and spread his arms so the boy could see him clearly in the prism of his scope, see his face, and recognize him as the old man's employee heading across to attend to business.

But instead the boy fired.

Somewhere between his ribs and his collarbone he felt a great upheaval, a tumult of molecules being rearranged and sloughed off in rapid succession, and in the midst of it a feeling like hitting your thumb so hard with a hammer that the pain is delayed and stays inert in your thumb for a long number of seconds before it flies up, and you have to lie down just to get yourself ready. That, until he hit the water. Then it hurt and felt cold all at one time, and the surface of the water seemed like a line bobbing in front of his eyes up and sideways and down again, like a lariat being snaked and twirled over the top of itself. And he could hear a loud and tremendous roaring and himself saying "Oh, oh," and tried to see above the water and beyond the rocking boat nearby, but couldn't.

Epilogue

In the Roosevelt Hotel in New Orleans he went with his father out of their room and into the dark, shaded corridor to where the elevators were, to go have oysters in the Sazerac Bar. And in the corridor there were men piled up against a doorway, straining and staring inside at something he could not see, but that was the object of someone's flash camera inside the room. And when his father got to where the men were, he looked in over their shoulders and said, "Look here." And the men parted the way and he stepped up to the door and looked around the painted jamb and saw a young man in his thirties with short blond hair and a square meaty face, lying face down half on his bed and half off, with his feet sticking straight up into the air like flagpoles, holding a pistol. The room was cool and smelled like cheap soap, and the man looked strange to be lying in that particular way. And he said to his father, "What's this?" And all at once the dark man with the camera reached to move the young man who was half on and half off the bed, and his father said, "Listen, now listen, and you can hear him rattle in his throat." And he listened and when the man with the camera moved the man with his feet on the bed in such a way that he was no longer lying on his nose, there was a faint sound from somewhere, like someone in the room had caught a fly in his throat and tried to cough it up without making any noise, and his father said, "See? See? Did you hear it?" And he wasn't ever sure if he had heard it or not.